THE
HORSE'S
MOUTH

The Horse's Mouth
is the concluding novel
of Joyce Cary's
First Trilogy, of which
the first and second
novels are
Herself Surprised and
To Be a Pilgrim.
This edition reprints
the definitive text,
incorporating changes
and corrections
made by the author and
Andrew Wright.

THE
HORSE'S
MOUTH

JOYCE CARY

 HarperPerennial

A Division of HarperCollins Publishers

The Horse's Mouth was originally published by Michael Joseph in London in 1944 and was first brought out in this country by Harper & Brothers in 1950. The revised edition, edited by the author and Andrew Wright, was originally published by George Rainbird, in association with Michael Joseph, in London in 1957; and this definitive version was reprinted here in *First Trilogy*, published by Harper & Brothers in 1958.

First Perennial Library edition published in 1965. First HarperPerennial edition published in 1990.

LIBRARY OF CONGRESS CATALOG CARD NUMBER 90-5505
ISBN 0-06-092021-1

90 91 92 93 94 AG/M 10 9 8 7 6 5 4 3 2 1

TO HENEAGE OGILVIE

THE
HORSE'S
MOUTH

1. I was walking by the Thames. Half-past morning on an autumn day. Sun in a mist. Like an orange in a fried fish shop. All bright below. Low tide, dusty water and a crooked bar of straw, chicken-boxes, dirt and oil from mud to mud. Like a viper swimming in skim milk. The old serpent, symbol of nature and love.

> *Five windows light the caverned man: through one*
> *he breathes the air;*
> *Through one hears music of the spheres; through*
> *one can look*
> *And see small portions of the eternal world.*

Such as Thames mud turned into a bank of nine carat gold rough from the fire. They say a chap just out of prison runs into the nearest cover; into some dark little room, like a rabbit put up by a stoat. The sky feels too big for him. But I liked it. I swam in it. I couldn't take my eyes off the clouds, the water, the mud. And I must have been hopping up and down Greenbank Hard for half an hour grinning like a gargoyle, until the wind began to get up my trousers and down my back, and to bring me to myself, as they say. Meaning my liver and lights.

And I perceived that I hadn't time to waste on pleasure. A man of my age has to get on with the job.

I had two and six left from my prison money. I reckoned that five pounds would set me up with bed, board and working capital. That left four pounds seventeen and six to be won. From friends. But when I went over my friends, I seemed to owe them more than that; more than they could afford.

The sun had crackled into flames at the top; the mist was getting thin in places, you could see crooked lines of grey, like old cracks under spring ice. Tide on the turn.

Snake broken up. Emeralds and sapphires. Water like varnish with bits of gold leaf floating thick and heavy. Gold is the metal of intellect. And all at once the sun burned through in a new place, at the side, and shot out a ray that hit the Eagle and Child, next the motor-boat factory, right on the new signboard.

A sign, I thought. I'll try my old friend Coker. Must start somewhere. Coker, so I heard, was in trouble. But I was in trouble and people in trouble, they say, are more likely to give help to each other, than those who aren't. After all, it's not surprising, for people who help other people in trouble are likely soon to be in trouble themselves. And then, they are generally people too who enjoy the consolation of each other's troubles. Sympathetic people. Who'd rather see each other's tears, boo-hoo, than the smile of a millionaire, painted in butter on a barber's shave.

Coker kept the public bar at the Eagle. About five foot high and three foot ·broad. Face like a mule, except the eyes, which are small and blue. Methylated. The Eagle is down on Thames-side and gets some rough ones. But see little Coker run a six-foot pug through the door, by the scruff and the seat, his ears throwing off sparks like new horseshoes. Coker has a small hand, but it feels like hot marbles. Coker has had a hard life. Long-bodied and short-tempered.

There were three chaps hanging round the door for the bar to open, and I asked 'em, 'Is it true about Coker?' But they were strangers. Come up on an empty gravel barge. They didn't know Coker. Just then I saw her coming along with a string-bag full of knitting and her slippers. Snugs for the snug. I smiled and raised my hat, took it right off.

'Hullo, Coker. So here we are again.'

'So you're out, are you? Thought it was tomorrow.'

'I'm out, Coker. And glad to see you. I suppose there aren't any letters for me?'

'Have you come to pay me my money?' said Coker, with a look that made me step back a pace.

'That's all right,' I said quickly, 'I'll pay you, Coker, I couldn't do anything about it while I was inside, could I?'

'As if you ever did. But you won't get any more.'

'I wouldn't think of it, Coker.'

But Coker was getting fiercer and fiercer. Working herself up. She squared at me as if she meant to give me a knock. And I took another step back.

'What about that lawyer of yours who was bringing a case? You told a lot of people. I should think they'll all want their money back now you're out again.'

'You'll get your money back, Coker, with interest.'

'Yes, I'm going to,' and she put the key in the door. 'Four pounds fourteen. I'm going to see about it Wednesday. And you're coming with me; to see that woman who's giving the evidence. And if you're having us on, it looks like another police job.'

The three chaps were looking, but what did Coker care? I like Coker. She doesn't give a curse.

'Why, Coker, I'll come with you. Yes, it's quite true we got the evidence. And the money.'

Coker opened the door and went through. When I tried to follow she shut it quick to about six inches and said, 'We're not open.'

'I'll sit in the passage.'

'Haven't you got any socks?'

'No, I don't need 'em.'

'I'm not going to get you any. So you can take 'em out of your pocket.'

'Search me, Coker.'

Coker thought a bit with her nose out of the door. Like a tit looking through a fence. Then she said, 'You made a nice fool of yourself. What did you go and utter menaces for?'

'I got in a state, Coker. I got thinking how I'd been done. And that always makes me mad.'

'You were lucky to get off with a month.'

'Yes, it did me good. It cooled me down. Come on, Coker, I'll sit in the passage. I don't want any tea.'

'And what about our licence? Wednesday morning at nine. Don't you forget, and keep off that telephone.' She shut the door. She was gone. I was surprised. I was surprised too that Coker was so keen on the money all at once. Bad sign. The three chaps were now about seven. Getting near opening time. I said to one, 'It looks like it's true about Coker. She's different.' 'I bubbeg your pardon.' 'Nunnever mind,' I said, catching it. I recognized him. Green eyes. Hay hair. Big flat nose like a calf. Schoolboy. One of the lot that went to the bun-shop just opposite where I used to live. Scholarship class. Talk about Ruskin and Marx. He had his satchel and I wondered what he was doing outside the pub when his nose turned pink and he said, 'Mr Jijimson.'

'Yes,' I said, 'Mr Jijimson, that's me.' 'I sspoke to you once last Christmas. 'Oh yes, of course,' though I didn't remember. 'Yes, of course, very interesting. How's school?' and I moved off. 'You said that William Bubblake was the greatest artist who ever lived.' 'Did I?' For I didn't want to talk to the boy. He wouldn't know anything about anything except a lot of words. Ask you a lot of questions, and when you answer, it's like shooting peas into a can.

'Sorry I can't stay,' I said. 'Busy.' And I made off. Sun all in a blaze. Lost its shape. Tide pouring up from London as bright as bottled ale. Full of bubbles and every bubble flashing its own electric torch. Mist breaking into round fat shapes, china white on Dresden blue. Dutch angels by Rubens della Robbia. Big one on top curled up with her knees to her nose like the little marble woman Dobson did for Courtauld. A beauty. Made me jump to think of it. You could have turned it round in your hand. Smooth and neat as a cricket ball. A Classic Event.

2. I could see my studio from where I stood, an old boathouse down by the water wall. A bit rotten in places, but I had been glad to get it. My trouble is I get big ideas. My last one was the Fall, twelve by fifteen, and you can't get room for an idea like that in a brick studio under two hundred pounds a year. So I was glad to get the boathouse. It had a loft. I took the planks off the beams at one end and got a very nice wall, seventeen foot high. When I had my canvas up, it was two foot off the floor, which just suited me. I like to keep my pictures above dog level.

Well, I thought, the walls and roof are there still. They haven't got blown away yet. No one has leant up against 'em. I was pleased. But I didn't go along in a hurry. One thing at a time. Last time I was locked up, in thirty-seven, I left a regular establishment behind. Nice little wife, two kids, flat and a studio with a tin roof. Watertight all round. North light. Half-finished picture, eight by twelve. The Living God. Cartoons, drawings, studies, two painter's ladders, two chairs, kettle, frypan and an oil stove. All you could want.

When I came back, there was nothing. Wife and kids had gone back to her mama. Flat let to people who didn't even know my name. And the studio was a coal store. As for the Living God, my drawings, cartoons, ladders, they'd just melted. I hadn't expected to see the frypan and kettle again. You can't leave things like that about for a month in any friendly neighbourhood and expect to find them in the same place. But the Living God with his stretchers and stiffeners weighed a couple of hundredweight. When I came back from gaol even the smell had gone. Coker said that someone said the landlord took it for the rent. The landlord swore he had never seen it. I daresay he had hidden it somewhere in an attic telling himself that it might be worth thousands as soon as I was dead, and the more I was worried, the sooner that would be.

The top of my boathouse suddenly nodded its head at me, as if saying, 'That's it, old man.' Then I saw that a couple of kids were taking a plank off the roof. More patrons, I thought. When they saw me coming, they slid off the roof and ran. But not far. Crouching round like a couple of wolves waiting for the old horse to drop. I didn't need to unlock the door. Somebody had done it for me by knocking off the hasp of the padlock. And when I opened it, two more kids got out of the window on their heads. 'Don't hurry,' I said, 'there's plenty of time before dinner.'

There was nothing inside except a lot of pools on the floor from last night's rain. And the picture. I got another surprise. A big one. It was still there. Why, I thought, it's not bad in places. It might be a good thing. The serpent wants to be a bit thicker, and I could bring his tail round to make a nice curl over the tree. Adam is a bit too blue, and Eve could be redder—to bring up the blues. Yes, yes, I thought, getting a bit excited, as I always do when I come back to work after a holiday, I've got something there. Adam's right leg is a gift, whatever you may say. Nobody has done that before with a leg. What a shape. I must have been tight or walking in my sleep when I knocked that off. And yet it's leggy all right. If that limb

7

could speak, it would say, 'I walk for you, I run for you, I kneel for you. But I have my self-respect.'

Just then a stone came and knocked out the last window-pane that wasn't broken already. And I heard a voice, 'Ya, mister, how did you like chokey?' Those kids had had a fright and they were getting their own back.

Next minute I heard a different kind of yell, and when I went to the window I saw them making for the street with young Nosy on their tails.

He came in two minutes later, blowing, with the sweat on his nose and his cap falling off the back of the head. 'It's a shushame, Mr Jimson. I hope they haven't done any damage.'

'Not to speak of. There's quite a lot left. And it's an expensive canvas. Make a good floorcloth for any scullery.' 'Why, it's all f-full of holes, and they've cut a piece out.'

For somebody had been shooting at the birds with an air-gun and there was a piece about a foot square cut out of Adam's middle with a blunt knife. 'What a shushame,' said Nosy, and his nose turned pink. 'You ought to tell the po-police.' 'Well,' I said, 'Adam hadn't got a bathing-dress.' 'It's disgusting.' 'So he was, and somebody has made him respectable. Some mother, I expect. Anxious about her children. There's a lot of very good mothers in this district. You'd be surprised.' 'But the p-picture's ruined.' 'Oh no, I can easily put in a patch. It's the little holes are the nuisance. Are you going to school yet?' for I wanted to get rid of him. I wanted to get on with my work. 'Nunno,' he said, 'it's dinner-time.' 'Don't you do any work in your dinner-time?' 'S-s-sometimes.' 'If you want to get that scholarship and go to Oxford and get into the Civil Service and be a great man and have two thousand pounds a year and a nice clean wife with hot and cold and a kid with real eyes that open and close and a garage for two cars and a savings' book, you'll have to work in your dinner-time. All the good boys round here work in their dinner-time.'

'They've been writing names all over Eve, Mr Jijimson. It's b-beastly, b-beastly.' 'Yes, they seem to have appreciated my picture a whole lot.' 'I wonder you can go on pa-painting, Mr Jijimson, for such people.' 'I like painting. That's been my trouble all my life.' 'I wuwish I could paint.' 'Now, young chap, you go home quick; before you catch anything.' And I chased him out.

3. Yes, I thought, but the trouble about a leg like that, it sticks out. It's like a trumpet in the violins and a trumpet doesn't mean anything by itself. Any more than a sneeze under the stage. And if I work any brass into the top left-hand corner, it will have to go into the right bottom corner as well, into Eve, in fact, and she'll come right out of the canvas into the stalls. Only way to hold her down would be to make the serpent's head scarlet.

Carbuncle. Blood colour. And about twice the size. But that's all wrong. The serpent has got to have a white head and sky-blue eyes. That's the feeling, anyhow. That's how I feel it. Let's see. And I went to open the locker where I kept my tubes and brushes. The padlock was all right. But when I opened the lid I got another surprise. Somebody had taken out a bit of plank from the outside and cleared the lot. There was nothing there but a cigarette tin. Well, I thought, it's natural. You can't leave brushes and paint around where kids can get them. They all love art. Born to it.

All the same, the situation had its comic side. Here am I, I said, Gulley Jimson, whose pictures have been bought by the nation, or sold at Christie's by millionaires for hundreds of pounds, pictures which were practically stolen from me, and I haven't a brush or a tube of colour. Not to speak of a meal or a pair of good boots. I am simply forbidden to work. It's enough to make an undertaker smile.

But then, I said again, as I walked up and down Ellam Street, to keep warm, I mustn't get up a grievance. Plays the deuce. I must keep calm. For the fact is, IT'S WISE TO BE WISE, especially for a born fool. I mustn't exaggerate. The nation has only got one of my pictures which was left it by will and which quite likely it didn't want; and only one millionaire has ever bought my stuff. Also he took a big risk of losing his money. Also he is probably far from being a millionaire. So I have no reason to feel aggrieved and ought in fact to thank God I haven't got corns and bunions.

Just then I found myself in a telephone box. Habit, I

suppose. I never pass an empty telephone box without going in to press button B. Button B has often been kind to me. It didn't give out anything this time, except an idea. I had some coppers, so I rang up Portland Place. Put a pencil between my teeth, and asked for Mr Hickson. The young butler answered in his voice like a capon's crow, 'Who shall I say?' 'The President of the Royal Academy.' 'Certainly, sir, please hold the line.' Then Hickson droned at me like a bankrupt dentist with toothache, 'Mr. Hickson speaking.' I kept the pencil well in front and gobbled, 'Mr. Hickson, I understand you possess nineteen canvases and about three hundred drawings by the celebrated Gulley Jimson.'

'I have a collection of early Jimsons.'

'Of which one small canvas was sold last year at Christie's for two hundred and seventy guineas.'

'Seventy guineas, and it wasn't mine. It belonged to a Bond Street dealer.'

'Even at that rate your nineteen canvases are worth at least two thousand pounds, while the drawings and sketches would amount to abount two thousand more.'

'Excuse me, but what name did you mention?'

'I am the President of the Academy. I understand that Mr Jimson is now destitute. And I was informed on the best legal advice that you have no right to his pictures. I understand that you conspired with a drunken model to rob him of this valuable property.'

'Is that you, Jimson?'

'Certainly not,' I said, 'I wouldn't touch the bastard with a dung fork. But I have to inform you that he means trouble, and he's a dangerous man when he thinks he's got a grievance. He is in touch with your accomplice Sara Monday, and he has powerful friends who mean to bring the case to law.'

'Then they will lose their money, as they have no case.'

'No doubt, Mr Hickson, you've got tip-top lawyers who could do down Magna Carta and George Washington. And you have my full sympathy. Such dangerous blackguards as Jimson oughtn't to be allowed to live. But I'm speaking as a friend. If Jimson doesn't get his rightful due in the next week, he fully intends to burn your house down, and cut your tripes out afterwards. He means it too. I have it from a mutual acquaintance. So I thought I'd better give you a straight tip.'

'If you're a friend of Jimson's, perhaps you'd better make him understand that he won't do himself any good by this sort of behaviour. He will only get himself another spell of prison, a very much longer one. As for his being destitute, if he is so, it is entirely his own fault. Good evening.' And he hung up. But he took the receiver off again. Because when I rang him again five minutes later, in a female voice, as the Duchess of Middlesex, the number was engaged. And it went on being engaged for half an hour.

This made me a bit impatient, and I began to be rough with the instrument. Till I saw a copper looking in at me. Then I pretended to take a call. And made my getaway.

In fact, I realized that I had been getting upset. I hadn't meant to say anything about burning Hickson's house down. Now, when I say anything like that, about shooting a man or cutting his tripes out, even in joke, I often get angry with him. And anything like bad temper is bad for me. It spoils my equanimity. It blocks up my imagination. It makes me stupid so that I can't see straight. But luckily, I noticed it in time. Cool off, I said to myself. Don't get rattled off your centre. Remember that Hickson is an old man. He's nervous and tired of worry. That's his trouble, worry. Poor old chap, it's ruining any happiness he's got left. He simply don't know what to do. He sends you to jug and it makes him miserable, and as soon as you come out you start on him again. And he's afraid that if he gives you any money, you'll come after him more than ever and fairly worry him to death. Simply daren't trust you. He's wrong, but there it is. That's his point of view. He daren't do the right thing and the wrong thing gives him no peace. Poor old chap. It's an awful problem for a poor old bastard that let down his guts about forty years ago, and has rolled in comfort all his life.

And I was so calm, that when I felt my pulse, it barely touched seventy-eight. Pretty good for a man of sixty-seven.

4. All at once I remembered the oilman. I owed too much at my colour-shop to get anything on tick, but I had often seen paint and brushes at the oilshop. So I went along and asked, 'How much for those little sample tins, interior decorator's stuff?' The oilman was a nice old chap. Bald head. Pince-nez. Looked at me and said, "Mr Gulley Jimson.' 'The same,' I said. 'The penalty of fame, so far as it goes.' 'Excuse me, Mr Jimson,' he said, 'I think we've got something of yours.' And he went into a glass dock where he kept his desk. 'I'd be glad of that,' I said, 'whatever it is.' 'Yes,' he said, 'I thought so,' looking in the desk. 'A little account.' 'Thank you very much,' I said, 'I'll send you a cheque.' And I went off quickly. But he came on nearly as quick. He was at the door sooner than I had expected.

Lucky thing there was a coal-cart at the kerb. I nipped under the horse and round the back of the cart. Stood there with my legs by the front wheel. Got a nice view of the oilman in the shop window opposite. He was a bit surprised. Looked up and down. Came out at last to have a look under the cart. So did I, the opposite way, and when he came back to the horse's head, I was round by the tail-board. He went in then and I went home top speed. I'd got an idea. The red cloud ought to be scarlet. Have a clash in the reds—pillar box and crimson lake. Get them moving. I'd only had time to borrow four pots from the oilman. He kept his books too well; didn't give me time to choose. But I had two reds, as well as a blue and a white. No brushes. All wired to cards. It's five years since I borrowed a brush from one of these shops round here. Too many young Raphaels on the grab.

But I made a pretty good stump brush out of a bit of rope and knocked out the idea for the two reds on the wall. Touch of scarlet in the clouds. Crimson apples. Eve terracotta with a scarlet reflection. Pretty good idea it seemed to me and kept that leg quiet. But I didn't look at it long. It had come up too quick. Ideas that shoot up like that won't bear the sun. They need time to make a root. I cut for the Eagle. To see if Coker was in a better

12

temper. And know if anyone could lend me a bed, a kettle, and a frypan. Or at least a frypan.

5.

No one in the bar but Coker. 'Is it Willy again?' I asked her.

Willy was Coker's young man. A warehouse clerk shaped like a soda-water bottle. Face like a bird. All eyes and beak. Bass in the choir. Glider club. Sporty boy. A sparrowhawk. Terror to the girls. Coker was church, teetotal and no smoke. Willy her only weakness.

Coker drew me a can and waited till I'd paid for it. My last bob. But she threw me a pair of socks across the altar. 'And they aren't Woolworth's,' she said. 'Don't you pop them or I'll cut your liver out.'

'Thank you, miss, I was wondering where I was going to put up. They've knocked out all my windows at home.'

'You're not going to stop with me again. I've no room. You'd better try a Rowton.' 'Rowton's all full,' I said.

Coker said nothing. But she was absent-minded. When she's got that look, as if she isn't sure if a suspender hasn't given way somewhere, she's usually friendly. I was just going to ask her for an advance of five bob on the fortune that was coming to me, when she said, 'I got them socks for Willy.'

'Not had an accident, has he?'

Coker thought a bit and her face was as blank as a sanitary brick. Then she said, 'He's gone off with a Blondie.'

'He'll come back if you want him.'

'Not him. She's a widow too. Five years older.'

'You'll soon get a better than Willy. The dogs leave sweeter bones on any doorstep.'

'Not me,' she said. 'Willy was a piece of luck. Due to the carols last Christmas—in the bad light.'

'You're still in the choir.'

'Never again, Mr. Jimson. No more religion for me. I hate God. It isn't fair to make a girl and give her a face like mine.'

'Don't let it get you down, Coke. Don't get in a state. That was my trouble, getting in a state.'

'I shall if I like,' said Coker. 'That's the only advantage

I've got. I don't give a damn for myself. Why, even when I was a kid, and I got my earache, I used to say, go on, ache; go on, you bloody flap. Give me hell. That's what I'm for.'

'Don't you believe it, Coker,' I said. 'You're young. You don't know. Things are never so bad they can't be worse. Don't you let anything get hold of you. You got to keep your independence. When I was a kid my father died and I went to live with an uncle who used to try which was harder, his boot or my bottom. And when my poor mother saw me cry, she would take me in her arms and say, "Don't hate him, Gull, or it will poison your life. You don't want that man to spoil your life." "No, mums," I would say, "I'd rather die." "So you won't hate him, my darling, you'll put all that bad feeling out of your heart." "Yes, mums, boo-hoo, tomorrow." "No, today, this minute." "Not this minute, mums, it's too soon." "Yes, this minute, you mustn't let that feeling stay one minute. It's a very bad poison." "Boo-hoo," I would cry, "but I can't help it, mums." "No, my dearest darling dear, my poor lamb, you can't help it, but God will help you. We'll ask Him now," and she would make me kneel down and pray for forgiveness.'

'Well, what had *you* done?' Coker said.

'She didn't mean I was to be forgiven—she meant that God was to put forgiveness into me.'

'He couldn't do that to me,' Coker said. 'Let him try, that's all. Yes, Captain Jones?'

A little old chap with bandy legs had come in. He put a shilling on the edge of the mahogany and gave it a slap with the flat of his hand so that it slid across to the other edge. Coker drew him a pint and gave him the change.

'Good shot, miss,' he said.

'He couldn't do that to me,' said Coker.

'Nor me,' said I, 'but my mother was a female-mother. Practical. She didn't rely too much on God. And when she got out a picture book and told me stories, I forgot my Uncle Bob and even my bottom. Yes, I would sit on my mother's knee and wonder why I felt sore.'

'Nice evening,' said the old man.

'No mother could make me forgive that Blondie,' Coker said. 'It would be a bloody crime not to hate her guts.'

'But wind's changing round,' said the old man. 'Look at

the smoke of that tug—easterly—we'll have blue sky and red noses tomorrow.'

'Don't let him get inside you,' my mother said. 'Don't let uncle reign in your heart—you want only happiness there. You want only joy and love and peace that passeth understanding.'

'So it does,' said Coker. 'It passed mine long ago.'

'Head wind for me if the old barge is ready,' said the little man, 'but the missus won't mind. She'll be able to keep me another day.'

'They tried religion on me,' Coker said. 'As soon as they saw I was growing out all the wrong way. They always try it on the flat-foot squaws. But it never would stick on this one, I had my pride. I said, "God has done the dirty on me and I'm not going to lick his hand for sugar left over from the horses."'

'Grace Darling, Florence Nightingale and the Rose,' said the old man. 'That's the fleet. Down on the tide with a fair wind to Gravesend or Burnham, and back by the train.'

'I thought you were Sunday school, Coker.'

'Mum sent me to Sunday school and I was Church till week before last. But I wasn't giving anything away. I kept myself to myself, thank you very much.'

'I'm a primitive,' said the old man. 'But I'm not one of the strict ones. My missus' Peculiar. She *is* strict. But she was born happy, thank God. She can't take anything too serious.'

'Mrs Jones is one of the lucky ones,' Coker said. 'Not a grey hair at sixty, and you'd take her for thirty from the back.'

'It was in the family,' said the old man, 'with deafness. Like bull terriers. She was stone deaf before she was forty. But she took it well. She's never got suspicious. Because it runs in the family.'

'I'd rather love a dog,' said Coker. 'He loves you back again. I saw such a nice pup yesterday. Think of all that love for ten and six—that's what they asked. And beat him all you like, he'd still think the world of you. It's nature.'

'The girls get it and not the boys. My boys have ears like a water-rat's, but the girl is a bit hard of hearing already— at twenty. Of course, you couldn't tell just at first go off. She's got her tricks to hide it. Smiles and looks nice when

15

she hasn't heard what you said. But it's hard on a girl. She knows what's coming to her.'

And I saw all the deaf, blind, ugly, cross-eyed, limp-legged, bulge-headed, bald and crooked girls in the world, sitting on little white mountains and weeping tears like sleet. There was a great clock ticking and every time it ticked the tears all fell together with a noise like broken glass tinkling in a plate. And the ground trembled like a sleeping dog in front of the parlour fire when the bell tolls for a funeral. 'Trouble is, you can always tell there's nothing in it,' said the old man, 'I mean the smile. It looks a bit empty when she hasn't heard.'

That's all very well, I thought, I could do the girls—their legs would look like the fringe on the mantelpiece, but how would you join up the mountains. There'd just be a lot of ground stuck on. Unless you had flowers. Yes, everlastings. Yes, and a lot of nuns pushing perambulators, with a holy babe in each. Yes, and every nun with a golden crown. Yes, and the nuns would be like great black tear drops. They could be the tear drops. And they wouldn't have feet. They would go on little wheels.

'I'd rather be blind than deaf,' Coker said.

'Not me,' said the old man, 'I likes to see the world. You can do without the talk.'

Yes, I thought. You've got the girls at the top red and blue and green, like a lot of little flowers burning and then the mountains blue-white and blue-green, and then the everlastings—they ought to be bigger than the girls, and then the little black nuns under them, black or green.

'Well, you can smell,' said Coker, 'and there's eau de Cologne and rum. And you wouldn't see yourself in the glass.'

Coker began to rub her tumblers, the old man took out a penny, polished smooth on both sides, breathed on it, rubbed it on his sleeve, and put it back in his pocket. Didn't feel he ought to play. Solemn occasion. I thought of the deaf girl and wondered if she was pretty. I wondered if she knew how to be happy. Why, I thought, if I were a pretty girl and going deaf, I'd be an artist's model. I'd be an artist. Concentrate on my work. Like Edison. But she wouldn't know. Who would tell her? And if you did tell her, she wouldn't believe you.

The wind was blowing the curtains at the little windows

behind the bar. I always like to see curtains blow, and feel the breeze from outside. The tide was flowing. A tug and four barges were going up like circus cars on a chain. The water was like frosted glass on the smooth side, not too bright. Over by the Surrey bank there was another flaw; as if somebody had breathed on the glass. But it didn't seem to be moving.

'Good night, miss,' the old man went out. But I caught him at the door. 'Excuse me, Captain?' 'Yes.' And I told him about the William Blake Memorial Association. I had been secretary of this Association for six months. Objects: to buy Blake's house in London. Hang originals on the walls. And have a caretaker to show the stuff and explain all about it. The idea was to charge sixpence a visitor. A hundred visitors a day would make two thousand a year.

'Blake,' said the captain, 'is that Admiral Blake?' 'No, William Blake, the great Blake.' 'Never heard of him.' 'Greatest Englishman who ever lived.' 'Was he? What did he do?' 'Poet and painter, but never had a chance. Didn't know how to boost himself.' 'Don't like all this boost.' 'Quite right. Blake didn't either. This memorial is for justice, that's all. We're selling five thousand founders' shares at half a crown down with three instalments at six months. It will pay a hundred per cent certain. And every receipt has the secretary's signature. In ink.' 'I don't mind all that, but I'll give you half a crown for your club if it's against boost.' 'Make it five bob and I'll elect you vice-president.' 'No, half a crown's enough,' and he put his hand in his pocket. But just then Coker put her tit's beak out of the door and said, 'Don't you give him anything, Captain Jones.' 'I thought it might be a swindle.' 'You'll never see your money back.' 'I knew that before, but what is this Blake?' 'Oh that Blake, that's just the tale.' 'I see, thank you, miss,' and he walked off.

I was angry with Coker. But she only said, 'I told you none of that in my bar.' 'It wasn't in your bar.' 'You old fool, and only out today.' 'It's all legal. And where am I going to sleep? If you won't let me make an honest bed ticket.' But Coker was in a bad temper again. She said only, 'Wednesday morning at nine. Don't you forget it. And keep away from the telephone.'

6.
It was half-past six, too dark to paint, turning very cold. Clouds all streaming away like ghost fish under the ice. Evening sun turning reddish. Trees along the hard like old copper. Old willow leaves shaking up and down in the breeze, making shadows on the ones below, reflections on the ones above. Need a tricky brush to give the effect and what would be the good. Pissarro's job, not mine. Not nowadays. Lyric, not epic.

Stopped at the corner and put on Coker's socks. Silk and wool; must have cost seven and six. But the trouble was, I had holes in my bootsoles and the pavement struck through. Went to a rubbish basket and got some evening newspapers. Shoved 'em in my boots. Shoved 'em up my trousers, stuffed 'em down my waistcoat. As good as leather against an east wind. Thank God for the Press, the friend of the poor. Then I went in and lit a match to have a look at the picture. I had a feeling it mightn't be there. And it wasn't there, only a piece of dirty yellow paint. It gave me a shock. There, I said to myself, I've spoilt my night's rest. Why couldn't I take it on trust? Act of faith. That's all it is really.

'Mr J-Jimson.'

'No, he's not at home.'

'I w-wondered if you'd like some coffee from the s-stall.'

'No,' I said, 'he wouldn't. He's gone to bed.'

The boy moved off. I went up to the picture on tiptoe and lit another match. This time it showed me a lot of dirty red paint. Like the skin on a pot of rust proofing. My God, I said, how and why did I do that? I must have lost the trick of painting. I'm done for. I'll have to cut my throat after all.

'Your c-coffee, Mr Jimson.'

'Mr Jimson has just gone out. He must have seen you coming.'

But the boy switched on his bicycle lamp; and came right in and put the coffee in my hand.

'Mr Jimson won't be back for some time,' I said. 'But he

18

asked me to tell you that you haven't got a chance. He isn't going to talk to you about art. He's committed arson, adultery, murder, libel, malfeasance of club moneys, and assault with battery; but he doesn't want to have any serious crime on his conscience.'

'B-but, Mr Jimson, I w-want to be an artist.'

'Of course you do,' I said, 'everybody does once. But they get over it, thank God, like the measles and the chickenpox. Go home and go to bed and take some hot lemonade and put on three blankets and sweat it out.'

'But Mr J-Jimson, there must be artists.'

'Yes, and lunatics and lepers, but why go and live in an asylum before you're sent for? If you find life a bit dull at home,' I said, 'and want to amuse yourself, put a stick of dynamite in the kitchen fire, or shoot a policeman. Volunteer for a test pilot, or dive off Tower Bridge with five bob's worth of roman candles in each pocket. You'd get twice the fun at about one-tenth of the risk.'

I could see the boy's eyes bulging in the reflected light off the boards, the colour of dirty water. And I thought, I've made an effect. 'Now go away,' I said, 'It's bedtime. Shoo.'

He took my cup and went away. And I struck another match to look at Eve's face. Oh my God, I thought, it's as flat as a tray. It's all made up. What a colour. Tinned salmon. Why did I do that? What a piece of affectation. What was I feeling about? And I felt all locked up. I wanted to knock my head on the walls.

The boy came in with another cup of coffee.

'For God's sake,' I said, 'Mr Jimson is not at home, and he doesn't like to be interrupted by impudent young bastards walking into his house as if it was their own.'

'Oh, Mr Jimson, but I saw they'd g-got buns.' And he gave me a bun with the coffee. 'I'm s-sorry Mr J-Jimson,' he said, 'but I don't know any other real artists.'

'Who told you Mr Jimson was an artist?' I said. And in my agony I took a bite of bun. It was a good bun and my impression was that the boy had given me the biggest, though in the dim light he might easily have juggled himself the big one. And I was touched. I oughtn't to have been touched because obviously the young blackguard was trying to get round me for his own purposes. With coffee

19

and buns out of his week's pocket money. But I've always had a weakness for boys like Nosy; ugly boys who aspire to martyrdom or fame.

'Look here,' I said, 'I'll tell you a secret. Jimson never was an artist. He's only one of the poor beggars who thought he was clever. Why, you know what the critics said about his pictures in 1908—that's thirty years ago. They said he was a nasty young man who didn't even know what art was, but thought he could advertise himself by painting and drawing, worse than a child of six—and since then he's gone off a lot. As he's got older, he's got younger.'

'Oh Mr Jimson, but they always say that.'

'Sometimes they're right, my lad. And my impression is that they were right about Jimson. He's a fraud. Don't you have anything to do with him. Let dirty dogs lie, and swindle, and so on.'

'But there are artists, Mr Jimson.'

'Yes, Jimson's papa was an artist, a real artist. He got in the Academy. He painted people with their noses right between their eyes. He started measuring up the human clock at ten years old, and he worked sixteen hours a day for fifty years. And died a pauper in quite considerable misery. Personally, I'd rather be eaten alive by slow worms.'

'What d-did he p-paint?'

'Pictures,' I said severely. I saw the way the boy's mind was going. 'Art. Jimson's papa may have been in the Academy and painted nicely, but his pictures were definitely art. A lot of artists have painted nicely. But I suppose you never heard of Raphael or Poussin or Vermeer.'

'Oh yes, they were f-famous artists—and there are s-still f-famous artists.'

'Jimson's papa was like that. Of course, when he started, he wasn't popular—rather too modern. He took after Constable and the critics said he was slapdash. But about 1848 he became fuf-famous, for about five years. His stuff was landscape with figures. Girls in gardens. With poetry in the catalogues. He used to get about two hundred guineas for a really nice girl in a nice cottage garden—hollyhocks and pink roses. He made two thousand a year at one time and entertained in style. His wife had three big receptions and a baby every year. But about 1858 a new lot of modern art broke out. The pre-Raphaelites.

Old Mr Jimson hated it, of course. And all decent people agreed with him. When Millais showed his "Christ in the Carpenter's shop," Charles Dickens wrote that the pre-Raphaelites were worse than the bubonic plague. And Mr Jimson wrote to *The Times* and warned the nation, in the name of art, that the pre-Raphaelites were in a plot to destroy painting altogether. This made him very popular. All really responsible people saw the danger of modern art.'

'The d-danger? But that's quite s-silly.'

'No, it's not silly. And it's time you went home to your mammy. By Gee and Jay, I'd like Mr Jimson to hear you say that his remarks were silly. Thank God he's absent tonight. Get out quick before he comes back and wrings your neck.'

The boy went out and I lit another match. As every painter knows the fourth look is often lucky. It is always a good plan, during an attack of the jimjams, to try at least four matches. A picture left about in the dark will often disappear for three matches, and come back again, at the fourth, a regular masterpiece. Something quite remarkable. But the match went out before I could see whether I was looking at genuine intuition of fundamental and universal experience in plastic forms of classical purity and simplicity, or a piece of barefaced pornography that ought to be dealt with by the police.

'Excuse me, Mr J-Jimson, I thought you might like a s-s-s-s,' and he gave me a sausage roll. 'It's so cold tonight.'

'You are a good boy,' I said, in spite of myself. 'And so I'm telling you something for your good. All art is bad, but modern art is the worst. Just like the influenza. The newer it is, the more dangerous. And modern art is not only a public danger—it's insidious. You never know what may happen when it's got loose. Dickens and all the other noble and wise men who backed him up, parsons and magistrates and judges, were quite right. So were the brave lads who fought against the Impressionists in 1870, and the Post-Impressionists in 1910, and that rat Jimson in 1920. They were all quite right. They knew what modern art can do. Creeping about everywhere, undermining the Church and the State and the Academy and the Law and Marriage and the Government—smashing up civilization, degenerating the Empire.

'Look at the awful disgusting pictures Jimson paints—look at that Adam and Eve—worse than Epstein or Spencer. Absolutely repulsive and revolting, as Dickens said about Millais. A shocking thing. Thank God Jimson's papa never saw it. It would have broken his heart if it hadn't been broken pretty thoroughly already, when the pre-Raphaelites got into the Academy, and he was thrown out.'

'How could they do that?'

'Yes, they could, because he wasn't an associate. He was just going to be when something happened and they threw him out instead. Bang. Three girls in three gardens. Lovely girls. Lovely pictures. But somehow nobody wanted any more nice girls in gardens. Not Jimson girls. Only Burne-Jones girls and Rossetti girls. So papa and mama and their numerous family had nothing to eat.' I swallowed the bun to hide my emotion. I didn't know whether I'd be able to live through the night without my picture. I'm never really comfortable without a picture; and when I've got one on hand, life isn't worth living.

'Mr J-Jimson, do you think it's a good thing to s-start in an art school?'

'Who's going to stutart in an art school?'

'Me.'

'Oh go away, go away. Go home.' And I chased him out. I wanted to be unhappy by myself. I wanted to grieve for Papa. That man suffered a lot. Even more than my poor mother who had to watch him suffer. For she had seven children to worry about as well, and children are a duty. Whereas a broken-hearted man with a grievance is only a liability, a nuisance. And he knows it too.

7.

Cold morning. My legs a bit stiff. Didn't look at Adam and Eve in case it hadn't come back. But went straight out.

Frost on the grass like condensed moonlight. Moon high up, transparent. Like snow mark in ice. Birds very lively. Sparrows fluffed out like feather dusters. Met friend Ollier delivering first post. Drop on his nose, a pearl, and two more on his moustache, diamonds. 'Hullo, Mr Ollier, know where I could get some coffee?' 'Good morning, Mr Jimson, if you would care to have one with me in about five minutes.' 'Thank you, Mr Ollier.' 'It's a pleasure, Mr Jimson, to be sure.'

Took a walk up and down to crack the joints. Sun coming up along a cloud bank like clinkers. All sparks. Couldn't do it in paint. Limits of the art. Limits of everything. Limits of my fingers which are all swole up at the joints. No fingers, no swell, no swell, no art. Old Renoir painting his red girls with the brushes strapped to his wrists. Best things he ever did. Monuments.

> The pride of the peacock is the glory of God.
> The lust of the goat is the bounty of God.
> The wrath of the lion is the wisdom of God.
> The nakedness of woman is the work of God.

And the nakedness of these trees, pavements, houses, old Postie's red nose and white moustache. 'Nice day, Mr Ollier.' 'A bit chilly for October. Bringing the leaves down.' 'You're right, Mr Ollier.'

'Coming to the meeting, Mr Jimson?' 'Another meeting?' 'Mr Plant's got a meeting on the tenth.'

Mr Plant was an old friend of ours. Plant and Ollier and three or four more had a society and held meetings. They got some schoolmaster or preacher or lecturer from the Workers' Education Association to give a lecture and smoked over him for a couple of hours. Chief idea for the married, to get away from the home for one evening; for bachelors, to find a home for an evening. There are a lot of these clubs in London. Some of them are simply habits, a few friends who meet regularly in a pub to discuss the dogs, religion, the government, and the state of Europe. I liked Plant's club because Plant had beer for his friends.

'Thank you, Walter,' I said. 'What's the subject?' 'I don't know,' said Ollier. 'But the last one was on Ruskin,' I said. 'How did you know?' said Walter surprised, as we went into the Korner Koffee Shop. 'Because it's generally on Ruskin, or Plato or Owen or Marx. But Ruskin comes first. I should think there must be about fifty meetings every night somewhere in London, on Ruskin.'

'He seems to have been a good writer,' said Postie, who is a modest man and never gives a definite opinion, out of politeness. 'Two coffees, my dear, and four bread and marg and marmalade.'

'So he was, a real artist at it.' 'And they say he knew a lot about art.' 'He was a real writer at it.' There was some coffee on the blue cloth and I pushed it about till it surrounded an interesting kind of shape. But I couldn't see what I could do with it.

'I thought Ruskin seemed to take a high view of art,' said Postie. 'So he did,' I said. 'He had private means. He needed something.' 'And Mr Plant takes a high view too.' 'Mr Plant's had a lot of bad luck in his life. Some take the high road and some take the low road.' I saw that the blue shape could be made into a kind of man, kneeling down like my Adam. But without any right shoulder. One line from the nape to the croup. A sweet line. I fell for that line. Here, I thought, why not. Bring the shoulder forward. Yes, bring his arm right out and have Eve pushing it away. Yes, have her doing the modest. Fending off the first pass. And that nice line will lie right up against the serpent—the serpent will have to come a little behind Adam to avoid two cylinders meeting at the vertical. All right, make the serpent fatter—fatter than Adam. Fat and stiff—erect. And all those red scales against Adam's blue-white flesh.

'Why, Mr Jimson, you're not going?' said Postie. I hadn't noticed it, but I was certainly going. 'I've got an engagement,' I said. 'Have another cup first.' Postie looked quite sad to see me go. He has a strong social sense. It goes with the moustache. Born for a dukedom. Perfect manners and no hurry. 'I'm sorry, Walter,' I said, 'but it's an important engagement—rather urgent.'

8. And I hurried round to the shed. Well, what, I said. It might be something. Probably not. But the fact was, I had got the feeling it was straight from the horse. And when I'd brushed out Adam's damned old knob of a shoulder and got him a new shape down the back, I had that feeling so strong that I sat on myself. Careful, I said, don't get too gay. Perhaps this damned old canvas is going to turn into something or other, perhaps not. Probably not.

Suddenly I got a pull from behind that nearly knocked

me down. There was Coker in her best. Nice tweed suit, man's shoes, little rat fur round her bull neck. No jewellery. Coker in her best, dresses county. Having no figure and no looks. 'What the hell you doing, Mr Jimson?' 'Nothing.' 'What's that blue thing? If it's a man it's more like a horse. Without any shoulder on one side.' 'It's just a picture, Cokey.' 'Well, I suppose I don't know anything about it.' 'I suppose so.' 'I suppose it's what you call art.' 'I suppose so.' 'And who was going to meet me at the bus-stop?' 'That was for Wednesday next.' 'This is Wednesday. I got the morning off on purpose.' 'You don't say so. What a pity. I've just arranged to meet a man about a picture. May mean a nice commission,' and so on. Pitching a tale. For the truth was, I wanted to get on with my work. And I knew very well what this new game of Coker's meant— trouble. Arguments. And very likely a lot of bad feeling. It was three years since I'd seen Sara Monday, and I didn't want to see her again. I hadn't the time.

'I'm sorry, Coker, but this is a real chance for me. I might get a couple of hundred out of it, pay you off.' 'Is this true?' 'On my honour.' 'You're such a liar, Mr Jimson.' 'Swear to God.' 'What time did you say?' 'Half-past nine at the Korner Koffee.' 'I'll wait.' 'You'll be late for opening time.' 'It's worth it if you're going to pay me my money.' And she stayed. I couldn't do any more work. Only pretending. Went round to the Koffee at half-past nine and put up a fuss because the chap hadn't turned up. Coker very suspicious. Wouldn't even stand me a coffee. And so to the bus.

All that idea had gone cold. It seemed to me I'd finally wrecked the picture. Adam looked like a frog, and why not? I wanted to give Coker one on the nose. But the only time I ever tried to give Coker a slap—and that was under provocation—she got in first with a clump which blacked my eye and nearly broke my jaw. And then kicked me downstairs. In the proper style. It's not really a kick when done by an expert. It's a punch with the foot. And the foot applied rather high on the crack. Coker shot me off the top step like a rocket, and I had so many bruises on me I couldn't take my trousers off or put my boots on or scratch the back of my neck, for a fortnight. It makes me laugh to think of it. I like Coker. She's a woman of character. There's something there that will stand the rain. But next time I have to deal with Coker on the level, I thought, I'll take a hammer with me.

'I don't know why you're so keen on this visit,' I said. 'You won't get much out of old Sara.'

'We'll wait and see,' said Coker. 'She wouldn't like to let it come into court, I should think—living with a chap who's not her husband and about ten years younger. And she's been in jug herself too.'

'And all this trouble for four pounds fourteen,' I said.

'I'm not letting them get away with it,' said Coker. 'Monday and Hickson, a nice pair. Why, they simply made a fool of you.'

Coker was getting hot, and I said no more. Coker had been working up the case for a long time, and when a woman gets the idea of justice, there's no teaching her any sense. That's why we don't have women judges. They'd be too strong for justice.

And, in fact, she went on getting fiercer and fiercer all the way. Working herself up.

'This Sara Monday,' she said, 'where did you pick her up? Is there a place for models or did you take her off the street?' 'She wasn't a model and I didn't pick her up. She was a married woman, and she picked me up.' 'What, you don't mean to say she went on the street?' 'Of course not, she didn't need to. It was in her own house when I went to paint her husband.' 'What, you don't mean to say she gave you the eye in her own house?' 'Two eyes and the aye-aye. Threw herself at me from the kick.' 'A married woman.' 'Married seven years, five kids.' 'Five kids,' said Coker. 'A woman like that ought to be hung on hooks.' 'You'd be surprised,' I said, 'the women that go for artists, especially artists that paint the nude. Makes 'em feel themselves in themselves, I suppose.' 'Don't you call them women,' said Coker, still working up her drill. 'A lot of whores, I say. And worse if they're ladies and haven't any call.' 'Sara had the call,' I said. 'Just getting up in the thirties and full blast on all cylinders. Regular man-killer. "Oh, Mr Jimson, I do love art," and she didn't know a picture from a bath bun. Never did. "Oh, Mr Jimson, how wonderful to be able to paint like that." Bending her neck, too, and spooning her eyes at me. She believed in butter, Sara did. Greasing the slides. I've known some liars and crooks, but Sara was the queen. Why, she couldn't ask you

26

to have some more cream without putting the comether in her voice and shooting off her eyes and jerking up her front.'

'Oh—it turns my liver.'

'And, what made me laugh, to see her at a tea party in her frills. "Some more tea, Lady Pye; another slice, Mrs Paddle. Oh, do try. Just a little bit of the angel cake." They all loved her. Sweet young British matron—guardian of the home.'

'Don't tell me about her,' said Coker, 'I can see her.'

'Family prayers. Down on her knees every night and morning. The Scripture moveth us in sundry places. And then hop-skip round to my studio. "Would you like me to sit?" "Not today, thank you, ma'am." "But you're drawing that figure out of your head." "Yes, ma'am." "Wouldn't it be better from a model?" "Depends on the model, ma'am." "Anything I can do to help?" And in two two's there she is in her skin.'

'I'd skin her.'

'Church on Sunday. Bible and prayer book in red morocco with gilt edges. Cold supper in the evening. Salmon, salad, lobsters, tongue, brawn, cold beef, stout, burgundy. Trifle with a pound of Devonshire cream and a couple of pints of old brown sherry. Evening hymns in the twilight. "Oh, Mr Jimson, what a lovely tune—it always makes me cry. What a sweet moon, shall we take a turn in the garden, to see if the tobacco has got another flower? Oh, Mr Jimson, isn't it a sweet scent—it goes to your head." Head was the word. And then the summerhouse and somebody had left the cushions in the deck chair.'

'Oh, the bitch,' said Coker. 'The whip is too good for them.'

'And afterwards, you know, Coker, she used to shed tears—real tears—and it was: "Oh, Mr Jimson, how did it all happen, I can't believe it, it all seems like a dream, doesn't it? Just a bad dream. And I'm so fond of my husband. He's such a true good man. Oh dear, I feel so awful—"'

'And you swallowed it all,' said Coker. 'Just like a man, encouraging the bitch.'

'Sara? Not on your life. I used to laugh at her tricks.'

'Yes, and let her grab you as soon as she'd murdered her husband.'

'Sara never grabbed me. Poor old Sara, she didn't have much of a success there, when she got too much of a nuisance I threw her out on her neck.'

'I believe you,' said Coker. 'Backwards. Look at you now. Hopping along with your nose stuck out in front like an old dog in the May moon—she'll grab you again if you aren't careful.'

'Never,' I said, pulling in my nose a bit and pushing out my stomach. For the truth was I had been getting up the pace. And yet I'll swear I never thought of Sara, except as a damned old nuisance. Spoiling a good day's work.

'Grab me? Sara? After all I know of her.' I said, 'Poor Sall, not likely. Why, talk of not letting your right hand know what your left hand was doing. Sara could commit adultery at one end and weep for her sins at the other, and enjoy both operations at once. She wasn't a woman—she was a bag full of women, and everyone worse than all the others.'

'I've half a mind to go back,' said Coker. 'I never knew she was as bad as that.' And she stuck out her front and made her heels rattle. Coker hasn't much chest. She's all of a piece like a ship's funnel. 'All right, Coker,' I said. 'That suits me. I don't want any trouble with the old devil.' 'Not on your life,' said Coker. 'You're not going to dodge out of it. Only thing is—I hope I'll be able to speak to the creature without showing what I think of her.' 'Say what you like,' I said. 'Sara won't mind—she's solid brass to the Adam's rib. Only way to touch Sara's feelings is to hit her with something harder. On the nose. Toko on the Boko. That's her only tender spot.'

'I couldn't do it,' said Coker. 'I couldn't touch her with a bottle-brush. It's psychology with me. A woman who could show herself off like that.'

9. But when we came to Sara's door it was new painted, and the door knob shining like rolled gold. Sara all over, I thought, you can see she's adopted that door knob—loves it like herself. Rub the little darling up and give it a chance to look its best. Sara for cleaning and washing. Loved slapping things

about. Getting off her steam. See Sara in her bath wash-ing herself. Like a cat. Almost hear her purr. I didn't know whether to draw her or to bite her. And I did give her one with the back brush which made her jump. Oh Gulley, what was that for? Just to let you know there's somebody else in the world. Good sketch I did of her—with the same back brush. Right arm in the air. Elbow cutting up against the window. Hair over left shoulder catching the light. Lime green outside. Head bent over to the left—line of the cheek against the hair. Lips pushed out. Eyes dropped. Looking at her breasts. Serious expression. Worship.

And all the same, she was a fine woman. She made me mad every way. Regular born man-eater. Coker gave me a nudge like a kick and the door came open. There was a fat old char with grey hair and a red face, breathing beer and suds. 'Why,' she said, 'it's not you, Gulley.' 'No,' I said, 'I'm Mr Gloster of Foster.' 'Well, isn't that nice,' she said.

She didn't smile. She only looked confused, like an old char when something happens out of her routine. 'You didn't see a little boy with white hair and blue stockings coming along the street? You might have heard him cough.'

'No,' I said, 'and how are you, Sara?' For I knew her well enough at a second look. She still had the build and the voice.

'Excuse me, Mrs. Monday,' Coker said, 'I think you heard from me. Miss D. Coker.'

'Yes, Miss Coker, of course. I was meaning to write to you only I've been so busy.'

All said like a duchess, so sweet you couldn't tell how it was meant, if you hadn't known that Coker was an en-emy. 'Excuse me a moment,' and she came bulging out of the door and went waddling down the street, calling, 'Dicky, Dicky.'

'A nice game,' said Coker. 'No, you don't, Madame. We've come and we stay,' and she pushed me through the door and into the parlour. Big armchairs. A lot of knick-knacks. Souvenirs of Brighton and Blackpool. Sara all over. Photographs of Mr Monday in a jampot collar. Photograph of Sara in her wedding dress. Silver frame that she gave me once for a birthday present to fit my favourite picture of herself in a tight bodice. A bun bursting out of

29

the bag. A Rubens Venus in a parcel. You could never get Sara into a fitted dress. You had to hang frills on her.

Sara came back, panting. 'Excuse me being so rude. I'm so worried about my little boy. My husband's little boy, I should say. Do sit down.'

'We came on business,' Coker said, standing up as stiff as a pillar box. 'As I wrote you, Mr Jimson is bringing a legal action against Mr Hickson for getting justice about nineteen paintings and over five hundred drawings. What we understand is you gave over this property to Mr Hickson for value which you had no right to receive.'

'That's right,' said Sara, 'but if you would just sit down a moment till I get the kettle on,' and off she went again. I sat down, but Coker gave me a look and said, 'Don't do that, Mr Jimson—that's just what she wants. If you sit down in her house it will all come out against you in the court.'

'Why,' I said, 'you don't know Sara. She's no idea of taking that kind of advantage. Don't need to. She's got better tricks than that.'

Sara came in again blowing like an engine, and said, 'Oh dear, I get so short of breath since I had the 'flu. Excuse me leaving you, Miss Coker. The kettle is just on. You'll have some tea, won't you? Yes, of course I meant to write a long time ago, but the children got away with my pen. You know what they are.'

'We came about these pictures, Mrs Monday. Which you sold to Mr Hickson, having no right to them.'

'That's right, Miss Coker.'

'I don't call it right. I call it a robbery.'

'That's right. Won't you sit down, Miss Coker. Why, Gulley, it's a real pleasure. Of course, Mr Hickson said the pictures weren't properly finished and we owed a lot of money all round, and Mr Jimson had gone away and I didn't know when he was coming back, so when Mr Hickson said he'd pay all the debts and give me a bit to carry on, just for some of the pictures lying about, I was in such a whirl I didn't know how to say no.'

'And you didn't think any of my pictures were worth twopence, anyway.'

'Oh yes, Gulley. I always thought you were a lovely artist.'

'Go on, Sall. What's the good of keeping it up? We're both tottering into the grave.'

And I had the old feeling all over again. I wanted to give her a tap. Just to knock the crookedness out of her. Not a hard one. She wasn't my wife any more. But just a tap, platonic.

I daresay I had it in my face for all at once the old rascal bent her great neck over to one side and said, 'You may well say that of me, Gulley. But you don't look a day older. Well, what a pity my husband is on duty this morning. He'd have liked to see you.'

'I came on Wednesday because Mr Robins told me he was on duty that day. And I thought you'd like to see an old friend without him being about,' said Coker.

This was from one woman to another. Telling Sara in one sentence that her husband wasn't a husband and that she didn't want him to meet anyone who knew too much about her. But it didn't shake Sara. She'd got used to the situation. No Duchess ever beat Sara in behaving like Nature when she chose.

'That's right,' Sara said. 'He's always away Tuesday night and Wednesday morning. It's a shame.' But she kept looking at me out of one eye as if to ask, 'How much has he changed?' An old woman's look. It surprised me. I'd never thought Sara could get so old.

'And how are you, Gulley? How's Tommy?' Meaning my son, Thomas William.

'Tommy is a scholar and a gentleman, and he's gone to China in a bank, so he needn't know me any more.'

'Oh, what a shame,' said Sara, looking out of the window and bending her ear that way for Dicky's cough. 'I never would have believed it of Tom.'

'Except that you put him up to it, and a good thing too,' I said, 'and I'll bet he writes to you every month.'

'And Liz and the babies?' said Sara, meaning my last wife and the two youngest.

'Gone off,' I said. 'Back to mama—when they put me away.'

'And when he'd spent all her money,' said Coker, 'and she hadn't got anything to eat.'

'I'm sure you never did so, Gulley,' said Sara, 'you were so fond of her.'

31

'You don't believe a word you say, do you, Sall?' I said.

'It's quite like old times,' Sara said, looking at me with both eyes and smiling for the first time. 'And how well you look,' meaning I looked so old and ugly she was sorry for me and wanted to stuff me up.

'So do you, Sall. No one would take you for thirty-five.'

'Oh yes,' said Sara. 'Oh dear yes,' giving a great sigh that shook her cheeks and chin and neck and bosom. 'You're being nice to me. But I know. I'm getting an old woman, Gulley. Well, I suppose it's only to be expected.' And she looked so broken down that I thought she was going to cry. 'Yes,' she said, 'when you really think, it's got a sad side, life,' and all at once she put her two hands on her thighs, elbows out, tossed up her head and straightened her back. And I knew that back. I saw it again, the big flat muscles under the skin, the lift of the shoulder blades and the dimples moving like little whirlpools over their spines; the lovely flexible turn of the flanks over the solid hips. Sara was smiling at me. 'What it was to be young,' she said. 'But there, those that don't know, no one can tell them.' Just as she might have looked and spoken thirty years before. It made me stare. As if that woman I'd known, all cream and gold and roses, had resurrected under that old skin. And then, before I could speak, she said, 'There's the kettle boiling. Don't come,' and heaved herself up with a groan, and waddled out, flat foot, with her crinkly old hand on her buttock, palm out. An old stump again. She left me staring. I daresay my mouth was open.

'You old fool,' Coker said. 'Why don't you stand up to her? She's turning you right round her finger.'

'Not me,' I said, 'and not Sara. I know her games.'

But the fact was, I was seeing Sara in her bath with the brush. And drying her feet, leaning down all back and arms with her hair falling over her knees, and a bluish light on the shiny flats round the spine—sky reflection—a sweet bit of brushwork.

And there was something else about the old boa constrictor that I'd forgotten. Till that moment when she squared up to me and threw me her old smile. Herself, Sara. The individual female. The real old original fireship. Yes. The old hulk had it. Still. A spark in the ashes.

'Not but what you can't get right down in the dirt if

you want,' said Coker. 'And splash yourself. So long as I get her evidence that she stole the pictures. And I will too, if I stop here all day and the guvnor has to open his own bar by his own graft and gives me the sack for it.'

'Don't worry,' I said, 'Sara won't give any trouble. That's not her method.'

Sara came panting in with the tea and a cake with a big slice out of it. 'I must apologize, Miss Coker,' she said, 'offering you a cake with a slice out. Any other day this week you'd have had a proper cake. But the truth was, Dicky kept on asking me and he has such a cough, poor lamb. And then you came. But it always happens like that, doesn't it? You'd think there was a special providence just looking out to catch any woman that tries to have things nice. I'm sure you've noticed it, Miss Coker.'

'I've noticed you keep off the subject of Mr Jimson's pictures.'

'That's right,' said Sara, 'I've been so worried about little Dicky's cough and his going to school, I couldn't think.'

'And you admit,' said Coker, 'you had no right to dispose of these pictures.'

'That's right,' said Sara. 'Well, Gulley, I can't get over it seeing you again. And how's dear little Liz and the new baby? But oh dear, you told me, didn't you. Let me fill your cup, Miss Coker.'

'And will you sign a paper to say you didn't ought to have agreed to Mr Hickson's swindling Mr Jimson out of his legal property?'

'That's right,' said Sara, getting up and looking down the street. 'Well, I could have sworn that was Dicky's cough.' And she sat down again in the old way; looking at the chair first, like a cat at the rug, and then giving it a pat, and then pulling up her skirts and then taking her seat. Taking her seat is the word. And then disposing her skirts, and pushing out her front and arranging her arms, and throwing up her top chin, and assuming a handsome expression. She hadn't got the face, but she still put on the expression. I'd seen her do the whole act a thousand times and wanted to give her a rap. Just to bring to her attention the existence of the forgotten man. A slap on the nap. And I pulled my chair up nearer. Took up a strategic position on the left flank.

'Why, Gulley,' Sara said, 'you never told me about your

painting. Is it going on nicely?' And again she looked at me with all her eyes and ears. Sara never asked me about my painting unless she was feeling tender. It was in the nature of a pass. And as Coker had her nose in her bag, I gave her a pinch—not a hard one. And Sara gave a little jump and a squeak and said, 'Oh, Gulley, you mustn't.' But then she turned quite pink and went on smiling at me with all her eyes. Like a girl of fifteen. Round eyes with a light inside. Light of youth, curiosity and devilry.

Well, I thought, here's another of the Jills in the box. But no woman really gets old inside until she's dead or takes to bridge. Scratch the grandmother and you find the grandbaby giggling behind the nursery door at nothing at all. Nothing a man would understand.

'And how are you really, Gulley?' she said. 'Tell me true. I want to know. How are your poor legs?'

'Still going on,' I said. And there we were smiling at each other. Just as if we'd never been man and wife. Just in pure original sympathy. The old Adam and the old Eve.

'And how are you really, Sall?' I said, patting her gently on the behind. 'But I can see Mr What's-his-Name—Robins, the present owner—I mean—takes good care of a valuable property.'

'Oh dear, he does. Oh yes. Too well,' said Sara, bursting out as honest as she always did when she was touched in the right place. 'I can't have a little cold or a little pain but he wants to send me to the doctor. Why only yesterday—' But all at once she noticed that Coker had taken her nose out of her bag and was making a point at us. Frozen. And Sara became at once the duchess again, easy and false as an old madame. 'But you know what it is, Miss Coker, ladies often have a little pain, but they keep it to themselves. And I shouldn't complain of being too well looked after, should I? It's only that I never could stand doctors. Well, they've got to find something wrong. Haven't they? It's only professional. But there was my friend Mrs Blomberg, just opposite—she used to have a little pain—I'm sure it was no more than I've had myself and thought nothing of, and she went to the doctor, and the next thing she was in hospital and they cut her up on Monday and we buried her yesterday.'

'As we came on business,' said Coker, 'perhaps we'd better get on with it.'

'Oh yes,' said Sara, and she gave another of her big sighs, like a burst tyre. 'But won't you have some more tea first—it's such a pity to waste a whole new pot.'

But Coker was not going to unbend towards us. 'Excuse me,' she said, 'but we haven't too much time. Here's a paper which, if you will sign, Mrs Monday, we will know where we are.' And she opened her bag and brought out a piece of paper folded up in a notebook. 'I left blanks for the numbers.'

'There were nineteen canvases,' I said, 'and about five hundred drawings.'

'Mr Hickson says seventeen.'

'That's right,' said Sara, looking at me all the time and trying to stop giggling.

'It isn't right,' said Coker. 'Where's the rest?'

'Well,' said Sara, 'one was the blacksmith's little girl and he kept on asking me for it till I had to let him take it, though I never liked him, Gulley, whatever you say. The way he looked at me from behind—every time I passed. But there, you wouldn't believe he meant anything.'

'And what about the other one?'

'I don't know,' said Sara. 'I never could find it—it must have got lost somewhere unless that blacksmith got hold of it.'

'It wasn't that one you liked so much,' I said, 'of yourself in the bath?'

'Oh, Gulley, I never liked it, you know. I never liked the way you painted me.'

'Always taking a peep at it,' I said. 'Admiring yourself in your skin.'

'Well,' said Sara, 'I must say I never had any trouble with my skin, like some people,' and she looked so pleased with herself and so hypocritical that I gave her another pinch. And Sara let out a squawk and said, 'Oh, I thought it was something biting. Excuse me, Miss Coker, if you knew what trouble you have in these nasty little houses to keep them out of the furniture.'

'Well, if you'll sign,' said Coker, turning rhubarb colour, 'I suppose we must be satisfied.' And she pushed the paper and a fountain pen under Sara's nose.

'Oh, you've brought a pen,' said Sara. 'Well, that is

thoughtful. I was so worried about not having a proper pen.' And she signed.

'Why,' I said, 'you've signed for nineteen pictures.'

'That's right,' said Sara, looking at me with all her feelings at once, and taking me in all over again.

'And you only gave Hickson seventeen.'

'That's right,' said Sara, cocking her head a little farther over to see if it improved my appearance.

'You don't care what you sign,' I said. 'You've always got something up your sleeve.'

'That's right,' said Sara. She wasn't even listening to me. Following out her own schemes as usual. 'Well, Gulley, I can't get over it. Seeing you like this. Such a lovely surprise. And you so young and gay.'

Coker was putting up the paper. 'Thank you, Mrs Monday,' she said. 'That's all we require. Now, Mr Jimson, if you've come to stay, it's all one to me. But I got to be in my bar some time this week.'

I got up. For I could see Coker was in a temper by the way she looked. Like a wooden figurehead on a ship that's had its bottom knocked out.

'Young,' I said, 'go on, you old treacle pot. You know very well I look a hundred without my teeth—nearly as old as you do,' and I gave her another pinch, a good one.

Sara gave a shriek and rushed out of the door, calling out, 'Dicky, Dicky, you bad boy.' You couldn't tell whether the shriek was for me or Dicky. Probably both. The old kangaroo could always shriek double.

'Well,' said Coker, 'if I said I was surprised at you, Mr Jimson, it wouldn't be true. I seen too many nasty old men and some of them didn't know any better.'

'Never mind, Cokey,' I said. 'It's only a how-d'you do with an old acquaintance. You're my steady.'

'Not me, thank you. I'm nobody's steady except my own.' And she went out. But not flouncing. Coker was always county in her county clothes.

Sara came bustling in pushing a kid in front of her. Skinny little chip with a blue face and red hair. Knobbly knees and no meat anywhere. Staring at us with pop eyes and sucking something in his left cheek. He wasn't walking. He was leaning back against Sara with his feet together; and Sara was pushing him along like a dirt shovel.

'This is Dicky,' said Sara. 'Oh, you bad boy. Where have

you been—with that cough? Say how do you do to the gentleman. This is Mr Jimson. He's an artist. A real Academy artist.'

'Academy?' I said. 'Since when? I may be dead, but I haven't admitted it.'

'Well, you were just as good, Gulley, in your day. You know you were. Now Dicky, where's your manners? You never seen a real artist before, have you? Mr Jimson paints real pictures, big ones in oil colours. Now Dicky, shake hands with the gentleman.'

Dicky put out his tongue. Only a little way. Because you could see he hadn't quite made up his mind what to do. Taken by surprise.

'Oh, Dicky,' said Sara.

'Leave the kid alone, Sally,' I said. 'What's he done to you? Good-bye, and lay off the beer before you blow up.'

'Oh dear,' Sara said, 'but you'll think so badly of him, and he can behave so nicely when he tries. Say good-bye to the gentleman, Dicky darling. For mother's sake. And perhaps I could find a peppermint ball.'

Dicky put out his tongue a little farther. But he was still a bit confused. And I gave him a pull on the ear. 'Go on, kid,' I said, 'you got the right idea. Why don't you bite me? That's the way to treat strangers.'

'Oh, Gulley, you mustn't,' said Sara.

'Never mind what mother says, you bite everybody and throw things at 'em. Make 'em respect you.'

'Don't you listen to the gentleman, Dicky,' Sara said. She was quite in a fluster. 'He's only joking.' And she said to me, 'You oughtn't, Gulley. It's a shame with a child. Here, run along and get yourself a piece of sugar,' and she pushed him out. 'You shouldn't, Gulley.'

I gave her a buss on her cheek and said, 'A nice tender chop,' and Sara took me by the arm, quite sentimental.

'Oh, Gulley, I do hope she looks after you properly—'

'She? She doesn't look after me. I'm my own man, Sall, at last. Yes, I've learnt something.'

'What, all by yourself?'

'Bachelor's castle, with barbed wire and spring guns.'

'Where is it exactly, just in case any of your old friends wanted to know?'

'Nowhere,' I said, 'just in case some of my old friends wanted to know.'

'Oh, go away,' said Sara, quite angry. 'As if I should take all that trouble—after all the trouble I'd had with you before.' And she went out calling for the boy. 'Dicky, Dicky, what are you doing with that sugar?' And just then Coker put her head in the door and said, 'Are you coming or am I going?' So I popped my silver frame off the mantelpiece in my pocket, and went out.

10. 'Giving your picture to the blacksmith,' said Coker. 'Why, I suppose it might be worth ten thousand pounds.' Coker thinks all good pictures are worth ten thousand pounds. 'And I bet she did away with that other one. She's got thief written all over her.'

'So she has,' I said, 'and there's plenty of room.'

'What you laughing at? Anyone would think you were sozzled,' said Coker. 'Pull yourself together, do.'

For the truth was I was a bit excited. I'd forgotten what Sara was like. The real Sara. The old individual geyser. And she'd gone a bit to my head.

'She looked like she's been on the street,' said Coker.

Wouldn't do Sara any harm if she had, I thought, she'd always be game for a laugh, and keep her floors clean.

> Because the soul of sweet delight can never be de-
> filed.
> Fires inwrap the earthly globe, yet man is not con-
> sumed;
> Amidst the lustful fires he walks, and polishes his door
> knob.

'Come up,' said Coker, for the truth is, I walked over the kerb at the end of the street, not noticing. And gave myself a shock. 'You aren't fit to be out by yourself.' And she took me by the arm and gave me a jerk that nearly dislocated my neck. 'Go on. You ought to be shut up. That's the fact.'

'That's right,' I said, just like Sara, to keep the woman quiet. 'For everything that lives is holy.'

'What are you talking about now? I declare you're off your loop.'

Amidst the lustful fires he walks; his feet become like

brass. His knees and thighs like silver, and his breast and head like gold. Old Randipole Billy on the ramp. Embracing the truth. Through generation to regeneration. The door of paradise. This way to the Holy land. Fall to rise again.

For everything that lives is holy. Life delights in life.

'Up with you,' said Coker, pushing me on the bus, and planting me between a navvy smelling like an old stable and an old woman with a sore nose and a basket full of pig's food.

> *And every generated body in its inward form*
> *Is a garden of delight and a building of magnificence,*
> *Built by the sons of Los;*
> *And the herbs and flowers and furniture and beds*
>   *and chambers*
> *Continually woven in the looms of Enitharmon's*
>   *daughters,*
> *In bright Cathedron's golden dome with care and*
>   *love and tears.*

That is to say, old Billy Blake dreamed dreams while Mrs Blake emptied the pot.

'A woman,' said Coker. 'That's what your Mrs Monday is. And in another minute I'd have said so.'

'That's so, Cokey. Female.' But I was thinking that Sara at about forty had been just what I wanted for my Eve. That falls every night to rise in the morning. And wonder at herself. Knowing everything and still surprised. Living in innocence. With Sara's eyes, young eyes. But not flapper's eyes.

'Wake up, old bones,' Coker said. 'It's a fourpenny fare to the junction.' 'I haven't got it, Cokey.' 'Then you'd better get out and walk. Think I'm going to stake you?' 'All right, Cokey,' and I got up. Seemed a good chance to get away and think.

Coker looked at me like corkscrews. Extracting. 'Where are you off to now? Back to your Monday?' 'Not much,' I said. 'I've had all I want from her.' The last person I wanted to see was old Sara, wasting my time with chatter. I wanted to think. I had a lot of ideas coming. Always like that after a party. Especially a party with somebody like Sara; all alivoh. 'Cheer oh, Cokey,' I said. But she grabbed

39

hold of my coat-tails and told me to sit down again. She didn't like to see me so pleased to get away from her. There's a lot of girl in Cokey. 'Want to get yourself run over, I suppose. Just before the case comes on.' 'I don't want to be run over. I'm too busy.' 'But don't you forget, it's another one and six you owe me—and fourpence for the other bus.' 'I won't forget.' 'You will, but I won't.'

Yes, I thought, all alivoh. Eve should be a woman of forty with five children and grey hairs coming, trying on a new velvet. Looking at herself in the glass, as if she'd never seen herself before. And the children fighting round the dustbin in the yard. And Adam smoking his pipe in the local. And telling lies about his spring onions. Works of passion and imagination.

There was a street market on the kerb. Swarms of old women in black cloaks jostling along like bugs in a crack. Stalls covered with blue-silver shining pots, ice-white jugs, heaps of fish, white-silver, white-green, and kipper gold; forests of cabbage; green as the Atlantic, and rucked all over in permanent waves. Works of passion and imagination. Somebody's dream girls. Somebody's dream pots, jugs, fish. Somebody's love supper. Somebody's old girl chasing up a titbit for the old china. The world of imagination is the world of eternity. Old Sara looking at a door knob. Looking at my old ruins. The spiritual life.

'Now where are you?' said Coker. And we got down at the bridge. White cloudy sky, with mother-of-pearl veins. Pearl rays shooting through, green and blue-white. River roughed by a breeze. White as a new file in the distance. Fish-white streak on the smooth pin-silver upstream. Shooting new pins.

'Well,' said Coker. 'Do you know where you are?'

'Make it five bob, Cokey,' I said. 'It's easier to remember. That's three and threepence, say three and six in round figures.'

'My God,' said Coker. 'You have got a nerve. Not one farthing—I need it too bad. One and tenpence for today is enough, with the bus, and all on top of the four-pound fourteen.'

'Make it a fiver, Cokey. Four pounds fourteen and one and tenpence. That's four and twopence you still owe me.'

'You get off before I call a copper. What do you want it

for? And don't forget Tuesday. Nine o'clock sharp. At the bus stop,' said Coker, 'or I'll know why and how.'

'Tuesday. What for?'

'Hickson.'

'I couldn't do it, Cokey. I can't afford it. I might shoot him or strangle him, and I haven't got the time to be hanged.'

'You be there or I'll be here. I'm not taking any more from any old tarts. I mean business, and that's Hickson.' But she gave me half a crown. Coker always barks loudest when she sees a bite coming. Because she knows she's going to get bitten. She can't resist a friend after she's bawled him out.

And I hopped into a pawn shop and took fifteen shillings on the silver frame. More than I expected. But Sara always gave good presents when she had the credit. I got some real colours and a couple of brushes at last, and made for the studio. I felt I could paint. As always after a party. Life delights in life. Especially with Sara.

11.

Next morning, of course, the canvas looked a bit flat. As always after a party. But when I got back my picture eye, I saw that Adam's new shape was right. Final. Eve was the trouble. She was a bit too clever, too artistic, too flat, more like a composition in line and colour than a real piece of stuff. But I didn't know why. I didn't know if it was the temporary effect of meeting Sara or the permanent result of losing touch with the real Makay. Losing the essential woman in the paint. I'll sleep on that one, I said. But I can do something to the foreground now, it's as empty as a beer jug with the bottom knocked out. All those nicely fitted receding planes amount to damn all but an art school dodge. And it struck me all at once, that what I wanted there was a pattern, not in the flat, but coming and going. Leaves, waves. Tufts of grass bending in the breeze. Flowers. I began the flowers, but they felt wrong. And all at once I made a thing like a white Indian club. I like it, I said, but it's not a flower, is it? What the hell could it

41

be? A fish. And I felt a kick inside as if I was having a foal. Fish. Fish. Silver-white, green-white. And shapes that you could stroke with your eyebrows.

'Oh Mister J-Jimson.' Oh God. There was young pink-nose looking in the window. Just going to school. Satchel on his back. 'Good morning, Mr Jimson.' 'Good morning, Mister poke-nose. Good-bye.'

I had no time to play and my temper was bad. I was a bit impatient.

For those fish were catching my fancy. School of herrings. In a shape something like a map of Ireland laid sideways. Cold green. Under the moon.

> *Ethinthus, queen of waters, how thou shinest in the sky!*
> *My daughter, how do I rejoice! For thy children flock around*
> *Like the gay fishes on the wave when the cold moon drinks the dew.*

All the green-silver noses in a row on the top of the water. But in the round. Knobs sticking out of the flat. Like worn boot nails in one of those green leather soles. And real fish eyes, glaring, bulging, astonished. I squeezed out some raw sienna on a plank and drew the rings on them.

'I've g-got a piece of canvas,' said Barbon. 'You there still?'

And there he was, inside the door. He'd just walked in. Nothing to beat the cheek of the shy, when desperate. Look out for cripples, stammerers, lame boys and ugly girls. The army of the frontier. Battalion of the damned. Do or die. Saints or snakes. Pink nose gave me a fright. 'Here,' I said, 'what you mean, coming into my house?'

Pink nose turned red and green in patches like a bad ham and said, 'Oh, Mr J-Jimson, I knocked—' 'Well, knock off.' 'But es-s-s-s,' and he began to sizzle like a steam engine. He opened his satchel and took out a piece of new canvas. He was looking at me with eyes like a sheep just before you knock it on the head. 'Ss-s—'

'Excuse you,' I said. 'No, I don't.' For I was getting in a state. 'What the devil do you mean?'

42

'To m-mend the hole, Mr J-Jimson—you s-said it could be glued.'

No good getting angry with the lopear. Only upset me all the morning. 'What the hell you think you're doing? Why aren't you working?'

'I'm just going to school.'

'But you're not working. You're thinking about art. Now look here, Nosy, you're on the road to ruin. Do you want to break your mother's heart, and your wife's heart, and your children's hearts, unless they're all bastards and stand on their own feet? I know what I'm talking about. My son Tommy was a scholarship boy—went to Oxford, and now he's a gentleman. A real gentleman with Christian feelings and a sense of responsibility and hand-made shoes, And born in the Institution. And how did he do it? From sticking to the books. And what you think would have happened to Tommy if he'd begun to play around with all this art nonsense? I told him. I said, "If I catch you drawing or painting, Tommy, I'll skin you with a blunt rake. Art and religion and drink. All of them ruin to a poor lad. Leave 'em to the millionaires that can afford to go to the devil first-class all the way. You've got to work for your living."

' "You needn't be afraid, Daddy," said Tom, "I haven't any taste for art." And, thank God, he did really hate the whole racket. Too polite to say so, but he thought me a dirty old faker, and his stepmother a slummock who would rather flop about in a wrapper listening to Wag-ner or Bee-thoven than wash her face or darn his socks. Tom went to a good school and it cured him of art before he was fifteen. And see where he is now. A gentleman and a scholar. Who doesn't know an illustration from a picture. And can't tell "God Save the King" from "Sleepers Awake." But here—that's enough.' For I saw that I was talking too much. Dangerous thing to tell people about yourself. They try to put you in their box. Keep you for the drawing-room cabinet. 'That's enough,' I said to Nosy. 'You get off quick. I've had enough of this.'

'But, Mr J-Jimson, I could this afternoon at tea-time. When you're at tea. And it would only take a m-minute. I wouldn't be in the way a bit, I promise.'

'You promise. Not to be in the way. That's a good one. Why, you're always in the way. Everyone is. But you know you are, and what do you care? Git.' And I shoved him out and banged the door. And got back to the fishes for an hour or six.

Then I had a disinterested look at them and they were not at all what I expected. Nothing ever is. But after a little reflection, I waked up about half-past two in the morning and perceived that their noses were not big enough and too near together. Water too bright. And soft. Had to be harder to get the plane flat.

The middle of the night is a good time for a man to study his picture because he can't see it then; and the new scheme worked out well. On Saturday morning it looked so good that I began to like it. I promised myself a bottle of whisky, if I could borrow the price. Whisky is bad for me. I hate the stuff. And so I only take it for the consequences, as a special reward for a lucky day's work. Yes, I said, admiring the fishes and already getting a little whiskified, by sympathetic magic; the fish are good; I am good; life is good; whisky, though bad, is good; when all at once I had visitors. Mr Plant and two other preachers. And you could see even by the way they walked and held up their chins that they were coming to encourage the fine arts. Out of a sense of duty. I hadn't time to run away, I could only pretend not to notice.

The first preacher was six feet high and had a nose like an overripe fig. I took him for a gospeller with Greek, learned, low and broad. The second was about five foot three inches high and had a face like a Landseer lion. Real orator's mouth, pug's nose, forehead reflecting the heavenly light. I knew him. He kept the tin chapel in Greenbank and his sermons made even leading-seamen cry. A real foghorn of salvation. As for Mr Plant, he's a bantam, half an inch shorter than Coker, and a great deal lighter built. He has a face like what Cardinal Newman's would have been if he had gone into the army instead of the Church, grown an Old Bill moustache, lost most of his teeth, and only shaved on Saturdays, before preaching.

Plantie keeps a cobbler's shop in an Ellam Street basement off Greenbank. They say he's the worst cobbler in four parishes, because his mind is so much on Plato and Owen, and Kropotkin and Spinoza, and Sacco and Vanzetti, that he never hits the right nail on the right spot. But people go on bringing their boots to be murdered by

44

him because he is offended if they don't. He can't bear disloyalty and unkindness. He's had so much of it.

Plantie is a very strong Protestant, that is to say, he's against all churches, especially the Protestant; and he thinks a lot of Buddha, Karma and Confucius. He is also a bit of an anarchist and three or four years ago he took up Einstein and vitamins.

There's a lot of religion about Greenbank; I mean real old English religion, which you don't notice any more than a badger unless you try to poke it. Then, of course, it will come up a little way towards the surface of civilization and bite you in half. It keeps itself to itself, and if you hear hymns coming out of a mews, or a terrace house down Blackboy's Yard, it may be Bunyan's great-great-great-grand-daughter teaching a class of young walruses to sing the International, or a dustman starting a revival among the Unitarian Prebaptists branch of the Rechabite nudists.

All the London prophets have strong followings round Greenbank; that is Bunyan, Wesley, Richard Owen, Prudhon, Herbert Spencer, W. G. Grace, W. E. Gladstone, Marx and Ruskin. The last two are a bit revolutionary and attract chiefly the sprouts like Nosy. A lot of the Ellam Street boys read Ruskin and catch ideas about beauty which cause a lot of trouble till the girls get hold of them and marry them and turn them into respectable Boorjoys. Ellam Street wives hate art worse than politics, and politics worse than other girls.

But preachers, being a class proof against domestic influence, often go on believing in truth, beauty and goodness, all their lives. Plantie was a very strong believer in all three, and whenever he could persuade anybody to see my pictures, especially another preacher, he would bring him in. As a public duty to art and God and the English nation.

The trouble is that though all good Protestant preachers round Greenbank including anarchists and anti-God Blackboys love beauty, they all hate pictures, real pictures. Each time Plantie sees one of my pictures, he gets a worse shock. This, of course, excites him to great enthusiasm, and makes me feel depressed. I don't care for people to admire my pictures unless they like them. So when Plantie began to cry out to the two other preachers, 'Look at that—beautiful, isn't it? Why, Mr Jimson, I think those fish are wonder-

45

ful—a wonderful bit of work. You could almost eat them.'
I felt a kind of gloom rise from my belly and darken my
windows.

'Mr Jimson has a picture in the National Gallery,' said
Plantie, blowing the trumpets of the Lord and art, with all
his might. 'He used to paint from the life, but now he
prefers Bible subjects.' Trying to tickle them with their
own breast feathers.

The preacher with the blue nose, who had been staring
at Eve like a bull at a picnic, now gave a loud sniff, and
Plantie, seeing that this picture was going to be more un-
popular with art lovers even than the last, made a great
effort. 'This one represents the Fall. Adam is on the left.
He is not quite finished down the back. Eve on the right
is kneeling down. The serpent on the left is speaking in
Adam's ear. The flowers at the side are daisies and marigolds. Really, Mr Jimson, I've got to congratulate you on
those flowers. Don't you agree with me?' turning towards
the bloodhound. 'Don't you think daisies are just right for
the Garden of Eden, Mr Dogsbody?' or some name like
that.

But the more he tried, the worse I felt. As if I had been
a happy worm, creeping all soft and oily through the grass,
imagining the blades to be great forest trees, and every
little pebble a mountain overcome; and taking the glow
of self-satisfaction from his own tail for the glory of the
Lord shining on his path; when all at once a herd of
bullocks comes trampling along, snorting tropical epochs
and shitting continents; succeeded by a million hairy goril-
las, as big as skyscrapers, beating on their chests with
elephant drumsticks and screaming, 'Give us meat; give
us mates,' followed modestly by ten thousand walruses a
thousand feet high, wearing battleships for boots, and the
Dome of St. Paul's for a cod-piece; armed in the one hand
with shield-shaped Bibles fortified with brass spikes, and
in the other with cross-headed clubs of blood rusty iron,
hung with the bleeding heads of infants, artists, etc., with
which they beat up what is left of the grass, crying, 'Come
to mother, little worm, and let her pat your dear head and
comb your sweet hair for you.'

The bloodhound then opened his mouth and bayed,
'Most interasting, Mr-ah-Mister Johnson. Of course, I know
nothing about art, but I wonder could you tell me if—ah—

the human form—anatomically speaking, could—ah—assume the position of the male figure. Of course, I know—ah—a certain distortion is—ah—permissible.'

I had to pretend to see a spot on Eve's nose and to rub it off with my finger. And I couldn't get out a word. It was most embarrassing. There was the poor chap doing his best, and I had to pretend to be stone deaf. Come, I said to myself, say something, anything. Something they can understand. That's all they want. Something about the weather. Something to knock a hole in this awful situation and let down the pressure. Come, I said, you're not one of those asses who takes himself seriously. You're not like poor Billy, crying out:

> *I've travelled through a land of men,*
> *A land of men and women too,*
> *And heard and saw such dreadful things*
> *As cold earth wanderers never knew.*

Which probably means only that when Billy had a good idea, a real tip, a babe, some blue-nose came in and asked him why he drew his females in nightgowns.

And making a strong manly effort, I opened my mouth, smiled my charming smile from ear to ear, and was just about to say that the weather was colder but on the whole the rain might be expected to keep off, or not, perhaps.

When Blue-nose gave another sniff and said, 'I notice that it is the fashion for modern artists to paint the female limbs very large. I must not say that there appears to be a cult of ugliness—I merely stand to be instructed.'

Luckily I noticed that the edge of Adam's big toe had become smudged. I rubbed a little while into the burnt sienna and touched it up. While old Billy cried:

> *And if the babe is born a boy, that is to say,*
> *   a real vision,*
> *He's given to a woman old,*
> *Who nails him down upon a rock,*
> *Catches his shrieks in cups of gold.*

Which means that some old woman of a blue nose nails your work of imagination to the rock of law, and why and what; and submits him to a logical analysis.

Having completed Adam's big toe, I touched up some

of his other members, and the bloodhound suddenly barked, 'Moost interasting, yaas. But I fearr that we are already la-ate for our engagement. Mr Fignose (or some name like that), I think we are expected at half-past five.'

Then they went out suddenly but without any loss of dignity; one of the first things a Daniel learns when he gets in the wrong den.

And little Plantie only stayed long enough to give me one subscription to the Blake Society, partly paid, to the amount of one shilling and sixpence, and to assure me that he would be back presently. 'Those gentlemen,' he said, 'were greatly impressed, and they're both on a lot of committees. They have a lot of influence.' He then hurried off to join the other preachers at the meeting.

And I took up a palette knife and asked myself if I should scrape out the picture or murder Blue-nose or only cut my throat.

But just then I noticed young Nosy dodging about in the background, and staring at the picture with eyes like another fish.

'How did you get in? Get out, I said. 'The door was open.' 'Let it open again, whiz.' 'But it's S-Saturday.'

The universal excuse of every schoolboy. It's Saturday. They break your windows. It's Saturday. They break your heart. It's Saturday. They break their necks and run you in for a funeral. It's Saturday.

'Never mind if it's Monday,' I said with great indignation. 'You've no business to walk in like that.'

Nosy reflected a moment, and then he said, 'Who were those people who didn't like your picture?' 'Preachers.' 'I w-wanted to kick them.'

I didn't want to encourage the boy, so I didn't answer, until I said coldly and deliberately, 'Don't you talk like that about my friends.' 'Your friends?' 'They came here out of love for art, and don't you forget it.'

'But they didn't like your picture.' 'Of course not. How could they? They haven't time. A preacher hasn't time to like anything or even to know anything, and you wouldn't have time either if you'd just been bitten in the backside by a mad dog.' 'B-but that man T-Thompson with the b-blue nose isn't mad, he's m-married a grocer's widow with m-money.' 'Of course he's mad. What is a preacher? An artist. Who rattles a lot of words against his ear to make

48

his babies laugh. And the babies cry boo-hoo, boo-hoo, God help us. So God sends a lot more mad dogs to bite them. You ought to weep for Blue-nose,' I said, beginning to scrape out the fish. 'Think of his agony when the late grocer's wife wakes him in the middle of the night to give her some consolation for being alive, and he hears the mad dogs, singing round the dustbins by the light of the moon. "Speech. Speech." "What's wrong, darling?" says the late grocer's wife, getting a bit impatient. "I was thinking of next Sunday—it's a great opportunity." "But you've got your sermon all ready." "Oh yes," says Blue-nose, "but I was wondering." "Now, you know it's a beautiful sermon, don't touch it, whatever you do. You'll only spoil it."

'Blue-nose doesn't say any more. Because he doesn't know whether it's a beautiful sermon or a lot of wind, wambling and wallowing among the ruined caves of the British Museum. But the mad dogs keep on singing, "Speech, speech. More wonderful speech." And Blue-nose keeps on trying to catch one of them by the tail, but they're always just round the corner. And when he sighs on the grocer's widow by accident, she bursts into tears and says he doesn't love her as he used to do last week.'

I was still scraping at the fish and Nosy was looking at me with eyes like another fish. 'What are you doing, Mr J-Jimson, you're s-spoiling it.' 'These fish stink. And what are you doing here, young man? How long have you been interrupting me?' 'I didn't interrupt you, Mr Jimson.' 'How do I know?' 'But you didn't know I was there.' 'How do I know?' 'But Mr J-Jimson, you're not going to take them all out?' 'All of 'em.' 'Why?' 'They're dead. They don't swim—they don't speak, they don't click, they don't work, they don't do anything at all.' 'But why don't they?' 'God knows. But he won't go into details. The truth is, THE OLD HORSE DOESN'T SPEAK ONLY HORSE. And I can't speak only Greenbank.' 'Horse,' said Nosy, with his eye revolving in different directions. 'Here,' I said, 'what are you talking about? You're doing it on purpose. Go away.' And I made a dart at him. But he didn't move. He was as obstinate as a three-legged donkey that means to get thistles if it costs him his life. 'But I like the f-fish, Mr Jimson. Are you s-sure they're wrong?' 'No, I'm not shushure of anything except that if you don't go away and shut up I'll have the stroke.' 'What stroke, Mr J-Jimson?' 'THE STROKE!

49

Nosy, the finisher, the cut-off. What you'll get some day with a hatchet.'

Nosy put this down as a piece of light conversation. And he didn't approve. His disposition was serious, noble and interfering. He held up a piece of new canvas and a glue-pot. 'Then, Mr Jimson, if you've finished painting perhaps I could mend the hole. It will only take a minute.' Saying his little prayer. And just when I was going to kill him, I felt my head turn round. And I thought, Blood pressure, my boy—be good, be magnanimous.

And I remembered that after all, it was always difficult to borrow a glue-pot. A wasting asset. So I said, 'All right, if you want to play. But I'll probably burn the whole bloody mess tomorrow.' More in sadness than in anger. Because of the bell ringing in my head.

12.

And I went out to get room for my grief. Thank God, it was a high sky on Greenbank. Darker than I expected. But the edge of the world was still a long way off. At least as far as Surrey. Under the cloud-bank. Sun was in the bank. Streak of salmon below. Salmon trout above soaking into wash blue. River whirling along so fast that its skin was pulled into wrinkles like silk dragged over the floor. Shot silk. Fresh breeze off the eyot. Sharp as spring frost. Ruffling under the silk-like muscles in a nervous horse. Ruffling under my grief like ice and hot daggers. I should have liked to take myself in both hands and pull myself apart. To spite my guts for being Gulley Jimson, who, at sixty-seven years of age, after forty-five years of experience, could be put off his intentions, thoroughly bamboozled and floored, by a sprout of dogma, a blind shepherd, a vegetated eye, a puffed-up adder of moralities.

Girl going past clinging to a young man's arm. Putting up her face like a duck to the moon. Drinking joy. Green in her eyes. Spinal curvature. No chin, mouth like a frog. Young man like a pug. Gazing down at his sweetie with the face of a saint reading the works of God. Hold on, maiden, you've got him. He's your boy. Look out, Puggy, that isn't a maiden you see before you, it's a work of imagination. Nail him, girlie. Nail him to the contract. Fly laddie, fly off with your darling vision before she turns into a frow, who spends all her life thinking of what the neighbours think.

> *And if the babe is born a boy*
> *He's given to a woman old,*
> *Who nails him down upon a rock,*
> *Catches his shrieks in cups of gold.*

The fog-bank was turning pink on top like the fluff trimmings on a baby's quilt. Sky angelica green to mould blue. A few small red clouds dawdling up, beige pink, like Sara's old powder puffs full of her favourite powder. Air was dusty with it.

And I thought how I used to powder her after her bath. I wonder she didn't kill me, the old Aphrodisiac. Fancy how once I was mad for that ancient hair-trunk. I ran after her skirts like a little dog, when she wouldn't have me. I wanted to cut my throat—or I thought so. And even when I got her at last, how I hung upon her. How I washed and dressed for her, and let her trot me about like her puggy on a ribbon. It was, 'Poor Gulley, don't forget your cough medicine. Now darling, what about your socks? I'm sure they're wet.' And when I was mad to paint, she was for putting me to bed ànd getting in after me. Stirring all that fire only to cook her own pot. Growing wings on my fancy only to stuff a feather bed.

> *She binds iron thorns around his head,*
> *She pierces both his hands and feet,*
> *She cuts his heart out at his side*
> *To make it feel both cold and heat.*
> *Her fingers number every nerve*
> *Just as a miser counts his gold;*
> *She lives upon his shrieks and cries,*
> *And she grows young as he grows old,*

The powder-puff clouds were getting harder and rounder. The sky was turning green as a starboard light. And I could see it. It came right in and made a considerable impression. It made me want to sing and hit the lamp-posts.

Poor old Sall's face the first time I hit her. She couldn't

51

believe it. Dear little Gulley to punch a lady on the neb. A flap on the tap. And when she'd done so much for him. Given up everything for him. What unkindness. What ingratitude. All those tactful arrangements and nice comfortable little formulas just thrown away.

How miffed she was. And how proud and stand-offish and self-righteous when she made it up again. Her face was saying, 'I'm ashamed of you,' and the rest of her calling out, 'Help, help!'

Not that I wasn't glad to have her back. That was when I did the first sketch of the bath picture, all the bath pictures. I suddenly got hold of the idea. Mastered it. Yes, I can remember the feeling; your brushes like a carpenter's tools. Yes, I found out how to get Sara on the canvas. Some of her, anyhow. And I was always at her, one way or another. The flesh was made word; every day. Till he, that is, Gulley Jimson, became a bleeding youth. And she, that is, Sara, becomes a virgin bright.

> Then he rends up his manacles
> And binds her down for his delight.
> He plants himself in all her nerves,
> Just as a husbandman his mould;
> And she becomes his dwelling-place
> And garden fruitful seventy fold.

As Billy would say, through generation into regeneration. Materiality, that is, Sara, the old female nature, having attempted to button up the prophetic spirit, that is to say, Gulley Jimson, in her placket-hole, got a bonk on the conk, and was reduced to her proper status, as spiritual fodder. But what fodder. What a time that was. Not that I noticed it then. I was too busy to enjoy myself —even when I was having the old girl, I was getting after some ideal composition in my head. Taking advantage of the general speed up in the clockwork. It's not really surprising that she was a bit jealous of the paint.

I was laughing at Sara's expression when she used to look at one of my pictures and try to find out why I'd taken such a lot of trouble to make that nasty mess. When three flat-face cads under the dog's lamppost at Ellam Street corner turned their dead cod-eyes and packet cigarettes towards me. Their faces said, 'Look at the old fool, he's drunk. Shall we push him down the gutter or isn't he worth it?'

I put out my tongue at them and dodged round the corner. I was still laughing but it was a different laugh. And I said, I musn't want to cut out the tripes of such as the Ellam Street corner boys; it's not their fault that they lack the spirit of prophecy and art. I am upset, in fact; only because I can't hit them all on the neddy.

Just then I saw the telephone box and went in to try button B. And I thought: what a game to ring up old Hickson again. I rang him up, and he answered before I'd finished speaking his name. A big surprise. So I told him I was the Home Secretary. Put a ball of paper in my mouth. To give the official tone. Told him I had instructed Scotland Yard to set inquiries in motion relative to certain dealings in the matter of the artistic productions of the late Gulley Jimson. The late was a good idea. After all, you wouldn't expect one of these high officials to know anything about art or artists. He would be acting on a report.

'I beg your pardon,' said Hickson, and I did the piece again.

'Excuse me, sir,' said Hickson, 'are you referring to works which I bought after the Exhibition of 1921, or the small unfinished canvases acquired from Mrs Monday in 1926,' and he spoke so humbly and politely he might have been a contractor with a battleship to sell. And I thought, Could he really be taken in? For of course, all this telephoning to old Hickson was a bit of a game. He nearly always spotted me, even if he pretended not to. And then he would try to get in a nasty one, on the side. Like telling me to warn myself against being a nuisance. And I would try to give the old man a prod or two, to keep him thinking. After all, he had got those pictures pretty cheap.

But this time he really seemed to be taken in. And I thought it must be the newspaper. Perhaps the Home Secretary really has adenoids; and these big bugs are always on the telephone to someone or other, especially millionaires. So I went on to say that the whole of his transactions *re* Mr Gulley Jimson's artistic output was under the gravest consideration by my technical advisers who took the most serious view of the legal anomalies involved by and for the same. I was prepared, I said, to allow for the time-factor, but I was led to think that according to my legal department, and the appropriate acts, there was at least a *prima facie* case—

'I beg your pardon, sir,' said Hickson. The paper was too big and made me so heehaw that the old man couldn't catch my words, and said, 'I beg your pardon' every minute.

So we went on for some time. And Hickson even asked me to hold the line while he found a letter from Sara which he wanted to read to me.

And I was just putting my hand over the receiver in case he came back too soon and heard me laughing, when there was a tap on the glass. Made me jump a foot. And when I opened, a young chap I didn't know pulled me out by the arm and said, 'They're after you. Plain clothes cop. Been asking down at the Feathers if you had been using their box. Alfred sent me to look for you.'

I didn't stop to argue. I got out and ran for it. I saw now why Hickson had been so sweet and reasonable and deaf for the last half hour. Been on to the local police station to look round the telephones. Probably sent out the butler to the street phone.

What surprised me, my legs were so shaky. Kept on trembling so I could hardly run. And my head was buzzing round. Why, I said, I'm not upset or anything. I'm not angry with Hickson. Or am I? Funny thing if a chap can get in a state without knowing it. And I was half-way along Greenbank, puffing like a steam car, when I thought: Why you damned old fool, you're running right into jug. That's just where they'll come for you.

And when I stopped I felt so queer I had to lean against the wall. Heart doing a hanged man's jig. Knees shaking like an old horse at the knackers. Cheeks jumping up and down all by themselves.

Anybody would have thought I was frightened to death. Funny, I thought, if a chap's body can be frightened and he not able to stop it. I don't care a blast for anybody. Let 'em jug me if they like. Let 'em put me away for five years—that will about finish me. It's only what I've got to expect. I'm ready for anything. But my face isn't. It'll give me away to the first copper. He'll take me up even if he doesn't know who I am. Loitering with a face. And I sat down on a garden wall to give my insides a rest.

Surrey all in one blaze like a forest fire. Great clouds of dirty yellow smoke rolling up. Nine carat gold. Sky water-green to lettuce-green. A few top clouds, yellow and solid as lemons. River disappeared out of its hole. Just a gap full of the same fire, the same smoky gold, the same green. Far bank like a magic island floating in the green. Rheumatic old willows trembling and wheezing together like a lot of old men, much alarmed at the turn things were taking, but afraid to say so out loud.

I could do that, I thought. These round clouds and the island in the sky, heavy as new melted lead. But what's the good of thinking about it? They've got me. For I saw that they had got me. And I began to feel better. That's that, I thought. They've got me. Here, I said to myself, that's all about it. Who are you to make all this fuss about yourself? Things are moving, that's all.

'Hullo,' young Franklin who drives the grocery van, still in his apron.

'Hello, Frank.'

'What's up? You look bad.'

'The police are after me.'

'What have you been doing?'

'Telephoning.'

'I should think you'll get about two years. And serve you about right,' said young Franklin, getting angry as if he were fighting somebody. 'You've asked for it.'

'That's it, Frank. How's the neck?

Frank was having trouble with boils. He had a plaster on his neck and was carrying his head all on one side. I like Franklin. He's about nineteen, and is just getting his first real worries. The girls he fancies don't fancy him; the ones he fancied last year and doesn't fancy any more are lying in wait for him with kisses and hatchets. Made a bit on the pools and lost a lot on the dogs. And his best friend did him out of a good job, because he wanted to get married. Three years ago he was a happy corner boy, living like a hog in his dirty little mind. Now he's been stabbed alive. He's seeing things. The old woman of the world has got him. Old mother necessity.

She cuts his heart out at his side
To make it feel both cold and heat.

He has a long old pale face like most boys of his age round Greenbank until they grow up and fatten up and give up.

'Neck,' he said, 'what's wrong with it?' Getting up another little fight with somebody invisible. 'It isn't necks.'

'Well, how's the revolution?'

'Revolution.' He spat on the kerb. 'That chestnut. Are you trying to be funny, or is it a joke?'

'Seen Walter?'

'I suppose he's at home.'

'If he's at home, it's no good asking for him. Is it?'

'Not much.'

A small boy came running along crying so hard that you expected him to turn himself inside out every sob. And when he came into the lamplight you could see he'd cried himself silly; his face was so blackened and swollen that you couldn't recognize it for a face.

'Beh,weh-heh,' he said.

Then he saw us and we looked at him; and he was surprised to find himself under observation. He pulled his face into a face shape, as quick as lightning, and went off without letting out another sound, so quietly and quickly I didn't know which way he'd gone.

'Young Dobson,' said Franklin, 'been catching it from his ma.'

'What for?'

'She married again. Got another kid and it's a bit queer in the head. So she wallops young Johnny. She'll murder him some day.'

'Why doesn't somebody do something about it?'

'Why don't they do something about anything—about Hitler?' said young Franklin.

The clouds had turned into old mahogany, heavy and solid. The fire underneath had burnt out—nothing left but a yellow streak like a gas flame seen through a kitchen blind. Cabbage-green sky with one star coming through like tinsel behind gauze. And over on the East the blue rising as thick as a forest.

'Coming?' said Franklin, who doesn't like to be alone. And we went along by Greenbank, into Peartree Lane, where Walter Ollier lives. Frank rattled the gate to give him the sign. The door opened, and we heard Mrs Walter screaming at him that if he went out, he needn't come

56

back. She didn't want to see him again, so long as she lived. As Walter came down the path, she put her face out of the door and said it all again, so that we could hear.

But we'd heard it all before. Mrs Ollier was a woman who didn't like Ollier to go out in the evening, or come back in the morning, or read a newspaper; or to do anything at all. She herself didn't do anything at all except open tins and smoke cigarettes, and she didn't like anybody else to do more. She wasn't on speaking terms with anyone in the world except Walter, and she always abused him. But then, young Franklin said, 'What would you do if you were a woman of that age without no ideas about nothing, no children, and nothing to do but open tins and smoke cigarettes? But what's the good of talking, nobody's going to do anything about it, or anything else either.'

'A bit nervous tonight,' said Ollier, apologizing for giving us some embarrassment.

'Ya,' said Frank.

'How's the boil, Frank?'

'Boil. What boil?'

'I thought it was a boil you had.'

'Had. Have. What of it? It's not the first, is it, I've always got one, if I haven't got two.'

'Been to the doctor?'

'Doctor? You can have doctors. What do they know? What did they do for your rupture?'

'Well, they say I'm an exceptional case.'

'So am I. That's what they always say. That's what you'll die of when your guts get another crick in them. That's what my ma died of. She was an exceptional case. Nobody's never seen anything like it before. Ya. Doctors.'

'It's a nice evening,' said Walter.

'You can have it, Walter. And keep it for an exceptional case.'

But I felt so old I wondered how my legs kept hanging on to my body. And I couldn't even think of what to do with the blank canvas. My eyes were dead as cod's and my ears only heard noises.

> An aged shadow, soon he fades,
> Wandering round an earthly cot,
> Full filled all with gems and gold
> Which he by industry had got.

And these are the gems of the human soul,
The rubies and pearls of a lovesick eye,
The countless gold of the aching heart,
The martyr's groan and the lover's sigh.

Well, I thought, I've filled a lot of canvases in my time.
Quite enough for any man. It's time I was done for.

And I remembered my father in the little Normandy
farm where we went to live, or starve, because starving
was cheaper in the Pas de Calais. Painting still more girls
in gardens. And a whole room full of them inside. He
wasn't going to be beaten by the wicked world and
modern art. How my mother kept him in paint and canvas
I don't know. But she did it even when we hadn't got shoes
to wear. Art came first. Even before the children. But
then, it was the art she'd been brought up to. It wasn't
modern art. It was real art, beautiful and moral art,
which is the same thing as what you've been brought up
to. And papa was part of her religion.

The proof was that she gave up all for him. She was a
belle of the season when she fell in love with papa's blue
eyes and little golden beard, and velvet coat; with a real
artist, who not only loved the good and the beautiful, but
painted them. Her family was shocked. But she had all
the will of a beauty. And besides, papa was making a lot
of money in the fifties. She was allowed to marry him, and
it was a great success. She set herself to serve art. But
nobody was shocked at that. That was the right thing in
those days. If mama had been a deb of these times, she
would have set out to have a good time; but in the
sixties, her idea was duty and devotion. Her vision was,
perfect service. And when papa stopped selling pictures
and she found herself with five children to feed and no
money, and a husband who was already brokenhearted;
when, that is, the old woman nailed her down on the rock
of necessity and cut her heart open she carried on with
duty and devotion. She went on worshipping real art,
papa's art, and she even went on having children, or where
should I be now? She went on conducting her life in the
grand classical style. Yes, that's what it was. And what a
technique when you come to think of it. Nothing like the
classical. A sense of form. None of your surface tricks; but
solid construction.

If I was only fifty or so, I declare I'd go back to school again, to the life class, like Renoir in his forties, and study nothing but form, form in the black and white, for two years. Just charcoal. See what my mother became in the years of misery; a great woman; a person in the grand style. Yes, by God, you need technique to make a good job of life. All you can get. You need to take necessity and make her do what you want; get your feet on her old bones and build your mansions out of her rock.

And she becomes his dwelling-place
And garden fruitful seventy fold.

Look at what Mick Angelo did in black and white or a chunk of rock.

'I hear you've been on the telephone,' said Walter.

'Yes, and the police are after me already. Smart work. They know their job, those coppers.'

'Does Mr Plant know?' said Walter. 'We ought to be making out what you ought to say. You'll have to have a story.'

'Story,' said young Franklin, quite losing his temper. 'Bloody lot of good that would be. He's done for himself, that's all. He'll get two years.'

'That's about it,' I said. 'I was warned. Serve me right. Playing the fool. I ought to get seven years.'

'They can't give you all that, Mr Jimson,' said Walter, who was upset. 'It wouldn't be right. What would they give you seven years for?'

'Being Gulley Jimson,' I said, 'and getting away with it.'

'It doesn't matter,' said young Franklin. 'Not if you look at what's happening to the Jews in Germany. Nor anybody anywhere.' And all at once he shouted out, 'Ahsitfeelin-todye, Chawly.'

All the Greenbank boys talk Greenbank as well as English. Frank's friend called back out of the dark, 'Cheeroarry, ah'llbeseeinyer.'

On the Surrey side the fire was dead. Clouds all in blue and blue-and-soot. Blue-black smoke drifting up like smoky candles, and a blue sky as blue as blue spectacles with long pieces of sooty cobweb floating high up. Stars coming through like needle-points; green-blue, and neon blue; and the river pouring quietly along, as bright as ink out of a bottle. All below as flat as melted iron, on three

59

levels: first, Greenbank Hard; then a step down to the river, and a step up to the towpath; then away to the edge of the plate. A flat earth. A few knobs of trees and houses popping up to make it flatter. And all above on one curve about ten thousand feet high. Sweet as the inside of a dish-cover. The cobwebs hung on nothing in the middle, to make it hollower.

As simple as Euclid. Grand as the field of glory. Almost a picture ready-made, I said. There's more than a sketch there—it's got some composition. And my fingers ached to do it. But I said to myself, time's up. You've had fifty years to play with. So what are you groaning about?

We'd got to the railing next the motor factory and Barberry Creek. It was half-tide, and there were three barges cockeye on the serge-blue mud. So that they tilted on the ramp. Like stranded whales with their waists in the water. And a brazier full of orange hot coke making a hay-green high light on their snouts. Two men and a boy moving about throwing shadows fifty yards long, right to our feet. Carrying long tar brushes, like brooms.

It made my mouth water. I could have eaten those personal chunks of barges and that sweet individual flank of mud. But I thought, only another sketch and there's a million every day. Self-indulgence. You damned old sorcerer.

Frankie and Walter were moving down the planks, and I went after them. The river came up to us and its surface dissolved away into blue-glass sky. But the stars were floating on the water you couldn't see. Gave the plane in the middle of nothing. Barges like cliffs hanging over our heads. Little Harry the watchman smoking his pipe by the brazier. Chin in right hand, right elbow in left hand. Eyes on the air. Didn't even nod to us. Pursuing the meditations of Harry.

Franklin called out 'Bert,' and one of the men gave us a shout. Came up with a little tar brush in his hand, like a whitewash brush. Bert Swope. Seventy-five or so. With his neck bent forward like a lizard. Long flat nose. White moustache, smoked like a kipper. Green eyes. A Greenbank walrus. Wears a jersey to show he's on the boats, and moleskins to show he's on the hard. Not to presume. Too proud and particular.

'In a minute—in a minute. Half a mo. Sno hurry.'

Bert had just put a patch on the bottom of a dinghy. He tarred it over and stood back to have a look at it. But when he stood back he couldn't see the whole effect. So he went to have a close look.

'Mr Jimson here is expecting trouble with the police,' said Ollier.

'Go on,' said Bert. Bert is an old bachelor, and doesn't believe anything he hears. 'What is it this time?'

'I've been telephoning again,' I said.

Bert went back to the brazier to take a dip of tar and gave the patch another brush over.

'What did you do that for?' said Bert.

'Just for the laugh. To make old Hickson jump.'

'Laugh,' said Franklin. 'Not much of a laugh when they put you away for two years.'

'It'll be a laugh for Hickson if they finish me off. He'll have killed me. And all legal. And he's got a lot of my pictures which will go up in value too.'

'Here,' said Bert, bending down to admire his brush strokes from another angle. 'What's the joke? What's happened really? Anything?'

'We must think up something,' said Ollier. 'Mr Plant will know. You can't go in again—not if it's only the same as last time.'

'It ought to be death without the option,' I said.

'What for?'

'For being an artist,' I said. 'For upsetting everybody. For thinking I'd get away with everything at once. And a medal for a good boy.'

'It's not what you'd call work,' said Bert. 'But what do I know?'

'It's more of a gift,' said Ollier.

'Like Frankie's boils,' I said. 'To keep him interested.'

'How do you start on that game, Mr Jimson?' said Bert. 'Just start?'

'No,' I said. 'It starts on you. Why I had a real job once, a job of work. But art got me and look at me now.'

No one said anything to this. Bert wasn't listening, and Franklin was angry, and Ollier was too polite and Harry was thinking as usual. Harry is a dwarf. A good-looking chap to the waist, but then two little twisted stumps. He got a wife once and gave her a baby; but she left him and took the baby with her, not because she didn't like Harry, but because the neighbours laughed when they went out together. Sensitive. A nice girl. She liked things nice.

13.

If, while I am dictating this memoir, to my honorary secretary, who has got the afternoon off from the cheese counter, I may make a personal explanation, which won't be published anyhow; I never meant to be an artist. You say, who does? But I even meant not to be an artist because I'd lived with one and I couldn't forget seeing my father, a little grey-bearded old man, crying one day in the garden. I don't know why he was crying. He had a letter in his hand; perhaps it was to tell him that the Academy had thrown out three more Jimson girls in three more Jimson gardens. I hated art when I was young, and I was very glad to get the chance of going into an office. My mother's cousin, down at Annbridge, near Exmoor, had pity on us, and took me into his country office. He had an engineering business. When I came to London in '99, I was a regular clerk. I had a bowler, a home, a nice little wife, a nice little baby, and a bank account. I sent money to my mother every week, and helped my sister. A nice happy respectable young man. I enjoyed life in those days.

But one day when I was sitting in our London office on Bankside, I dropped a blot on an envelope; and having nothing to do just then, I pushed it about with my pen to try and make it look more like a face. And the next thing was I was drawing figures in red and black, on the same envelope. And from that moment I was done for. Everyone was very sympathetic. The boss sent for me at the end of the month and said, 'I'm sorry, Jimson, but I've had another complaint about your work. I warned you last week that this was your last chance. But I don't want to sack you. You might never get another job, and what is going to happen then to your poor young wife and her baby? Look here, Jimson, I like you, everyone likes you. You can trust me, I hope. Tell me what's gone wrong? Never mind what it is. I'm not going to be stupid about it. Is it debts? You haven't been gambling, I suppose. Is your petty cash all right? Take a couple of days off and think it over.'

But of course I couldn't think of anything except how to get my figures right. I started as a Classic. About 1800 was my period. And I was having a hell of a time with my anatomy and the laws of perspective.

> *Her fingers numbered every nerve,*
> *Just as a miser counts his gold.*

I spent my holiday at a life class, and when I went back to the firm, I didn't last two days. Of course, I was a bad case. I had a bad infection, galloping art. I was at it about twelve hours a day and I had a picture in the old Water Colour Society that year. Very classical. Early Turner. Almost Sandby.

My wife was nearly starving, and we had pawned most of the furniture, but what did I care? Well, of course I worried a bit. But I felt like an old master. So I was, very old. I was at about the period when my poor old father was knocked out. I'd gone through a lot to get my experience, my technique, and I was going to paint like that all my life. It was the only way to paint. I knew all the rules. I could turn you off a picture, all correct, in an afternoon. Not that it was what you call a work of imagination. It was just a piece of stuff. Like a nice sausage. Lovely forms. But I wasn't looking any more than a sausage machine. I was the old school, the old Classic, the old church.

> *An aged shadow soon he fades,*
> *Wandering round an earthly cot,*
> *Full filled all with gems and gold*
> *Which he by industry had got.*

I even sold some pictures, nice water-colours of London churches. But one day I happened to see a Manet. Because some chaps were laughing at it. And it gave me the shock of my life. Like a flash of lightning. It skinned my eyes for me, and when I came out I was a different man. And I saw the world again, the world of colour. By Gee and Jay, I said, I was dead, and I didn't know it.

> *Till from the fire on the hearth*
> *A little female babe did spring.*

I felt her jump. But of course the old classic put up a fight. It was the Church against Darwin, the old Lords against the Radicals. And I was the battleground. I had a bad time of it that year. I couldn't paint at all. I botched my nice architectural water-colours with impressionist smudges. And I made such a mess of my impressionist landscapes that I couldn't bear to look at them myself. Of course, I lost all my kind patrons. The first time, but not the last. But that didn't upset me. What gave me the horrors was that I couldn't paint. I was so wretched that I hardly noticed when we were sold up and my wife went off, or even when my mother died. It was a good thing she did die, or she would have had to go to the workhouse. And really, I suppose she died of a broken heart at seeing her youngest go down the drain.

Of course I was a bit upset about it. I thought my heart was broken. But even at the funeral I couldn't tell whether I was in agony about my poor mother's death, or about my awful pictures. For I didn't know what to do with myself. My old stuff made me sick. In the living world that I'd suddenly discovered, it looked like a rotten corpse that somebody had forgotten to bury. But the new world wouldn't come to my hand. I couldn't catch it, that lovely vibrating light, that floating tissue of colour. Not local colour but aerial colour, a sensation of the mind; that maiden vision.

> *And she was all of solid fire*
> *And gems and gold, that none his hand*
> *Dares stretch to touch her baby form,*
> *Or wrap her in her swaddling band.*
> *But she comes to the man she loves,*
> *If young or old, or rich or poor;*
> *They soon drive out the aged host,*
> *A beggar at another's door.*

I got her after about four years. At last I got rid of every bit of the grand style, the old church. I came to the pure sensation without a thought in my head. Just a harp in the wind. And a lot of my stuff was good. Purest go-as-you-please.

And I sold it too. I made more money then than I ever did again. People like impressionism. Still do, because it hasn't any idea in it. Because it doesn't ask anything from them—because it's just a nice sensation, a little song. Good for the drawing-room. Tea-cakes.

But I got tired of sugar. I grew up.

And when they showed me a room full of my own confections, I felt quite sick. Like grandpa brought to a nursery tea. As for icing any more eclairs, I couldn't bring myself to it. I gradually stopped painting and took to arguing instead. Arguing and reading and drinking; politics, philosophy and pub-crawling; all the things chaps do who can't do anything else. Who've run up against the buffers. And I got in such a low state that I was frightened of the dark. Yes, as every night approached, I fairly trembled. I knew what it would be like. A vacuum sucking one's skull into a black glass bottle; all in silence. I used to go out and get drunk, to keep some kind of illumination going in my dome.

> *He wanders weeping far away,*
> *Until some other take him in;*
> *Oft blind and age-bent, sore distrest,*
> *Until he can a maiden win.*

And then I began to make a few little pencil sketches, studies, and I took Blake's Job drawings out of somebody's bookshelf and peeped into them and shut them up again. Like a chap who's fallen down the cellar steps and knocked his skull in and opens a window too quick, on something too big. I did a little modelling and tried my hand at composition. I found myself wandering round the marbles at the Brit. Mus. and brooding over the torso of some battered old Venus without any head, arms or legs, and a kind of smallpox all over the rest of her. Trying to find out why her lumps seemed so much more important than any barlady with a gold fringe; or water-lily pool.

> *And to allay his freezing age*
> *The poor man takes her in his arms;*
> *The cottage fades before his sight,*
> *The garden and its lovely charms.*

Good-bye impressionism, anarchism, nihilism, Darwinism, and the giddy goat, now staggering with rheumatism. Hail, the new Classic. But you might say it was in the air about then, at the turn of the century when the young Liberals were beginning to bend away from *laissez-faire* and to look for their Marx, and science took a mathematical twist, and the old biologists found themselves high and dry among the has-beens, blowing their own trumpets because no one else would do it for them. And I studied Blake and Persian carpets and Raphael's cartoons and took to painting walls.

But I rubbed most of them out again. They looked like bad imitations of the old masters; or made-up, pompous stuff. They didn't belong to the world I lived in. A new world with a new formal character.

I had a worse time than the last time. I drank more than ever. To keep up my self-respect. But it didn't have the same effect. I was gloomy even in drink. I didn't seem to be getting anywhere very much. If there was anywhere to get to.

> *The stars, sun, moon all shrink away,*
> *A desert vast without a bound,*
> *And nothing left to eat or drink,*
> *And a dark desert all around.*

And of course no one would buy anything. They didn't know what I was driving at. I probably didn't know myself. I was like a chap under witchcraft. I didn't know if I was after a real girl or a succubus in the shape of a fairy.

> *The honey of her infant lips,*
> *The bread and wine of her sweet smile,*
> *The wild game of her roving eye,*
> *Does him to infancy beguile;*
> *Like the wild stag she flees away,*
> *Her fear plants many a thicket wild;*
> *While he pursues her night and day,*
> *By various arts of love beguiled.*

The job is always to get hold of the form you need. And nothing is so coy. Cézanne and the cubists, when they chucked up old doddering impressionism, caught their maidens. But the cubists did it too easily. They knocked them down with hammers and tied up the fragments with wire. Most of 'em died and the rest look more like bird-cages than forms of intuition and delight. Cézanne was the real classic. The full band. Well, I suppose poor old Cézanne did more wandering in the desert even than me —he wandered all his life. The maiden fled away so fast that he hardly caught her once a year. And then she soon dodged off again.

> *By various arts of love and hate,*
> *Till the wide desert planted o'er*
> *With labyrinths of wayward love,*
> *Where roam the lion, the wolf and boar.*

I painted some cubists myself once and thought I'd got my maiden under padlock at last. No more chase, no more trouble. The formula of a new classical art. And of course a lot of other people thought so too. A lot of 'em are painting cubistry even now; and making a steady income and sleeping quiet in their beds and keeping their wives in fancy frocks and their children at school.

> *The trees bring forth sweet ecstasy*
> *To all who in the desert roam;*
> *Till many a city there is built,*
> *And many a pleasant shepherd's home.*

Cubiston. On the gravel. All services. Modern democracy. Organized comforts. The Socialist state. Bureaucratic liberalism. Scientific management. A new security. But I didn't live there long myself. I got indigestion. I got a nice girl in my eye, or perhaps she got after me. After 1930, even Hickson stopped buying me. And tonight it seems that I can't paint at all. I've lost sight of the maiden altogether. I wander weeping far away, until some other take me in. The police. It's quite time. I'm getting too old for this rackety life.

14. The chaps, except Harry, were all watching Bert while he gave a last coat of tar to his pet patch. Harry kept his eye on the air. Looking after his own affairs.

'Here,' said Frankie, working up a rage as if he'd been diddled. 'What are we stopping for? We haven't got all night, have we? Are we going to get on with it, or aren't we?'

Bert, still keeping his eyes on the patch, put on his coat,

a real old Greenbank walrus coat, with a yoke, double-whipped seams, and two cuts behind. Built about the same year as the Crystal Palace.

'All right, son,' he said, 'all right, all right, all right.' He struck a match and held it over his job to see what it looked like by matchlight. 'All right, all right, I'm coming,' and he walked backwards till the boat was out of sight. Then he turned and marched off, poking out his head like an old dog smelling for corners.

'When we see Mr Plant, he'll know what we ought to tell them,' said Ollier, who was worrying about me all the time. But I don't mind Ollier worrying about me because he never intrudes. He's got a lot of self-control on account of his manners.

'You needn't mind about all that,' said Franklin. 'He's finished, anyhow. Done for himself, and why not?'

Young Franklin is a nice chap. He takes things hard. That's why he likes to see the worst occur.

'That's it,' I said. 'And I'd rather go quietly.'

It was Mr Plant who had helped me in my last trouble. Came running straight from work with his spectacles falling off his nose and his hands as black as Wellingtons. 'What's this, Mr Jimson?' 'I've been had up, uttering menaces.' 'It's a scandal. If ever there was an innocent man, it's you, Mr Jimson.' 'Oh no,' I said, 'it's all right, I did it.' 'But look at the provocation—we must have a lawyer.'

This didn't suit me at all. In all my life I'd always tried to keep out of court. 'We don't want too much publicity, Mr Plant, something else might come out.' 'So that's what they're counting on,' said Plantie, turning pale with indignation. 'It's persecution. But I know the man who'll settle 'em.' 'We don't want any lawyers in it, Plantie.' 'But it's a duty, Mr Jimson. And if we don't get justice in the court, we'll go to parliament. I know the man we want—he acted for that poor lad, Rockway.' 'Who strangled girls?' 'That's it, poor lad, poor lad.' 'He got off, didn't he?' 'Yes, we got him off. But he was never the same again—a scandalous case.' 'I remember the papers liked it.' 'That's it, scavenging. If only we could have kept the whole thing quiet, the poor chap might have had a chance. Only eighteen. But the publicity went to his head. And of course he got into trouble again.' 'They shut him up?' 'Shut him up—that was ten years ago. Awful to think of.' 'And the girls?' 'The girls?' said Plantie, and he looked at me with his mouth open, and his forehead crumpled right over the top. Quite confused. He had overlooked the girls and he didn't know quite how to deal with them. He hadn't got the right tools. He wasn't using Spinoza then, but some kind of old Bible cement mixer. 'The girls,' he said at last. 'Poor things. Awful, terrible.' And he shook his head like an old dog bothered by a horsefly. 'It's a mystery.' And he cheered up a little. 'Yes,' he said, 'if we only knew, there's a meaning in it.' 'That's it,' I said, 'it means that girls are liable to be strangled by young devils like Rockway. Always were and always will be.' 'No, no,' said Plantie, 'there's a meaning in it. And anyhow,' he said, cheering up still more, 'we did get the poor young lad off, and we'll get you off.' 'No justice for me,' I said. 'What I need is special consideration on account of age and rheumatism and my services to the British nation in the future —about the year 2500. When they'll probably need a few good artists in their history or they won't be in history at all.'

But, of course, Plantie wouldn't listen to me. He has a lot of old English feelings under all his foreign philosophies, just as he has a lot of the real old English religion under all his fandangos. He loves to fight the law. 'No, no,' he said, 'no compromise with those rascals.' And he got up meetings and took subscriptions till my name stank for miles round. And he hired that lawyer G—, who looked like a crystallized choirboy, only his head was quite bald. He came to see me in my old studio and when I had told him all about myself and my little jokes, he said, 'I see, Mr Jimson, we'll have to concentrate on character.' 'No you haven't,' I said. 'Remember I'm an artist. And you know what that means in a court of law. Next worst to an actress.' 'That's what I mean,' he said. 'And I believe you're a modern artist.' 'Very nearly,' I said. 'Yes,' he said, 'it's a difficult case. We can only stick to character and hope for the best.' And when he got into court he began at once to throw dirt on Hickson. It was wonderful. That man was a poet. The way he made it seem that poor old Hickie had been a bloodsucker in buying my pictures cheap, and that he'd been exploiting poor devils like me all his life.

No, I nearly got in a state in that case, because of all the nonsense they talked, and all the lies they told about poor old Hickie. Not knowing anything about art or pictures or Hickie or me, and what was worse, not caring. I was just going to start on to tell that chap what I thought of him, and twice I tried to put some sense into the court and make it understand that a picture wasn't a bag of flour that goes up and down in the market; that it was a highly complicated question which had to be handled by experts and not too many of them all at once. Hickie and me would be enough for one afternoon.

But when I saw them all so serious and reverent, and even the police with their hats off as if ready for prayer, I said to myself: Don't be a fool, Gulley, they're doing their best and they couldn't do any better. They know it isn't justice and they know there can't be any such thing in this world, but they've got to do their job which is to keep the handles turning on the old sausage machine, and where would the world be without sausages?

So I said nothing. And in the end I got a month, instead of seven days, which was the usual equivalent. But it was a great victory for Plantie. It made him happy for weeks and gave him a big reputation round Greenbank. The real British hero. The man that whopped Old Woman the Law and frightened the magistrates.

We had turned east along Greenbank. The moon was coming up, as if somebody had flashed a torch under the far edge of the dish-cover. A fog of white light seeping up into the blue air. Overhead the sky was as black as Prussian blue. The stars were sparkling like electric cars. And the river crawling along, the colour of pig iron, like a stream of lava just going solid.

I could use the dome, I said, with that bite out of it, where the moon is rising. Like a dark cathedral with one chapel in the apse lighted up. I should like a sharper edge at the junction. Probably get it when the moon actually sticks up her nozzle. She'll throw a halo. A vault, and the vault will give the measure and the architecture of the dome. Yes, I said, by Gee and Jay, I should like to do that dome, the heavenly height, the eternal roof, the everlasting muffin-dish, heavy as the hand of fate, solid as the Bank of England, and glorious as the first of things. The Primary. Rap your knuckles on it and it makes a noise like a turnip.

'Hullo, hullo, hullo, hullo,' said Bert, 'where you coming to?' For the fact is, having my nose in the air, I didn't see the kerb. And when Bert had put me on my legs again, there was little Plantie standing waiting for us, under a lamp, under the dome, looking so neat and small that it made you smile. Like a fly in black amber.

Plantie in his best blue suit, with a clean collar, barmaid's, three sizes too large. With an electric-blue lightning bow tie hooked on to the stud. Bowler, eyebrows and moustache all brushed different ways.

'Good evening, Mr Jimson. Good evening, all.' His eyes were running out of their holes and then running back again, like children at the nursery door, just before the party.

'Going to a meeting?' I said.

'I've got a meeting,' said Plantie, and he tried to stick out his chest. 'Professor Ponting is speaking at my place. Professor Ponting from America.'

'What—the professor of plumbing?' said Bert.

'He's a great authority,' said Plantie, putting one finger down the back of his collar to see if the stud was holding.

'What's he authority of?'

'He's known all over Germany,' said Plantie, giving his tie a poke to see if it was still there. Plantie was obviously in a state. This was his great day. He'd got a professor to talk to his meeting.

'Nice evening, Mr Jimson,' and he looked round quickly to see if it was a nice evening.

'Very nice,' said Bert. 'Bit of all right, all right. What about that wet?'

Plantie let out a sigh, but in the middle of the sigh he snatched off his bowler and gave it a fierce look to teach it not to come unbrushed until after the meeting. Then he put it back again, and said, 'Beautiful, beautiful. Never saw such stars.' And he looked quickly up to make sure that there were such things still to be seen.

'Hitler would laugh,' said Franklin.

'Come on, son,' said Bert, taking his arm. 'Come on, come on, come on.'

'But it strikes a bit cold through the pavement,' said Plantie, slapping down his feet to see if it was a pavement that struck cold.

'Come on,' said Bert, taking his other arm. 'Come on, come on.'

'I've got to go and get things ready for the meeting,' said Plantie.

'No, you haven't. Not for another half hour.'

'No,' said Plantie, 'or say twenty minutes.' And we all went into the Feathers.

'Have one with me, Mr Jimson,' said Plantie. 'It's my turn.'

I said, 'Since last Christmas,' but he didn't answer. Put up his hand and ordered cans round. Napoleon on the field of battle. A glorious day. Mine not to reason why.

I like little Plant. A regular old King Walrus. Genus, Chapellius. Species, Blue-suitius, Bandy-leggus. Steady as a burst barometer. Putting one foot in front of the other. On account of the curl in his legs.

Plant's father was a plumber. Old family trade. Good business and plenty of money. Plantie was going to be a plumber. But he joined up for the South Africa. Mother died and papa married a widow with kids. No room for Plantie at home after the war. He went into boot trade, built up a nice little business, married a nice little wife. Then the Great War. Democracy in danger. Joined up again under the Derby scheme. Nice little wife hooked up with a conchie, sold the business and got clear away with everything. Plant got one bullet in the knee and one in the stomach and had fourteen operations. Every time he found a job his leg gave out, and he had to go to the hospital. Took to drink and broke the other leg. Then pulled up his socks, quarreled with his minister, and took to cobblery and anarchism. Religion had always been in the family. His father had been a lay preacher.

'That's a fine picture of yours,' he said, putting down his can like a law of Moses. 'Great subject, the Fall.'

'I'm giving up art,' I said. 'It's a bit late, but I may still learn to respect myself before I die.'

Plantie shook his head and felt for his tie. He was wounded in his fundamentals and it make him feel that he couldn't trust even elastic to hold.

'You saw Jim, Mr Jimson?' said Alfred from behind the bar.

'Yes, thank you, Alfred.'

'Thought you'd better know.'

Alfred isn't a gossip. But he would like to be. He looks like a white rabbit powdered pink in front. His eyes are as blue as skim milk. He was born to be a village baker's wife and tell the news warm, with the new loaves.

The door banged and my hand did a jump, all by itself, slopped the beer over my nose.

'It's all right, Mr Jimson,' said Alf. 'They won't come here, and Jim wouldn't breathe a word.'

'Both of you are good at keeping secrets—like onions on the breath,' I said. 'Got to be in my job,' said Alf, wiping a glass out with his forefinger. 'See nothing, hear nothing, say nothing. That's the golden rule for the bar. You needn't be nervous.' 'I'm not nervous,' I said, 'it's my legs. But if the coppers don't come for me pretty soon, I'll knock your windows out. 'I know what you mean,' said Alfred. 'It's the suspense working on the imagination. A lot of chaps get in wrong due to the suspense.' 'What's this?' said Bert, 'Who's in suspense?' 'The Lincoln murderer,' I said, 'this morning.' 'Mr Jimson is joking,' said Plantie, 'he knows better than that. He's an artist and an artist knows the value of life.' 'Buyers or sellers?' I said. 'What offers for the celebrated Gulley Jimson? Sound in wind and limb except for arthritis, conjunctivitis, rheumatitis, sinovitis, bug bitis, colitis, bronchitis, dermatitis, phlebitis, and intermittent retention of the pee.'

Plant shook his moustache at the air. He was being grieved. I like grieving Plant. Always trying to rescue me from myself. To convert me to a wiser view of life. I don't like converters. You never feel safe with them. They've always got some knuckleduster up their sleeve. Always working round the flank for a dash at the scullery window. Got to lock up everything, and even then they keep on squinting through the keyhole.

'Mr Jimson doesn't mean it,' said Plantie, turning red. There was still a bit of the old Flanders sergeant in Plantie. 'For what is an artist for, but to make us see the beauty of the world?'

'Well,' I said severely. 'What is art? Just self-indulgence. You give way to it. It's a vice. Prison is too good for artists—they ought to be rolled down Primrose Hill in a barrel full of broken bottles once a week and twice on public holidays, to teach them where they get off.'

The moon was coming up somewhere, round the corner from the side bow window, making the trees like fossils in a coalfield, and the houses look like fresh-cut blocks of coal, glittering green and blue; and the river banks like two great solid veins of coal left bare, and the river sliding along like heavy oil. It was like a working model of the earth before somebody thought of dirt, and colours and birds and humans. I liked it even better than the dome of glory. I liked it so much that I wanted to go out and walk about in it. But of course I knew it wouldn't be there. You never get the real world as solid as that. It was a trick of the light. Alfred's old white cat, jumping on the wall, spoilt the weight of it. I had to put up my can to blot her out.

'I respect artists,' said Plantie, 'they give their lives to it.'

'And other people's lives,' I said. 'Like Hitler.'

'Hitler,' said Frankie, not angry but sad; as if he couldn't bear much more. 'Who said Hitler? Is he on the wireless or isn't he? Why do they all go on talking *all* the time?'

'Do you think there'll be a war, Mr Moseley?' said Alfred. Mr Moseley had just come in. A smart young man of fifty with a face like a raspberry, and suits and shoes so beautiful that they make you look again. Visions that reveal clothes to you. Mr Moseley is a prophet. He sells racing tips and takes bets. 'Yes,' said Mr Moseley, 'of course there'll be a war.' 'I believe you're right, Mr Moseley,' said Alfred. 'You bet I'm right. Double and split.' 'But do the Germans want a war?' 'Don't know what they want till they get it,' said Mr Moseley, 'and then they want the other thing.' 'I believe you've said it, Mr Moseley.' 'Everyone likes a change,' said Mr Moseley, 'to keep up the circulation.'

'But what I can't understand is, what Hitler really wants,' said Walter. 'Doesn't want anything,' said Mr Moseley. 'He's got ideas. That's the trouble. When a chap gets ideas, you look out—' 'I believe you're right, Mr Moseley,' I said. 'He's got ideas that chap. And he wants to see them on the wall.'

Mr Moseley gave me a look but didn't say anything. I didn't blame him. I couldn't expect a suit like that to talk to my overcoat. And I was thinking of Artist Hitler.

But when they find the frowning Babe,
Terror strikes through the region wide:
They cry 'The Babe! the Babe is born!'

> *And flee away on every side.*
> *And none can touch that frowning form,*
> *Except it be a woman old;*
> *She nails him down upon the rock,*
> *And all is done as I have told.*

'Since you've said it,' said Franklin, 'what is it all for—what's the good of art? You can have it. It's just another racket, it's a put-up job from start to closing time.' 'That's it, Frankie,' I said, 'a put-up job.' 'And they know it too,' said Frankie, turning quite white and breaking into a sweat with indignation against the enemy. 'The buggers know it —just like the bloody parsons know it. And the bloody government. Putting it over. Taking advantage.' 'That's it,' I said, 'they're all at it, like ticks on a mad dog. When he's too busy charming the moonshine to scratch himself in detail.'

Plantie looked at his watch and looked at us all round. Then he moved his moustache and eyebrows and spectacles in an earnest way, and said that he'd have to be going. But no one said they'd go with him. Not even Ollier. Plantie always makes the same mistake. Asks people to go to his meetings. Even Ollier, who thinks as little of himself as any hero of the war before last, would never go to Plant's meetings when Plantie asked him. He was always there. But he went under his own steam.

Plantie looked at me again; then pulled up his trousers and trundled out. You could see he was afraid that nobody would come to his meeting.

'Poor old Plantie,' said Bert. 'Gone to put on his braces for his uplift.' 'Meetings,' said Franklin. 'What's the idea? That's all I ask. What's the real idea? What are they getting at?'

'They aren't getting it, they're giving it,' I said. 'A chap has to get rid of his ideas somewhere, or they'll turn sour and give him a pain.'

All at once Alfred gave me a wink and I saw a nice young man standing beside me in a tweed coat. Student you would have said. Except for the way his shoulders filled the sleeves. And the look in his eye. Like a filing clip. He touched my arm and stepped back from the bar. 'Hello,' I said, 'it's Bill Smith.' But my legs were going away from me. Seemed to be nothing in my trousers but

75

the draught. I just floated after the smell of tweed. 'My old friend, Bill,' I said, 'how are things at Botany Bay?' 'Mr Jimson?' he said, confidentially, as if speaking through a ventilator to the prisoner next door. 'No,' I said, 'that's my first cousin once removed. He moved out just now. He's an artist who's always getting into trouble with the police. Shall I go and call him back?' And I went out. But the copper came along. And outside he took my arm. 'Excuse me a moment, Mr Jimson.'

'Which Mr Jimson?' 'Did you at six-thirty this afternoon send a telephone message of a threatening character to Mr Hickson, 98, Portland Place?' 'I only said I'd burn his house down and cut his liver out.' 'You know what will happen to you if you go on at that game.' 'Yes, but what will happen if I don't? What will I do in the long evenings?' 'Mr Hickson doesn't want to prosecute. But if you go on making a nuisance of yourself, he'll have to take steps.' 'Would he rather I cut his liver out without telephoning?' 'Put yourself in his place, Mr Jimson.' 'I wish I could, it's a very nice place.' 'Well, you heard what I said. Do it again and you're for it.' 'That's a good idea. I'll call him up at once.' A hop, step and jump for the Feathers. But there they were in a row, Ollier, Swope and Franklin, looking at me.

'What's up?' said Bert. 'Who was the chap?' 'C.I.D.' 'Well, I wondered.' 'And you could see he was changing his mind just because I'd told the truth.' 'What did he want with you?' said Franklin. 'It's a painful subject, Frankie, super-tax.' 'I knew I'd seen him before,' said Bert. 'Schoolmaster, ain't he, Jimmy, got run in last year for drunk and—' 'It's seven struck,' said Ollier, changing the subject. 'I'm off for the meeting.' 'What's it about?' said Bert. 'Religion and humanity.' 'That's a good one, son. That's all right,' said Bert. 'For those it's all right for.' And young Franklin turned round and walked off very fast. But he went round the lamp-post and walked back again. They come to most of the meetings. Both being on the loose. I've seen Bert, in his white coat with the yoke, and four other old walruses from Greenbank, at a meeting on the Gold Standard. But it was an open-air meeting. Bert couldn't go to the Gold Standard indoors. He likes something to bite on; religion or the white slave traffic. All alive at seventy-five. But he's a bachelor. Driven in on himself. Banked down and still burning, the fire in the hearth.

15. Plant has two rooms down an area in Ellam Street. Shop in front, sitting-room behind. We went in through the shop. Smell of boot polish like a lion cage. Back room with an old kitchen range. Good mahogany table. Horsehair chairs. Bed in corner made up like a sofa. Glass front bookcase full of nice books. Chambers's Encyclopaedia. Bible dictionary. Sixpenny Philosophers.

I made off to the dark corner by the back window looking out on the dustbin. There was a nice old comfortable sofa for a snooze. Or to flirt if I felt flirty and anything came in to flirt with. Dirty in the cover, but good springs in the seat. But I hadn't got settled before Plantie came running up to me. 'Are you all right, Mr Jimson?' 'I'm all right.' 'You know your way to the—' 'Yes, I know my way to the—' And then he was off again to shake hands with the Rev. Such or the Mr So. He had four dog collars there, including Cabbage-nose. A great day. He was in such a fizz that he couldn't contain himself. I saw him twice make his way to the— And then up he comes again. 'You all right, Mr Jimson?' 'I'm all right, Mr Plant.' 'That's all right, Mr Jimson.' 'I know, Mr Plant. Down the yard.' 'Good meeting, Mr Jimson.' 'There's a lot of it.' 'Yes, there's twenty-two, not including Walter or myself.' 'What does that old woman come for?' 'Why not?' 'Women generally have something better to do.' But Plantie was away again. He always goes off his head at a meeting, charges up and down like a sergeant on a field day, and gets his collar up at the back.

The people kept floating in. Like fish in an aquarium full of dirty brown water, three dimensions of fish faces, every one on top of the other. Bobbing slowly to and fro, and up and down. Goggle eyes, cod mouths. Hanging in the middle of the brown. Waiting for a worm or just suspended. Old octopus in corner with a green dome and a blue beak, working his arms. Trying to take off his overcoat without losing his chair. Old female in black with a

77

red nose creeping about in the dark corners like a craw-fish, shaking her bonnet feathers and prodding her old brown umbrella at the chairs. Young skate stuck up the wall with bulgy white eyelids and a little white mouth. Never moving. You'd think he was glued to the side of the tank. People kept falling over and sitting on me. I took a chair into the scullery to be out of the way, and shut the door to be at peace. For I knew where Plantie kept bottled beer, under the scullery draining-board.

But pretty soon the chairs came knocking up against the door. Just as I was opening the first bottle they knocked it ajar. As the people in front made themselves comfortable and stretched their legs and pushed backwards to snatch a little floor from the people behind. As happens at all meetings, except in a church with good Christian traditions, where they screw the pews to the floor. In the end they pushed one chair backwards right through my door, and when I tried to push it back again, Plantie got up and began to shake his moustache and introduce Professor Ponting, who turned out to be the moon-coloured young gentleman against the wall; the skate.

'Ladies and gentlemen,' said Plantie, 'we have tonight the great privilege—'

I pushed the chair forwards and the Christians pushed it back; ten to one. But still I might have got the door shut if just then the old crawfish hadn't come working sideways along the row, apologizing and groaning, and sticking her umbrella into everybody's eyes; until she got her backside wedged up against the scullery door. Then everybody began to hiss at her and she got her umbrella jammed between a chair and an old man's waistcoat, and some good Christian, looking carefully the other way, gave her a hard shove with his shoulder and she tumbled into the scullery. She fell on the empty chair, panting like a steamboat, and then began to push her dress about and pull her bonnet and jerk her legs and elbows, as old women do when they're flustered. But all at once she felt me just behind her and gave a jump and turned half round. And I said, 'Sara.'

'Oh Gulley,' she said. 'You did give me a start.' And she went on panting and heaving and pushing herself about. 'Oh dear, I do get so breathless.'

'And what are you doing here, Sall? In a bonnet too.'

'Well, didn't you get my card, or my letter?'

I remembered then that I had had a card from Sara, care of the Eagle, saying that she had to visit an old friend's grave on the Saturday in my part of town, and not to trouble about being in, as very likely she wouldn't have time to call. A real Sara card, meaning just the opposite. And then there had been a letter. But I had forgotten to open it.

'There was a card,' I said. 'But it said not to expect you. So I didn't tell my staff to prepare dinner.'

'The Eagle said you were here. But I didn't know about the meeting. And then I couldn't find you. Oh, Gulley, aren't you glad to see me, when I've come all this way?' Now I looked at Sara, I could see she was in more than a fluster. It wasn't only that her nose was redder than before, but her eye was wet. And her panting wasn't all due to exercise.

'Have another one with me,' I said, holding up the bottle.

'Oh no, Gulley, I couldn't. I've had enough already. Well, you can see I have—what with the worry and the cold wind. And how are you, Gulley?' she said, looking at me as if I were a landscape about twenty miles away. 'How are you? In that awful shed all alone with no one to look after you.'

'I'm all right, Sara,' I said. 'Don't you worry about me. It's how you are.'

'Oh, I don't know why I came. And look how late it is. But being only a mile off, at the graveyard, and wondering how you were managing—'

I poured out the bottle into two glasses and held out one to Sara. Her hand closed round it, without noticing. The sensitive plant. 'And it being Fred's day on. Oh dear, what's the time—?'

'Eight, just gone. What time is Fred coming home?'

'Ten, but I'm getting back by half-past nine. Not a minute after. Not while the poor boy's so upset.'

'And what's wrong with Fred?'

'Oh everything—but it's really his stomach, poor mannie. And his married sister that lives opposite. She never liked me doing for him. Though how he would do for himself, I don't know. As nervous as a maiden. It's those engines in the yard. Running backwards when you're not looking. Oh dear, I shouldn't have come, should I?' But she kept looking at me like a young lass when she first feels her front and wonders what she wants.

'He's a bit jealous is he, your Fred? Well, I'm not surprised. I should think he'd better.'

'I've been good to him, Gulley, truly I have. But you oughtn't to have come like that—not to the house, I mean.'

'How did he know?'

'There's plenty to tell him down our street—not forgetting the sister. And of course he likes to know who comes to the house—it's natural for a man. And where I am.'

'And where he is.'

'Oh dear,' said Sara, taking a pull at the porter, as if by accident. And wiping her mouth with the back of her hand. Reflex action. 'I oughtn't to have come, really. It does make you feel old, acting silly. But it seemed such a chance. Don't you hate to feel old, Gulley?'

'No, what I hate is to feel young, and then my arms and legs go back on me.'

'Oh, it's different for a man. But I feel so old, I could cry. And I feel it all the time. Everything seems to say to me: You're an old woman, Sara Monday. No more fun for you in this life. You'd better go and bury yourself.' And there were tears in her eyes.

'We're not so old, Sara.'

She shook her cheeks at me. 'An old apple and an old wife have but a creaking life.'

'Why Sara, what's wrong with you? Tough as an old saddle.'

'I don't know,' said Sara. 'But I'm so breathless Fred keeps on saying I ought to go to hospital.'

'What for?'

'Well, I had a little pain—in my inside.'

'Growing pains. Was it your stomach?'

'That isn't it—it's one of those pains you can't quite tell where it is.'

'I know them. Forget them, Sall.'

'So I should if only Fred would forget them. But he'll drive me into hospital at last and then they'll find something. Trust them. Oh, those hospitals. They gave little Morris Hagberg the wrong anaesthetic only last week— burnt his throat to cinders—that's two in a month.' And she looked so sadly at me I was quite surprised. 'Come, Sara,' I said. 'You never used to talk like this.'

'And there was Rozzie—I'll never forget Rozzie lying there in the infirmary without her leg.'

Rozzie was an old friend of Sara's and of mine, who had died in the workhouse infirmary after an accident.

'Well,' I said. 'Don't go and get run over by a bus on the way to the local, like Rozzie.'

'Rozzie crying because they wouldn't even let her have her stays or put a little powder on her poor face. Oh, Gulley, if I could trust you to keep me out of those hospitals and infirmaries, I believe I'd go off with you.'

So that's it, I thought. She wants a change. The last flutter of the old candle. But no, I'm too busy.

'I should think he's fond of you, Fred,' I said.

'But he's so set on those places. He's so scientific. And what does he know about how a woman feels to be dragged about on a slab like butcher's meat, and left to die among strange walls, in sheets that never belonged to any human soul, much less her own self. I'd rather be drowned or poisoned.'

I put my arm round the old thing. 'Come, Sall, you're not dead yet.'

'It's not the being dead—it's the dying. And being so helpless. Look at poor Rozzie, she was so big and gay. She was bigger than I was, and never cared for anything till she lost her leg and her money.'

'Rozzie wasn't so tough as you are, Sall. She may have been bigger and noisier, but she was softer.'

'All the same, Gulley, you'd have picked Rozzie first if you could have got her.'

'Never,' I said. Though, in fact, I had been on pretty close terms with Rozzie and there were times when I did prefer her to Sara. Her hips and legs were better, and her temperament more placid. You always found Rozzie where you left her, and she didn't intrude on your private character, like Sara. She stayed on the outside.

'You proposed to Rozzie once?' said Sara.

'Never,' I said, which was true. I hadn't proposed because it hadn't been necessary. 'Do you ever go back to the grave?' said Sara, and I knew she had found out something. 'I have been,' I said. For in the last two years I had had a kind of understanding with my son Tom, who was also Rozzie's only son, to keep her grave decent. 'That is,' I said, 'I've passed that way. It's a short cut to the Red Lion.'

'It wasn't you left all the flowers last year on her funeral day? The sexton said it was a gentleman in a blue overcoat.'

'A gentleman—come, Sall. I haven't been a gentleman for forty years.'

Sara shook her head at me. But she was a little more cheerful. 'Poor Rozzie, she had a terrible skin. It was a cross to her.' 'Oh terrible.' 'And her face was all crooked.' 'I remember.' 'Her mouth was on one side.' 'Poor Rozzie.' 'She was a dear,' said Sara, 'and I wish I'd gone to see her oftener in the infirmary.' 'Don't blame yourself, Sall, it's all over long ago.' 'That doesn't make it any better. Oh dear, I wish poor Rozzie was back again. I'd be a better friend to her.' 'No, you wouldn't, because you wouldn't know she was going to fall under a bus and die in the infirmary.' 'That's true, I wouldn't,' said Sara, and she gave a great sigh. 'Oh dear, why can't we know before?'

'And there's another thing,' I said. 'Rozzie would never have lasted as you have done. She was too soft and too lazy. She would have been an old woman by now.'

'And so am I an old woman.'

'Come on, Sall,' I said, squeezing my arm round her. 'Drink up, and you'll feel better.'

'Drinking up won't do any good to thoughts. They're too deep.'

'No, but it'll do good to your feelings, and then your feelings will do good to your thoughts.'

'Oh, Gulley,' said Sara, taking off the rest of her glass. She was crying and smiling all at once. 'You'll be the ruin of me all over again. Why, look at me, coming all this way, and upsetting Fred and everything. I ought to be pole-axed.'

'I hope you haven't been imprudent, Sara,' I said.

'A lot you care,' she said, 'but there, if you were a woman, you'd know what it feels like to get older and older, and to know that nothing will ever happen to you any more. Nothing nice, that is.'

'Go on, Sall,' I said. 'You're not so old as all that or you wouldn't be here today.'

'Oh no, Gulley, it's because I'm old I'm acting so silly; yes, and it's worse than just coming out of my way. Well, you didn't get my letter, and a good thing too. I kept on thinking of the good times we had. Oh dear, you were a bad husband to me, Gulley, but you did know how to enjoy yourself, and I do like people that know how to enjoy themselves, man or boy. And, oh dear, look at your boots and your socks. Well, I meant to bring you some socks, but then I wasn't sure if you wouldn't think I was being a nuisance and trying to make up to you after the last time.'

'Bring me all the socks you like, Sall. I've no meanness about me. I'll never refuse a gift from a friend. I'd take 'em even from my enemies, if they offered. So thank you, my dear, and drink up.' And I filled her glass.

'No. No, Gulley, it's bad for me. Though why I should want to do good to myself I don't know. Oh dear, that time at Bournemouth. With that sweet sunset the first day. Roses and violets. And the waves just whisking the pebbles. Oh dear, and the policeman nearly caught us—'

She dipped her nose again, and then gave a sigh like a grampus when he breaks surface. I gave her old stays another tender pressure; I doubt if she felt it through the armour. And the voice of the skate came through the yard window.

'The boundless possibilities of human happiness when guided by those natural loves and fraternal sympathies planted in the soul.'

'Oh well,' said Sara, 'I suppose I'll get used to it in time. Time slow but sure will all your troubles cure.'

'The nature of man is love. Look at the little helpless child, born so utterly dependent. Dependent only on love.'

'He speaks nicely, the young man,' said Sara. 'I shouldn't think he'd been married, do you? I'm glad it's about religion. I haven't been to a church for a long time, I've been so busy.'

'And so it is to love alone that Nature entrusts her most important task. Love, the source and guarantee of all our hopes.'

'That's right,' said Sara. 'Though goodness knows, children are a work too. But it would be better in church. Church is more homely. Well, after all, it is the house of God. Yes, I always liked church, even on a week-day, and it saves time without a sermon. Oh dear, that awful service when Rozzie died—in that cemetery chapel. I'd rather drown myself than a pauper funeral.'

'Come, Sara, you've had a good innings—you've squeezed the lemon. Three husbands and five children—not counting the stand-ins, the Freds and the Dickies—it's a lot of happiness for one woman.'

'Don't talk of happiness like that, Gulley, as if it was all over. I never was happy unless I was with you, and you gave me a chance. I always say there was no one like you for gaiety. Oh dear, when I saw you on that Wednesday, it did bring back the old times, and what times they were.' And there she was looking at me as if she could eat me without sauce, the old crocodile. I've set the tow alight in the old cask, I thought. It's the last flare of the old bonfire; and there may be a lot of combustible there still. You can't tell by the bung, I'll get my face singed unless I'm careful.

'And you couldn't have done better than Fred for a quiet billet,' I said.

'Yes, indeed. Fred is a good home. Only for the worry about the bills. Well, what if there are a few little set-offs, after four years? Why, I always give him the best of everything. And if we had to get rid of the lodger, that wasn't my fault. There! jealousy as they say is the mustard to a good meat. But I wish I'd met you first, Gulley, in my maiden time.'

'You made a very good match with old Monday—plenty of money and he doted on you.'

'I'll never say a word against him. And, indeed, I blessed myself, Gulley. I thought I was well enough. But now I know better. You know what it is with a man like that—so nervous and weak in his spirits. You have to be keeping it up all the time and working at yourself lest you fall away—and then with the children coming as fast as mine did, it was work, work, work, and no end till they got married and my dear Edith went to China, and so it was good-bye. But there, I knew it was ordained. And if I didn't know what was due to my teens and had to learn artfulness and contrivance in my bridal moon when even the plainest pug may give herself the right to put off her brains with her suspenders. What did I know but it went with the service? Like the second housemaid to clean the upstairs door handles, and thank God and my dear good mother if I was foolish I was dutiful and took my gaiety as the tinker's donkey takes grass, between the kicks and the hard pull-ups.'

'In that kingdom of love which is the home, does any father ask for laws to assist his authority? Does the mother send for the police?'

'I like the young man, he ought to be a preacher,' said Sara, stopping. 'Yes, indeed,' she said, giving another gentle sigh that made her stays creak like an old shutter. 'I ought to go to church—it always did me good. But then the people will look at you if you're keeping house for a widower, or perhaps I only think they do.'

'And Fred didn't like the lodger?'

'Now, Gulley, you mustn't think anything against the poor man—he was old enough to be my father almost—and a great wen on his neck. And if he was with the Cleansing Department, I always think it a shame the hard dirty work they have which somebody has to do. I'm sure Fred would make enough fuss if the dustbin wasn't emptied. But there, I'm not going to say anything against Fred, being particular. I'd always rather Sir Whimsy in a clean shirt, than Master Easy to lie in dirt.'

'Meaning me,' I said, for I remembered how Sara had made me set up a night-shirt instead of sleeping in my winter drawers.

'Oh no, Gulley, for you know how I took you; you hadn't got a whole pair of trousers. Well, I've never been sorry, for if I hadn't gone to you, I would never have known the true sweet joys of life. But there, you're laughing at me. I know I'm acting silly. It's being old and seeing Rozzie's grave and thinking of the hospital, and perhaps I've had a drop. Well, I know I've let myself go, Gulley. You may well look at me, a regular old jelly. Sliding round like aspic on a hot plate. Yes, I always needed a man to peg me down, a real man. And I only found one. But, I mustn't say that, must I? And now it's all over, I'm only fit for a warning.'

'Don't say that, Sara,' I said, giving her another squeeze. And meaning it. For you couldn't help liking the old trout. The very way she was speaking; easy from her soul as a jug runs when you tilt it to a wet lip; it made me tingle all over; it made me laugh and sing in the calves of my legs. It made my toes curl and my fingers itch at the tops. It made me want to go bozo with the old rascal. What a woman. The old original. Clear as a glass-eye and straight as her own front. The very way she worked her great cook's hand, jointed like a lobster, round her glass; and lolled her head on one side, and turned up her eyes and heaved up her bosom when she sighed, enjoying the feel of herself inside her stays; it made me want to squeeze her till she squealed.

'Don't believe it,' I told her. 'You'd still walk away from any hop-pole girl, in a light breeze. You've got the genius, Sall, if that's what it is.'

'Oh dear, but they were good times, weren't they—sweet, lovely times.'

'And not so bad now—does Fred go out every Tuesday and Saturday night?'

'But, Gulley. You wouldn't have to come to the house again. It's the sister—she watches all the time, and it does upset Fred so much when anyone comes, it's not fair to a man with his delicate stomach—'

'No, and you don't want to lose a good home, do you—and I don't blame you. Why should you with your mornings off and every Saturday?'

'Oh, Gulley, you make me feel like twenty-five again, in my first ripening. I never knew a man like you to hold a woman. You used to make me feel quite queer,' and she drank her drink quickly so as not to spill it and tried to put her head on my shoulder. But her neck wouldn't bend so far, and she only managed to hook on to my coat seam by one eyebrow.

'Nature, that supreme creator intended man for happiness and peace, in the enjoyment of all her beauties—' the skate was saying.

'It all helps,' said Sara, 'but not unless there's some kindness on both sides—and perhaps when Nature goes out, the kindness comes in. I think we're both kinder sort of mankind than we used to be, Gulley. When we had our nature more fidgety, and indeed it may be intended for peace in our old age—'

'Damn old age,' I said. 'I'm not old, and if I wasn't so busy and had the money, I'd take you to Brighton tomorrow.'

'Too busy,' said Sara. 'Oh well, I suppose that's a good

thing. But, oh dear, how I used to hate that word. Why, even on our honeymoon at Bournemouth, it was always. "Just keep like that a minute, Sara, while I catch the slant of the left shoulder." '

'Well, Sara, and I wouldn't mind drawing that shoulder again—when you come to me next week. I shouldn't be surprised if your back and thighs weren't as good as ever they were.'

'Oh dear, I could never make out whether it was me or my flesh that you wanted—that was the beginning of all our trouble.'

'Who made the trouble? It was nag, nag, nag—'

'I never nagged you, Gulley. I would never do such a thing to a male body. I've more contrivance than that, I hope. And who hit me on the nose? Well, look at it even now.'

'It was the only way to teach you to keep it out of my business.'

'Well, perhaps I made too much of the nose, Gulley, but you know a woman has her feelings, especially a young woman, before she learns sense.'

'You were forty when you hooked me.'

'Ah, but that is the youngest time—I mean in your feelings—that's when a woman acts her youngest and silliest. Well, I was a silly girl I know, but I couldn't bear for you to hit me on the nose—it wasn't the pain, it was making it so red and ugly. Well, I always knew my nose was my weak point—'

'Point—'

'There you go,' and Sara began to laugh and cry at the same time. 'Oh, isn't that you all over? Oh, it's cruel. Well, I know it always was too soft and spready, and you know you did make it worse. I'm sure you broke the gristle—yes, if I've got to carry about this awful sponge now, it's because of you.'

'And a few score hogsheads. Come, Sara, fill up and don't let it stick to the glass. You and I were a pair of fools, but that's no reason why we should go on being foolish—you come along next Saturday and bring some beer, and I'll do a nice sketch or two and give you a copy. You always liked to keep a drawing of yourself. I daresay you have some now.'

'You only want me for a cheap model, Gulley, I know.'

'The best model I ever had. Why, Sara, they're giving thousands for those old sketches of you in the yellow bath. And you've got it about you still,' and, in fact, I could have painted the old trollop that minute if I could have got her clothes off. There was always something about Sara that made me want to hit her or love her or get her down on canvas. She provoked you, and half of it was on purpose.

The skate was working himself up. 'On the one hand the home; a little sketch or picture of that paradise which Nature meant for the whole world.'

'Yes,' said Sara, sighing again, and a tear or perhaps a drop of porter sweat rolled off her nose into the glass. 'That's what I always felt—if only people could be sensible and not so jealous and spiteful—there's such a lot of happiness that God meant for us.'

'And what do we see about us?' cried the skate, working himself up and answering his own questions like the end man at the nigger minstrels. 'Nothing but crime and hatred and wars—'

'And just when you get some sense,' said Sara, 'and know that you can't have happiness brought up on a hot plate, you're old and it's too late—'

'And why? Because of property,' said the skate, 'that institution of the devil. The love of things, which is the enemy of God's love—'

And old Plantie began beating his great walrus flippers together and shouting, 'Hear, hear.'

'There,' said Sara, 'I knew the young man wasn't married—but he does speak nice. It's the voice—like burnt sugar.'

'I daresay, Sara,' I said, 'you've got a bit laid by yourself. So that even if Fred does turn nasty—'

But she got quite agitated. 'Oh dear, what's the time—?'

'That's all right, Sara, drink up and we'll catch the bus—but first you can come round to my place and I'll show you where I hide the key.'

'You really think I'd better come?' said Sara, quite shaky.

'Not if you're afraid for your virtue.'

'Oh dear,' and she was giggling like any dairymaid in the straw-house. 'Don't talk so. It's not nice at our age. I'm too old.'

'You wait and see who's too old—and we'll have a bit of supper somewhere.'

'Well, of course, Gulley—you must let me give you supper, and I'd have brought something over today only I had to get away quick when that sister was out at her shopping, and there's some shirts too that Fred thinks are tight in the neck. I'm sure you could do with some winter shirts.'

'Property, that devilish invention to which we owe every evil, envy, hatred, thievery, the police, and all the cruelty of law, armies, navies, war—'

There was more clapping, and Sara drank up her glass in order to clap for herself. The old blancmange was dissolving in sentiment and drink; her nose was on fire and her little grey eyes were swimming, and while she slapped her fat hands together, all her chins and her neck and her front shook up and down and even her backside quivered in the tight black bombazine, or whatever it was.

But all at once she saw me looking at her, and just like the old Sara she knew at once what was in my mind and said, 'Well, aren't I a picture of fun? But there, when you're old, what can you do? If you don't feel anything about anything, you might as well be dead.'

And I gave her another hug. For she had got round me so far that I was all on the jump, and ready to carry her off that minute. Though I ought to have known I was much too busy for females, except in the way of work. 'Don't you mind, Sara. Go on being Sara. Let yourself go. Act how you feel, and if they laugh, who cares? Why, they laugh at me. And I laugh back. That's one advantage of turning into a damned old scarecrow. Drink up, old girl, and we'll laugh at 'em together.'

Just then there was a scruffling next door, like the beginning of a dog-fight, and next moment the whole meeting got up and began to sing Jerusalem. So Sara jumped up too, and began to sing as loud as she could, stretching up her neck and shutting her eyes, like a prize tenor.

Till we have built Jerusalem
In England's green and pleasant land.

'Well, I always did love that song,' she said. 'It's the tune, I suppose, and whatever you say about Jews, they're good family people.'

'Come on, Sara, there's only one bottle left.' And I poured out.

'Oh, Gulley, I couldn't—I'm quite swimming, well, I suppose we can't get out till the people have moved.'

'And very comfortable here, too,' I said, getting a firmer grip. For the truth was that, what with memories and beer, and Sara herself, we were both a bit glorious and we seemed like young things again, in our forties. And we fell to kissing, and so on. And Sara was half laughing and half crying. And our chairs fell over against the wall.

However, after a time, I found that I had my head jammed under the scullery shelf and I was nearly smothered with Sara who seemed to spread her bombazine all over me and I had a stabbing in my thigh that I thought must be my sciatica, till I realized it was Sara's umbrella jammed in between the legs of our chairs. So I began to wriggle out of the clinch, and Sara said, 'Oh, oh, mind my hat—oh dear, oh dear, I've got the cramps,' and then when we saw each other, she was more crying than laughing. 'Oh dear,' she said, 'I'm ashamed, Gulley, you can laugh, but we're too old. And dressed in my Sunday blacks for poor Rozzie. No, it's not right—it's so uncomely. No, you can't get over it, Gulley, being old. Well, if I had a beauty cure perhaps, and a tea-gown like some old actress and was in a nice room with silk sofas and flowers, but there, I'm talking silly. I'm too old, and look at my stockings, I know half my suspenders are pulled right out. I feel all to pieces, and what's the time—you don't say it's half-past ten?'— and the old lady began to get in such a fluster that I was afraid she'd have hysterics.

She grabbed up her umbrella and made for the back steps. I ran along with her and tried to soothe her down. 'Come, Sara, you needn't run—you'll blow up.'

'Run, why I'm lucky if I catch the last bus, and Fred home any minute now, and perhaps that sister with him. Oh, you don't know, or you wouldn't have come to the house, Gulley. They ferreted it all out—what with that girl Coker and Hickson, yes, even about the pictures.'

'Well, Sall, if Fred does turn you out, you come along— come back to me.'

'Oh, he wouldn't do that. Not Fred. He couldn't be so stupid. Why, what would happen to Dicky, yes, or Fred himself? With that nasty herring gut of a creature. Is that my bus? Well, it can't be helped, I can't run any more. Oh, I've got such a pain, whatever did I drink all that beer for?'

But I got her to the bus stop at last and while her bus was driving up, she came to her senses for a minute, as Sara always could, in the most exciting situations, and she took me by the coat and turned up her eyes and said, 'I shouldn't have come, Gulley, should I? Just upsetting us both. But we were happy, weren't we, and I'll bring those socks and shirts, and there's an old overcoat too, or if I don't dare to come out so far again, I'll post them to you. Only don't come to the house or write. It's not safe, truly it isn't. And look after your chest. You ought to have more woolies for winter, you know you ought. I'll put some in, chest thirty-two, it used to be. Well, if they're too big now, they'll shrink. And if I can't come again, we were happy Gulley, weren't we? I mean in the good times—we were the happiest couple. Oh dear, here's the bus—you'll never say we weren't the happiest couple. Even if you did spoil my nose. Oh, I thank God for that time, and you were a sweet husband when you liked.'

'Come on, Sall,' I said. 'Get up, old lady.' For I thought she would dissolve away on the pavement.

'Yes, I thank God for it. We've got something better than noses, haven't we. We've got our memories and they last better than any nasty flesh.'

And she had me nearly as flustered as she was. As the bus moved off I was in two minds about jumping on the platform and running off with her. And after the bus had gone, I walked down to Greenbank in a high state of enjoyment. What an evening. And I couldn't get the old girl out of my eye or my feelings. I kept on seeing her hand tilting the glass, and the turn of her body from the waist; stiff enough, but I could see the woman inside; the real old Sara that had made me mad, and especially with the brush.

Yes, I thought, and that's what I've been missing in my Eve, something female, something that old Cranach had, yes, something from Sara. And not just the hips either, and the high waist; it's something in the movement; and as soon as I got back to Plantie's I opened one of his old encyclopaedias and began to draw what I wanted on the end-papers; the everlasting Eve, but all alive-oh. She came out strong like Sara, the Sara of twenty years ago.

16.
When Plantie came down the steps from seeing his Prof to the Tube, I put Sara in my pocket and the encyclopaedia on the shelf. Then I helped Plantie to pour all the odd bottles together into a jug and we sat down in front of the fire to try the mixture. While Plantie talked of Ponting and Proudhon and Comte and Spinoza.

The trouble of staying with Plantie is the talk. These old blue-suit walruses are great ones to talk. I knew a dustman down Brocket Yard who would talk all night about the number of the beast. But he was one of the old school, with a bowler hat like a paddle steamer. Plantie's great hobby-horse is Spinoza. The reason I suppose is that Spinoza was all for making the best of a bad job. And Plantie, having had a hard life, is the same way of thinking. Motto:

KEEP YOUR PECKER UP, OLD COCK. HERE'S THE
CHOPPER COMING

'To contemplate the glory of creation,' said Plantie, blowing clouds of smoke like a chimney on fire. He'd taken off his collar and tie and boots, and was prepared to be happy. I said nothing for fear of provoking provocation. But I drank the more. A good mixture. There was some gin in it as well as lime-juice and lager, black-strap and wallop.

Plantie put one foot on the fender and wagged his big toe, and said, 'Yes, Mr Jimson, the greatest of philosophers.'

This was provocation. Because Plantie knew I didn't like Spinoza. I used to, of course. In the year when I couldn't paint and went to the devil, and philosophy, science and the newspapers; I fell for old Ben Spinoza myself. Like everyone at first sight. The old Eye got me. And I, too, went round offering provocation. I once bit a man who didn't like Spinoza; or perhaps he'd never heard of him, and didn't want to hear. I remember he was trying to grind out my guts with his knees. He was some kind of idealist; took a real interest in fundamental things. But just after that I began to read Blake. And Blake led me back to Plato, because he didn't like him, and the pair of them took me forward to black-and-white drawing and formal composition. And soon after that I got too busy for amusement; and stopped reading anything but judgment summonses.

Spinoza is one of the most popular London philosophers, especially in the East End, and round the Isle of Dogs, but he is not so strong in Greenbank, which belongs more to the upper river cultural sphere. In Greenbank they drink in Plato and Ruskin with the Oxford bath water. Postie has always been a Platonist and a Dark Blue. Bert Swope was a passionate Dark Blue. On the Boat Race day of 1930, Swope tore the favours off two Cambridge men from Poplar and threw them into the river. He would have been a leading Platonist if he had ever heard of Plato. But about 1933 or 1936, Plantie who had read all the philosophers, began to take a special interest in Spinoza. Anarchists who love God always fall for Spinoza because he tells them that God doesn't love them. This is just what they need. A poke in the eye. To a real anarchist, a poke in the eye is better than a bunch of flowers. It makes him see stars.

Plantie has had a hard time and so he likes to be told that in God's sight he is dirt. Plantie has been kicked about the world like a football, and so he likes to be told that he isn't any better than a football, except to kiss the foot that kicks him. It makes him feel more brisk and independent. It gives him confidence in himself. To say, 'I can take the worst they've got.'

When you tell a man like Plantie that he isn't free except to take it as it comes, he feels free. He says, 'All right, let 'em all come.'

But I didn't like Spinoza. I haven't got any self-respect, and besides, I'm an optimist. I get a lot of fun out of fun, as well as the miseries. And so when Plantie tried to convert me to dignified independence I quarrelled with him. We didn't speak for some weeks or months. And since Plantie is a good man and therefore a bit of a nagger, he's tried at least three times a year since to provoke me on Spinoza. But now that I'm broke I can't afford to quarrel with my friends, and I've worked up a technique to avoid arguing about Spinoza. I don't say anything at the time, but afterwards, and only to myself.

'He kept free,' said Plantie. 'Yes, one of the greatest and noblest men who ever lived. Because with it all, with the glass dust, and all the people who wanted to burn him alive for a heretic, he kept his happiness.' Plantie wagged both his toes, and blew out such a cloud of smoke that I wondered we didn't have the fire brigade. He was working up his happiness. 'What he said was, "Life is a gift, and what right have we to complain that we weren't given it different." No, he never complained against good or bad luck or any nonsense like that. Any more than you do, Mr Jimson.'

This was a pass at the scullery window. But I only took another pull at the jug. For the truth was I wasn't hearing Plantie, only his words. So I listened like an angel. Grinning like Essex clay in a June sun. Plantie's voice stroked me down like a warm breeze; while I swam in mixed lager, and contemplated the new Sara-Eve like another golden fish in the same pond.

I said nothing and thought nothing and never felt any of the injuries the old blowhard was aiming at me, under cover of his hospitality. And all I remember after half-past eleven is Plantie's toes going like a sewing machine, and Plantie's moustache shaking up and down in a cloud of blue smoke, like the burning bush, and his bald head shining pink, while he talked about the evils of property and the police, and the joys of Nature and the contemplation of its beauties.

Then I woke up in Plantie's bed with a rug over me and breakfast ready on the stove. Plantie was tap-tapping away in the front shop. He always works on Sunday. Being a man of strict principles.

But I had a head like a dog-fight and a mouth like a vacuum cleaner, and, worst of all, the feeling of too much society.

A nice way to spend my life, I thought, at parties. And I felt so damned ill that I only wanted to get to work.

When I wished Plantie good morning, he looked at me over the top of his iron spectacles that he wears in the shop and said, 'Coming back?' gruff and short as always in the workshop.

'Thank you, Mr Plant,' I said. 'But I shall be pretty busy from now on, and I think I'll sleep on the job. Get the early light.'

Plantie knocked in another clag, and said, 'You can't sleep in that place of yours.'

'Yes, thanks, not badly.'

Plantie knocked in two clags. And I was fretting to be off. I'd had enough of talk and people for a week. Talk is not my line. It gives me a stomach-ache. When I've talked a lot, I know I've told a lot of lies, and what makes it worse, not even meaning to. When you're talking a lot you haven't time to get the words right. Talk is lies. The only satisfactory form of communication is a good picture. Neither true nor false. But created. Yet I couldn't go until Plantie was ready for me to go because I'd slept in his bed and eaten his breakfast. And he wasn't ready yet. I knew that by the stiff way he worked his hammer and stuck out his moustache.

'What about supper?' he said at last.

'I'm afraid I'm engaged for supper.'

Plantie knocked in another clag, but I could tell he'd given me up, by his free style. 'So long, and thanks,' I said. 'Good-bye, Mr Jimson,' said Plantie. 'It's a pleasure.'

And so we parted friends. But I had wasted the day. I sat and looked at the canvas most of the morning. And what I did that afternoon I took out next morning. I could see there was something there, but it kept on fleeing away from me. I began to think I'd never paint anything again. I'd lost the artfulness. And even in the dark, I couldn't see my way. I only got a headache in my feet, and corns on my brain. Going round and round.

What I say to an artist is, WHEN YOU CAN'T PAINT— PAINT. But something else. So I knocked up a little sketch of Sara on a piece of plank. Sara as she was, broad as a door. And it went very well. It went so well that I forgot my feet, I forgot my head. And just as always happens, this other job of Sara, which had nothing to do with my picture in hand, began to bend round and give me ideas on that picture too. I began to get so many ideas about it that I should have started all over again if the light hadn't failed. Then I noticed my rheumatism, and my backache, and my poor feet. But I was lucky enough to meet Postie Ollier outside the Eagle, and he stood me a pint and a

95

stand-up supper. He also tried to take me home to Plant's. Postie is one of the vice-presidents of the save Jimson from himself society. But he can't ask me to his own place, because he married beneath him, and his friends have to be his wife's friends too.

'Mr Plant is expecting you,' he said. But I knew I couldn't do with any more talk.

'Thank you, Mr Ollier,' I said. 'But I shall be very comfortable in my own quarters.' And I ran away from him in case he pressed me.

Constable night. Broken lumps of cloud whirling across a knife-coloured sky like wreckage on a Thames flood. Moon running over the house fronts like a spotlight. When it fell on the willows, they trembled like girls caught in dark corners waiting for their young men.

> These lovely females form sweet night and silence
> and secret
> Obscurities to hide from Satan's watch-fiends
> human loves.

The rain came down like glass bead curtains, glittering across the black arches. It swayed in the wind and rattled against the stones.

Shed pouring through the roof. Pools on the floor. No oil in the lamp, no matches. And a couple of cold sausages. Got into my night-dress of newspapers. Knock on the window and Coker shouted over the noise of the rain, 'Who's there, is that you, Jimson?'

'No.' 'What are you doing there?' and she poked her head through the window. 'Going to bed.' 'You can't sleep there, you old fool, in a pool of water. I hear you coughing from Greenbank Hard.' 'I've been coughing for thirty years. 'You're a bloody nuisance, that's what you are. Where am I going to put you this time of night?' 'I'm all right, Coker.' 'You ought to be in the Union, that's the truth of it.' 'You can't put me in the Union. I'm a householder.' 'Oh come on, and don't talk so much. But you'll have to sleep on the floor, and I've only one blanket.'

'I've got my coat.' 'Sopping wet, I should think. Oh dear, what I ought to do is to leave you to go to the Union.' 'If I go to the Union, I shan't be able to paint, and you won't get your money.' 'I won't get my money out of your painting, I'm getting it from Mr Hickson.'

Coker lived on the top floor in Dahlia Road. Nice respectable villas come down to social life, and bare wood stairs. Top landing full of buckets, chests of drawers, jugs and pots. Coker pushed me into the room and stopped to tell some neighbour what she thought about a bucket. 'Nobody's going to slip their buckets on me. It's been four buckets for six months. It was three before that, and then there was the agreement. And now there's five. All right, but if it's five tomorrow night, somebody's bucket is going out of the window.'

Slice of a room, all furniture. Big bed. Four dining-room chairs piled up. Dining table on its side against the wall. Coker's summer coat hanging on one leg. Bird cage on the other. Radiogram as big as a chicken-house. Roll of stair carpet. New carpet, brown. Tins of cleaning stuffs, furniture polish, on the mantelshelf.

'Whose furniture, Coker? Yours or Willie's?' 'Mine,' said Coker. 'Catch Willie spending his money on anyone but himself.' 'Heard anything about him lately?' 'Dancing at the Palace with his Blondie every night.' 'I should say good riddance. Nothing but trouble to you all the time.' 'Don't you comfort me. Willy was worth trouble. He's a dead loss. And forty pounds' worth of furniture, all my blankets, two pairs of double sheets, six face towels with initials. It's enough to make a girl put herself in the water.'

'Don't you be a fool Coker. Think of all the cups of tea and buttered scones you'd miss.' 'Don't you be afraid, I'm not drowning myself. Not while the Blondie's alive. Somebody ought to hate that bitch, and who'll do it if I don't?' 'It's a mug's game, Coker, especially for a woman. You can't get your own back. And I'll tell you why. It isn't your own when you get it. It's moved on.' 'I don't want my own back. I want to be like I am, hating that dirty tart. Why, look at all my poor chairs with their legs in the air. Like a lot of dead dogs, poisoned off. Don't you talk to me about forgiveness or I might get cross and give you a smack.' 'It's not forgiving. It's forgetting.' 'That's enough, or I'll get my mother up. Look at the floor, you old bone. You're wet to the skin. It's coming out of your boots.' 'Only my overcoat.' 'Take it off then. Don't stand goggling like a last week's bloater.' 'I did a good job today, Coker, one of those lucky days.' 'Lucky if you don't get pneumonia. Nice fool I'd look with you dead on my hands.' 'That job is going to be good—as good as anything I ever did. And better.' 'There, I knew, it's right through to your shirt.' 'The fact is, Coker, I'm first-class.' I was surprised when this popped out. But as it had come out I thought I might as well let myself go. 'Don't you tell anybody else, Cokey, but I'm one of the big fish. In a hundred years, fifty perhaps, the National Galleries will be paying fifty thousand pounds for a Jimson. And they'll be right. Because my stuff is the real stuff.' 'And nothing but rags under your shirt—you'll freeze one of these days.' 'The fact is, Coker, I'm a genius.' 'I shouldn't wonder if you hadn't a temperature this minute.' 'You think I'm talking nonsense.'

Coker was pulling me about like a rag doll and swearing at me. 'You're a nuisance, that's what you are—I suppose you'll have to come into the bed. Nice tale for the neighbours. But they'll talk, anyhow. Here, take your trousers off and turn 'em the other way round, they're dry anyhow. Back-before I mean.' And she pushed me down on the bed and began to pull my trousers off. Coker never had much patience.

'You don't believe a word I say, Coker.' 'Lift up your bottom—how can I get 'em off when you keep on sitting down?' 'You wonder how I know that I'm one of the greatest artists that ever lived—of course there are a few hundred of 'em—but that's not so many among thousands of millions.' 'Yes, yes, you're a wonderful man.' 'All right, you can laugh.' 'I'm not laughing. Why, Mr Plant told me two years ago.' 'What did he tell you?' 'That you were a real genius. Don't you worry, everybody knows it round here. Even the kids say, there's the professor.'

'What do they say that for?' 'Well, they think you're cracked, who wouldn't? Get in now and over against the wall and keep over. I'll put a bolster down the middle to make sure. 'What do you mean by a genius?' 'I'm not going to wait all night. And turn your face to the wall while I get ready.'

Coker undressed and knelt down to say her prayers. I took a peep to make sure, and when she got up I said, 'I thought you hated God, Coker.' 'So I do.' 'What do you pray for?' 'He's our Father, isn't he?' 'That's a funny reason.' 'Not so funny as you're a nuisance. Here, let me feel your head. I bet you got a fever. Nice bit in the papers if you croak in my bed. Oh well, it would happen to me. It's a wonder I got my legs the same length, and don't squint. Now you go to sleep.'

Coker put a loop of string on the switch; laid a bolster down the middle of the bed, and got in on the other side. Then she pulled the string and the light went out. Light went out and the moon came in through the curtain making a pattern on the blanket like water. And I felt as gay as Garrick. It's a joke, I thought, that I should have such happiness in my life and this poor kid should be damned from the kick. It makes you laugh. 'What did you pray for, Coker?' 'Mind your own business.' 'You ought to look for a nice widower of fifty with a wooden leg. Make allowances on both sides.' 'If you're being funny, I'll give you a smack.' 'You got the furniture, all you need is a husband.' 'Who wants a husband? I wouldn't mind if I never saw a man again. A dirty lot of crooks.' 'You were going to marry Willie, weren't you?' 'Willie was different. He was a gentleman.' 'Who walked off and left you in the mud.' 'He didn't know what he was doing, poor boy, when that Blondie got him. She's well known.' 'Did you pray for Blondie to get trouble?' Coker didn't answer. 'If Blondie knew how she'd got on your mind, she'd laugh.' 'Let her; she won't laugh if I get her where I want her.' 'Where does she live?' 'I'm trying to find out. What she wants is a splash of acid.' 'You'd get seven years for that.' 'It would be worth it.' 'Don't you believe it—she'd be burning on your brain the rest of your life. She'd come back, in the acid.' 'I shouldn't mind if I'd got justice.' 'You can't get justice in this world. It doesn't grow in these parts.' 'You're telling me.' 'It makes you laugh.' 'What does?' 'The damned unfairness of things.' 'It doesn't make me laugh. More like crying.' 'Or cry, just as you like.' 'Suppose you let me go to sleep.'

And in five minutes she was as deep as a diver. I sat up to take a look at her. Face like a child. Breathing like a baby. She turned over like a child. Sudden earthquake. Gave a sigh, threw one arm over the blanket. Deep all the time. And what a forearm. Marble in the moon. Muscled like an Angelo, but still a woman's. Nothing obvious. Modelling like a violin solo. The sweetest elbow I ever saw, and that's a difficult joint. No fat above the wrist but a smooth fall into the metacarpals. Just enough structure to give the life and the power. Bless the girl, I thought, she's a beauty, and she doesn't know it. I could have kissed

Coker for that elbow. But what would be the good of that? She wouldn't believe me if I told her an elbow like that was a stroke of genius.

And I thought, that's the forearm I want for Eve, with Sara's body. Sara as she was about thirty years ago. Sara's forearms were always too soft. Cook's arms. Mottled brown. Greedy and sentimental arms. Lustful wrists crested like stallions, with venus rings. But Eve was a worker. The woman was for hard graft. Adam the gardener, the poet, the hunter. All wires like a stringed instrument. Nervous fibre. Eve smooth and thick as a column, strong as a tree. Brown as earth. Or red like Devon ground. Red would be better. Iron ground. Iron for the magnetic of love. English Eve.

> *And this is the manner of the daughters of Albion*
> *   in their beauty.*
> *Everyone is threefold in head and heart and*
> *   reins, and everyone*
> *Has three gates into the three heavens of Beulah*
> *   which shine*
> *Translucent in their foreheads and their bosoms*
> *   and their loins*
> *Surrounded with fire unapproachable: but whom*
> *   they please*
> *They take up into their heavens in intoxicating*
> *   delight.*

When we got up I tried to do Coker's arm from memory on the back leaf out of her prayer book. But it didn't have the feeling. It wanted to be in the round. 'I wish you'd let me paint you, Coker,' I said. 'It's your arm I want.'

But Coker didn't even answer. 'Hurry up and finish your tea.'

'What's the hurry for me?' 'We've got a visit to pay.' Then I noticed that Coker was putting on her county suit. 'You're not going to take me to Sara's again.' For I didn't want to see Sara again, especially after the night at Plant's. I hadn't the time at my age. 'No,' said Coker, 'we've finished with that one. Now it's Hickson's.' 'A bit quick, isn't it?' 'That's the idea, to get there before she can tip him off.' 'Sara wouldn't do that—she gave us all the evidence we wanted.' 'A double cross in each eye and a plant in her smile.' 'I couldn't go today, Coker, I've got work to do that can't wait.' 'What do you mean, can't wait? You haven't got an opening time. Nobody's going without his beer because you're on the outabout.' 'I got an idea and I got to get it down.' 'Ideas will keep without ice.' 'Not unless you turn 'em into paint—they go soft at the edges, or melt into grease and water.' 'You can always get new ones.' 'I don't want new ones, I want this one. And I'll never get it again.' 'Then you'll get better. Here, give your boots a rub with the newspaper. I never saw such boots.' 'They're on the big side for warmth.' 'And what are the cracks for?' 'Ventilation.' 'It's not a joke. What do you think people think of you going about like an old tramp out of the Union?' 'They think nothing of me, and that's a comfort.' 'Don't talk silly.' 'Do you like to see people thinking about you? I didn't think you had so much vanity, Coker.' 'Put on your hat and don't fall over the apples like last time.' And she had me in the street before I could think of another excuse. 'It's bad when they think well of you, Cokey, because you get to think too much of yourself. And it's bad when they think badly of you because you may get to think badly of them. Take your mind off your work.' 'Where are you going to?' 'Gentlemen.' 'Be quick then—we got to catch Hickson before ten.'

I went down the steps, walked through the passage and came out at the other end. But Coker was waiting for me at the top of the steps. She jumped on me like a lion. 'I thought so—now why shouldn't I give you a smack.' 'Didn't I come up the same way?' 'No, you didn't, and you didn't do anything down there either. There wasn't time. Why, you old fool, I knew you wanted to make a getaway as soon as you spoke. A monkey at the zoo could look more innocent.' 'I can't come to Hickson's today, Coker.' 'Don't you talk to me about your ideas. I'm not Mr Plant. You may be a genius, but you need boots and a new overcoat or you'll be dead before next winter. And a dead genius stinks as high as any other flat fish.' 'It's like this, Coker. I've had trouble with Hickson. I like Hickson, but he upsets me. And I'm at rather a tricky place in my work. Suppose we go and see Hickson and he begins to talk his nonsense, and we have a row. It might put me off the work. I don't say it would but it might. And then I might have to scrap the whole job and where would we be then?' 'You needn't speak to Hickson. Good thing if you don't after the way you talked to that Monday woman.' 'Then why do you want me along?' 'Because you're my only bona fides.'

I took a step backwards down the stairs. I knew Cokey was too much of a lady to chase a man into the gentlemen. Cokey saw the idea and she said, 'Come this once and I'll stand you a couple of quarts at a gill a time.' 'I don't want quarts.' And I took another step down. 'What do you want then?' 'I could do with a bladder of flake white, a viridian, a cobalt and chrome yellow. Also a No. 12 brush.' 'How much does it come to?' 'A few bob.' 'All right.' 'There's a colour shop just off High Street—not fifty yards off.' 'Can't you wait till we come back?' 'Something in my pockets would keep me from going through the ceiling at Hickson's.' 'All right, come on. You're a winner, you are.' 'That's a bargain.' 'Cross my heart. I shan't strangle you, though that's just about what you deserve.'

I came up then and we went along and got the colours. Twenty-three bob surprised Coker. But she surprised me. She paid down on the nail and said only, 'Caught again. But you're not going to say I went back on you.' 'No, I shan't, Coker. I think a lot of your character, especially your arms, and I wish you would sit for your arm. The left one. We could do it now in less than half an hour. I want it for my picture.' 'What about Hickson?' said Coker, and she stopped in the street and looked at me. 'All right, Coker, but you're taking a big chance. Why not telephone? Let me telephone.' 'I've telephoned already. He's expecting us. Are you coming on or are you going back on me after skinning me of twenty-three bob?' 'All right, Cokey. It will probably finish me off. But what's it matter after all? I mightn't have been born.' 'You might have been born with more sense.'

We took a bus to Oxford Circus. And I kept on moving till we got the front seats on top. Coker didn't want to move, but when I moved she had to move. 'I like the front window,' I said, 'for the view. As good as a Rolls. Better; higher and not the same responsibility not to run over the poor.' 'Yes,' said Coker, 'and when you've made me come with you and push in and push out, somebody's stuck his umbrella in my stockings. It's a wonder if I haven't two ladders this minute.' 'I wouldn't be a girl for a million pounds.' 'I wouldn't be a man if I was Clark Gable with twenty-five suits and forty pairs of shoes. I'd rather be the lowest woman in the world than the top man.' 'That's loyalty to the sex.' 'No, it's feelings. If you men were women for five minutes you'd know and you wouldn't want to change.' 'I thought you didn't like to be a woman.' 'I don't like being myself. But I'm not going to let up on it. I got my pride.' 'Yes, you've got your pride—it makes you a doormat for a sot like Willie.' 'Willie's not my pride. He was my chap, and he was good to me. You leave Willie out of it, you hear.'

It was a grey morning. Air skim milky. Grey sky, grey street, and the houses dodging by like a grey paling. Green-grey face just over the chimney pots, where the sun was hiding. Fat sulky face with one fat eye, three-quarters closed. Gave it a look as if it had something on its mind. Old black rooks flapping along the sky and old black taxi-cabs flapping down the street.

'That's all right, Cokey,' I said. 'Well, you can't help it, can you. You're as God made you, more or less, with some interference from Daddy.'

Coker thought a moment and moved her little beak up and down. Then she said, 'I'm not expecting anything from anybody.' 'I'm glad of that,' I said, 'I was afraid you might be.' 'Might be what?' 'Expecting.' 'Mind your own business.' And I could feel she was trying to think of something cruel, something that would stab me to the heart, so I said, 'Never mind, Cokey. Say what you like. If it lets the pressure down. I can take it.'

Cokey thought again. But her temper had changed. And she said at last, in her bar voice, 'No one expects anything of a man, except mess and talk.' 'What do you expect of a woman?' 'Everything she can give and a smile.' 'Don't you give it, Coker, not everything.'

And Coker turned fierce again. But just when she was going to cut me to the soul, she changed her mind again and said, 'I might—I got my pride.'

I gave it a minute to cast its warmth upon the conversation, and then I said, 'I hope you didn't give anything to Willie you couldn't spare.'

Cokey didn't answer, but her mood was still lofty and calm. 'If Willie had wanted to chop off your legs with the meat hatchet, I suppose you'd have lain down on the scullery floor and lent him an apron to keep his trousers clean.' 'I'd rather my neck than my legs. And I'd rather he stuck a skewer in my heart than either. I don't like mess —but why not? Even my legs. I've got a lot of pride.' 'So you have, Coker. And it makes me anxious. Might get you into a lot of trouble.' 'I'll take it on.' 'Pride is a good chest protector but a bad bicycle,' I said. 'Its wheels only go round. And you want to get right away from that dirty lot of ordures, Cokey. You want to forget Willie and Blondie; and go on to the next thing. There's plenty of it, waiting to say how do you do, and it smells nicer.'

Cokey said nothing to this. She was feeling her wings; touching up her county scarf.

'I like you, Cokey,' I said. 'But the reason I tell you is that a friend's troubles are one's own troubles, and I don't like trouble. I could fall for you, Cokey, if I had time. And I don't like to see that Blondie getting on your mind, poisoning your springs. The worse she is, the worse for you. Well, I tell you, there's some fellows I daren't even remember their names, or I'd get ulcers on the brain. You take a straight tip from the stable, Cokey, if you must hate, hate the government or the people or the sea or men, but don't hate an individual person. Who's done you a real injury. Next thing you know he'll be getting into your beer like prussic acid; and blotting out your eyes like a cataract and screaming in your ears like a brain tumour and boiling round your heart like melted lead and ramping through your guts like a cancer. And a nice fool you'd look if he knew. It would make him laugh till his teeth dropped out; from old age.'

But Cokey only heard the first bit and she didn't listen to that. She only felt it, and it caused her to lean her right shoulder about a quarter of an inch in my direction. Approach to confidence. 'I tell you, Mr Jimson,' she said, 'a girl needs it with a face like mine. She needs a lot of pride. Every time I see it in the glass or shop window it gives me a smack where it hurts most, and every time I see it in another girl's face, it sticks a knife into me. Yes, even girls that I could pity, they shoot me full of hot needles.' 'And you shoot them?' 'Yes, I shoot them. It isn't what you mean to do, it's the flashback. First time it hit me was about when I left school. At fourteen. Like a kick, and the kicks went on coming so quick I didn't have time to put up a guard. Makes a kid think.'

We were passing the gardens and the trees were lifting up their skinny black arms to the dirty sky like a lot of untouchables asking for a blessing from heaven. Which they knew they wouldn't get.

'I mean a girl, of course,' said Cokey. 'Nothing makes a boy think.' 'Only about what he can get or eat. Not about himself.' 'I wasn't thinking about myself. I was wondering who gave all the flowers to a totty like I won't say who and all the kicks to me, just because my features weren't out of the matchbox.' 'The delight of the eye beats home comforts any day. Even a chap like Willie has his poetical side. He forgets himself when he sees a real peach. That's what you're up against.' 'Don't I know it? Men are a lot of fools.' 'Or artists.' 'If Willie marries that Blondie she'll make him wish he was dead.' 'He won't want to change his poison, if she keeps her looks.' 'She's a bad heart.' 'Good hearts are sixpence a packet, but peaches are rare.' 'What do they make us for?' 'Quantity production and take the pick—goodness is a throw away.' 'I got my pride, thank God.' 'It gives you a centre, but I find it cold for the guts.' 'Who said I wanted the heat?'

Hickson lives in Portland Place, top end, near the Park. Coker rang and I said, 'It's your responsibility, Coker. I didn't ask for it.' 'All right, it's my responsibility.' Man in a blue suit opened the door and showed us into a little room full of whatnots. Hickson has collected everything. I suppose it was that or drink. Man went off. 'Who was that?' Coker said. 'Hickson's man. Always in a blue suit.' 'How could I tell he wasn't a gentleman?' 'You're not meant to, first time. Look at this.' And I showed her the Japanese netsukes on the mantelpiece, real old ones. Carved all over with the wrinkles on the soles of their feet. 'Magnify them fifty times and they'd be monuments. It's chunky work. And yet look at the detail.' 'Too foreign-looking for me.' 'That's why Hickson likes 'em. He hasn't got any imagination either.' 'Well, what are they for?' 'Imagination.' 'I pity the girl who has to dust this room.' 'So do I if she hasn't got any more imagination than you have.'' Coker said nothing. She was preening herself for Hickson, pulling down her coat, looking down the backs of her stockings, to see if the seams were straight. Admiring them. Real silk. Coker was very particular about her stockings.

For Eternity is in love with the productions of
time.

'What are you doing?' Coker said, turning round. She'd been looking at herself in a picture-glass. 'Nothing.' 'Take those things out of your pocket. You old fool. Do you want to do five years?' I took out some of the netsukes and put them back on the mantelpiece. All but the best, which Hickie couldn't have appreciated, anyhow.

17. Just then Hickson's man opened the double door and asked us to come into the next room. The big drawing-room. And right in the middle of the wall my picture of Sara standing in the sun beside a flat bath. Right foot on a chair. Drying her ankle with a green towel. Sunlight throwing the window squares on her back and thighs. Giving the section. Solid as stone, but all in light without shadow and all direct painting. Eight by five. I hadn't seen it for fifteen years and it nearly knocked me down. 'Look at that,' I said to Coker. 'Where's your Rubens now or Renoir either?' 'Who did it?' 'I did.' 'Who is it, not that Sara?' 'What's it matter who it is?' 'How she could show herself—and such a lump too. It's disgusting.' 'It's a work of genius. It's worth fifty thousand pounds. It's worth anything you like because it's unique; and Hickson knows it too. Or somebody's told him. He's put it in the place of honour. Middle of the wall between Goya and Tiepolo. Best light in the room. And the frame. Take a look at the frame, Cokey. That's old Spanish, or I'm a Dutch doll with my eyes painted on the outside. What'll you bet?' 'What do I know?' says Coker.

She was pinching the curtains and running her hands over the chair coverings. Like all those visitors who are requested not to touch. Might as well ask a woman not to look. Women have three sets of eyes. In their fingers for curtains and stuffs. In the backs of their heads for their back hair. And all over them for any other woman. The eyes in the front of their face are not used for seeing with, but for improving the appearance. Hang the thickest veil in front of them and a girl of seventeen will still see the other woman, through two doors and a brick wall, with the various organs of perception existing in her skin, which changes colour, her breasts which tingle, and her brain which performs evolutions of incalculable direction and speed.

'Have you seen this picture, Cokey?'

'I see it,' said Coker, poking her finger into a Gobelin's chair. 'This old stuff, it's worn to shreds.'

'And this frame. Look here.' I went up and took out my penknife and gave a prod. 'There you are, look at that.' For my knife had gone right in. 'None of your composition there. It's just what I said. Carved wood. Every bit of it. And he got it to fit. No, look there. That's a new bit specially carved to match and fitted in. Hickson took a lot of trouble for my picture, didn't he?'

Coker was turning up a corner of the carpet. 'It's a hand-made carpet. I'll say that for it.' I gave her a push on the behind with my foot and made her jump round. But she saw it was a friendly act.

'Here, what are you doing?' 'Look at my picture, Cokey. That's all my own work.'

'I saw it before.'

'No, you didn't. You didn't even think about it.'

'What I think is fifty thousand pounds for a fat totty in her kinsay is a crime. And I wish I had Mr Hickson in the back kitchen for five minutes with one or two of the girls. Like Nelly Mathers that's got five under seven and her man run off with a girl in the Pools. Thinks he'll get a prize.' 'That's not a fat totty. It's a picture. It's a work of genius.' 'Yes, a dirty picture, if you ask me. If it was a postcard and some poor chap tried to sell it he'd get fourteen days.' 'It's you've got the dirty mind, Cokey.' 'You tell me it would be all the same if that was a chair or a bunch of flowers.' 'No, it's bigger. It's got a woman's quality as well as its own.' 'A totty's.' 'Every woman's that ever was.' 'You can count this one out.' 'You don't know what a picture is, Cokey.' 'I know what this is. A virility pill for millionaires. At fifty thousand saucepans—'

But my head was blowing off like a champagne cork. I forgot myself. I gave myself a smack on the top and I took Coker by the arm. 'You're a friend of mine, Cokey, and I'll tell you what I never told anyone before.' 'Yes, that you're a genius. I know that one.' 'No, that's a secret. I don't tell secrets because they come round again like crooked arrows and shoot you in the back. But this is the truth.' 'Did you never tell the truth before?' 'Not since I was a kid.' 'Why not?' 'Because when you tell the truth, you kill it. And it changes into something else. Into a corp. I once shot a kingfisher with a catapult. Knocked him off a twig into a bunch of reeds. And he looked like a piece of cheap satin.' 'You look like you're tight, old man. Take a hold of yourself before Hickson comes.' 'No, I won't. I'm a genius.' 'So you said yesterday.' 'That was because I didn't really believe it. Now I know. And I'm not only a genius, I'm an artist. A son of Los.'

'Los?'

'Los was the Prophet of the Lord.'

> And the sons of Los build moments and minutes
>   and hours
> And days and months and years and ages and
>   periods, wondrous buildings;
> And every moment has a couch of gold for soft
>   repose,
> And between every two moments stands a
>   daughter of Beulah
> To feed the sleepers on their couches with ma-
>   ternal care.
> And every minute has an azure tent with silken
>   veils;
> Every time less than the pulsation of an artery
> Is equal in its period and value to six thousand
>   years,
> For in this period the poet's work is done.

'You haven't got six thousand years this afternoon.' 'Half a minute of revelation is worth a million years of know nothing.' 'Who lives a million years?' 'A million people every twelve months. I'll show you how to look at a picture, Cokey. Don't look at it. Feel it with your eye.' 'I'm not a snail, am I?' 'And first you feel the shapes in the flat —the patterns, like a carpet.' 'You told me that one before.' 'And then you feel it in the round.' 'All that fat.' 'Not as if it were a picture of anyone. But a coloured and raised map. You feel all the rounds, the smooths, the sharp edges, the flats and the hollows, the lights and shades, the cools and warms. The colours and textures. There's hundreds of little differences all fitting in together.' 'The bath towel isn't too bad, I can see that—it's got the look of huckaback.' 'And then you feel the bath, the chair, the towel, the carpet, the bed, the jug, the window, the fields and the woman as themselves. But not as any old jug and woman. But the jug of jugs and the woman of women. You feel jugs are like that and you never knew it before. Jugs and chairs can be very expressive.'

*And every space smaller than a globule of man's
   blood opens
Into eternity of which this vegetable earth is
   but a shadow.*

'Say it again.' 'No, I can't stop. It means a jug can be a door if you open it. And a work of imagination opens it for you. And then you feel with all the women that ever lived and all the women that are ever going to live, and you feel their feeling while they are alone with themselves —in some chosen private place, bathing, drying, dressing, criticizing, touching, admiring themselves safe behind locked doors. Nothing there but women's feeling and woman's beauty and critical eye.'

'I'll admit she might think twice about those legs.'

'Those are beautiful legs.' 'Then they ought to have an elephant for Puss in Boots.' 'Not in a principal boy, you silly, in a picture. Those legs are divine legs, they're ideal legs.' 'So long as you're pleased with them, old man.' I'd like to give you one, Cokey. You'd drive a lamp-post mad.' 'What have I done? I never said it wasn't a nice bit of work. I always said you were clever, do you think I'd have any patience with you if you weren't? I'd shove you in the first dustbin.' 'You can't teach a woman.' 'Why do you want to teach me?' 'I'm trying to teach you a big happiness.' 'To look at a fat totty in her bath. I'm not a man.' 'No, you're an obstinate bloody fool.' 'That's enough before you get rude.'

I made a run at her, but she lifted her fist. So I thought better of it and took a walk across the room. And I forgot my wrath. That's the advantage of Cokey. She's dangerous. If you hit at her, she'll hit you first and harder. So that you don't lose your temper with her. It isn't safe. The best friend I ever had.

Sara looked different from the other end of the room.

The formal composition appeared. Rather better than I had expected. But nothing to my real pictures. No, I thought, it's a masterpiece in its own kind. But it's not the kind I like. It's the real stuff. But in a small way. Lyrical. Impressionist. And say what you like, the epic is bigger than the lyric. Goes deeper and further. Any of my wall pictures is bigger stuff than that.

Hickson came in. Hickson had got older since I saw him last. Small and dry, black suit hanging off his back like a sack. Looked like a little beetle on its crooked hind legs. Poking out his head as if too heavy for his neck. Long white face, all folded with misery-wrinkles like a sick albino bloodhound. Big bald head and a couple of tufts of white wool. Eyes like a pair of half-sucked acid drops. Rolled them from me to Coker and back again. Then lifted up his hand half-way and let me shake it. Like shaking a piece of cold bacon fat. 'Miss Coker,' he said, in a kind of thin flat voice, like some chemical squeezed out of him by the weight of woe. 'Jimson. Glad to see you.'

'How are you, Mr Hickson?'

'You came about those Jimsons I bought in '26.' He sighed so much you could hardly understand him.

'That's it, Mr Hickson,' said Coker, 'and if you don't mind, I'll sit down.'

'Oh yes,' he sighed. 'Sit down. We'll all sit down.'

'We saw Mrs Monday on Wednesday last and she signed a paper to say she had no right to dispose of the pictures.'

'Oh yes, she told me.'

'When was that? She's been quick.'

'On Wednesday. She telephoned. Mrs Monday and I are old friends.'

'I thought she was a double-crosser. But we've got the paper, Mr Hickson. Of course we don't want to make trouble. We'd rather have a settlement without any lawyers coming in, wouldn't we, Mr Jimson?' But I saw there was a row coming, and I pretended not to hear. I got up and had another look at Sara.

'A fine thing, Jimson. Finest you ever did,' he said. But I pretended not to hear. I was staying outside this. And I wanted to look at the picture. It surprised me. Especially the shoulders and back. Sara in that picture is reaching her arms forward. You don't see the torso. Mostly left shoulder and upper arm, a bit of back and the supporting flank.

Coker was talking about the paper again, asking Hickson how much he paid for the pictures at the sale.

'There were several sales, you understand. Mrs Monday left some canvases with a friend.'

'I'm sure she did. But for the lot—'

'Seventy for the first two—then forty-five, about three hundred pounds—the whole of Jimson's debts came to considerably more than four hundred.'

'And how much is that worth?' pointing at Sara with her umbrella.

Hickson put up his shoulders and made a face like a man who's had a piece of ice dropped down his neck. 'Who can say?'

'Fifty thousand pounds,' said Coker.

'Hardly. It may be worth that some day. All I can say now is I wouldn't take five thousand for it.'

'And what did it really cost you? Five quid?'

'Sixteen pictures for three hundred pounds. Say about nineteen pounds each.'

'Mrs Monday said seventeen.'

'There were about twenty but Mrs Monday wanted to keep a few canvases and I agreed to let her have them.'

'You hear that, Mr Jimson?' But I kept my eye on Sara.

'Nineteen pounds each,' said Coker. 'Nineteen pounds for that big picture,' pointing at the bath picture. 'Why, this frame cost more.'

'That is a very fine frame. It cost me a hundred and fifty pounds, and it was very cheap at the price.'

'Mr Jimson was cheaper, and he hasn't got boots on his feet. What a hobo would call boots.'

Hickson screwed himself up again. Like a white parrot in its death agony.

'Well, what about it?' Coker said. And she turned to me again. But I dodged round and took another walk down the room. 'Don't go walking like that, Mr Jimson,' she said to me, 'come here and show your boots.' But I was taking a long eye at Sara's left shoulder. The one holding the towel. It got the right light from the top corner of the room. Showed the modelling. More subtle than I had believed possible for myself fifteen years before. The insertion of the deltoid between triceps and biceps was a beautiful job. It almost did justice to the arm. A lovely place in any arm and enough to make you laugh or cry in Sara's. To wonder at the glories and the mercies of God. As Mr Plant would say.

Coker and Hickson were getting confidential. And Hickson was saying, 'I don't think you understand the whole position, Miss Coker.'

I moved off to the other side of the room. And took Sara from the new angle. And called up Coker's arm for comparison. Yes, I thought, the Coker forearm is a marvel. But the upper arm's much too tight. Too anatomical. A man's arm. And a vaccination mark right on the join. Like the pivot of a machine. As if on purpose. Like a piece of silly smartness daubed on a piece of real understanding. Amateurish. Sara had too fine an instinct to be vaccinated on the arm. On any junction of muscle. She had the vision of an artist, even if it was only fixed on herself. Her upper arm is as clean as a baby's, and that valley under the deltoid as sweet as a snow valley on the Downs. Yes, Mr Plant, I said Mr Spinoza might look there and thank God to be alive, even if he had his lungs full of glass dust.

'Mr Jimson,' said Coker, quite loud, too loud for her manners. But I was reflecting deeply on matters of real importance. Anyone but Coker could have told that by the vacant gaze of my eye. And the way I held my head on one side. I was deaf to the world. Yes, I said to myself, when you see a piece of stuff like that, spontaneous, it brings you bang up against the facts of life. Which are beauty, and so on. So, I said, Plantie's Spinoza had the right stuff in him when he said that it was all my eye to talk about justice. Being alive was enough—to contemplate God's magnificence and eternity. That was happiness. That was joy. On Sara's top arm I blow an angel's trumpet. Oh certainly, Mr Plant, old Ben had some good tricks—aces up both sleeves.

But my point is this, I said. Contemplation is not the doings. It doesn't get *there*, in fact.

And Hickson was saying to Coker, 'But leaving the question of value on one side, these pictures didn't belong to Mr Jimson or to Mrs Monday. They were seized for debt. If you will wait a minute, I can show you the papers—'

I went a little farther off. For I didn't want any interruptions. Things were too critical. Yes, I said to myself, I've got something. Contemplation, in fact, is ON THE OUT-SIDE. It's not on the spot. And the truth is that Spinoza was always on the outside. He didn't understand freedom, and so he didn't understand anything. Because after all, I said to myself, with some excitement, for I saw where all this was leading to. Freedom, to be plain, is nothing but THE INSIDE OF THE OUTSIDE. And even a philosopher like old Ben can't judge the xxx by eating pint pots. It's the wrong approach.

Whereas Old Bill, that damned Englishman, didn't understand anything else but freedom, and so all his nonsense is full of truth; and even though he may be a bit of an outsider, HIS OUTSIDE IS ON THE INSIDE; and if you want to catch the old mole where he digs, you have to start at the bottom.

Hickson was telling Coker all about the sale or sell or whatever it was. 'Of course, a sale of Jimson's pictures in a remote West Country hamlet would have yielded only a few shillings, so when Mrs Monday appealed to me—'

I took a turn down the room. It was a long room. I got away among a lot of little tables covered with gold and enamel snuff-boxes. Set with diamonds and rubies and painted by Boucher, and so on. Knick-knacks.

But what you get on the inside, I said to myself, is the works—it's SOMETHING THAT GOES ON GOING ON. Hold on to that, old boy, I said, for it's the facts of life. It's the ginger in the ginger bread. It's the apple in the dumpling. It's the jump in the OLD MOSQUITO. It's the kick in the old horse. It's the creation. And that's where it's leading me. Right up to that blasted picture of mine.

And I kept looking at the snuff-boxes, so as not to see Coker glaring after me and beckoning with her county umbrella. The Fall is a frost, I said. It's iced all over. It's something contemplated from the outside. It doesn't get under your skin. No, not so much as Sara's back over there. It's not an event; it's a tea-party.

For what happened, I asked myself, turning my back on Coker, and putting my left and best eye to a nice little Leda by Nattier, what happens to any girl when she falls for the first time; what happens to a thousand Eves and Adams every night of the week somewhere under the willows or the palm tree shade—it's a long way from a tea-party. It's not pleasure, or peace, or contemplation, or comfort, or happiness—it's a Fall. Into the pit. The ground gives way, and down you go, head over heels. Unless, of course, you know how to fly. To rise again on your wings.

There was a visitor's book, nicely bound in morocco, lying on a buhl desk with pens and inks. I took a few blank pages out of the end and carried them over to one of the little tables where the light was good. And began to scrawl some figures that had come into my head. Eve under the willows. And the everlasting maiden, Oothoon. The eternal innocence that thinks no evil. Yes, I thought, there's Billy again. Handing me the truth. Even when I wouldn't take it. That's what he was saying all his life. A tear is an intellectual thing. And a joy. It's wisdom in vision. It's the prophetic eye in the loins. The passion of intelligence. Yes, by Gee and Jay, I thought. The everlasting creation of delight. The joy that is always new and fresh because it is created. The revelation ever renewed, in every fall.

> *Oothoon wandered in woe*
> *Along the vales of Leutha seeking flowers to comfort*
>   *her;*
> *And thus she spoke to the bright Marigold of Leutha's*
>   *vale:*
> *'Art thou a flower? art thou a nymph? I see thee now*
>   *a flower,*
> *Now a nymph. I dare not pluck thee from thy dewy*
>   *bed!'*

Leutha's vale being the valley of desire; and the marigold her own virginity.

I took another sheet and let my hand run over it. But I couldn't make out why I gave poor Eve-Oothoon a head as big as her body, and little fat legs, and why she had her hands over her ears. Unless she was trying not to hear Hickson and Coker who were getting quite excited over the papers.

And now, I said to myself, we have the marigold.

> *The golden nymph replied, 'Pluck thou my flower,*
>   *Oothoon the mild,*
> *Another flower shall spring, because the soul of sweet*
>   *delight*
> *Can never pass away.'*

And this, you see, I said to myself, was before the Fall, before innocence gave herself to passion and the knowledge of herself. For in the next verse Oothoon-Eve, who is all womankind, plucked the flower, saying:

> *I pluck thee from thy bed,*
> *Sweet flower, and put thee here to glow between my*
> *   breasts,*
> *And thus I turn my face to where my whole soul*
> *   seeks.*

That is, to the passionate Bromion, to her lover, who is passion in the spirit.

> *Bromion rent her with his thunders; on his stormy bed*
> *Lay the faint maid, and soon her woes appalled his*
> *   thunders hoarse.*

I drew Bromion for some reason as something like a gorilla, but with eyes like a lemur, and tortoiseshell spectacles. I did him in blue ink. But he looked like a comic, so I had to start again on a new sheet.

Hickson and Coker were adding up accounts. 'Yes,' said Hickson, 'I should think Jimson has had about three thousand pounds from me altogether. I used to pay him two pounds a week, under no obligation whatever—'

So you said, old boy, I thought, and it ought to have been five. But I was not going to be drawn into a foolish argument. I'd other and bigger fish to fry, and I cleared off some more of the snuff-boxes and spread out my papers.

Now the idea is this, I said to myself, making a blot and spitting in it, in order to draw Bromion's face the right shade of blue. That the soul of innocence, maidenhood, could never be destroyed so long as it lived in the free spirit. For it would always be new created in real virginity. The virginity of the soul which never allows experience to grow stale. Which never allows custom to hide the wonders of love.

So that the virgin Oothoon cannot understand the jealousy of Theotormon, which is chastity; her own as well as everybody else's.

> *And folded his black jealous waters round the adulter-*
> *   ate pair.*

Theotormon is Oothoon's jealous touch-me-not which hates her own passion, or Bromion.

> Oothoon weeps not, she cannot weep. Her tears are locked up.
> But she can howl incessant writhing her soft snowy limbs,
> And calling Theotormon's eagles to prey upon her flesh:
> 'I call with holy voice! Kings of the sounding air,
> Rend away this defiled bosom that I may reflect
> The image of Theotormon on my pure transparent breast.'
> The Eagles at her call descend and rend their bleeding prey.
> Theotormon severely smiles: her soul reflects the smile,
> As the clear spring mudded with feet of beasts grows pure and smiles.

And then Oothoon again:

> Why does my Theotormon sit weeping upon the threshold
> And Oothoon hovers by his side, persuading him in vain?
> I cry: arise, O Theotormon, for the village dog
> Barks at the breaking day, the nightingale has done lamenting,
> The lark does rustle in the ripe corn, and the Eagle returns
> From nightly prey and lifts his golden beak to the pure east
> Shaking the dust from his immortal pinions to awake
> The sun that sleeps too long. Arise my Theotormon. I am pure,
> Because the night has gone that closed me in its deadly black.

And the night took a shape in my eye like a map of Australia. Inside this dark shape Oothoon and her gorilla, that is Eve and Adam, were fitted together in a nice compact mass while the tree of knowledge in red ink with blue leaves was throwing down a shower of tears and little red apples over them. I didn't know why I wanted the

116

tears till I remembered the fish. I suppose, I said to my-self, I need a small regular pattern somewhere to give mass to the big forms.

I did most of this cartoon in finger painting with two inks and spit. The red ink did not thin so well as the blue. But it gave a lovely pink, transparent as a sunrise.

All at once Coker began to call out, 'Mr Jimson, Mr Jimson.'

I didn't hear. I was busy blackening the night; the dark shape round the pair. That needed a lot of ink. But the effect was astonishing. 'Mr Jimson, will you come here— or must I come and fetch you?'

'Yes, Miss Coker.' For I could feel Coker was exasper-ated. I stuffed Oothoon into my pocket and went down the room. 'Mr Hickson tells me you've had about three thousand pounds from him. In loans and by the week.'

'I shouldn't wonder,' I said. 'Mr Hickson has been a good friend.'

'What I say is he's had pictures from you worth about twenty times as much, and you say the same.'

'It's a difficult question,' I said. 'Very.'

'You didn't say that when you got us to subscribe for the case,' said Coker, turning pink, 'you said you'd been robbed, you said he's got away with a hundred thousand pounds of your pictures. Yes, and now he says himself he wouldn't take five thousand for that totty over there he gave nineteen for.'

Hickson gave a kind of groan and I felt like groaning myself. I don't know anything more exasperating than talk-ing about pictures or picture values to people like Coker, people who don't even know the language.

'It's not so easy as all that,' I said severely. 'What do you mean, for instance, when you say a picture is worth five thousand pounds or five hundred or five bob? A picture isn't like chocolate, you can't eat it. Value in a picture isn't the same thing as the value in a pork chop.'

'No, no,' Hickie moaned with enthusiasm and grief. 'Not at all. It's not the same thing.'

'Here, what do you mean?' said Coker, as red as a brick. Friction always made Coker warm, and I was sorry for her. After all, how could she know about art?

'You don't understand these things, Coker,' I said, in a kindly way. 'For instance, one might say that pictures

117

haven't got any value 'at all in cash. They're a spiritual value, a liability. Or you might say that they hadn't got any real value till they're sold. And then the value keeps on going up and down. I should think Mr Hickson must have spent a lot of money on pictures that he'll never get back again.'

'About half a million pounds,' Hickson groaned. 'Including commissions to artists who never delivered any pictures at all.'

'Yes, and you've made about double,' said Coker.

'Oh no, Cokey,' I said. 'Mr Hickson has been a great patron of art, and real patrons never get their money back. Not in their own lifetime, anyhow.'

'Why, anyone would think you were standing up for him,' Coker said.

'I think he's been a good friend to English art.'

'And is it true all those pictures you left behind were seized on a judgment summons?'

'Very likely, Cokey. I certainly owed money.'

'So you've been telling me a lot of lies and borrowing money from me and Mr Plant and a lot more, on false pretences.'

'Well, Cokey,' I said, 'what I said was that Hickson had got my pictures cheap.'

'No, you didn't, you old crook. I tell you what, Mr Jimson, you deserve that I should send for a copper and give you in charge.'

'But excuse me, Miss Coker,' Hickson said, 'we had a suggestion to make.'

'Yes, I'm coming to that. But I feel so cross I could bite myself.'

'I was explaining to Miss Coker,' Hickson said, 'that I had to stop your weekly allowance because you kept on telephoning threats against myself and my servants.'

'Yes, yes,' I said. For I was in a hurry to get home and see how the Fall looked in the light of my new ideas. 'And I did time for it, didn't I?'

'I am an old man,' Hickson said, 'and a sick man. I don't mind much if you do murder me, and you can write as many threats as you like. But I can't bear all this telephoning. It disturbs the servants. One man has given notice already.'

'I hadn't thought of that,' I said. 'It's a point.'

'I must have servants,' said Hickson, 'or my life wouldn't be worth living.'

I felt deeply for the old boy. What a position. 'I quite see that, Mr Hickson,' I said. 'It's a perfect nuisance. It's intolerable.'

'And if you could undertake not to telephone or to damage my property, I should be prepared to continue the allowance.'

'At two pounds a week?'

'Yes.'

'Make it three,' I said. 'I shan't live more than another two years, not with my chest and blood pressure. And look here, I'll sign a paper giving you the right to these pictures.'

'They are mine.'

'I meant, the moral right. To eighty thousand pounds worth of masterpieces.'

'I don't want any such paper, but I will make it three and also pay any outstanding debts up to fifty pounds.'

'And give me ten pounds down.'

'Yes, out of the fifty.'

'Very well, Mr Hickson. Split the difference and it's a bargain—ten pounds down, fifty-five to come and three pounds a week, shake hands on it.'

Just then the man servant came in and said something in Hickson's ear. Hickson excused himself and went out. Then he shut the door. And Coker flew out. 'My God, you old crook, you. I've a good mind to do it to you—and I will too.' She came towards me, and I thought it wise to withdraw. 'Don't be so hasty, Coker,' I said. 'Look at what we've got. By behaving like gentlemen. Kept our self-respect and avoided all bad feelings—and raised him a pound a week on my old allowance.' But Cokey kept on after me. She was hurt in her feelings, her pride.

All at once she stopped and said, 'What did he go off for, what's up?' She ran to the door, and put her head out. 'He's telephoning.' And she turned on me again. 'Here, have you been up to anything? What have you got in your pockets? I thought you seemed a bit bulgy.'

She made for me again, and then ran to a side window and stuck out her head.

119

'Don't be so suspicious, Cokey,' I said, 'I didn't think you could be so mean. After the nice way Mr Hickson has behaved.'

'A copper's car's just turning the corner,' she said, pulling in her head again. And if she had had whiskers they would have been quivering like radio wires.

'Nonsense, Cokey. Mr Hickson would never treat me like that. You're imagining things.'

'Come on,' Coker said, and she grabbed me by the arm. 'Come here, you old fool.' She ran me down to a side door and out on to a landing. Then we went down a service stair into a basement and opened an area door.

'There you are,' she said, 'what did I tell you. A copper's car at the area railings.'

'I don't believe it,' I said. For I couldn't believe that Hickson would play me such a trick.

'Soon as he goes in, we'll make a run for it.'

'It's all nonsense,' I said. 'That's not a copper's car,' and I went up to look. But Coker was right. A copper got out of the car and went up the steps. When I saw that I lost my temper and went out in the road and threw a snuff-box through a front window. Coker caught my arm. 'Stop, stop, don't do that.'

'It's an insult,' I said, for I was in a great rage. 'And after the way I've backed him up and sympathized with him.'

'You took his things.'

'Only a few dirty little netsukes, so far as he knew. He didn't know about the snuff-boxes.' And I sent another through the big window of the drawing-room. Coker ran off. I went on throwing things so quick there were three boxes in the air at the same minute and the windows were exploding like fireworks. Then the door opened and I saw the copper and the man coming out; and old Hickson waving his fins like a penguin in despair. So I sent the last box, a heavy diamond one, at his head, and ran for it.

I'm sixty-seven, but I'm light and I can still run. I might have beaten that copper if he hadn't blown his whistle. But then coppers started up all round me. They seemed to come out of the street gratings, and drop from the sky. And they all took hold of me at once and nearly pulled my arms off.

'That's enough,' I said. 'Be careful what you're doing. I'm Mister Gulley Jimson, and I shall put this matter into my lawyer's hands. First-class lawyers. For false imprisonment and assault. Obviously you don't know who I am. Call a taxi.'

I got six months for this piece of carelessness. I knew I was making a mistake when I put those snuff-boxes in my pocket, just to get them off the table. And foolishness when I lost my temper. Blood pressure is one of my worst enemies. A traitor in the camp. It would be too good a joke to let him blow my brains out from the inside.

18. Those six months

in gaol turned out well. Carried me over the spring and cured my winter cough. Gave me time to get Hickson off my mind. Time to think, and read. Learnt the good bits of Jerusalem by heart. Nothing like poetry when you lie awake at night. It keeps the old brain limber. It washes away the mud and sand that keeps on blocking up the bends.

Like waves to make the pebbles dance on my old floors. And turn them into rubies and jacinths; or at any rate, good imitations.

> Albion gave me to the whole earth to walk up and
>   down, to pour
> Joy upon every mountain, to teach songs to the shep-
>   herd and ploughman.
> I taught the ships of the sea to sing the songs of Zion.

A good verse carries you off to sleep. Like a ship in full sail. Why, you can hear the water under the side as it sings, and as you drop off, you can smell the spices of the cargo. Sleep in the land of Beulah. And when I got my first mail, three old bills and a demand for the rates, there was among them a letter forwarded from the Eagle, in what looked like Coker's hand. I had never seen her hand, but the writing was like a child's, very big and clear; written with the blunt end of a poker.

19 Capel Mans,
Kensington.
9/2/39.

Dear Mr Gulley Jimson,

You will excuse, I hope, my temerity in writing to you without a proper introduction. Mr Hickson, who is happy in the possession of so many of your finest works, was good enough to let me have your address. I have called twice, but understand that you are away in the country. So I venture to write.

I do not suppose that my name is known to you, especially as I have been abroad for some years on account of ill health. But it is known, favourably known I hope, to serious students of British Art. Among my publications are The Early Work of John Varley and many articles in the Press. I also carried out for Messrs Robson and Hicks the descriptive catalogue of the pictures at Wimley Hall before the sale.

I have long been among your most ardent admirers. And Mr Hickson agrees with me that the time is long overdue for a considered appreciation of your magnificent contribution to British Art. What I should venture to propose is a biographical and critical study of your whole artistic development. The title that occurs to me, subject of course to your approbation, is The Life and Works of Gulley Jimson. This seems to me preferable to Gulley Jimson, Master-Painter. The latter no doubt would have a greater appeal to modern tastes, but it does not seem to me sufficiently dignified for the kind of work which I have in mind; and which, I venture to suggest, would alone be suitable to one whose name and genius have in his lifetime, obtained so distinguished a fame among connoisseurs of contemporary European art.

I have the honour to be Sir,
Yours ever respectfully,
A. W. Alabaster.

When I read this letter I thought that it was a bad joke. Several of the young bastards at the Ellam Street school were quite up to it, especially the bit about the early work of John Varley, and the last paragraph. But then I thought, All the same, people must write such letters, and artists must get them too. How do I know that it isn't the proper thing, even to the words. Temerity and ardent, words like that. They may be just like please and thank you in those circles. And as for fame, a lot of people have heard of me by now. Hickson's always showing off his collection to all sorts of people, from all over the world. After all, I said, it's happened before. And it's happened to men who were less than nobody at all. Just the imitation of a bad smell. So even if I were nobody and a good for nothing, it might happen to me. Just like this. Fame! And then I couldn't believe it again. No, I said. It's one of those young imps down Ellam Street, Nosy has been talking about me. The Life and Works of Gulley Jimson. Why, nobody could believe it. It even sounds like a joke; or a take-off.

And then one night I waked up and thought, after all, I am a genius. God damn it, of course I am. And why shouldn't a genius be discovered like this? Even if Alabaster is a crackpot or a ninny. We all know what the world is. Free for all. And the winner is the chap who gets knocked out first and comes to while the others are still asleep. Yes, I said, this old cabbage stalk has come out on top of the heap, and Mr Alabaster, M.A., who has just been let out of Colney Hatch, has crowned it with a wreath borrowed from a dog's funeral. Mr Gulley Jimson, his life and work. Old horse, you are now famous. The dealers will be running after you with cheques in one hand and smiles in the other. You will have commissions to pick. And the walls will come waltzing to your big front door. As many as you like.

As I was an artist, I had been put on to painter's work, whitewashing. Latrines, etc. A nice job. Though I had had some trouble to get the mixture to my liking. I like white-wash on the blue side to bring out the brilliance of the colour. And while I was putting on a second coat, I kept on thinking: Well, you're famous now. The celebrated Gulley Jimson. But I never got quite used to it. My belief is that nobody does. It never seems quite true. Or if it seems true, then it doesn't seem just what you had been led to expect.

Fame isn't a thing. It's a feeling. Like what you get after a pill. What's happening now, you think. Or is it too soon? Nothing's happened at all. Yes, there's something now—a sort of crick in the upper guts. No, that's the old dent, which the pretty barmaid made, at the Bricklayer's Arms, when you overheard her ask who was the dirty little old runt in somebody else's overcoat. Yes, you say, I suppose you're right. You were getting talked about then too, and that's how you mistook the sensation. But ha, what about this—a sort of emptiness round the liver and confused noises in the cerebellum. Not a bit of it, old boy, that happened to you when you saw your name in the newspaper and underneath were the words, 'Mr G. Jimson's work shows a progressive disintegration and is now quite incomprehensible.' Well then, old chap, you'd better give it up. Wait a minute, what about that creeping twitch in the diaphragm. That might be fame, or it might be a touch of suppressed heartburn.

And mounting a seat to which so many bold heroes had retired for private meditation and the planning of new campaigns, I slopped another bucket of whitewash on the bricks.

The famous Gulley Jimson. Why not? Fame is a grass that grows in any dirt, when no one's looking. And a man can be famous without knowing it, like all of them in the beginning. And fame, I thought, if it's true, has its advantages. It will bring in cash. And I remembered a canvas I had seen in Ikey's junk shop, just off High Street, a big one. Fifteen by twenty. 'Birth of Moses,' by Antonio Something, 1710, Italian style, turnips and gravy; standing in a sort of shed he had in the yard, with some other big canvases and a lot of old frames.

I've bought a lot of small canvases in Ikey's, cheap. Ikey's is a shop that never has any luck. It changes hands about every six months. It has murdered more people than even the haberdashers opposite, between the Co-operative and the Bank. One time there was a dog that would rush at people's legs whenever they tried to get into Ikey's. Ikey was then a smart young man with long yellow hair and knotty fingers; a connoisseur of real Chinese china. Every time the dog barked he used to rush out and have hysterics. I put a *Times* down each leg, and when the dog nipped me, he got such a surprise that he couldn't believe his teeth. He staggered away in silence. He must have felt like a gourmet who bites on a stick of asparagus and finds it solid drainpipe. And I walked in and bought a fine junk shop Romney with a few holes, etc., and some boot-marks on the lady's face, for two-and-sixpence. Of which the two was not perhaps altogether British mint silver. But the young gentleman was in such an excited state about the dog and about the bad condition of business that you could have paid him in a Bank of Engraving note and taken change. I often wished I had, for a week afterwards he hanged himself over the stairs.

But the place wasn't empty long. When I called again only a week later, Ikey was a widow like a cottage loaf, with a face like Julius Caesar and pale green hair. Due to some bleaching powder guaranteed to make grey hair into a veritable crown of snow. She was very high and mighty. She'd put capital into Ikey's and had a family to support. She felt deserving, and she didn't like the rest of the world which was probably not half so deserving. She asked me twenty pounds for a Constable, two trees, four clouds, and a little piece of dog-shit in the foreground. The usual junk shop Constable, value four-and-six. Or with two bits of dog-shit, and a spot of genuine synthetic cobalt blue between the two bottom clouds, five-and-six. With frame, string, and patent hook ready to hang, five-and-ninepence.

Twenty pounds didn't shock me from a widow. Widows always ask too much, especially if they've got all their capital in the business. The unwidowed asking price for a small back street Constable is fifteen guineas. I offered her half a crown, meaning to meet her half-way, at three-and-ninepence, when she walked off to another customer. And she wouldn't even listen to offers. I had to take another canvas, of the same size, while she wasn't looking, and it wasn't worth the expense. For it turned out to be rotten, and I couldn't go back again to Ikey's until the widow was sold up. Which was nearly a year. And meanwhile I had to paint on old sacks, which are expensive to prime and difficult to stretch.

If Ikey's is still there, I said, when I come out, I'll buy that big canvas. No more walls for me that fall down or get knocked full of holes by charwomen's brooms. Give me canvas now I can afford it. The works of Gulley Jimson. Canvas is more portable. All the National Galleries like you to paint on canvas. They can't hang walls. And I began to think what I'd do with that canvas. Supposing of course that Ikey's hadn't sold it or been blown up or burnt down or turned into a shoe-shop. Which was almost certain. Yes, you could bet on the shoe-shop. Fifteen by twenty gave a chap some scope. I used to wake myself up at night, painting in my sleep. The movements, on a canvas, threw my blanket right off on the floor. I thought, I could do something good on fifteen by twenty. Masterpiece by the famous Gulley Jimson as reproduced in the art publication, Gulley Jimson, His Life and Works, by Professor A. W. Alabaster, M.A.

I used to lie awake on the plank, all smiles. And when I said to myself, what's the joke, Gulley, I thought, the Life and Works, etc. And the real joke, I said, will be if somebody is pulling your leg. In any case, I thought, there's a big catch somewhere, or why would it happen to me?

When I came out, and as I was passing along High Street on my way home, I just threw a glance out of the corner of my eye down Gas Lane, and there it was, the sign brighter than ever, Isaacson and Waller, Antiques. I got a shock. Well, I thought, if Ikey's is true, Alabaster must be a particularly nasty trick. I'm going to get a kick in the stomach that would paralyse an elephant. Not that it would worry me. No, I've had some. I'm not a wild ass of the desert. I'm an old hoss. I know something. I've been ridden by the nobility and gentry. Millionaires have cut an important figure on my back. Hickson kept me in the stable for years and trotted me out for his visitors. His Gulley Jimsons, his pride and his joy. My stomach has had two kicks a day for sixty years, one to put the saddle on and one to take it off. It can take anything. And eat its own hay. And organize its own kicks. And save up a bite that will take the bloody pants off the seat of government. If it likes.

And all that gilt, I thought, walking past. I'll bet some smart West End firm has bought up Ikey's and cleared out all the old junk. They'll be selling antique furniture direct from the factory and old Masters of the highest class as painted in Paris for the American market and varnished with real mastic.

But when I went into the shop I saw at once that all was well. Ikey was now a little man shaped like a flower stand. With bandy legs and bottle shoulders. Draped in a black coat, two sizes too large. Cobwebs on his knees. Face like a cod on the fishmonger's slab. Colour like a new potato. No hair except on the backs of his hands. Gentle, cultivated voice. He's half dead already, I thought, Ikey's have him by the throat. And I said, 'Afternoon, Mr Isaacson. Very glad to see you again, as an old customer.'

He looked at me for a moment and said in a mournful voice, 'Yes, sir, of course. I knew you at once.' 'And how are you?' I said. 'You look fine. Business good? Tell me, Mr Isaacson, have you got a good Morland? A genuine one. I mean the real thing.'

Ikey looked at my boots, and I said quickly, 'Not for myself. I don't buy pictures, I paint 'em. In fact,' I said, trying it on the dog to see if it was real meat, 'I'm Gulley Jimson.' 'Oh yes,' said Ikey. 'Yes, I knew you at once, sir,' and he moved his mouth just like a smile. 'I expect you've seen my portrait in the book,' I said, anticipating things a bit, 'Gulley Jimson, His Life and Works.' 'Yes, of course,' said Ikey, still stretching his mouth. 'By Professor Alabaster, M.A.' 'Yes, no,' said Ikey, suddenly taking away the smile again. 'I don't know—I didn't see any name on it.' And he closed his eyes as if he had such a pain that he couldn't bear it another minute.

'Professor Alabaster is the great collector,' I said, 'and he's looking for some good genuine stuff, oils.' If you want to buy something in a junk shop, ask for something else. As laid down by old Clotheswitz. It causes the enemy to concentrate on the wrong flank and upsets his communications. Often he can't say anything at all.

'Oh yes,' said Ikey, opening his eyes again very slowly.

'And he's very keen on Morland,' I said. 'You haven't got a little Morland?' It was safe to ask for Morland. Every junk shop in England has two or three Morlands from one-and-sixpence, with horse and stable in a real wood frame, to seven-and-sixpence with added straw, figure, one tree and label of the Duke of Devonshire's collection at Chatsworth.

Ikey had two. Nice brown ones. The first had a horse, stable, dog, man and tree. The second was more important. It had a stable, a dog, a horse, a peasant, a tree and a gate.

'That's not bad,' I said to Ikey, 'I like the gate. It's real. I like the way it opens. How much is that one?' 'Thirty guineas, sir.'

That didn't shake me. Thirty guineas is the usual price of a seven-and-sixpenny Morland, with gate.

'That's cheap for a genuine Morland,' I said. 'Can you

give a guarantee? I couldn't advise Professor Alabaster to spend thirty guineas on a genuine Morland without a guarantee.'

'Oh yes,' Ikey breathed in a faint voice. 'Of course. It comes out of the Wallace collection.'

'Well, even if they did throw it out, I might bring the Professor to see it. The horse's knees are very genuine. How much did you say?'

'Thirty-five guineas, sir,' said Ikey. 'The frame is original.'

'Make it pounds.'

'Couldn't take anything less than guineas, sir. It would fetch a hundred and fifty guineas at Christie's. Only needs a little cleaning and restoration.'

This was fair enough. A hundred and fifty guineas at Christie's is a reasonable junk-shop valuation for a hand-painted Morland with real hair on the horse's belly, done with a dead match. 'Well,' I said, 'I daresay the Professor might meet you. What's that old brown thing there in the rubbish shed?'

'An old Master, sir. Splendid piece of work. Antonio Ruffiano (or some such name) "Moses in the Bulrushes." Out of the Shillingford Castle collection.'

'I'll give you fifteen bob. I want a piece of old canvas to cover a toolshed.'

'That picture is worth five hundred guineas, without the frame,' said Ikey. He was indignant. He still had some kick in him, in spite of two months at Ikey's. 'And with the frame I wouldn't take five hundred and fifty.'

I turned away and put my nose up against the Morland. 'Here,' I said, 'do you guarantee that this is a genuine Morland? I mean a genuine genuine Morland. The Professor is an expert you know. You can't fool him with fakes.'

'Absolutely genuine, sir.'

'Well, look at that rustic—he's been repainted. And he's not wearing a Morland hat either.'

'That's a genuine real Morland, sir,' said Ikey. But he spoke as from the grave. He was near his end. 'The hat is one of the most genuine passages in the work.'

'Well,' I said, 'I don't like it.' And I was just going out of the shop when I stopped and pointed at the Ruffiano. 'I'll tell you what, I'll give you sixty guineas—and take it away tonight. Providing it's sound, of course, and a genuine Ruffiano.'

'Couldn't do it under a hundred, sir.'

'Split the difference and say seventy-five. Or look here, you're right about the frame. It's a good frame.'

'Hand-carved pear, sir. You couldn't get such a frame for seventy-five guineas by itself.'

'That's what I say. Fifty guineas is much too little. Split the difference and say sixty pounds for the frame alone. At least I'll let you have it for that. And that leaves two guineas for the canvas. Forty-two bob.'

'Im-possible, sir.'

'Well, say fifty bob for both of 'em.'

'Both of them?'

'Yes, the Ruffiano and the Morland.'

Ikey closed his eyes as if he was about to pass away again. Then he said, 'Five guineas.'

'Make it pounds,' I said.

'All right, sir, pounds.' We were getting to business at last.

'Split it and call it two quid and look here, I'll give you back the Morland frame. It doesn't fit anyhow. Thirty-nine and sixpence.'

In all such negotiations the proper financial course is the double entry. You get out and then you get in again. So that the enemy doesn't know whether you're advancing backwards or he's retreating forwards, or you're retreating forwards while he's advancing to fresh positions in the rear. This confuses him, as he hasn't time to look up the rules of war; or if he does remember them he can't quite see how they apply to the situation.

Ikey was trying to find out how we stood when I said quickly, 'Well, perhaps that is a bit too cheap for the Morland frame. Put it at a shilling. That's giving you more than it was worth when it was new. So I'll owe you thirty-nine bob.'

'No,' said Ikey, making a strong recovery.

'Well, I tell you what. I'll give you the Morland back. Thirty-four bob. And I'll guarantee that Mr Alabaster will pay twenty-five guineas for it certain, and very likely fifty. He doesn't care what he pays. He's an expert. He'll get it all back twice over.'

'Thirty-nine for the Ruffiano. That's the lowest price,'
said Ikey.

'We'll make it guineas, Mr Isaacson. I always deal in
guineas. Thirty-one and sixpence. And I'll do the insurance
and packing at my own expense. Twenty-eight bob cash
on the nail.'

'All right, sir,' said the old rascal suddenly. He would
probably have paid me to take the Ruffiano away. 'Cash on
the nail.' I felt I'd been done. I hadn't expected him to
take twenty-eight.

'Very well,' I said. 'Done. And the two-and-sixpence for
carriage makes it twenty-four-and-six. Cash on the nail.
Tomorrow. But I'll tell you what, I'll take Antonio off
your hands now.' I knew a coalman, friend of Swope, who
would fetch me the canvas in his empty cart for one-and-
six. And I still had nine-and-six of my prison money.

But Ikey suddenly turned obstinate. He wouldn't let the
picture go without the cash.

'Very well,' I said, 'I've done my best, and I can't do
more. Not if you go back on your bargain. But I must say
I'm not used to this kind of treatment.'

'You said cash,' said Ikey, 'and two-and-sixpence from
twenty-eight bob is twenty-five-and-sixpence.'

'We'll split it,' I said. 'If that's your trouble. Nobody can
say I'm not ready to meet you. Call it twenty-four-and-
ninepence.'

'All right," said Ikey. 'But cash.'

'On the nail,' I said, 'tomorrow.'

But he wouldn't trust me. And it wasn't because he
meant it. It was because he'd turned sour. And I hate a
man who can't do better for himself than to turn sour. I
appealed to him, 'I'm only an artist,' I said. 'I don't understand business. I get swindled all the time. There's two
Bond Street dealers at this moment who've made thousands out of me. And look at my boots. But I do understand that business is built on confidence between man
and man. If you don't know how to trust, Mr Isaacson,
you'll never be in Bond Street.'

'No, I won't,' said Ikey. And he closed his eyes and died
again.

'More likely the workhouse,' I said.

'I think so too,' said Ikey.

'Throwing away the substance for the shadow,' I said. For I was upset. I'd wanted that canvas. If I'd had only a pound, I'd have given it to the barnacle. 'No faith, no pluck to take a chance,' I said. 'The mistake of all the men who fail in life.'

'That's it,' said Ikey, opening his eyes just enough to see my way to the door. He looked very ill. He might fall dead any minute. 'All right,' I said, 'I'll be in tomorrow to take the thing away.' 'And bring the money,' said Ikey. I saw the old boy never expected to see me again. And I thought: If the old chap holds on for another fortnight, I'll get that canvas for ten bob. But probably he won't—he'll hang himself or fall down dead. Because I never had a better chance of a big canvas. It was the finest I ever saw. Smooth painted all over in the best classical period before the bitumen came in. Not a crack anywhere. There's nothing like a real old Master for an undercoating.

The very touch of that canvas was enough to make my hand sing. I felt the colour flowing on to it as sweet as cream. My God, I said, I'll put the Fall on to it. Trouble with the Fall—it's not big enough. All at once I had the feel of the Fall. A real fall. Fire and brimstone. Blues and reds. And I saw green fire in the top left next the red tower. And the red tower opened to show a lot of squares full of blue and green flames. Symbols of something. Generation would do. Or a lot of little flames like men and women rushing together, burning each other up like coals. And then to carry the pattern upwards you could have white flowers, no, very pale green, moving among the stars, imagination born of love. Through generation to regeneration. Old antic propriety falling down on his nose and seeing constellations. Yes, the destruction of old fly button, the law by the force of nature and the unexpected entry of the devil as a lyrical poet singing new worlds for old. The old Adam rising to chase the blue-faced angels of Jehovah. And beget a lot of young devils on them.

> *A mighty spirit leaped from the land of Albion,*
> *Named Newton: he seized the trump and blowed the*
> * enormous blast*
> *Yellow as leaves of autumn, the myriads of angelic*
> * hosts*

Fell through the wintry skies seeking their graves,
Rattling their hōllow bones in howling and lamenta-
    tion.
Then Enitharmon woke, nor knew that she had slept;
And eighteen hundred years were fled
As if they had not been.
She called her sons and daughters
To the sports of night.

Science destroying the law of the old Panjandrum. The fall into manhood, into responsibility, into sin. Into freedom. Into wisdom. Into the light and the fire. Every man his own candle. He sees by his own flame, burning up his own guts. Oh to hell, I said, with the meaning. What I want is those green flames on a pink sky. Like copper on a dying fire.

Thundery day along Greenbank. All the willows standing still with their leaves pricked. Dusty green. Pale lilac shadows. Tarred road reflecting the sky. Blue to make you jump. A great cloud over on the Surrey shore. Yellow as soap and solid as a cushion. Shaped like a tower about a mile high and half a mile thick, with a little Scotch pepper pot in front. Dresden blue behind full of sunlight floating like gold dust. River roughed up with little waves like the flat side of a cheese grater. Dark copper under the cloud, dark lead under the blue. I could use that cloud in the Fall, I thought. It's a solid square. To give weight in the top left-hand corner, opposite the Tower. Salmon on pink. It's an idea worth trying.

The people kept looking at me, but I didn't notice I was noticing them till a kid turned round and said 'Ya,' as if I'd insulted him. Then I realized that I was laughing. Enjoying myself, I suppose. Yes, I thought, I'm enjoying myself. The famous Gulley Jimson, whom nobody knows, is perceived laughing like an old goat and skipping like a young ram. Who cares, I said. The advantage of being old and ugly is that you needn't care a damn for anybody. Or even somebody. You can grin when you feel like grinning. And skip when you feel skippy. So long as your boots don't fall off. Second childhood. People make allowances, including yourself. Which is you in particular. Anonymous you.

    'I have no name:
    I am but two days old.'

> *What shall I call thee?*
> *'I happy am,*
> *Joy is my name.'*
> *Sweet Joy befall thee!*

The next kid that came along, I smiled upon him. Out
of pure benevolence. 'Hullo, Tommy,' I said. But he
turned pale and burst into tears. Must have been too young
for social occasions. About six or ten. Necessary limits to
fellow feeling and universal brotherhood.

The pepper pot had floated off the Tower and turned
into a grey monk in a rugged gown, creeping across the
sky with his hands on his breast. Blue-grey on a sandy
desert with a lot of rusty bones along the edge. Nice, but
no good to me. No, but I had the cushion in my mind. And
I thought, I'll be painting in half an hour. Say an hour at
the longest. And the Eagle this evening. And I might mention Alabaster to Cokey to see if she really did send that
letter on, and if she saw him again.

19. The boat-shed
came in sight. New tin chimney sticking through the roof
and quite a lot of smoke coming out. Glass in all the windows. Green curtains. Gave me a surprise. Knocked on
the door and Coker let me in.

'Hullo, Cokey.'

'Oh, Mr Jimson, where you dropped from?'

'Chokey, Cokey.' And I looked at her. About the eighth
month at a first guess, and her face shrunk up to a peeled
walnut. White as wax except her little nose which was as
pink as blotting paper. Seeing how it was with Coker, I
couldn't bring up Alabaster. You don't talk money and
medals at a funeral.

'How are you, Cokey?' I said.

'Just how you see,' she said.

'How's that?'

'Can't you guess?'

'I always said Willie was a hound.'

'You let Willie alone.'

'Who got round you then—the roundabout?'

'Nobody got round me. I'd like to see them. Willie never did anything to me, poor boy, that I didn't let him.'

'I'm surprised at you, Cokey,' I said. And this was true.

'Oh, what's the good of talking to a man. We had the ring two months. And Willie so he couldn't sit still for two minutes. And all the competition there is. I took a chance, that's all. And a fair chance, too, for a girl like I am with a real catch like Willie was.'

'You never wrote me.'

And I thought, now she'll remember that letter, and Alabaster. But she answered that she didn't want to bother me. 'I knew you couldn't pay my money back.'

'And what are you going to do about it, Cokey?'

'What can a girl do? She can't creep up a drainpipe till she's human size again, can she? God didn't make her a spider. His idea was to make a girl and give her socks all the time and then some. First thing is, I lost my job. You can't blame the Guv'nor. The Eagle is a respectable house. Then I got remarks passed, so I couldn't bear hardly to walk down the street. Then I had to leave my lodgings because I couldn't pay the landlord. And then my mother came and gave me such a doing on both ears that I had to sleep on my back.'

'I heard she was a cruel woman.'

'Of course she's cruel. After the life she's had. I wish some pot would fall off a chimney and knock my napper in.'

It frightened me to hear Coker speak like that. She's an honest girl. She always says what she means, and means what she says. But I could see she was just about as miserable as a girl can be. 'Come now, Coker,' I said. 'You'd never do anything silly. Things will come out all the same in the end.'

'Listen to you. I wish you were like me for two minutes. And you'd know whether anything can come out the same again or anything like it. Come, if you want to be a friend, why don't you tie a brick round my neck and push me in the river?'

'I'm surprised at you, Cokey.'

'So am I. I'm surprised at myself. What I been through without doing murder on someone.'

'Well, don't do it on yourself.'

'Who said I would? I only said what a nice birthday present it would be if someone would stick me in the gizzard with a pig knife. But it won't happen. No such luck. And you needn't pull a long face at me. I asked for it, didn't I?'

'You didn't ask for Willie.'

'I mean, being born a girl. That's what I say. Here I am, another bloody girl. Come on, knock my teeth out. Turn my hair grey. Make me look like something that the dog got out of the dustbin. I can take it. Ain't I a woman?'

'Well,' I said, 'I'm glad you did come here. We'll be very comfortable, won't we?' For when I looked round I saw how the place was changed. All cleaned up. Coker's furniture piled in a corner. New linoleum on the floor. Old sheet hung in front of the picture to keep the dust off. Two little tables, a horsehair sofa and a couple of straw armchairs. New coke stove with a japan chimney. 'You made it very nice here, Cokey,' I said. 'And I can sleep in the loft.'

'You can't sleep anywhere here. Mother'll be back from shopping in about ten minutes, and you'd better not let her catch you. She won't have a man in the place. And she doesn't like artists either.'

'Can't sleep here? Whose house is this?'

'Mother's. She paid all the back rent and she's paying the rent now. She couldn't take me home in this state, to get herself pitied, could she?'

'But Coker, where am I going?'

'Couldn't you go to Mr Plant's till you find somewhere?'

'No, I couldn't. I can't paint in a basement, can I. I got my work to do. No, I'm stopping here. It's my home. I don't mind you staying, Cokey, but this is my home.'

Just then a little woman about three inches smaller and five stone lighter than Coker came into the room. Very respectable in a black satin cloak and a bonnet. Old style. A little thin white face like a child that's been starved. And big blue eyes with pink rims.

She was muttering to herself so that I couldn't understand her. 'Good afternoon, Mrs Coker,' I said. 'I'm Mr Jimson.'

'No, this is too much,' said Mrs Coker as if talking to herself. 'No, I don't see why I should,' and all at once she

135

turned on Cokey and gave her a whack on the side of her head with her shut fist. It sounded like two croquet balls knocked together.

'Oh Mum,' Coker said, 'I only just got up.'

Mrs Coker gave her another whack on the other ear and muttered something. Coker lay down on the sofa and put her hands over her ears. She was trembling like a horse when you beat it and it can't go on. Mrs Coker came after me and murmured under her breath, 'Out you go—you hear—I'm not standing any more.' She was shaking all over. 'I can't stand any more. Dirty wasters coming in here. It's more than flesh can bear. Go on, you hear.' And all at once I got a knock on the ear that nearly made my eyes fall out. 'Go on,' said Mrs Coker. 'Quick, too. I'm a respectable woman, and I can't be expected to stand everything. Out with you.' And I got a right and left. Next minute I was outside, and the door banged behind me so loud that the whole shed went out of shape.

It made me laugh. Then I took a bottle out of the dustbin to operate on the windows. But before I could do anything I saw I was going to be angry. No, old man, I said, you can't afford luxuries. You're too old. It's fun to play the fool, but an old chap has got to hold on to wisdom and Christian virtue. Yes.

IT'S GOOD TO BE GOOD.

It pays all the time. Don't let 'em rattle you or you might as well take a dive into your coffin. So I walked away a little, with the bottle in my hand, and I thought: as for Alabaster, I expect he's dead. Or gone away and Coker didn't want to tell me. Yes, that's the way it would happen. Life and Works of Gulley Jimson. In one volume. Unpublished, without illustrations. Delivered gratis at the dead letter office, to Mister Nobody.

All the same, I thought, why should Mother Coker get away with it? I might throw the bottle through the window and move off quick before I heard the crash. Nothing to stick in the mind. And I took aim. I'm a good shot with a bottle. Trick is, don't swing it by the neck. Take it by the body and throw it like a dart.

But then I thought, I've got to get my picture out safely. I've got to paint somewhere. Better not smash up my own property. And I noticed the sky on the windows. Surprising effect. And when I turned round I saw my tower had broken up into a lot of copper bars, like puffs of sulphur smoke. And the sky behind was like the middle of a gas flame, blue fire. That's more like it, I thought, I could do something with a sky like that. And the water underneath was like, melted golden syrup. All smooth waves, with the light inside as well as outside, except under the sky where it was white fire. You couldn't see it for the sparks. Gorgione might have made that sky, I thought. And probably he did. He made me see it. But he didn't make the water. I should like to do it—you'd have to use a glaze to get the double lights. And so I was thinking about the water and how I should do it without any impressionist tricks, when I came to Ellam Street. But I wasn't sorry to catch sight of old Plant's signboard fixed to the area railings. It was an interruption, but I wanted to know how to get old Mrs Coker out of my studio; or at least, how to take my picture from her. Old Plant might be an old nuisance, but he was a good friend, and he knew the Law. He would talk all night about his Spinoza and his Swedenborg and his Comte and his Robert Owen and revelations and revolutions; but I didn't need to listen. I could carry on with the Fall.

So I hopped down the area steps. But it was getting dark in the area, the blind was half down in the window; and when I opened the door I came plump upon a great fat woman in a vest and knickers brushing out a little girl's hair; and about six other children were rolling on the floor, and all of them were screaming as if they were being murdered.

I couldn't believe my eyes. Till the woman made a run at me with the hair-brush and screamed louder than all the kids together. 'Nothing today. We don't take nothing at the door.' And she banged the door in my face.

I had a look to make sure I'd come to the right house. But there was Plant's board still fixed to the railings. So I opened the door again and asked, 'Where is Mr Plant?' But the woman and all the children set up such a scream that it was like engine whistles. Then the woman rushed at me with the brush and said, 'I get the police.' 'Where is Mr Plant?' I said. 'He was here twenty years.'

'Nobody called Mr Plant. We took it from a lady called Johnson.'

'I want Mr Plant.'

'Go away. I tell you nobody hear of Mr Plant.' So I went up the steps again, and when I looked at the board it said 'Mrs Slumberger. Wardrobes bought for cash.'

I couldn't believe it. I rang at the ground floor and a man came out. I asked him what had happened to Mr Plant, the shoemaker.

'Plant,' he said. 'Oh yes, I remember him. Old cobbler in the basement. Nice nuisance he was with his tapping and his shoe polish stink. Why, isn't he there?' 'No,' I said, 'even the board's changed.' The man came down and looked at the board and said, 'Funny, so it is. Never noticed it before.' Then he looked again, and he said, 'Here, did he ever have his name on the board?'

'It's been there for about twenty years.'

'I been here fifteen, and I bet you he never had his name on the board.'

'Of course he had his name on the board—C. Plant. Bespoke bootmaker. Repairs a specialty.'

'Well, all I say is, funny thing I should forget it so quick.'

'Yes,' I said, 'I don't know.'

I went along the streets to see if I could catch Mr Ollier on his round. Till I was beginning to think that Ollier had gone too. I was beginning to feel as if I'd been away seven years and everybody and all the houses had been changed. When just after six, I came on Ollier emptying a pillar box.

'Hullo, Mr Ollier.'

'Well, Mr Jimson. This is a pleasure.'

'What's happened to Plant? He hasn't come into a fortune?'

'No, he ran a needle into his hand and it got poisoned. It's a bad business, Mr Jimson. You know what Mr Plant is. No doles for him. No insurance. No unions. Never would take anything from the government. And even with his friends, he always liked to give more than he got. Never kept anything back and never saved.'

'Plant was one of the old sort.'

'It's a rare old London family, the Plants. Goes back three hundred years, father to son. Craftsmen every one of them. It was a Plant made some of the clocks for Nelson's fleet.'

'But what's happened to the old man? Hospital?'

'Hospital and more. They took his hand off.'

That surprised me for a minute. Then I saw the idea. 'Yes,' I said, 'that was what would happen to Plant. No other way to get him except knocking him on the head with an obelisk. Take off both his legs and he'd be whistling. But his right hand. They knew his weak place.'

'Of course he didn't look after it properly,' Ollier said. 'He didn't go to the hospital till his thumb was like a saveloy. He said he was too busy.'

'That's very neat, yes. That's the way it would happen to Plant. Just a prick like what he's had a thousand times before. They'd studied him. They knew he wasn't one to fuss about himself or break his promises to the customers. How does he take it, Ollier?'

'Badly. I haven't seen him since the sale. I think he keeps dodging me so that I shan't try to do anything for him. It's hard for a man like Plant.'

'Where does he sleep?'

'I did see him coming out of that sixpenny doss back of Ellam Street. But it mightn't have been Plant. I looked the other way in case.'

'You were quite right, Mr Ollier. It wouldn't do for you to see him. Not until you lose your legs under a bus or get a stroke.'

'That's true, Mr Jimson. But if you would take him my respects and tell him that I'm missing the club, I'd be obliged. It's made a big hole in my life, that club stopping. It's like a door shutting over me. The last door.'

'I'll tell him.' Then I made for the sixpenny doss in Ellam Street. I had two-and-sixpence left of my prison money.

20. The sixpenny doss is a double-fronted villa called Elsinore standing back from the road. Front garden has been laid down in cinders and the back garden is a builder's yard. The owner is a retired army man, a bony man with a long face like a sheep and a little black moustache. His head is bald and shaped like a tea cup. He has big round blue eyes which are always watering, and he looks as silly as a sheep. But he keeps good order. No lights and no noise after twelve, and if you don't like it you must go.

Bunk beds are sixpence. They aren't exactly spring, but they are better than sacks. More like wire hammocks made of chicken wire. And there is always a kettle boiling in the kitchen. Frypans and teapots and tin cups free up to nine o'clock in the morning and after six at night. Between tea and six the house is closed to the sixpennies. But there are cubicles for residents at a shilling a day, with slot meters for light and heat.

Room for twenty-five sixpennies and ten residents, and he's nearly always full because of the lights and because he'll take letters and let you write a letter from the address. Of course he has a lot of letters that aren't called for. He keeps the old ones in a sack and I think he burns them after about six months. Residents, who are half of them beggars in the letter-writing way, say he knows postal orders through an envelope by the smell, and takes his share. But I don't believe it. I think the man might burn postal orders in letters but he wouldn't take them. He wouldn't bother. Not the kind that cares about money or anything else. He bought the business because it was cheap, and he keeps it going because it is going.

Time to go to Elsinore is early, at six when the doors open. I got there after seven and the kitchen was full already—about nineteen people fighting for the three frypans. They always fight for the pans, between six and eight. If you miss your chance at six, the only thing to do is to wait till nine when the rush is over. But the sixpenny customers at the doss are mostly young fellows passing through, going for jobs along the waterfront or doing a wander. Quite well-off tradesmen who would rather spend their money on clothes and girls and cinemas and fags than a bed. There was one used to come regularly in a car. Left it in the yard outside. The residents said he was a burglar who robbed villas out by Richmond, but no burglar would sleep at a doss. Too much police supervision and too much notice by the other customers. And these young fellows had no time to learn the way to do things. So there was always a riot at seven.

I edged round them till I came to the far corner next the larder, and there was an old man sitting on a box, with an old green bowler hat, and a face like a French cheese, chalk and green, hollowed out and folded up like a mummy. And a long greenish moustache hanging down over his collar. Hump on his back as if it were broken.

I knew it was Plant because it had one arm stumped off at the wrist in a stocking. But I didn't recognize him.

'Hullo, Mr Plant,' I said. But he didn't hear me. He got up and dived into the crowd, pushing and butting till he got near the range. Somebody had just put down a frying pan there. Old Plant and a young man in a blue jumper with his braces outside got to the pan at the same moment. They argued. Then Plant gave it up and came back to the corner.

'Hullo, Mr Plant,' I said.

'I was there first,' Plant said. 'That's the second time I missed it.'

'A bad time for frying pans at Elsinore,' I said. 'Now at Myrtle View this is a good time. Because Myrtle View is nearly all residents at a shilling a day and they have their own pans.'

'But I'm next,' said Plant. 'He said so.'

'That's all right, Mr Plant,' I said. 'You're next or the one after. What's it matter? Plenty of time before tomorrow morning.'

Plant thought a bit, then he gave a start and looked at me. 'Mr Jimson,' he said, 'so you're back—but why aren't you at your own place?'

'Mrs Coker has taken it over for Miss Coker's lying-in.'

'She can't do that, can she?'

'She has done it. It's funny, isn't it?'

'I don't call it funny. What, taken the roof from over your head and your working place?'

'Yes, a funny turn. I didn't expect it. Not that one. And the old lady gave me two bonks on the ear that nearly burst the drums.'

'What for?'

'That's it, what for? It's all part of the idea.'

'It's a scandal,' said Plant. 'You ought to go to the magistrate.'

'And how are you, Mr Plant?'

Plant gave a start and lifted up his stump to rub his nose. And to let me see it. But I didn't look. I didn't want

141

to pity a man like Plant. Hurt his pride. Or make him feel sad. I wouldn't have liked it myself, from anybody. Pity is a whore. It gets inside you and sucks your blood.

'Ollier told me he'd been looking for you. Wants a club meeting.'

Plant waved his stump in front of my nose. 'This is a funny business, if you like.'

'That's what I said when I heard. A real surprise. It makes you laugh.'

'Didn't make me laugh. It made me think.'

'You ought to get a job, Mr Plant. Why not a watchman? Nice job in the summer.'

'No, I don't want a job. I want to think. What I feel is, it can't be wasted—a thing like this. It means something.'

'Why should it mean anything? Does a kick in the stomach from a blind horse mean anything?'

Old Plant shook his head. 'It can't be wasted. It's a revelation. It makes me feel like I never knew anything before.'

'What do you know now, Mr Plant?'

He shook his head. 'That's where the thinking comes in.'

'You don't think that needle was sent from God to poison your hand?'

'No, Mr Jimson. But it might have taught me something. It might have been a revelation to me.'

'I understand that, Mr Plant. It was the same with me when I got my nose broken. When I was eighteen, my sister Jenny came home from school. I liked that very much. Jenny and I were the two youngest and we were great friends. We enjoyed each other more than anyone else in the world. And when my mother had to go into hospital for an operation she said, "You look after Jenny —I can trust you." "Jenny doesn't need looking after," I said. "Oh no," said my mother cheerfully, "but she's very attractive—look after her." And I said I would look after Jenny. And I went on as before enjoying myself with the girl. I was pretty good at enjoying myself. As good as any baby. But Jenny was even better. She had enjoyment to give away; so that you felt it all round her, even while she was walking down the road, and breathing the air.'

But old Plant wasn't listening. He had his eye on the nearest frypan.

'I've been thinking about your Spinoza,' I said. 'It's this question of rejoicing in the glory of God,' I said.

Plant gave a kind of sob and lifted up his stump as if he wanted to hit someone with it.

'That's all right,' I said. 'Give it another month or two and put a hook on it, and you'll be able to give a chap like that something to remember. Hook his tripes out. You'll always find him when you want him. He comes here every week or two to meet the girl down the High Road. Tells her he stops at an hotel.'

'I wouldn't mind if they didn't know it was my turn.'

'What I wonder is, Mr Plant, your Spinoza didn't go blind. He only died at forty from breathing glass dust. Not a healthy job grinding lenses.'

'He died independent,' Plant said. 'Never owed anything to anybody. And not a surly chap. No, he was the happiest man that ever lived, the God drunk man.'

'Well, why didn't he go blind?'

'Why should he?'

'That would have been the kind of thing to happen to your Spinoza, Old Diamond Death.'

'What do you mean, Old Diamond Death?'

I didn't know what I meant till Plant asked me. But then I saw the diamond flashing different colours off every facet, and never moving from its place. The cold eye. Now if he had been set in the top of a drill, I thought, to bore the rock—he would have got hot—the sparks would have flown—

'Spinoza was the most independent man that ever lived,' said Plant, 'never asked for anything of anybody. He'd rather have died, and he did die. And mind you,' said Plant, getting fierce all at once, 'a happy man. In the contemplation of the majesty and glory of God's being.'

'Old Million Eye.'

'What do you mean Old Million Eye?'

'I don't know.'

But I once saw a photograph of a fly looking at an electric bulb. It didn't move, and neither did the bulb.

'Didn't need anything,' said Plant. 'Why, anyone can contemplate. You haven't got to ask anyone to learn to enjoy the wonder of the world.'

'But why didn't he go blind?'

'It wouldn't have made any difference. His vision was inward. No, he could snap his fingers at the lot of 'em.'

'He couldn't have gone on making his lenses. Interesting job.'

But Plant wasn't listening. He'd got his eye on the frypan and suddenly he made another rush; just as the young man in the blue jumper took his fried bread and rasher out of it and put them in a tin plate. Plant snatched the frypan and shouted 'Thank you,' and he made a push at the fire. But another young chap in a dust-cloth shirt said 'Thank you,' and snatched it out of Plant's hand, so neatly, that it was gone before he saw where. Then the first young chap knocked his hat over his eyes, gave him a push that sent him flying back into the corner and said, 'Go and scrape yourself, you bum.'

Plant hit the wall so hard that he didn't know where he was. When I picked him up, I saw that his nose and mouth were bleeding. I propped him on the box and said, 'Yes, no doubt about it, Jenny had an angel's blessing.'

The angel that presided at her birth
Said, 'Little creature, born of joy and mirth,
Go love without the help of anything on earth.'

Plant went on moving his lips, and then I saw they were moving by themselves. The old man was crying. It surprised me. And then I thought, But it's natural. He's got a sense of justice. Poor old chap. And he can't get over it —not at his age.

'But of course she was a popular girl,' I said. 'The boys liked her. Because she was happy. And one of them, not exactly a boy, but a man of about thirty-five, with a wife and four children, made a nuisance of himself. He used to lie in wait for her and walk beside her through the town, telling her that she made all the difference to him, and so on. The usual story from a married man of thirty-five to young girls. And usually the truth. He was a thin chap in spectacles with a long bald head, and no chest to speak of. Looked like a consumptive lay preacher. But he was one of our engineering staff. Draughtsman. Name of Ranken.'

Plant wiped his nose on his stump and gave a sigh. He was getting over his bereavement.

'And one night when Ranken was a bit too pressing in the back lane, Jenny gave him a slap. She had plenty of

144

spirit. And when she came in, she told me she was tired of Ranken. "He's always waiting for me," she said, "and it's a nuisance." So next evening I went out and there was the chap in the lane, waiting. And I told him to clear off. I remembered my responsibilities and I swelled up my chest, which wasn't very much, but at least it was bigger than his, and I said, "You leave my sister alone, you blankety blank."

'He was a head shorter than I was and I made myself plain.

' "Why?" said he.

' "Because you frighten her and because you're not fit to have anything to do with a decent girl." "It's a free country," he said. "I'll do what I like." "No, you won't," I said. "Why not?" said he. "Because if you do I'll break your neck," I said. "Just you try it," said he. And the next day he came after Jenny again, and pulled her about in the back lane. So she called for me and I ran out and said, "All right, you've asked for it," and I made to hit him. But before I could hit him he hit me three or four times; he broke my nose and knocked out my front teeth. You see, Mr Plant, he'd learnt how to do it. He'd done a bit of boxing. And then he knocked me out and fractured my skull on the pavement. I was three months in hospital. And when I came out, he'd run off with Jenny to London. She had a bit of money, you know, in the Post Office. She thought him the finest man in the world. She thought I'd been unkind to him; that everybody had been unkind to him. Well, of course, Ranken had had his let downs. Who hasn't at thirty-five? Especially fitters and draughtsmen, and scientists, and garage mechanics. All of them have got ideas that ought to have made their fortunes and fame, if only some firm had taken them up. But it wasn't any good telling Jenny that England was full of Rankens and all their boxes were full of neglected genius. She didn't believe it. There was only one Ranken in the world for her. And she'd hardly speak to me for having been so nasty to him and provoking him to crack my skull.'

Mr Plant had stopped crying. But he wasn't listening to me. He shook his head. 'They talk about accidents happening, Mr Jimson. But it isn't all accident. When it's one that finishes you off. It's too big.'

'Big enough. You should have seen Jenny after the first

145

year with her darling Robin—skin and bone and her eyes coming out her head. But of course not admitting anything. "How goes it, Jenny, you look a bit low?" "Me, I'm all right. It's only that poor Robin does have such awful luck."

'It made me swear, Mr Plant. But I was young then. Young and innocent. I didn't make allowances for other people doing what they liked, as well as myself.'

'We ought to be grateful, if we only knew,' said Mr Plant.

'That's it. Go love without the help, etc.—a first-class tip for the six o'clock. Last race.'

Just then I noticed that the young chap in the dust-cloth shirt had put his coat down on the back of a chair. Near the stove. And he was engaged in tearing a teapot from another young chap, a smaller one. So I went over and poked the fire and played with the shovel. And a coal flew out. Then I went over to Plant and said, 'Come along, Mr Plant. I've got half a dollar. Let's go to the good Pull-up and get a cut off the joint with two veg.'

Old Plant shook his head. 'I owe you ten bob,' I said.

'Do you?' said Plant, a bit suspicious. But he got up. As we were going out of the kitchen, we heard a lot of shouts and awful curses. 'Why, what's up?' said Plant.

'Somebody's coat on fire. Burning nicely. Might have had a live coal in each pocket.'

'In each pocket? How could that happen?'

'I don't know,' I said. 'But it's a pity. Poor young fella. Going to see his girl. What a shame.' And I was sorry for that young chap. So as not to be too excited. Taking a chance like that. Might have got something on my mind. Vengeance is mine, saith the Lord. Safer to leave it to Him. He won't do anything about it. It's not His game. He's too busy getting on with the next thing. But why should you know?

21.

I didn't tell anyone about Alabaster because I didn't believe in him any more. Effect of daylight. Anyone can believe anything in chokey, or at night time, but daylight makes even generals look like fairy tales.

I wasn't surprised therefore, when, just for the joke, I telephoned 19, Capel Mansions, and was told that Professor Alabaster didn't live there. The porter had never heard of him. Nor even of Mr Alabaster. Unless his name was Bastard. No, I said, it wasn't Bastard. That was a pity, the porter said, because a Miss Bastard had once lived next door about seven or eight years ago. Yes, I said, it was most unfortunate. And I hung up.

And when I came out of the box, I was relieved. No doubt about it. I examined my diaphragm and its sensations were undoubtedly those of relief and repose. The fact is, I said to myself, as I turned towards the studio, I have escaped a lot of trouble—and perhaps a great misfortune. Suppose this Professor had come true, suppose he'd made me famous, what then? Every time I wanted to get on with my work, ting-a-ling, somebody at the door, wanting their portraits painted; or whong, whong, somebody on the telephone, wanting me to go to a party. And what would I get out of it? Nothing but worry and kicks. For the benefit of Prof. Alabaster. No, I said. I'm well out of that racket. My job is to get that old woman out of my house, and the new canvas in.

My plan to get Mrs Coker out was to make her think the place was unlucky. Women are very superstitious. I had already written her a letter in large print.

MRS COKER. A WARNING. DON'T LET THAT BLACKGUARD JIMSON PERSUADE YOU INTO TAKING HIS ROTTEN OLD SHED. IT IS HAUNTED BY THE SPIRITS OF THE BOGG FAMILY, WHICH DIED OF FEVER THERE AND WAS EATEN BY THE RATS.

And in the evening I went along that way and scratched on the walls with a long stick. Mrs Coker ran out with a poker in her hand. But I was well away by then. It was important that I shouldn't be seen.

On the next night I put a lot of dry brown paper through the scullery window and dropped a match on it. There was such a smoke that you would have thought the place was on fire. Mrs Coker came out again coughing and sneezing and shouted for the police. She didn't expect the police to hear. She wanted to frighten me. The silly old woman

147

didn't consider that the fire might well have been caused by rats. Rats have caused a lot of fires by gnawing matches, or if they haven't, every old woman believes they have. I should have liked to tell her so. But it was difficult to compose a letter which wouldn't give me away. Finally I sent this.

I SEE YOU HAD A FIRE LAST NIGHT. THIS IS DUE TO THOSE PLAGUE RATS. THEY MADE A FIRE BEFORE GNAW-ING MATCHES WHEN THAT SCOUNDREL JIMSON LIVED THERE. BUT OF COURSE HE KEPT IT DARK MEANING TO GET SOME MUG TO RENT THE PLACE.

Next night the old woman was popping out every minute with her poker and walking round the shed. On guard. The plan was working well. But what worried me was the state of Ikey's health. For, I thought, it would be just my luck if old Ikey dropped dead and that canvas was sold or cut up for floor-cloth.

I had been several times to take a look at it. You could see the top corner of it through a crack in the yard door, which gave a view of the shed. And every time I saw it, I liked it better. But every time I saw Ikey, I liked him worse. He was going to pieces at a fearful rate. As sure as I'm Gulley, I thought, the very day that old Mrs Coker throws in the towel and goes, Ikey will take spirits of salt or simply fall dead in his dust of ingrowing despair. Which, statistics show, kills more people every year than all the other kinds of heart disease put together.

I thought of going in and telling the old jelly fish that if Ikey's was killing him, he'd only got to go bankrupt and he'd soon find that bankruptcy itself can be a pleasure. I'd been bankrupt four times. There's nothing like a good smash for getting rid of small worries, the things that don't matter, but peck a man to death.

I thought of it, I say. Or I think I was thinking of it, on the Wednesday morning. But when I was peeping through the front window to see if he was alone, all at once his face came floating up quite close to me. And it was as blank as a whitewashed wall, as stupid as a corpse that's been a week in the water; more wretched than an old clubman at an empty bar with nothing to talk to but the whisky advertisements. And you see him looking at them as if he had forgotten how to read and they might hold the secret of the universe.

No, I said, it's no good. It's no good telling the poor old bladder that life is sweet, brother. Because he doesn't want it to be sweet. He's tired of enjoying anything by himself. He hasn't got the jump to laugh by accident. The grace of God can't reach him even through a Nellie Wallace. No, he can't go on. Why should he? He doesn't even get paid for it. He'll take prussic acid and there'll be another crash, and this time the landlord will put a match to the whole thing and take the insurance money. And it would be a moral act. Ikey's is a death trap.

So I was walking along in a dejected spirit, for I couldn't work, when, just as I was turning into Greenbank, to take a long view of the studio and see if the enemy's flag was still flying, I mean, smoke still rising out of the chimney, a nice young gentleman came walking along. And he was watching me all the time. Not with his eyes. He was too polite. But with his left ear and left elbow.

He wasn't a detective. Though he wore a neat brown suit and a brown hat. He had too long a neck and he turned out his toes. He was walking like the front legs of a French pug. He had round shell spectacles and his expression was intellectual as well as watchful. That is to say, he looked so that any good vet. would have said, at a first glance, that poor dog has worms.

What does that poor animal want with me, I wondered. Can he be a brother artist? He looks as if he might be capable of a wash-drawing in sepia; or decorating bookends with transfers.

Suddenly the young man gave his neck a twist, as if to shake a fly out of his ear; his large brown eyes, melting like jelly on a warm afternoon, filled with respectful delight, and off came his chappo. 'Excuse me, sir, but are you, by any chance, Mr Gulley Jimson? I called at your studio twice last week.'

Alabaster, I thought, and I nearly laughed in my own face. Here was my professor, a kid just out of school. One of the up and at 'em boys, looking for a stepping-stone to higher things. 'No,' I said, 'my name is Henry Ford, incognito.'

But he had outside information. He knew me. 'My name

is Alabaster. I don't know if you received a note of mine. I'm afraid it was never forwarded. But I am a student of art, I have written much on the British School, and I have long been a fervent admirer of your magnificent works.' 'How do you do?' I said. 'How are you? Quite well, I hope.' 'Yes, thank you. It was a great pleasure to me to see Mr Hickson's wonderful collection.' 'Yes, Mr Hickson has been a collector all his life. What he hasn't collected isn't worth the investment.' 'And he and I agreed that it was a crying scandal that your splendid art is so little known outside a limited number of connoisseurs.'

'Mr Hickson wants to bull the market, does he?'

'He thinks it is quite time there was a proper appraisement of your contribution to art.' 'He'll have to be careful. He may do a lot of harm. He tried to get up a Jimson boom once before, in '25. But first of all the General Strike broke out and then his publicity agent had an attack of delirium tremens and got converted and wrote that in his real opinion I was anti-Christ, and one of the chief causes of the decadence of British youth.'

'I think I remember something of that disgraceful agitation.' 'It did me a lot of good. I got several offers from dealers. I made money that year.'

The Professor smiled quickly like one who says, 'the eccentricities of genius. But really it's a pity.' Then he became very serious again, and in fact almost blue, and said, 'Mr Jimson, I have been planning for some time, subject to your approval, of course, and I hope, assistance, a definitive biography, and a descriptive and appreciative catalogue of your art, with reproductions of principal works.'

Reproductions of principal works was a good one. If I hadn't been in company, I should have lain down on the pavement and kicked my legs in the air. Was he real? I couldn't make up my mind. I was pretty sure he wasn't really real, by something in his left eye. It seemed to say, I call myself Alabaster, but God knows what I am really. Probably an optical delusion due to public indigestion.

'That's a nice idea, Professor,' I said. 'Are you an experienced biografter?' 'I wrote a short life of old Crome for my book on his early work.' 'How long?' 'About forty pages.' 'I didn't know old Crome lived as much as that. I should want about four hundred at that rate.' 'A full life might occupy a second volume.' 'Did old Crome have any reproductions?' 'No, there was only a frontispiece.' I stopped at the corner of Ellam Street and drew myself up. 'I shall want reproductions.'

The Professor at once realized the decisive nature of the occasion. Or rather, he was as nearly sure of it, as he could be of anything. He said firmly, 'Most certainly.' 'Coloured ones,' I said. 'That was what I planned,' said the Professor. But his left eye was wondering again, as if the whole thing was a bit of nonsense.

'With lace edges,' I said. 'Lace edges?' said the Professor, and I think a button fell off his trousers. 'Like tarts,' I said, 'and hams. The best quality. If we're going to do the thing at all, we ought to do it well. We don't want to make any mistakes. I know a chap, a friend of mine, who used to paint girls for magazine covers. The best class of girls, eleven feet high with eyes as big as eggs. Well, one morning he put on his best suit, called a taxi and drove to the Tower Bridge, where he took a pint of poison, put ten pounds of lead in each pocket, tied his legs together, cut his throat, shot himself through the head and jumped over the parapet.' 'Poor fellow,' said Alabaster. 'Yes, indeed. He was always a drifter. Never worked things out. Never had a real plan. They saw through this job at once, picked him up, pumped him up, sewed him up, plugged him up and got him back to work in six weeks.' 'I suppose he just went and did it again.' 'No, he'd lost his nerve. One of the nurses married him soon after. He made no resistance and we thought that after all he was dead. But his wife was a nice girl. She brought him alive, and now he's doing those girls again to support his beloved family and he looks just like St. Lawrence frying over a slow fire. He'd like to scream all the time, but he knows the agony is going on too long.' 'I'm afraid there are many like that among the commercial artists.' 'Yes, and if I am going to be a commercial artist, I shall want my gridiron upholstered in the best brass nails.' 'Nobody could call you a commercial artist, Mr Jimson.' 'Blow the trumpets, sound the drum, Tantara, Boom. Twelve reproductions in colour. Why not twenty-four?' 'The only question is one of expense.' 'That doesn't matter in a case like this.' 'Certainly not.' 'We're aiming at the highest class of publication.' 'Of course, an edition de luxe.' 'And neither of us is paying for it.' 'Exactly, but of course the publishers,' the Professor hesitated to wound my ears with the facts of life. But he took a deep breath and threw his heart across the ha ha, 'Publishers are sometimes apt to take a business view.' 'Reproduce some of Hickson's Jimsons and make him pay for the whole edition.' 'Mr Hickson has already given me his support.' 'Have you got it in your pocket?' 'No, it is to be paid over only on the completion of the publisher's contract.' 'Got a contract?' 'Not yet.' 'Got a publisher?' 'I have approached three.' 'How far did they run?'

Mr Alabaster smiled as if to say, The unbending of greatness. How delightful. He said that he expected an answer from Muster and Milligan. 'Never heard of them.' 'A new firm, but very enterprising.' 'Will they pay?' 'It would not be usual to pay an advance.' 'I meant, me.' 'I don't think, Mr Jimson, the artist usually receives any direct financial benefit.' 'Then I don't mind.' 'You will receive a great deal of publicity.' 'Favourable publicity this time.' 'Most certainly.' 'That means paying for drinks instead of selling pictures. In my experience, Professor, fame is not only the ruin of artists, it busts them.'

Mr Alabaster shook his head as if to say, How true. Meanwhile we were walking along Greenbank towards the Eagle. And I began to draw in my steps in case we should pass the door, before Alabaster noticed the sign and remembered that the bar was open. 'I like your idea, Professor,' I said, 'The Life and Work of Professor Alabaster, by Gulley Jimson.' 'You mean the Life and Works of Gulley Jimson.' 'It's the same thing, I give you a job and you give me a job. Let's talk it over. What we want is a quiet spot.' And having reached the Eagle, I lingered so much that the Professor shot two yards ahead before he found himself alone. He noticed this and said, 'I should like that very much. Where shall we go?'

I reflected a moment and answered, 'I hardly like to suggest a public bar, but I notice the Eagle is close by, and though it is but a primitive place with a small bar and very hard chairs, it is a free house. The beer is said to be drinkable.'

'The only difficulty is that I am forbidden by my doctor to drink beer.'

'I understand that the Eagle frequently has whisky, rum, and gin, as well as beer.'

'I was hoping that we might find more congenial surroundings at your studio.'

'I'm afraid my studio is in process of cleaning. We should not be comfortable there. Why not come and try the lemonade at the Eagle?'

Mr Alabaster opened his mouth and looked like a fish that is gaping for air on the bank. His eyes had a dusty expression, like a London pool. I thought, I've seen that look before. What does it mean?

'Perhaps in your lodging, Mr Jimson. Even in a temporary lodging.'

'No chairs at all,' I said. 'The Eagle has chairs, though they are upholstered in oak.'

'It is very awkward,' Mr Alabaster said, and then suddenly I knew his look. It was the look of a man who can't pay for a drink. 'By Gad,' I thought, 'I believe the Professor is broke.'

So I took an inventory of the smart young gentleman and there was a piece of his shirt sticking out of his trousers, a little piece no bigger than a sixpence but blue as the North star. Indication to mariners. And when I looked longer I saw that his shiny brown boots were down on one side like torpedoed ships. There was a fringe on the back of his trousers like old flags after the battle and the breeze, and his collar had an edge like a splintered mast.

'Why should we not adjourn to your flat in Kensington, Professor,' I said. 'I am afraid I have given up my tenancy,' said the Professor. 'Yes,' I said, 'I phoned and the porter was sure your name was something else and you'd been living somewhere else.' 'I wasn't exactly a resident,' said Alabaster. 'I was staying with a friend.' 'That's much the best plan,' I said. 'I prefer it myself. Let us visit your friend. He may be out.' 'I'm afraid he is away. But I should be delighted with any accommodation, Mr Jimson. Your lodgings, even if there aren't any chairs.'

We walked on. And I thought, the Professor is broke, but I like him. There's a kind of little lamb who made thee about him, which is very attractive. And though he is probably a blackguard who would sell his own mother to

153

the bone factory for half a crown and cut a blind man's throat for glory, he is such an unsuccessful blackguard that you can't help mothering him, poor snake.

'My address for the moment,' I said, 'is Elsinore, Ellam Lane.' 'Is it close?' 'You can see the chimney-pots from here, that large villa with the fire-escape.' 'A very wise precaution.' 'Yes, I never take a house of that size unless it has a fire-escape. Right turn. There you are, Professor. My bedroom is on the top floor—the window with the gent's pants drying on the sill. I prefer a top bedroom for the airing.' 'So do I.'

It was about half-past seven and I said to the Professor, 'Just about my dinner time.' 'Don't let me intrude on your arrangements.' 'Certainly not, I hope you'll stay.' 'It's very good of you. But it's really too late,' said the Professor, and I thought, where have I heard that voice before, like wind blowing through the cracks of an empty church. 'Oh, not at all,' I said. 'The dining-room is downstairs. For convenience. The staff nowadays so dislike stairs.' 'Yes, of course, quite so. You are too good. If I might wash my hands.' 'The arrangements are downstairs, next the dining-room.' 'Thank you so much, I really feel that I am imposing on you.' 'The imposition is a pleasure all round.' And I thought: Yes, of course I know that voice, the chap is hungry and doesn't know what to do about it. 'This way, Professor.' 'I can't say how much I appreciate this hospitality.'

And we came into the kitchen where about fifteen chaps were eating, each trying to turn his back on all the others at once; and to cover his plate. For to have anyone look on your food in a common lodging-house kitchen is a misfortune. The envious eye makes you forget the taste even of Wiltshire ham. And the critical eye which is the evil eye turns a cheap kipper into sulphuric acid and old leather.

I had a quick look round and there was old Plant in his corner, arms crossed, hat over his nose like a Roman helmet. Looking as if to say, Let 'em all come. On guard. The sentry of Pompeii. With pepper and salt in his pockets and the cup on a string under his coat; and a kettle between him and the wall behind. A kettle with only two small holes we got off a dump.

'All safe, Mr Plant?' though he was safe enough in his

back corner. 'All safe, Mr Jimson,' with the look of the Pompeian when they dug him out of the ashes. Making quite a thing of it.

'Mister Plant,' I said, 'Professor Alabaster. He's coming to dinner.'

'With pleasure,' said Plant, taking a side glance at my pocket.

'The Professor is my biograbber,' I said. 'He said snap and my fame is his bed and broad.'

'I hope you will get some recognition at last,' said old Plant. 'I shall be recognized by the starry wheels,' I said, forgetting myself. 'You are an art critic in the papers, sir?' said old Plant who thinks a lot of papers though he thinks he doesn't. 'Yes,' I said, 'the Professor is an art-cricket. He knows the game backwards, from Zuloaga to Alfred the Great.' 'You don't believe in art criticism?' said Alabaster. 'Yes,' I said, 'it exists. I even knew a critic once. A chap who could criticize pictures. Yes, he even knew what a picture was.' 'What is a picture?' 'A picture, that's the trouble really.' 'What papers did he write for?' 'He didn't write. He swore. His language was so bad that his wife and family deserted him. They were also starving.' 'What did he do then?' 'He decided to live for his mission as critic, so to support himself, he took up cricketism. Balls and bats. His special branch was the googly. The slowness of the hand deceives the sly.'

The Professor reflected a moment. He was thinking of his dinner. As one in a dream, which might still turn out not to be a dream, he said, 'The googly.'

Poor chap, I thought, he's such an inefficient scoundrel that he doesn't know the simplest motions of his craft. 'I'm surprised,' I said, 'that as a cricket you don't know the googly. Slow balls right off the wicket with a break from the blind side. You start, let us say, on the modern spirit with a touch of surrealism, come in sharp on the superb Sargents in the collection of Sir Burrows Mouldiwarp. Then you mention that great offers have been made for the Mouldiwarp pictures. But Sir Burrows has up to now, in the interests of the nation, rejected all temptation to part with his unique gallery, and down goes the wicket, middle stump. Next day all the papers reveal that the Mouldiwarp collection is to be dispersed, on account of the death duties.'

155

The Professor fired up. The smell of kippers was biting him in a new place. 'Mr Jimson,' he said, 'if you think that I have any motive in this project which I have suggested to you except the desire to make your superb work better known to the public—'

'Hickson's work,' I said. 'And why not? It's all in the game. Hickson is a business man. And I'm a painting man. He makes money for fun and needs art to keep him alive. I paint pictures for fun; and need money to keep me alive. He wants to boost his pictures and get fun out of them, and I want to get some money and paint new pictures. And you want a job.'

'I see you have the lowest opinion of my motives,' said the Professor. 'Not at all,' I said. 'Not the lowest, I've known a lot of real artists in my time and some of them were geniuses in their way.'

Somebody was frying a chop and the smell began oozing through the kippers. It reached us like music from the never-never land. I hadn't eaten a chop for two years. Too much fat and bone for true economy. But to the Professor, brought up probably in luxury, it came like the wind of the desert to a wild barb. You could see his nostrils expand and drink it in, especially the lean. It went to his head. He became excited. 'Mr Jimson,' he said. 'Since you have mentioned it yourself, I might perhaps be allowed to suggest that you are suffering, no doubt temporarily, from some financial embarrassment.' 'Not at all,' I said, 'I'm used to it.' 'But do you realize that the art dealers would give very good prices for your work? I know one who would pay any sum for a fine example.' 'I've had any sum before and worked out at nothing less expenses.' 'You don't know your value.' 'How much is it? Mention some sum.' 'That would depend, of course, on the work. If the gentleman I mention could see a specific picture.' 'Certainly, Prof. If your friend would run down to Ancombe in Devonshire, he'd find the finest thing I ever did, and they'd give it to him.' Alabaster took out his notebook. 'At Ancombe, Mr Jimson?' 'Yes. In the village hall. On the end wall under four coats of white-wash.' 'Oh, a wall painting.' 'Yes, but I used oil paint on a special plaster. Very durable.' 'I'm afraid my friend couldn't remove the wall.' 'Well, then there's another one, nearly as good, in Bradbury, near Leeds. I should think you could have it for seven-and-sixpence.' 'Is that on a wall?' 'No, on canvas.' 'Perhaps I could have particulars.' And out came the notebook again. 'Jacob and his wives stealing away with Laban's flocks.' 'A very interesting subject.' 'It came out well.' 'And you say the canvas is in Bradbury?' 'Last I saw of it, it was covering a screen in a barber's shop—they'd cut it down a bit and given it a coat of black japan, but you could still see Leah's eyes and a bit of Rachel's left leg coming through.' 'What vandalism.' 'Of course my biggest work is the Holy Innocents, but I'm afraid your friend couldn't have that. It's in the hall of the Therapeutic Society, near Cheapside. But one of the Colonial governments took over the building and it didn't like the babies because they hadn't any trousers on. So it said the plaster was dangerous and knocked it about a bit with a hammer. And most of it fell down.' 'I think I heard of that scandal.' 'Well, why not? After all, they'd bought the house, so why shouldn't they do what they liked with the decorations?' 'Works of art ought to be sacred to civilized people.' 'These people were civilized. They all wore trousers and they never spat on the floor. They used the fireplace.'

'I can't treat that sort of thing lightly, Mr Jimson. It makes me furious.' 'It doesn't worry me, Mr Alabaster. What I say is, anyone who goes in for art deserves what he gets. If he ends up in the Academy, then he ought to thank God that he escaped worse. He might have been sweeping out a lavatory in Leicester Square. And if he ends in the workhouse he ought to say to himself: After all, I've been out for a good time. And I've had a damn good time too. And if I'm not in a lunatic asylum or jug, it's only because no one took the trouble to set the police on me. I wasn't good enough.'

'You are too modest, Mr Jimson—your work hasn't the reputation it deserves. What you need is a business manager.'

'Bring in the business, Prof., and I'll pay you your whack.'

'Excuse me, but I am not in the art business. I am a critic. But it is precisely as a critic that I happen to know how dealers regard your work.'

'Bring along your friend and we'll sting him both sides at once.'

'I know he offered Mr Hickson two hundred guineas for the "Lady in her Bath".'

'Sara in her skin. That wasn't a picture. It was a piece of stuff. But I have a real picture to sell.'

'He would give you two hundred for any important work.'

'Make it three hundred, and I'll give you half.'

'I really had no idea of such a thing, Mr Jimson—but in the circumstances—'

'We're both broke, Professor. So why worry about a few hundred here or there.' 'Half is too much.' 'Not if I get the other.' 'Say the usual agent's fees.' 'Thirty-three-and-a-third per cent with a cut for the frame.' 'It's really too much, I feel ashamed.' 'Don't do that, Professor. Buy yourself a new suit and be a new man. We're in this together. You tell the tale and I make the hokey pokey, works by the celebrated Gulley Jimson.' 'I resent very much the suggestion that there is any ulterior motive in my action.' 'You're quite right, Professor. To resent. Stick to the rules. Crickets ought to resent suggestions. All they have to sell is somebody's good name. Quick, Mr Plant, there's a gap in the stove.'

Plant got up and took my frypan from under him. I found it hanging outside a shop in High Street market. Fell into my hand. Cheap tin. Regular swindle. But good enough for rough work. Old Plant always sat on it. 'You'll bust it in, Mr Plant,' I said, 'if you lean your weight on it.'

'But I don't lean my weight. Trust me. The trick is, to sit a bit sideways and forward. I could show you, but it's not so easy as it looks. I hit on it myself, by accident.'

Well, I thought, Old Plant is a bit of an artist after all. Life and Work of Godfrey Plant. Creation of dignities and responsibilities.

> *Some sons of Los surround the passions with porches*
> *of iron and silver,*
> *Creating form and beauty around the dark regions of*
> *sorrow,*
> *Giving to airy nothing, a name and a habitation*
> *Delightful, with bounds to the infinite.*

'I'll leave it to you, Mr Plant,' I said. 'Couldn't leave a pan in better hands.' And I took out of my pocket four portions of fried fish with chips done up in a paper bag.

They give you a bag with anything more than two portions. And a packet of lard.

Then I made for the fire. All the frypans were pushing at each other over the red, joggling together, and the owners swearing and glaring hotter than the fire. I had to put my pan on the black of the stove. But it was hot enough on the draft side to melt the fat. Then I took a little cocoa tin with a nail hole in the lid, as if for salt and pepper, and gave the fat a sprinkle. But I had some wet rags in that tin, and when I shook it, drops of water flew into the fat. And it began to splutter and shoot like a British square attacked by wild zulus. So the boys on the red gave a jump.

'Ow,' said one. 'What you playing at, you old bastard? That was my eye.'

'I don't know how it is,' I said, 'but this fat always shoots. Because of the adulteration. But what does the government do for the poor, nothing.'

'Wow,' said another. 'Here, you swine. Your bloody pan has burnt my nose.'

'I'm sorry, gentlemen. It's this here fat. But if I get it on the red a moment, I'd soon have it done.'

"It bleeding well better, or I'll shove it down your neck and all. Hi, ow wow, what you doing?'

'Well really, gentlemen, you see how it is—it's worse than ever.'

'Get it on the red, for Christ's sake, and finish with it before you burn our bloody eyes out.'

'Thank you, gentlemen, you are very kind.'

So I got my billy on the red and in two minutes that fish began to curl and smoke blue, and the chips shone like bars of gold in champagne.

'Come on, Mr Plant,' I shouted. 'Where's that bread?'

'Here,' they said. 'You clear out. Scram, you old stinker, you smell.'

'What I want to know,' I said, in a soft voice, 'who's that stranger with the thick chin over by the window?'

And they all looked round. 'Thick chin?'

'Looks to me like an inspector.'

So they looked again. And Plant came up panting with two rounds of bread. And the castor. Which was in his charge. In went the bread. And the salt and pepper to taste.

Then one of the boys gave me the shoulder and said, 'That's enough,' and he looked me in the eye. 'None of that, you Union crab, or I'll smash your face in.'

'I beg your pardon, Mister,' I said, 'but suppose I got a jog and this pan should slip out of my hand, fat might go anywhere—why, I knew some hot fat once, burnt a chap's eyes out. Nice young chap just like you.' Looking him in the eye. And he didn't smash my face in. He only gave me another little push and said, 'Yes, I'd like to see you.'

'If you could,' I said. 'That other poor young chap didn't have any eyes—not much face either.'

Then he pushed me off the fire. But I thought: No good giving him a poke. Lose my dinner. And it's time enough. The fish are nicely hotted. Another minute and they'd have gone dry.

'Here you are,' I said, carrying the pan to the corner. And Plant brought out the cutlery. Two forks, a knife and a skewer. Fork for the Professor. Knife and fork for Plant. Skewer and fingers for me. Fingers before forks. Especially with chip potatoes.

I divided up the odd fish and odd toast so quickly that no one saw which was which. Passing the brown. Someone had two pieces of toast. 'How do you like it, Professor?'

'Excellent. Marvellous. Tell me, Mr Jimson, can one sleep here?'

'Sometimes. After dinner. Flea's dinner. Sixpence a night.'

'I really think I might try it. Just for the night.'

'That's all you'll get,' I said. 'For sixpence.'

'I had an invitation, but there was a mistake about the dates. So I found myself free. And I can't say I'm sorry.'

'Social engagements are a terrible bore,' I said, 'but they'll want their sixpence in advance at this Ritz.'

'I suppose it wouldn't be possible for you to add to your kindness and lend me fourpence?'

'Of course I can. Out of that three hundred pounds you are getting me for the Fall.'

We lent him fourpence between us. And stood him a breakfast. And he vanished with the fourpence. 'Well,' I said, after a week, 'I'm surprised. I knew the Professor wasn't quite real, but I thought he was a stronger dream than that. I expected that he was going to hang around my pillow long enough to distinguish him from asthma.'

22. Then one morning I had a letter dated from Capel Mansions. On a good solid paper without deckle edges or rough grain; a lordly paper.

Dear Mr Gulley Jimson,

I am staying here for a few days with my friends Sir William and Lady Beeder, who are both distinguished lovers of art and great admirers of your work, which they have seen at Mr Hickson's.

I don't know if you have a picture available at the moment, but I feel that Sir William would very much like to see some of your latest work. He is, I may say, rather more advanced in taste than Mr Hickson, and possesses examples of all the modern schools, including some symbolist work in which I believe your murals were pioneers. Sir William is a wealthy man and a generous patron of all the arts.

Perhaps you would let me know if you have any recent work to show and we could then arrange a suitable date and place for a private exhibition.

Yours most sincerely,
A. W. Alabaster

And he enclosed four penny stamps.

'Look at this, Mr Plant,' I said. 'What do you think of it?'

'It's just what he said. That he was waiting to go to a friend.'

'That's what I can't make out. It looks almost as if he had been telling the truth.'

'I liked that young man,' said Plantie, who was getting more like himself every day. 'I felt all the time that he was a sincere lover of art.'

'So did I. That's what made me careful. But Capel Mansions, it's a big modern place, isn't it? High rents.'

'Go and see him at his friends'.'

'Yes,' I said. 'But suppose the Professor is straight and his friends are really the sort of people who would give me money, real money for a picture, a real picture. That's to say, a real Jimson.'

'Why not?' said Plantie, folding his arms and looking fiercely at a little old man about ten yards away, who had no more idea of stealing a frypan than washing his face. 'Why shouldn't they buy one of your pictures? I agree with the young gentleman. You don't think nearly enough of yourself, Mr Jimson.'

'It's not what I think of myself,' I said. 'It's what this Beeder thinks of himself. Does he think himself cleverer than all the other millionaires who never buy a picture till the dealers tell 'em that the price will be more next week? And if so, what sort of a fool is he?' And I went away. I liked old Plantie, but he was always too encouraging. As if he thought I was just going to hang myself, or jump into the river.

I wanted to think. I saw that this was a turning point in my life. Or probably not. A thousand pounds, I thought, or let's say fifty pounds, it would set me up for life. I could get a new studio, a good one with a roof as well as a wall. Even twenty pounds would give me a fresh start. Of course, I thought, it's not a likely tale. I haven't sold a picture for fifteen years, and my last big commission was from that old woman in Ancombe, who was more or less mad. Or she wouldn't have given me the job. And as for the Professor, he may be straight in places, but that's all to the bad. You know where you are with a complete liar, but when a chap mixes some truth with his yarns, you can't trust a word he says. All the same, I thought, even ten pounds, I'd be painting again.

So I took Plantie's advice and cleaned the top of my boots with a newspaper and went to call at Capel Mansions. Fine large new buildings in the playbrick design. Fine large old porter in the Victoria R.I. style. Everything right. He pushed me down the steps without any hesitation. Quite right. And it took me some time to persuade him that I had been asked to call. Then he phoned the flat. The Professor himself came down to receive me and to apologize. Quite right too. So did the porter when he heard I was a distinguished artist.

'Don't mention it,' I said. 'You did the right thing. I'll tell Sir William that he can have every confidence in you. After all, if a man can't get his money's worth in fidelity, what would the world be coming to? What is your pub?'

'Well sir, I sometimes go to the Red Lion, just round the

next corner.' 'I'll come and have something with you.' 'I don't get off till twelve.' 'I'll wait. That's a bargain.'

The Professor was nervous and I thought probably he had lost some more buttons off his trousers. He looked as if he could no longer rely on them. On the other hand, he was cleaner than ever and had more oil on his hair. 'You wrote to me just in time,' I said. 'I have just completed the finest thing I ever did. It only wants a touch. An important work. Nine by twelve. Of course a lot of people are after it, and the Chantery trustees would jump at it for the nation. But what I always say is that private patrons, really generous and beneficent men like Sir William, ought to be encouraged. Especially if they are millionaires. Artists owe a debt to millionaires that can never be repaid, except in cash. For, of course, Sir William will get it all back as soon as I croak, even before.' 'What is the subject of the picture? Oh, of course I oughtn't to ask that. But I want the general nature of the work.' 'Meat,' I said, knowing that the Professor wouldn't like the idea of the Fall. 'Human meat, in appropriate attitudes, with surrounding vegetables. A thousand is the price—guineas —that's unframed. But I could supply a fine carved frame for another hundred. That, of course, would also be guineas, or say a hundred and ten pounds with a guarantee of genuineness.'

'It isn't the picture called The Fall?' said the Professor. 'Certainly not.'

'What Sir William wants, I think, is one of those magnificent nudes.'

'I'm talking about nudes.'

'But ah, if I'm right, this picture you speak of is one of the more recent works—more in the style of Gauguin.'

'Gauguin, who is Gauguin? You don't mean that French painter who did dead dolls with green eyes in a tin landscape? I couldn't paint in his style unless I became a Plymouth brother with the itch, and practised on public house signs for fifteen years. Hullo, how much higher are we going?'

'Beeder lives in the attics. The best flats are at the top, for the view.'

But I wasn't quite reassured until I saw the flat. Luckily the Beeders were out to tea and I was able to look round. A real hall, a big studio with gallery, a little dining-room off the studio, two bedrooms and chromium bathroom. Usual Persian rugs and antiques, vases, marbles, African gods, American mobiles, Tanagra, and rock crystal ashtrays. Old portraits in the dining-room, modern oils in the studio, drawings in the bedroom, water-colours in the hall. Usual modern collection. Wilson Steer, water in watercolour; Matthew Smith, victim of the crime in slaughtercolour; Utrillo, whitewashed wall in mortarcolour; Matisse, odalisque in scortacolour; Picasso, spatchcock horse in tortacolour; Gilbert Spencer, cocks and pigs in thoughtacolour; Stanley Spencer, cottage garden in hortacolour; Braque, half a bottle of half and half in portercolour; William Roberts, pipe dream in snortercolour; Wadsworth, rockses, blockses, and fishy boxes all done by self in nautacolour; Duncan Grant, landscape in strawtacolour; Frances Hodgkin, cows and wows and frows and sows in chortacolour; Roualt, perishing Saint in fortacolour; Epstein, Leah waiting for Jacob in squawtacolour. All the most high-toned and expensive. 'I can see your friends are rich people,' I said, 'that is, really nice and charming. I like them very much already.' And I had a look round the bedrooms. Silk underdrawers in Sir William's wardrobe. And nothing but silk. Piles of fine white handkerchiefs. 'I suppose he is the sort of man who has a clean handkerchief every day,' I said. 'He dresses very simply,' said the Professor, who was hovering over me like a guardian angel in case any small savage article might rush into my pockets and bite me in the dark. 'Perhaps we'd better go now,' he said. 'Where?' I said. 'To see the picture.' 'Oh no,' I said, 'there's plenty of time. And besides, I want to meet Sir William.' 'Oh, I'm afraid he won't be back for a long time.' 'When do you expect him back?' 'Not till dinner time at least.' 'That will suit me perfectly. I haven't got an engagement to dinner.' 'Oh, but it's quite likely he won't be back till much later.' 'How much later?' 'Midnight.' 'It's a nuisance, as I had a kind of understanding with the Archbishop of Canterbury to be in about dinner time if he called. But Sir William comes first. I never disappoint a millionaire if I can help it. Not if I have to sleep on the sofa.'

The Professor looked as if not only his trousers but his pants were coming down. I led him back to the studio, made him sit down, I offered him one of Sir William's cigarettes. 'All this,' I said, 'gives me a lot of confidence in the Beeders. Living in a studio and buying pictures. I suppose they love artists.' 'They are very interested in art.' 'I said artists. Clean ones, of course.' 'They do entertain artists.' 'More than once?' 'Lady Beeder is herself an artist.' 'That's not so good.' 'She is not at all bad. She is an amateur of course.' And both of us paused for reflection.

'Of course,' I said, 'with all this money.'

'But some of her water-colours are quite excellent, in the traditional style.'

'Of course, with all this money. The best advice. The best of everything, in fact.'

The Professor made an appeal with his eyes. 'The Beeders are two of my oldest friends. Especially Flora, that is, Lady Beeder.'

'So they ought to be,' I said. 'With all that money. You stick to them, old man. Clasp them to your soul with bands of steel—say steal. But I suppose they find you useful too. The lady asks your advice about her painting.'

'She is really very keen.'

'Look here, Professor,' I said. 'What we want to do is to get up a Life and Works of Lady Flora Beeder and sell her the first refusal for five hundred pounds down. That's two-fifty each.'

'Not Lady Flora Beeder. Lady Beeder.'

'That's all right. You can put in the stops. I'll do the works. But cash on the nail.'

'Are you serious?' The Professor was surprised.

'Of course I'm serious. Look at my boots.'

'But, Mr Jimson, it would be quite impossible to bring out a Life and Works of Lady Beeder. No publisher, no reputable publisher, would touch it.'

'Then we'll get one of the other kind. Come on, Professor. You've no imagination. Business is business. I'm in this with you. What about the Life and Works of Gulley Jimson?'

'Do you compare yourself with Lady Beeder? Gifted as she is, she is hardly—'

'Nobody would know the difference. Not if it was done properly. Of course, we want the best paper, and a lot of coloured reproductions, and gilt edges and an introduction by the President of Something, or a Professor of the Fine Arts. But expense is no object. She's got the beans. Damn

165

it, Professor, for five hundred down and expenses we'll put her on the Roll of Fame. We'll roll her on the floors of eternity for a year or two. Of course, when people try to hang their hats and umbrellas on a Beeder, they may find a sort of an absence. But by that time it will be too late. She'll be in all the public galleries, and the only thing the directors can do is to put her in the sun, over a ventilator, where the rain comes through the bricks, or store her with the Turners in the Tate basement until the Thames comes up again and gives her a wash of dead dog and sludge. She'll still be in the best company.'

'My dear Mr Jimson, it can't be done.'

'I see, it isn't cricketism. Well then, why not give an exhibition for her, and let her buy in about half and stick red tabs on them—and put some paragraphs in the paper about the finest type of English traditional art, solid achievement rather than flashy cleverness, a reverent approach to Nature—and so on. If that isn't cricketism, what is?'

But the Professor thought I was joking. No imagination, nothing of the artist. And the thought struck me perhaps after all he was an honest cricket. A straight bat. The noblest work of Gog.

'I thought you and I were going into business together,' said I, 'to coin me cash.'

'Is it possible,' said the Professor, 'to serve Mammon and Art at the same time?'

'It is,' I said, 'or there wouldn't be any art. Through cash to culture. That's the usual road. What's the difference between little Bob who likes pictures to chuck stones at and Nosy Barbon who would walk ten miles to meet a bad painter—about two hundred pounds in school fees, paid by the state monthly with war bonus. The history of civilization is written in a ledger. Who are the most enlightened people in the world—the rich. What is the most Christian nation: the one with most of the money.'

The Professor was shocked. 'You are joking, Mr Jimson. You would not like me to put such things in your biography, as considered statements.'

'I hope you will,' I said. 'If you don't, I'll do it myself. The best of everything for everybody is what I want and it costs millions. Hell is paved with good intentions, but heaven goes in for something more dependable. Solid gold.

With walls of jasper, etc. We got to build Jerusalem, and that needs a lot of finance. Pure hearts are more than coronets. I should think so. It takes about a thousand years of good education to turn them out and even then the process is not yet foolproof. We haven't got the money for the necessary research, let alone repairs to the laboratory. And the most expensive thing in the world is a work of genius.'

'Most of the French impressionists were poor men, poorly rewarded. And of the expressionist school, many were almost starving.'

'All the French impressionists lived in a country where the government paid millions a year for training artists and buying pictures. True, when it got any real artists, it spat on them and starved two or three of them to death. But you can't expect a government to know what original art is. The nature of Bats is to comprehend Balls, and nothing else. But what a government can do is to encourage art schools and bad artists, and when you get a lot of art schools and bad artists, you get a lot of people trying to steal an idea from somebody else and the people they steal from are the original artists. So you get an encouraging atmosphere for original art.'

'I'm afraid the post-impressionist school was received with contempt and derision, even in France.'

'I didn't say the original artists got encouragement in their own lifetime—that's impossible. What I said was you got an encouraging atmosphere for original art, after the artists are dead. When Van Gogh was painting his masterpieces, the clever ones were beginning to admire Manet— that was very encouraging to Van Gogh, and if it wasn't, what did he care? And when Van Gogh was dead and rotten, and his pictures were being bought at thousands a piece for public galleries so that students could get ideas from them, Matisse and Picasso and Braque were bad jokes, but how encouraging for them to hear Van Gogh who was nearly as mad as they were, appreciated in all the best drawing-rooms. That's what I say (I said) if a government wants original art, great art, it only has to pay a lot of crickets and professors and brokendown screevers to talk Balls about art to a lot of innocent children, and teach them how to draw and paint so badly that their own mothers are ashamed of them; and beg them to go in

167

for something more respectable like selling gold bricks or white slaves. Because they won't leave off. And half of them become like Herod, devoured by worms, and the other half like Job, so rotten in their limbs that they can't find rest anywhere. And the first half go prowling round looking for something to stop up their bellies, and the second half go creeping about on all fours looking for somewhere to rest their miserable carcases. And so they gather at last in the graveyard and dig up some poor pauper with their teeth and claws and say, "Lo, he was a genius, starved to death by the government." And so he may have been. Or perhaps not. Everybody makes mistakes. Even a generation devoured by worms at government expense. But unless you spend millions you don't even get mistakes—you have nothing at all. Just a lot of social economics lying about like army disposal after the war before last or the war after next.'

Just then the Beeders came in, Sir William and Lady. Big man with a bald head and monkey fur on the back of his hands. Voice like a Liverpool dray on a rumbling bridge. Charming manners. Little bow. Beaming smile. Lady tall, slender, Spanish eyes, brown skin, thin nose. Greco hands. Collector's piece. I must have those hands, I thought, arms probably too skinny but the head and torso are one piece. I should need them together.

Lady Beeder was even more charming than her husband. 'I'm so delighted, Mr Gulley Jimson—I know you hardly ever pay visits. I did not dare to ask you—but I hoped,' and she asked me to tea. People like that can afford it. Nothing to them to send their cushions to the cleaners.

What I like about the rich is the freedom and the friendliness. Christian atmosphere. Liberty hall. Everything shared because there is too much. All forgiveness because it's no trouble. Drop their Dresden cups on the fireplace and they smile. They are anxious only that you should not be embarrassed, and spoil the party. That's their aim. Comfort and joy. Peace on earth. Goodwill all round.

When I first met Hickson, I could have kissed his beautiful boots. I loved them for themselves, works of art, and he was so full of goodwill that it came off him like the smell of his soap, linen, hair cream, tooth wash, shaving lotion, eyewash and digestive mixture. Like the glow of a firefly. Calling for something. Until he got burnt up, poor chap. A flash in the dark. For of course the rich do find it hard to get through the needle's eye, out of heaven. And to spend all your life in paradise is a bit flat. Millionaires deserve not only our love but our pity. It is a Christian act to be nice to them.

When Lady Beeder asked me if my tea was all right, I said, 'Yes, your ladyship. Everything is all right. I am enjoying myself so much that you will have to throw me downstairs to get rid of me. I think you and Sir William are two of the nicest people I've ever met. You have lovely manners and lovely things, a lovely home, and very good tea. I suppose this tea costs four-and-sixpence a pound, it is worth it. Genius is priceless.'

The Professor kept coughing and making faces at me, but I wasn't afraid of embarrassing nice people. I knew they would be used to unfortunate remarks. Rich people are like royalty. They can't afford to be touchy. *Richesse oblige.* And, in fact, they kept on putting me at my ease; and paying me compliments all the time. And when I told them how I had been turned out of my studio by the Cokers they said they hoped that I would come and stay over the week-end, to keep the Professor company while they were away.

'I'm sorry we can't offer you a bed beyond Monday, but we have only two bedrooms.'

'I could sleep on the sofa,' I said.

'Oh, Mr Jimson, but we couldn't allow you to be so uncomfortable.'

'Then why shouldn't Sir William sleep with the Professor and I'll sleep with her ladyship. You can count me as a lady—at sixty-seven.'

Alabaster turned green and coughed as if he was going into consumption. But I knew I couldn't shock cultured people like the Beeders. They get past being shocked before they are out of school, just as they get over religion and other unexpected feelings.

'A very good idea,' said Sir William, laughing. 'I am greatly complimented,' said the lady, 'but I'm afraid I should keep you awake. I'm such a bad sleeper.'

'Perhaps,' said Sir William, getting up, 'Mr Jimson would like to see some of your work, my dear.'

'Oh no, Bill, please.'

'But Flora, that last thing of yours was really remarkable—I'm not suggesting that it was up to professional standards. But as a quick impression—'

'Oh no,' said her ladyship, 'Mr Jimson would laugh at my poor efforts.'

But of course they both wanted me to see her work and say that it was wonderful. And why not? They were so kind, so good.

'Why,' I said, 'amateurs do much the most interesting work.'

The Professor began to hop about like a dry pea on the stove. He coughed and made faces at me, meaning, 'Be careful, be tactful, remember these people are used to luxury of all kinds.'

But I laughed and said, 'Don't you worry, Professor, I'm not pulling her ladyship's leg. I wouldn't do such a thing. I have too much respect for that charming limb.'

Sir William got out an easel and a big portfolio, in red morocco with a monogram in gold. And he took out a big double mount, of the best Bristol board, cut by a real expert, with a dear little picture in the middle. Sky with clouds, grass with trees, water with reflection, cows with horns, cottage with smoke and passing labourer with fork, blue shirt, old hat.

'Lovely,' I said, puffing my cigar. 'Only wants a title—what will you call it? Supper time. You can see that chap is hungry.'

'I think the sky is not too bad,' said she. 'I just laid it down and left it.'

'That's the way,' I said. 'Keep it fresh. Get the best colours and let 'em do the rest. Charming.'

'I'm so glad you like it,' said she. And she was so nice that I thought I should tell her something. 'Of course,' I said, 'the sky is just a leetle bit chancy, looks a bit accidental, like when the cat spills its breakfast.'

'I *think* I see," said her ladyship, and Sir William said, 'Of course, Mr Jimson, you do get skies like that in Dorset. It's really a typical Dorset sky.'

I saw the Professor winking at me so hard that his face was like a concertina with a hole in it. But I didn't care. For I knew that I could say what I liked to real amateurs and they wouldn't care a damn. They'd only think, These artists are a lot of jealous stick-in-the-muds. They can't admire any art but their own. Which is simply dry made-up stuff, without any truth or real feeling for Nature.

'Yes,' I said, 'that is a typical sky. Just an accident. That's what I mean. What you've got there is just a bit of nothing at all—nicely splashed on to the best Whatman with an expensive camel-hair—'

'I *think* I see what you mean,' said her ladyship. 'Yes, I *do* see—it's most interesting.'

And she said something to Sir William with her left eyelash, which caused him to shut his mouth and remove the picture so suddenly that it was like the movies. And to pop on the next. A nice little thing of clouds with sky, willows with grass, river with wet water, barge with mast and two ropes, horse with tail, man with back.

'Now that's lovely,' I said. 'Perfect. After de Windt. Look at the wiggle of the mast in the water. What technique.'

'My wife has made a special study of water-colour technique,' said Sir William. 'A very difficult medium.'

'Terrible,' I said. 'But her ladyship has mastered it. She's only got to forget it.'

'I *think* I see what Mr Jimson means,' says she. 'Yes, cleverness is a danger—'

And she looked at me so sweetly that I could have hugged her. A perfect lady. Full of forbearance towards this nasty dirty old man with his ignorant prejudices.

'That's it,' I said. 'It's the jaws of death. Look at me. One of the cleverest painters who ever lived. Nobody ever had anything like my dexterity, except Rubens on a good day. I could show you an eye—a woman's eye, from my brush, that beats anything I've ever seen by Rubens. A little miracle of brushwork. And if I hadn't been lucky I might have spent the rest of my life doing conjuring tricks to please the millionaires, and the professors. But I escaped. God knows how. I fell off the tram. I lost my ticket and my virtue. Why, your ladyship, a lot of my recent stuff is not much better, technically, than any young lady can do after six lessons at a good school. Heavy-handed, stupid-looking daubery. Only difference is that it's about something—it's an experience, and all this amateur stuff is like farting Annie Laurie through a keyhole. It may be clever but is it worth the trouble? What I say is, why not do

171

some real work, your ladyship? Use your loaf, I mean your brain. Do some thinking. Sit down and ask yourself what's it all about.'

And both of them, looking at me with such Christian benevolence that I felt ready to tell them almost the truth, went off together.

'But Mr Jimson, don't you think—of course, I'm not a professional, that the intellectual approach to art is the great danger?'

'Destructive of true artistic feeling,' Sir William rumbled. 'Don't you think, Mr Jimson, that the greatness of the French impressionists like Manet and Monet was perhaps founded on their rejection of the classical rules?'

'Oh Lord,' I said. 'Listen to them. Oh God, these poor dears—and didn't Manet and Monet talk about their theories of art until the sky rained pink tears and the grass turned purple—didn't Pissarro chop the trees into little bits of glass. And Seurat put his poor old mother through the sausage machine and roll her into linoleum. What do you think Cézanne was playing at, naughts and crosses, like a Royal Academy portrait merchant, fourteen noble pans in exchange for a K.B.E.? Jee-sus,' I said; for they were so nice and polite, the lambs, that they didn't care a damn what I said. It passed right over them like the brass of a Salvation band hitting the dome of St Paul's. They were so rich and Christian that they forgave everybody before he spoke and everything before it happened, so long as it didn't happen to them. 'Jee-minny Christy,' I said. 'What you think I been doing all my life—playing tiddly winks with little Willie's first colour-box? Why friends,' I appealed to their better halves, 'what do you see before you, a lunatic with lice in his shirt and bats in his clock (this was for her ladyship on the maternal side), a poodle faking crook that's spent fifty years getting nothing for nothing and a kick up below for interest on the investment (this was for Sir William on the side of business commonsense), or somebody that knows something about his job?'

Her ladyship and Sir William both smiled and laid their hands on my arm.

'Dear Mr Jimson,' said she, 'don't think I don't agree with every word. I can't say how grateful I am—'

'A great privilege,' Sir William rumbled, 'and believe

me, we know how to appreciate it. Yes, most valuable and illuminating.'

'But dear me,' said her ladyship, 'it's nearly half-past eight.'

'Good God,' I said, 'I haven't got in the way of your dinner?'

'Not at all,' said Sir William. 'We dine at any time.'

'Perhaps Mr Jimson will stay to dinner,' said she.

And I stayed to dinner. I knew it would be good. The rich, God bless them, are supporters of all the arts, bootmaking, dressmaking, cookery, bridge, passing the time of day. We had seven courses and six bottles. But Sir William, poor chap, was a teetotaller and his wife drank only hock for the figure. A half bottle for half a figure. So the Professor and I shared the rest. He had a glass of claret and a suck of port, I had wine.

23. And after the fish, I began to swim. My eyes were opened and I saw the light. The candles kept growing into silver porches, and the flowers walked under them like green girls with chorus hats. Their flames looked at me like the eyes of tigers just waking from sleep. Lying on their sides and opening one eye at a time. Tiger, tiger, burning bright. A ravening brute with a breath like a rotten corpse and septic claws. This beauty grows with cruelty.

'You've got a nice wall there, Sir William,' I said. 'I should like to paint tigers on it. With orchids. Flycatchers and flesh eaters. Flowers of evil. Millionaire eats a poor baby for breakfast and contemplates the beauties of creation. Art lives on babies. It would cost millions to save a few thousand babies a year. Got to teach the mothers first. Then the grandmothers. Then the grand professors. How much will you give me for the tigers? A hundred guineas? All right, I start tomorrow. Through roast grouse to spiritual joy. Joy is goodness. Do you believe in Spinoza, Sir William? To accept all the works of creation with humble delight.'

Sir William began to move his mouth which made him

look so like a sheep chewing gum that I burst out laughing.

I could see old Spinoza with round spectacles and a white apron polishing a lens and looking at my tigers. On a ground of tall brown tree trunks as close together as a chestnut fence—a few tufts of green at the top. No sky. No blue, no vision. Orchids sticking out of the ground with thick stamens like lingams modelled in raw meat. Beauty, majesty and glory.

'I think she's got the toast better tonight, Bill,' said her ladyship in a little mild soft voice. 'It's not right, of course, but it's edible.'

'Much better,' said Sir William. He took a piece of toast and reflected deeply. 'Yes, distinctly better.'

The green girls began to dance under the silver porches and shake their silver hips. A lot of impudent hussies. And I swallowed down two glasses of nice burgundy. Oh land of Beulah,

> *Where every female delights to give her maiden to her*
> *   husband:*
> *The female searches land and sea for gratifications to*
> *   the*
> *Male genius, who in return clothes her in gems and*
> *   gold*
> *And feeds her with the food of Eden; hence all her*
> *   beauty beams.*

'Won't you have some more wine, Mr Jimson?'

And I saw a face close to mine more beautiful than true. What eyes. Grey like a night sky full of moonlight and pencilled all about with radiating strokes of blue-grey like the shading of petals. Darkening to the outer edges of the iris as if the colour had run there and set. A white as bright as a cloud; lashes, two pen strokes of new bronze, dark as sunrise before a single ray reaches the ground. And what a nose, what lips. Eve. Fearful symmetry.

A voice so sweet that I could not hear the words begin to speak. Too full of woman. Too enchanting. I sat with my mouth open, grinning like Circe's pig. Her eyebrows were not plucked. Only brushed and oiled. Feathers of an angel's wing.

'Have you any family, your ladyship, I mean kids?' 'No, I'm afraid not.' 'Of course not.' For children were not born in the land of Beulah. 'You think I haven't done my duty.'

'Yes, of course, your duty is to be rich and happy.' 'But we're not really rich, you know.' Looking at me as if to say, Friend, I give you my confidence. Beautifully done. 'My husband suffered terribly in the slump.' 'Poor chap.' 'Yes, terrible.' 'And yet I suppose it did some good. It made people think about the poor.' 'Round and about.' 'I don't think any government will allow all the unemployment again.' With a serious look full of sympathy and political wisdom. Burnt sugar on the caramel pudding. 'The slump,' said Sir William, 'certainly did much to push forward social legislation.'

'Like the Great War,' said the Professor.

'Oh, don't speak of that terrible time,' said her leddyship. 'I was only a child, but I still remember the Zeppelins.'

'Yes, the war was perhaps not an unmixed evil,' said Sir William. 'It gave us the League. It taught us to be prepared.'

They made me laugh so I choked and nearly lost half a glass full. It was all so rich. Sir William patted me on the back. 'I should like to do some sunflowers among the tigers,' I said, 'turning towards the tiger's eyes.' 'Yes, yes,' said Sir William. He thought I was drunk. 'A hundred guineas,' I said, 'that's the bargain.' 'Good out of evil,' said her ladyship, in a thoughtful mood. Italian school. Touch of Giorgione. 'How true that is.'

'Yes,' I said, 'like winkles out of the shell. We give you the pin, and the winkle likes it.'

'Oh but Mr Jimson, speaking seriously, don't you think —in a deeper sense?' And she turned her lovely eyes on me. Spanish school. Religious touch. Spot of Greco.

'You're quite right, M'dam,' I said. 'An expert can do a nice job, even in the worst case. A girl of thirteen in our village, a deaf mute, had a kid, drowned it and swallowed about a pint of spirits of salt. But they cured her and shut her up. She was a bit off, of course, and rather violent.'

'But do you think mad people really suffer?' With a note like a dove that has laid a double egg. Oh the darling, I thought. Oh daughter of Beulah.

> *She creates at her will a little moony night and silence*
> *With spaces of sweet gardens and a tent of elegant beauty,*

> *Closed in by a sandy desert and a night of stars shin-*
> *ing,*
> *And a little tender moon and hovering angels on the*
> *wing.*

'Do try some more of the sweet, Mr Jimson.' Sweet, sweet, I can cut up a sweet with anybody. 'And some more burnt sugar.' Wonderful land of Beulah. 'You're quite right, your ladyship. The doctors had a wonderful chance with that little girl. Good out of evil.'

'That's another advance we owe to the Great War,' said Sir William. 'Medicine. Especially in mental cases, and plastic surgery.'

'Yes, a time of progress. That kid's mother had been a bit slow too, and a bit deaf, and she married a chap who was a bit slower and a bit tubercular. Well, no one else would take her. And they had fourteen children who were all rather more than a bit slow or deaf or crippled or all three, a regular museum. It was a miracle that they grew up at all. Scientific miracle. It's a marvel the babies that doctors manage to save nowadays.'

'A terrible story. But science is advancing all the time, isn't it?'

'Yes, of course, and it will get on quicker still when we have more idiots in the population.'

'Don't you believe in science, Mr Jimson?'

I began to laugh. 'This place is called Beulah. It is a pleasant lovely shadow, where no dispute can come because of those who sleep.'

'I'm afraid you are a cynic, Mr Jimson.'

'No, but I'm not a millionaire. Don't you ever stop being a millionaire, your ladyship. It would spoil your art.'

'But we are poor. Really quite poor. Or we wouldn't live in a flat like this, would we, William? With only one bathroom.'

'Talking of bathrooms, I have something to ask your ladyship. I should like to paint you.' 'Not in my bath?' 'No, in the nude.' 'But I am fearfully thin, Mr Jimson.' 'I want the bony structure to go with the face.' 'I'm afraid my husband wouldn't approve.' 'He needn't look.'

'Goya,' said the Professor, 'painted the Duchess of Alva in the nude and also clothed.'

'I know the pictures,' said Sir William. 'Wonderful work —what brio—'

'Wonderful,' I said. 'The girl has no neck in the nude and no hips in her chemmy. Yet there they are, distinctly something.'

'Don't you like Goya, Mr Jimson?'

'A great man who painted some great stuff—too big for a dinner party. The Queen's nose in the court picture is alone a very serious matter.'

'A lyric artist,' said the Professor.

'On the brass.'

But Goya was making too much noise. The Queen's nose in the court picture began to trumpet at me and the walls of Beulah trembled. 'Don't talk about him,' I said. 'Let me look at your missus and give me some more port. When shall I paint you, M'dam, I'm free tomorrow afternoon.'

'I'm afraid I have an engagement.'

'No, not one you can't put off. And this is a great chance, you understand. Wouldn't you like to be immortal, like Goya's Duchess?'

'Have some more port, Mr Jimson,' said Sir William.

'With pleasure.' But I couldn't help laughing. For I could see he was put out. He was pipped. And he was only a dream in Beulah.

'We must think of your wonderful offer,' said her ladyship.

'Yes,' said Sir William, warming his brandy glass, and his voice was warm again, his voice sleepy. 'It is an honour.'

> *And every moment has a couch of gold for soft repose,*
> *And between every two moments stands a daughter of Beulah*
> *To feed the sleepers on their couches with maternal care.*
> *And every minute has an azure tent with silken veils—*

I did not feel sleepy. Far from it. Dreams were moving in front of my eyes like festivals of Eden. Land of the rich where the tree of knowledge of good and evil is surrounded with golden rabbit wire.

'Yes,' I said. 'I shall paint you in Beulah, ma'am, and your loom and your tent, it will only cost you a hundred guineas; and fifty for the Professor—cheap for immortality.'

24. When I left for home after dinner, some time after, the Professor was holding one arm and Sir William the other.

But I could not tell whether they were throwing me downstairs or protecting an honoured guest from a dangerous fall. We went home to Elsinore by car, perhaps by taxi, and somewhere on the way we were joined by Nosy Barbon. I think the Professor called for him. They seemed to know each other. And Nosy took me up to bed.

In fact, finding that I had difficulty in staying in the bed, which was narrow, and that some of the other guests were irritated against me on account of my being happy while they were in low spirits, he stayed all night.

I was grateful to the boy, but I wished he had let me wallow, especially when, in the morning, I found him much depressed; at a time when I was also depressed.

'What are you worrying about now?' I asked him.

'About m-mother,' he said. 'I expect she sat up all night for me. She's such a worrier.'

'So are you,' I said. 'So it's her own fault.'

'Oh, but m-mother is a t-terrible worrier.'

'I expect she's fond of you,' I said. 'Some mothers are fond of their children. It's natural.'

'She's fond of me, but I don't think she likes me very much.'

'A lot of mothers don't like their children much. It's natural. Women are so critical. The personal point of view.'

'She hates me to do any drawing and painting. I was wondering.' And he stopped. I knew that he wanted me to go home with him and speak to his people for him. Tell them he wanted to be an artist. But my head was bursting, my eyes were burning, my legs and arms were shooting like sore teeth, my mouth was like a dirty shoe, and I wanted to get back to work. 'That's enough nonsense,' I said. 'I've wasted enough time and energy on doing the polite—the sooner I can get hold of the Fall and finish it, the better. Especially if I can sell it to Beeder.'

'Perhaps if you could come round with me,' said Nosy.

'Why,' I said severely. 'Why didn't you go home last night?'

'You seemed so ill I was afraid you would fall out of bed and hurt yourself.'

This made me feel more severe still. For I saw that Nosy was inclined to make heroes and sacrifice himself to them. Like my sister Jenny, who nearly killed me a hundred times with exasperation. When I saved up fifteen pounds, out of my lunches, to buy her a set of teeth, since her own had dropped out for want of looking after, she gave the money straight to her husband to be wasted on some new working model. And when I saw her still without teeth and found out what she had done with the money, she said only, 'But I thought you wanted to please me.'

'Of course I did. I didn't starve myself for six months to amuse Robert.'

'But darling, you did please me; you gave me great happiness—that fifteen pounds was like a gift from God. It was a gift from God since it was your goodness and love that gave it to me and saved poor Robert from despair. He was absolutely desperate when your letter came.'

'He's always desperate. All inventors are desperate unless they have a million in the bank and a tight hold on some managing director. Robert has no more hope of selling his invention than a cockroach of getting into Simpson's cheese.'

'But darling, only last week he showed the new model to Rackstraws who are one of the biggest firms in the country, and they were delighted with it. It was the most sensitive governor they'd ever seen. And it only wanted a little simplification to be a commercial proposition.'

But I was too disgusted to argue with her. I wanted to cry. And then of course she wanted money. She had been too proud to beg from me at first, but love soon changed all that. Mother and I clubbed together and we raised a few pounds. All my savings went in those three years. Before I was married and had a natural protector of my bank book. And it made no difference that the new model

179

of Ranken's Regulator was a great success. Not to their happiness. Because it simply proved to Ranken that he ought to get ten thousand a year and a factory for himself. And Jenny, of course, began to see that he'd never be satisfied. She began to feel what life was like when you live it with a man with a grievance. Like being swallowed by a very big lazy shark, who can't stop if he wants to, because his teeth all point one way, towards the dark.

And of course Mother and I never got our money back. Even when Ranken began to draw an income. He didn't pay debts. He thought the whole world couldn't pay him enough to make up for its injustice to him. He went on spending everything he could raise on new models. But we went on lending money to Jenny. Because she was devoted. All of us danced on Ranken's string because Jenny was devoted. It made me so hot even to remember it that my head began to fry. And I shouted at Nosy, 'Here, what do you think you're after? Didn't I tell you to go home?'

'Oh yeyes,' said Nosy, alarmed. 'It was all my own f-fault.'

'And haven't I told you a hundred times not to come chasing after me—let me alone, and get on with your job.'

'Oh yeyes,' said Nosy, looking as if he was longing for a rabbit hole into which to dive.

'And haven't I told you that if you don't win that scholarship next month, you deserve to be pushed down the nearest drain?'

'Oh yeyes,' said Nosy, so terrified that he had shrunk down about half size, except the nose, which was double, being full of anxiety.

'Then git-go,' I roared, 'and never let me see you again till next year.'

'B-but you will come and say something to Mother?' said Nosy. And, in fact, I saw that I had made a little mistake. Nosy was frightened all right, out of his wits, but not out of his character. Which was just the same, only more so. Devoted and pig-headed. As if hammering made it tougher.

'You see,' said he greatly excited, 'it would make such a lot of difference if you spoke for me. Because Mother knows you're a famous artist.'

'Then she knows wrong. How does she know?'

'I told her.'

'How do you know?'

'Mr Plant told me first.'

'If you don't get that scholarship your parents ought to throw you out. After all they've done for you. And you ought to be shot for a fool, which is worse than murder. Only four more years scratching at the books and a nice government job for the rest of your life. Four years half work in exchange for fifty or sixty of no work on a regular income and a pension after. Made for life. Not another worry in the world.'

'But I *can't* be a government official—I want to be an artist.'

'Do what you like when you get that job. But make sure of it first. How can you be an artist without money? Why, look at me. I've been painting for fifty years, and at this moment I don't even possess brushes or paint. No, you can't go in for art without money from somewhere. Art is like roses—it's a rich feeder.' I talked quite brilliantly for a long time. But at the end of it, there was Nosy, with his red watery eyes, and his ugly face looking so ugly, and worried and miserable and obstinate and devoted, that I couldn't resist him, and I let him take me back to his home.

Neat little terrace house with a little front garden. Fifteen feet by ten. With four beds about the size of frypans and a piece of crazy paving just big enough to stand on.

Nosy had a key and took me in. Parlour in chintz with a good mahogany table. Bookcase of Dickens and Thackeray. Couple of French bronzes on the mantelpiece. Gilt clock. Brass grate. Pictures—family enlargements. Death of Nelson. Trade union card with religious and royal emblems. Mr Barbon came in. Middle-sized walrus with a squeezed up face and a head like a wedge of cheddar. Forget-me-not eyes in a couple of tit nests. A bit stooped. Blue suit with tight sleeves. About 1912. Hands like coal grabs. 'How do you do, sir? It is very kind of you to come.' 'Not at all.' 'I know your time is valuable.' 'Not a bit.' 'A famous gentleman like you, sir.' 'Not just yet.' 'But it's about my boy, Harry. My Minnie is a bit worried. You know how it is with mothers, and Harry's the youngest.' 'I know, I've had two boys myself.' 'Oh yes,' he said, not noticing what I'd said. 'Oh yes, it's hard on the mother. Our eldest went into the Air Force—got killed in an accident.' 'A lot of accidents everywhere. Babies drinking out of kettles, children going under lorries.' 'Yes sir, we're not the only ones. We oughtn't to complain, really. But of course you know what mothers are.' 'I know, I've had two.' 'Oh yes, of course,' he said, not hearing a word I said. 'Yes, of course, but Harry being the youngest, and he's been such a good son. Clever too. All his teachers thought no end of Harry. They said he was sure of a scholarship. This next September. An Oxford one. It would make the boy's fortune, you might say.'

And he went on telling me what a nice, clever good boy Harry was. And how he had always been his mother's comfort. But now she was worrying. I knew what women were.

Somebody came in at the front door, and Mr Barbon turned himself out of his chair and turned himself out of the door. Like a crane on a turntable. His arms were long enough. Going up and down. And the hands closing from all round like iron grabs. The door handle disappeared quite slowly, but you expected to see it come right off. Soft muttering outside like an old-fashioned donkey engine. And a woman's voice saying that she wouldn't, and she didn't. Mrs Barbon came in. Small and soft, neat nose and smooth white hair. Pretty face once but too short in the neck. She gave me a look as if she would like to poison me, and Mr Barbon said, 'This is Mr Jimson, Mother,' gave her a little push to make her do the polite. But she went back a bit and said, 'So you said,' keeping her eyes on me. Barbon swung round one of his grabs and pulled her sleeve. 'Mr Jimson is a friend of Harry's, Mother. He's the famous artist.' 'So you say, Tom. Do leave me alone.' 'Perhaps we'd better sit down,' said Mr Barbon. 'I don't want to sit down,' said Mrs Barbon; and then she said to me, 'I think you might have let the boy alone, Mr Johnson. Instead of spoiling his chances.' 'I beg your pardon, Mrs Barbon.' 'No, you don't care. Now you've got hold of him. You just turn him round your finger how you like. Ruining his whole life and breaking his father's heart.' 'Well, Mrs Barbon, I didn't—' 'And I may as well tell you I think a lot of artists ought to be stopped. The government ought to do something about it.' Well, I was sorry for the poor girl. It was a terrible thing for her to see her only darling suddenly fly off to the devil, just when he was going to make her proud and happy for her old age. Who would be a mother? 'I quite agree, Mrs Barbon,' I said, 'it's a bad business.' 'Then why do you go on at it for?'

'But, Mother,' said old Barbon.

'Please let me say one word, Tom. Without interrupting all the time. I think it's a shame, Mr Johnson, or whatever your name is. I think that a decent man ought to be ashamed to get hold of a boy like Harry who anybody can see is not fit to look after himself and young for his age and keep him running about on his errands when he might be doing his work and working up an honest Christian job and a proper life.'

'Quite right, Mrs Barbon. I—'

'Because you'd better know I don't call this a proper job for anyone that respects himself or wants to respect himself.'

'Quite true, Mrs Barbon. I've advised Harry several times to—'

'It isn't a job at all. It's a mean swindle by lazy good-for-nothings and won't-works.'

'I told Harry several times,' I said, 'that he ought to be working for his scholarship.'

'And what sort of living will he make as an artist?'

'None at all,' I said. 'I don't suppose he has any talent whatever.'

'That's all you know about it,' said Mrs Barbon. 'He took the art prize only last year and he got two bronze medals from the Art Society,' crushing me for my blindness to Nosy's genius.

'Even then, Mrs Barbon, an artist's life is very uncertain. It would be far better for the boy to get his scholarship first.'

'Then why have you stopped him working all these weeks—his masters say he spends half his time dodging round your studio or going to galleries and looking at pictures.'

'I didn't know—'

'And then last night—never coming home at all.'

'I was taken ill, and he very kindly—'

'All I can say is that if you want him, you'd better take him,' said Mrs Barbon, trembling all over. 'I don't want any more to do with a son of mine that goes about with such people and breaks his father's heart.'

'But, Mother,' said old Barbon.

'Will you be quiet, Tom. I know you want to smooth everything down and smooth it up as if it didn't matter. But I say, it does matter if the boy ruins his whole life and turns into a nasty dirty swindler and good-for-nothing and breaks your heart after all you've done for him.'

'But, M-mother,' said Nosy, going over to her, 'it's not t-true that artists are s-s-swindlers.'

'Do let me alone, Harry,' said the woman, closing her eyes as if exhausted by unreasonable interruptions. 'What do you know about it? Of course, nothing I say will make any difference—I know that already. You'll just go your own way. And treat your poor father like dirt. I don't mind. So if you don't choose to give any kind of explanation, Mr Johnson, or even say you're sorry for what you've done, perhaps you would go and leave us alone. As for Harry, he can go with you if he likes. But if he does, I don't want him back again.'

'But, Mother—' said old Barbon. Mrs Barbon then left the room, shutting the door behind her very carefully, and Mr Barbon apologized for her. 'She's a bit upset, Mr Jimson. Harry being the only one left. And, of course, we don't really feel like that about artists. It's an honourable trade. Only we were wondering if Harry would do any good at it.'

'Probably not, Mr Barbon. Very few people do any good at any of the arts. And I haven't seen any sign of genius in Harry. What he wants to do is to get his scholarship. That's safe.'

'S-s-safe,' said Nosy, hissing like a snake.

Mr Barbon then thanked me very politely for my visit and I came away. And Nosy came with me. But I gave him a lecture about the way he was treating his mother. 'She's right,' I said. 'If you go on like this, you'll ruin your own life and hers. You're breaking her heart as it is.'

But Nosy only looked more obstinate. What did he care about breaking his mother's heart? Not much more than a runaway horse cares for a shop window. Which he doesn't see, anyhow.

'B-but she's so unreasonable,' he said. 'If nobody is allowed to be an artist, art would stop.'

'Not a bit of it,' I said. 'You can't stop art. You just try, that's all. You'll always have amateurs. That is, everybody.'

'But are they any g-good?'

'Yes, the professional ones are good, the others are awful.'

'How do you become a professional amateur?'

'You give all your time to the job, and even then it's not enough.'

'Then what's the d-difference?'

'A big difference. The amateur has cash in the bank and goes on having it when he's a professional. That's what I tell you. Get some cash in the bank and then you can go in for art and be as bad as you like. You'll still be happy. Because the worse you are, the better pleased you'll be with yourself, and you'll be able to afford a nice little wife and nice little babies and nice little parties and nice little friends, and you'll get into some nice little society and get a whole lot of nice little compliments from all the other nice people.'

'But I don't want to be s-s-safe,' said Nosy.

'That's because you've had too much of safety. But it's not so safe as you think—safety. And when you've lost it, you can't get it back. Run along now and get down those books. And I tell you what, I'll teach you all about art.'

'What?' said Nosy.

'Yes,' I said. 'You get that scholarship and I'll teach you all about art. That is, all that one person can teach another, which isn't much.'

'You really mean it, Mr Jimson?'

'On my honour. Or I'd better say, on your honour.'

The boy seized me by both hands. 'Oh, Mr Jimson, how c-can I thank you?'

'We'll see about that when you've had your instruction. Now, off you go, and tell your ma I sent you.'

He turned away and actually ran towards home.

25. I turned up Ellam Street and made for Elsinore. My job, I thought, is to get that picture out of Mrs Coker's grip—to get her

185

out of the studio. Sir William must see the thing soon or he'll forget all about it.

And I was worried about the picture itself. Of course, a picture is always a worry. It's worse than a child for getting itself into trouble, and breaking your heart. But my recollection of the Fall was that Eve's legs were all wrong. You don't want a lot of agitation in the rising lines when the horizontal planes are so active. As far as I remember, I thought, those legs are too rococo for a landscape which ought to be as massive as rocks. Original forms. Solid ideas.

On the other hand, it seemed to me that the general organization was not bad. I had a feeling at the back of my notions that it would be better than I expected. I must have a look at the thing, I thought, if it costs me a black eye.

Now the truth was that, though I had sent letters to Mrs Coker every day, and even managed, on one dark evening, to put three rats through a side window, I hadn't yet taken the last decisive step. My idea was, if she wouldn't go by persuasion, to remove my picture and then take the windows and door off, and possibly some of the roof. Make a ruin of the place. And when she had been blown out, and rained out, I would go back again. I'd often lived in ruins before.

And I had formed, by careful observation, a pretty good idea of Mrs Coker's habits. She went shopping at any time she fancied, and she was usually away for an hour. So I only had to watch her off the premises, and then get to work with a screwdriver. And it had better be today, I thought, if I'm going to sell the Fall. I have no time to waste. I must close with the Professor at once before he gets thrown out again, or his Sir William has a fit. And the Fall will certainly need touching up, even if I pass those legs.

But I had bad luck. I waited there all that afternoon by the Eagle, and still Mrs Coker remained in garrison. I saw her now and then empty a bucket into the dustbin or throw a piece of coal at a cat, but she did not go shopping. Then it began to rain chandeliers in the afternoon sun; big drops which went through the thin spots in my overcoat like shot through blotting paper. And when I was trying to take cover against the side wall, down came young

Barbon, fizzing like a ginger beer bottle. He annoyed me. 'What the hell,' I said. 'Didn't you swear to go home and leave art alone and do some real work?'

'Oh, but Mr Jimson, I did work. And you know it's my holidays now. Since last week.'

'Holidays? The only chance you'll ever get to do your own job. As it ought to be done. My boy Tom always worked in the summer holidays. It's the best time to work because there's no masters to waste your time.'

'I d-did work, Mr Jimson. But I saw you going down Greenbank, and I thought you were going to paint on the Fall.'

'I wish I could paint on the Fall,' I said. 'But I have to wait till my lady guest goes out before I can even see the damn thing.' And like a fool I told him all about the Cokers. I am always inclined to talk too much to ugly boys, because they are so modest and so keen on everything and because they ask such a lot of questions. Of course, as soon as I explained the case to young Barbon, he got so excited that he could hardly speak. He was so sympathetic that I wanted to jump into the river. I like a little sympathy in the right place, but a lot of sympathy always makes me feel as if I had lost my clothes and didn't know where to hide. And when I had explained my plan for removing the doors and windows he rushed off to borrow a hatchet and screwdrivers and wanted to start at once. I had to tell him that this matter was more serious than that. 'There mustn't be any violence,' I said, 'or the thing wouldn't be legal. First we have to take formal possession, and then we can remove the doors and windows. That is the way bailiffs do it. But we must establish possession first so that if Mrs Coker calls in the police, we shall be able to make them think we thought we were on the right side of the law. We've got to have a case.'

But Nosy went on getting so excited and stammered so much that I could hardly speak. And so I began to get in a state and I should have ended in committing some foolish crime if Mrs Coker, about five o'clock, hadn't come out in her bonnet, with a string bag and Cokey's umbrella, and hurried away to the shops.

Nosy and I were at work in less than a minute. Nosy started on the windows outside with the screwdriver. But I went in to get the picture down. And there was Cokey in a blue pinafore like a landslide, perched on the side of a chair and knitting a pair of baby's drawers. 'Hullo, Cokey,' I said. 'How are you now?'

'I wish I wasn't anything or anywhere either. You better look out, Mr Jimson.'

'Your mother's off to the shops. I saw her this minute.'

'Yes, but she might come back. She's got a way of coming back. Especially since last week. What did you go and write those letters for?"

'Why does she think that I wrote them?' I said. For I was annoyed. Women are so unreasonable. They're always jumping to conclusions.

'Well, you did. Didn't you?'

'Your mother had better be careful making statements like that. Which she couldn't prove. They're slander.'

'Well, don't write any more,' said Cokey. 'They only put her in a temper, and then she takes it out of me. And I've got enough on my plate as it is. The time you put the rats in, she broke her umbrella over me.'

'Your mother is going to get a lesson,' I said. For I could see Nosy at work on the window hinges from the outside where Cokey couldn't see him. 'And I've come to claim my property.'

I began to take down the dining-room chairs piled against the sheet at the end of the room.

'If you're looking for your picture,' said Cokey, 'it isn't there.'

'Where is it then?' I gave a dive and pulled the sheet on one side. There was nothing behind but the boards. I was so surprised that I felt quite queer. As if someone had kicked me in the stomach.

'Where is it then?' I said. 'If the landlord took it, I'll go to law. I'll have damages off him. It's work in hand. Even a bailiff can't touch work in hand.'

'It wasn't the landlord. It was Mother.'

'Then it's robbery. What's she done with it?'

'She cut it up and mended the roof with it. Why, didn't you notice—'

I looked up to listen. And you could hear the rain rattling on the canvas like shot on a drum.

'You know how the boards used to leak,' said Cokey, 'but of course she had to have the canvas tarred over—it's made a lovely job.'

I felt as if the top of my skull was floating off, I was quite feeble. To lose the Fall like this, suddenly; it was like being told your home and family had fallen down a hole in the ground.

I looked at Cokey. There she was like a blue bag tied round the neck with string, with a white wood knob for a face. Calm as you please. I took my breath and said, 'You thought I'd done two years work on that picture to get it ready for the roof?'

'No,' said Cokey. 'But I didn't care. Not after Mother had talked to me for a bit. If Mother wanted to cut me into slices with a saw knife, she'd only have to talk to me for a bit and I'd go down on my knees and ask her to get on with the job. You don't know Mother's talk. It's chronic.'

'That picture was worth thousands of pounds, and I had a buyer for it. I'll run your mother in for five thousand pounds. The spiteful old devil.'

'Don't you call Mother names. She's had a hard time and don't you forget it.'

'What's that got to do with my picture?'

'What's the good of pictures to poor Mum. Pictures never did anything for her. Pictures never gave her what she'd a right to expect, did they?'

'What about my rights, Coker?'

'You don't need any rights. You're a man. But you won't be, if Mother catches you here again.'

'You've changed, Cokey, you used to think a lot of my pictures.' For I was still feeble. I really thought I should cry. I didn't know how I could live without the Fall.

'Changed,' said Cokey. 'Well, you've only got to look at me.'

'I mean in your feelings.' My legs were so weak that I was sentimental. Cokey's bosom would probably have felt like old tins and door knobs, but I was ready to fall on it.

'My feelings,' said Cokey, 'I feel like I want to do murder or something, and so would you if you'd taken about a barrel full of pink pills and pints of oil and jumped off tables and run around carrying trunks on your head and fallen downstairs and all for nothing. Well, I should have known. God had something up his sleeve, ever since Willie made his first pass at me behind the church. It was too good to be permanent. I'm not complaining. But if I should have an accident with a bus or a traction engine, don't let anybody send flowers. Send along a pickaxe to bash my head in and make a good job of it. Put me in a sausage machine and can me into cat's meat and write Bitch, second quality, on the lid.' 'Why, whoever called you a bitch, Cokey?' For I was still feeling soft. 'They'd better not, but they think it. And the ones that don't think it, laugh.' 'After all, Cokey old girl, this little development of yours isn't so very uncommon in the neighbourhood. I should think there must be half a dozen young ladies in the same temporary difficulty down Ellam Street alone, on any day of the month.' 'And you think that makes it any better—to get mixed up with that lot of dirty sluts?' 'They can't say anything.' 'Oh, can't they, the worse, the more. And think! You can hear them from here.' 'Well, I don't see you need mind what a lot of nasty natured women say or think about you.' 'Oh go away, do, Mr Jimson. You men make my guts wind. And there isn't room.'

26.

And just then Nosy came in by the back door to tell me that Mrs Coker was coming in by the front one. So I went away by the middle window. Nosy followed half a minute later with an ear like scarlet fever. But he didn't seem to notice it. 'I g-got f-four windows off,' he said, 'and hid them in the ditch. D-did you get the picture?'

'No,' I said, 'the picture is caput. The Fall is finished.' And I told him what Mrs Coker had done to my picture. And the boy was so astonished that I thought he would have a fit. 'I can't b-believe it,' he said. 'N-no, I can't believe it,' and his grief was real. It seemed that he had given his heart to that picture. 'It's awful,' he said. 'How did she d-dare? The h-horrible old b-brute.' And he began to get angry. For he was truly suffering. He had lost his first love. His nose was as red as beetroot, and his voice sounded like a little dog shut into a cellar. 'It's a c-crime,' he said. 'It's t-terrible to think of.' He was young for a real grief. Irreparable loss.

It was raining warm dishwater out of dirty rags, and

when I took off my hat because it was dripping down my neck, a quart fell into my waistcoat.

'B-but what can you expect of p-people like that?' said Nosy, getting angrier and barking at the stones. 'They don't d-deserve to have artists. We B-British are a l-lot of b-bloody fffphilistines, we aren't f-fit to h-have g-great artists born among us.'

'Go on, Nosy,' I said. 'Blow up the British like a true Briton. Blackguard them as much as you like. They're old. They don't expect anything better. They're used to it.'

'It's true,' said Nosy. 'They d-don't d-deserve to have great artists.'

'Nobody does,' I said, 'but they go on getting them whether they like them or not.'

For the fact is I was beginning to feel very lively. You might say, gay. I couldn't believe it at first. And so I went on being dejected.

'A wonderful picture like that,' said Nosy. 'P-put on the r-roof.'

'A serious thing for me,' I said. But I almost burst out laughing at Nosy's indignation. And I decided to give way to my gaiety. It's not an easy thing to do when you have a real grievance, and if I had been fifty years younger I shouldn't have done it. But for some time now I had been noticing that on the whole, a man is wise to give way to gaiety, even at the expense of a grievance. A good grievance is highly enjoyable, but like a lot of other pleasures, it is bad for the liver. It affects the digestion and injures the sweetbread. So I gave way and laughed.

'W-what is it?' said Nosy, quite terrified. He thought I was going mad with grief.

'I was laughing,' I said.

'You are too g-good, Mr Jimson, too n-noble. You oughtn't to f-forgive a crime like that—a crime against s-s-civilization. I'd like to cut that old woman's throat. I'd like to cut the whole B-British throat. The d-dirty fffphilistines.'

'Not exactly noble, Nosy,' I said. For it's dangerous to be thought noble, when you're only being sensible. It causes fatty degeneration of the judgment. 'The fact is, I was sick of that god-damned picture.'

'It was the f-finest picture I ever saw,' said Nosy, getting angry with me. 'You m-mustn't s-say such things.'

'I never knew how I hated it,' I said, 'till now. I've disliked all my pictures, but I never hated one so much as the Fall.'

'Mr J-Jimson,' said Nosy. 'No p-please—it's not a j-joke.' The poor boy was in agony. I was blaspheming against his faith.

'But what I do like,' I said, 'is starting new ones.' And the very notion made me feel full of smiles. The vision of the nice smooth canvas in front of me, say the Ruffiano, newly primed in white, and then the first strokes of the brush. How lovely the stuff is when you've just put it down. While it's still all alive and before it dies and sinks and fades. Paint. Lovely paint. Why, I could rub my nose in it or lick it up for breakfast. I mean, of course, paint that doesn't mean anything except itself. The spiritual substance. The pure innocent song of some damn fool angel that doesn't know even the name of God.

'I love starting, Nosy,' I said, 'but I don't like going on. The trouble with me is that I hate work, that's why I'm an artist. I never could stand work. But you can't get away from it in this fallen world. The curse of Adam.'

'N-no, p-please, Mr J-Jimson. You know you have s-sacrificed your whole life to art, and no one works harder. I've seen you myself working all day and never even s-stopping to eat.'

'I was probably altering something or taking something out, that's a way of starting new. But not a good way. It only leads to more trouble. More problems, more work. No, you want to start clear, with a clean canvas, and a bright new shining idea or vision or whatever you call the thing. A sort of coloured music in the mind.'

And the very words made me grin all down my back. Certainly an artist has no right to complain of his fate. For he has great pleasures. To start new pictures. Even the worst artist that ever was, even a one-eyed mental deficient with the shakes in both hands who sets out to paint the chicken-house, can enjoy the first stroke. Can think, By God, look what I've done. A miracle. I have transformed a chunk of wood, canvas, etc., into a spiritual fact, an eternal beauty. I am God. Yes, the beginning, the first stroke on a picture, or a back fence, must be one of the keenest pleasures open to mankind. It's certainly the greatest that an artist can have. It's also the only one. And it doesn't last long—usually about five minutes. Before the first problem shows its devil face. And then he's in hell for the next month or six months or whatever it may be. But I didn't tell Nosy why I felt so cheerful. He wouldn't have understood. He would have been shocked. And it is easy to offend the faith of the little ones. It also does a lot of harm.

'A m-m-masterpiece,' said Nosy, flipping a pear-drop off his cutwater. He was getting hysterical. Everything at once was too much.

'Talk sense, Nosy,' I said. 'It wasn't even finished.'

'A m-m-m-masterpiece,' said Nosy. As if I had been trying to strangle his first-born. Which was just what I was doing. 'Go on, Nosy,' I said. 'It couldn't be. Nothing is a masterpiece—a real masterpiece—till it's about two hundred years old. A picture is like a tree or a church, you've got to let it grow into a masterpiece. Same with a poem or a new religion. They begin as a lot of funny words. Nobody knows whether they're all nonsense or a gift from heaven. And the only people who think anything of 'em are a lot of cranks or crackpots, or poor devils who don't know enough to know anything. Look at Christianity. Just a lot of floating seeds to start with, all sorts of seeds. It was a long time before one of them grew into a tree big enough to kill the rest and keep the rain off. And it's only when the tree has been cut into planks and built into a house and the house has got pretty old and about fifty generations of ordinary lumpheads who don't know a work of art from a public convenience, have been knocking nails in the kitchen beams to hang hams on, and screwing hooks in the walls for whips and guns and photographs and calendars and measuring the children on the window frames and chopping out a new cupboard under the stairs to keep the cheese and murdering their wives in the back room and burying them under the cellar flags, that it begins even to feel like a real religion. And when the whole place is full of dry rot and ghosts and old bones and the shelves are breaking down with old wormy books that no one could read if they tried, and the attic floors are bulging through the servants' ceilings with old trunks and top-boots and gasoliers and dressmaker's dummies and ball frocks and dolls-houses and pony saddles and blunderbusses and parrot cages and uniforms and love letters and jugs without handles and bridal pots decorated with forget-me-nots and a piece out at the bottom, that it grows into a real old faith, a masterpiece which people can really get something out of, each for himself. And then, of course, everybody keeps on saying that it ought to be pulled down at once, because it's an insanitary nuisance.'

'I d-don't care w-what anyone says,' said Nosy, still angry with me. 'It's a s-shame. It's a wicked s-shame.' He was shivering and steaming like a sheep just out of the dip. It was his first great sorrow. Without remedy. And the rain was coming down like soda-water bubbles out of new cottonwool in tufts. It fell slowly in a neat pattern and didn't make a sound. We came to the end of Greenbank and stopped. Nosy looked round as if to say, 'Where shall we go?' But I hadn't the price of a beer, and so there was nowhere to go.

'The f-finest picture,' said Nosy. And he looked as if he might cry at any moment. He hadn't got used to the never-more feeling.

'The rain's over,' I said, and we turned back. 'No,' I said, 'it's a providence,' and I pulled out the top of my trousers in front to let the water run off my belly. 'That picture has had me by the throat for the last two years. Choking my life out—the worst enemy I ever had.' And as we came to the end of Greenbank we turned back again. The little rain-drops were smaller and closer. They were falling like a cold steam; slow and white, which was wetter than water. It was as if the air had turned into soda bubbles. The sun came through like through a frosted window, and the sky was like the top of the sea to a fish's eye; Roman candles and blue fire. There was more water in my boots than outside.

'B-but why should everything and everybody be always against real g-greatness,' said Nosy, 'real jj-genius?'

'Well,' I said, 'suppose you were just sitting down in a quiet corner behind the dustbin with a jug of beer and a wasp came and stung you on the bottom, how would you like the wasp?'

'Look at Keats and S-Shelley, and Hopkins and S-s-Cézanne and Van H-h-Gogh and you.'

'And me,' I said. 'What about me?' I was upset. To get a smack like that just when I was feeling gay.

'L-look at the way they t-treat you—it's awful,' said

Nosy. 'You haven't even anywhere to live—it's aw-awful—it's t-terrible.' And Nosy really was in tears, or perhaps it was only the rain down his beak which made him make such comic faces.

And I felt almost like crying myself just because he was crying. Over my own woes. And yet, as I say, I was in particularly good spirits. There, you see, I said to myself, talk to anybody in a friendly way and in half a minute he'll be pitying you and then you'll be pitying yourself and damning the world and all the rest of the nonsense. Getting in the worst possible state. And you can say good-bye to work for another week. And I flew out at Nosy. 'What the devil do you mean, young man? Who's treated me how? What's terrible? If you had a little more sense and decent feeling,' I said, 'you'd realize that I've been very well treated. Quite as well as I deserve. Why, I haven't an enemy in the world, except, of course, that blasted picture. But a special providence in the shape of Ma Coker has now delivered me of that. At least I hope so. I daresay the snake will need another knock or two. Cut it in four pieces and it will try to bite and spit poison in your eye at one end and tie itself round you at the other. That picture was a curse to me. It left me no freedom to paint. To paint,' I said, and my fingers closed on a brush and executed a sweet stroke, from left to right, my favourite movement.

And all at once I knew why I was sick of the Fall. And I knew what I wanted to do. That blue-grey shape on the pink. The tower. The whatever it was, very round and heavy. Something like a gasometer at full stretch without its muzzle. Or possibly an enamel coffee-pot. And chrome yellow things like Egyptian columns or leeks or dumb-bells or willows or brass candlesticks, in front; and to the left, also round but much smoother, a fat pillar or glass rolling-pin coming out of green waves or mountains or crumpled baize—very dark green with a broken surface. And a strong recession. A dark red below, curving up towards the right, a beach or range of mountains or German sausage. The pink, rather misty, volcanic eruption or cottage wallpaper. And a swag of red across the top left, clouds of volcanic smoke, or a plush curtain. All very solid. But not hard. Three-dimensional. With great attention to texture. 'And besides,' I said to Nosy, 'I've got a far better thing all ready.' It wasn't all ready, but I felt that it was going to be ready in five minutes. 'All ready in my eye.'

'A b-better thing?' said Nosy, in a doubtful voice. Like a child whose oldest boat has just gone down the drain, when you tell him that you've got something much nicer in the cupboard. 'But it wouldn't be the F-Fall.'

'Yes,' I said, for why shouldn't I call it the Fall? 'It might as well be that as anything else. The blue tower could be Adam and the red wave Eve, and the yellow things the serpents.' 'Yes,' I said, 'it's going to be the Fall, only much better. Much solider. I've learnt a lot since I started that last Fall. And I know what was wrong with it. It wasn't immediate enough. It didn't hit you hard enough. It wasn't solid enough.'

'S-solid enough?' said Nosy. 'No,' I said, 'what was the Fall after all. The discovery of the solid hard world, good and evil. Hard as rocks and sharp as poisoned thorns. And also the way to make gardens.'

'G-gardens?'

'Gardens. Adam's work. You have to make the bloody things and pile up the rocks and keep the roses in beds. But you don't get the thorns in your tender parts, by accident—you get them in your fingers, on purpose, and like it, because a garden, as old Randypole Blake would say, is a spiritual being. Why,' I said, quite surprised by my own eloquence in inventing all this stuff, 'it happens every day. The old old story. Boys and girls fall in love, that is, they are driven mad and go blind and deaf and see each other not as human animals with comic noses and bandy legs and voices like frogs, but as angels so full of shining goodness that like hollow turnips with candles put into them, they seem miracles of beauty. And the next minute the candles shoot out sparks and burn their eyes. And they seem to each other like devils, full of spite and cruelty. And they will drive each other mad unless they have grown some imagination. Even enough to laugh.'

'I-m-m-m,' said Nosy.

'Imagination, understanding. To see behind the turnips, to enter into each other's minds. My first girl had a face like a pig, and only one eye. She was a trifle soft too, and about twenty years older than I was at fifteen. She used to clean out the pigsty and byres, and she never washed.

When we had our first quarrel, I called her bitch and bastard, which was all quite true. But she chased me half a mile with a fork. And I thought I should never forgive her. At fifteen I had a lot of dignity. But when I needed her again, I thought things over and I understood that the woman, though a pig to look at, and worse to smell, had some feelings of her own. Even some self-respect. So I went and apologized and gave her a present of some of my mother's flowers. And she burst into tears and said I was an angel. The Fall had given her imagination too, and we made it up and were very happy several times and had some more fork fights and made it up again till my uncle caught us and had her sent to an institution where she pretty soon died. She was used to sleeping in ditches and middens, and she couldn't bear comfort. But she gave me my first taste of real knowledge, the knowledge of good and evil, heaven and hell, and she taught me that love doesn't grow on the trees like apples in Eden—it's something you have to make. And you must use your imagination to make it too, just like anything else. It's all work, work. The curse of Adam. But if he doesn't work, he doesn't get anything, even love. He just tumbles about in hell and bashes himself and burns himself and stabs himself. The fallen man—nobody's going to look after him. The poor bastard is free—a free and responsible citizen. The Fall into freedom. Yes, I might call it the Fall into Freedom.'

'F-f-free,' said Nosy, with his eyes starting out of his head. For he didn't know what I was talking about.

'Yes,' I said. 'Free to cut his bloody throat, if he likes, or understand the bloody world, if he likes, and cook his breakfast with hell-fire, if he likes, and construct for himself a little heaven of his own, if he likes, all complete with a pig-faced angel and every spiritual pleasure including the joys of love; or also, of course, he can build himself a little hell full of pig-faced devils and all material miseries including the joys of love and enjoy in it such tortures of the damned that he will want to burn himself alive a hundred times a day, but won't be able to do it because he knows it will give such extreme pleasure to all his friends. He's in hell, that is, real hell—material hell, nailed to the everlasting fire with a red-hot clag; and his

197

kicks and wriggles are enough to make a cat laugh. In fact, they are the chief amusement of all the other citizens in the same position.'

'The f-f-fall into f-f-f,' said Nosy, trembling all over and twitching his nose like a rabbit in front of a doubtful lettuce.

I threw the water out of my hat and once more it fell down the opening of my waistcoat. This was due to carelessness. But I was so pleased with the enjoyments of genius which to angels look like torment and insanity, that I said to myself, gurgle, oh navel; freeze, you belly; trickle and shiver, old spout, I haven't time to worry about your troubles. Down slaves, and weep. For I am the king of the castle. 'Yes,' I said, 'the Fall into Freedom, into the real world among the everlasting forms, the solid. Solid as the visions of the ancient man. And that's what I'm going to do in this new Fall. Adam like a rock walking, and Eve like a mountain bringing forth, with sweat like fiery lava, and the trees shall stand like souls pent up in metal; cut bronze and silver and gold. With leaves like emerald and jade, cut and engraved with everlasting patterns sharp as jewels, as crystals, and the sun like a ball of solid fire, turned on a lathe.'

'Yes, yes,' said Nosy. 'I s-see, a kind of dream.'

'Dream be damned,' I said. 'It's got to be real.'

'But will it l-look real?'

'To hell with looks,' I said. 'Nobody ever saw the real— but you can feel it— By God, I feel it now. For the first time in about two years since that bloody picture first got hold of me. Yes, I feel it—the solid forms of the imagination.'

'Solid,' cried Nosy. 'Imagination.'

We had come to the other end of Greenbank. And it was raining scullery taps. Out of a sky like a battle. Great jagged lumps and balloons of water, with oyster domes and a green splash. We stood among fountains, under waterfalls. And Nosy looked round thinking, 'Where are we going to?' 'You'd better go home, Nosy,' I said. 'You're wet.'

But he knew I couldn't go anywhere. So we turned back.

'Solid imagination,' said Nosy. 'Yes, I s-s-s-see.'

'What do you sus-see?' I said. For I felt I had been talking too much. Dangerous to talk too much about your work. It fixes it. It nails it down. And then it bleeds. It begins to die. 'What I'd like to sus-see is a studio—and paints and brushes—in fact, some cash.'

'I s-see the idea,' said Nosy, giving a loud sneeze.

'How can you see an idea?' I said.' 'You must be a clever chap. Can you see the price of a pint in my pocket?'

'I sus-see what you mean.'

'You must be a bloody conjuror. I didn't mean anything—'

'But Mr J-Jimson, you s-said you see—'

'I see my picture. In fact, I don't sus-see it. I only imagine it, and probably I'm imagining all wrong. But what the devil, you're wet through. You'll catch cold. And then what about that scholarship—time you went home. Good-bye, Nosy.'

'B-but, Mr J-Jimson,' and I thought he would grab me by the coat. 'You *did* mean something else—you were talking about the truth—the real—'

Yes, I thought, I knew I was talking too much. And I said, 'That's enough, Nosy, or too much. You cut along home to your mother and change your socks. It's opening time, and I rather think I see Mr Ollier going into the Eagle.'

'And you said about religion,' said Nosy, making eyes at me as if I was a slot machine with the wisdom of the world at a penny a shot. 'You go home to your mammy where you belong,' I said, 'and get on with the books. Or you'll come to a bad end.' And I gave him a push and made a dart for it into the Eagle.

It wasn't Ollier. But Bert Swope was there and he stood me a pint in exchange for rude remarks about the state of my boots, trousers, coat, etc., and the way I smelt. I like Bert. He's always a tonic when one has been talking too much.

27. When I went back to Elsinore that evening, there was the Professor waiting for me. Sir William had made an offer—one hundred to three hundred guineas. I told him at once that all I wanted was an advance of a hundred pounds. For a new studio and materials. 'I have the best thing I ever did all ready. It only needs putting down.'

The Professor looked like a judge; judicious. This meant that he didn't know what to say.

'I've even got an option on the canvas. Twelve by fifteen.'

The Professor looked like an angel. Illuminated. This meant that he saw how to wriggle out of a difficulty. 'It's a big thing,' he said.

'Big in every way,' I said. 'The very biggest.'

'I'm afraid Sir William wouldn't have room for it. What he really had in his mind was something of the same nature as that magnificent thing at Mr Hickson's.'

'What, the Bath?'

'He would give three hundred guineas for anything of that quality.'

'I haven't painted stuff like that for fifteen years.'

'You don't know perhaps where one might be found? Perhaps one of your early patrons might care to sell?'

'I hadn't any early patrons—except Hickson and one or two speculating dealers, who cashed in long ago. But if Sir William wants to make an investment, I'd let him have the new Fall for a thousand—that's guineas, of course. And what's more, I'll give him a frame, a real carved one, for another hundred—guineas again.'

But the Professor looked like a maiden lady, about to retire after the picnic, behind a bush. 'I'm very much afraid,' he said, 'that Sir William will say he hasn't room. He specially mentioned one of the Sara Monday period. Not necessarily a large one. Sir William's object is always quality.'

'The best English meat,' I said. And I was going to tell the Professor that his job as cricket and my partner was not to act as pimp to Sir William, but as salesman to me. To sell my work while I was doing it.

But suddenly I had an idea. And I said to the Professor, 'I don't think much of Sir William's taste, if he'd rather have a study from the nude than a real picture. But I believe I might be able to get him what you call one of the Sara Monday period, and a good one too. One of the best I ever did of the old skin.'

The Professor looked like a choir-boy when the paid tenor comes in wrong. Bursting out of his collar with joy.

'Splendid. Good news, indeed. And if it's anything like as good as Mr Hickson's Bath I think I could suggest to Sir William that three hundred and fifty wouldn't be too much.'

'Guineas?'

'Guineas, of course.'

'And how do we split?'

The Professor looked like a Protestant saint when the cannibal offered him the choice of taking six wives or being boiled alive. He wanted to mortify some flesh, but he didn't know which. 'Really, Mr Jimson,' he said, 'I had no idea—'

'What about the other fifty, if you get it?'

'No, no, I couldn't take a commission.'

'No, of course not. But I tell you what, I'll form a committee and give you a token of esteem. That's either a marble clock or a cheque. Or both. Think it over and let me know. And a handbag for your wife.'

The Professor looked like a horse about to receive the nosebag. Smiling but thoughtful. 'I haven't yet committed that rash act.' 'There you're wrong,' I said. 'A good wife would make a man of you, provided that all the raw materials are available.' 'I fear I couldn't support a wife.' 'Then let her support you. All my wives supported me. It's a very good plan. It gives them a serious interest in life, and it leaves you free to get on with your work.'

But the Professor shook his head and smiled; and went round the corner and wrote it all down in his notebook. Epigrams of the late Mr Gulley Jimson. 'With reference to this flash of the typical Jimson wit, it might be added that Mr Jimson was exceptionally fortunate in his matrimonial ventures, if we can venture such a description.'

But I couldn't wait till next morning. I was in such a fret. For my idea was that if Sara still had any of the canvases which Hickson had left with her, she wouldn't have them long. Some dealer would hear about them and jump in with an offer.

I borrowed a shilling from Plant, and I was on the bus next morning by half-past nine. By good luck it was a Tuesday, so I could hope to find the old contriver alone. I didn't want to have any difficulties with the husband.

But when I rang Sara's bell the door hopped open about six inches and a yellow woman put her face in the crack.

A face like the breast bone of a chicken, all nose and hard cheek.

'No brushes, no cleaning stuffs, no buttons and nothing to give away,' she said, and began to shut again.

I put my foot in the crack. 'Excuse me, madam, does Mrs Monday live here?'

The door hopped open again rather wider than before and the yellow bird snapped her beak at me. 'No, she doesn't. She's gone, and if it's one of her bills, it's nothing to do with us. She hadn't any right to order on credit.'

'You don't know where she's gone, do you?'

'122, Chatfield Buildings, down the allotments. Mr Byles. Ask for Mrs Byles, I should think. Not that she's any right to that name,' but she shut the door so quickly that I couldn't use my foot.

Chatfield Buildings were a long way off, getting towards the river. Six sets of yellow tenements—standing up among a lot of little houses like six rusty corned beef cans bogged in a muddy pool, full of blue ripples. Half a mile of concrete road led up to them across a brickfield; and about twenty acres of allotments, straight as a drainpipe. Rows of little trees had been planted on each side, but half of them were dead, kicked to pieces by kids or scratched to death by cats. And the allotments were in their April state, a bit bare except for regiments of bean sticks and rows of tool-houses like drunken paupers staggering about in the mud; some on their noses, some on their knees, some with felt hats, some with whitewash hats, some in rusty tin.

When I had travelled across this land of Ulro, I found the buildings on the other side of a road, behind a lot of high railings, like an isolation hospital. They stood in a little desert of asphalt, where some kids were running about making a noise like a battle in a railway tunnel.

122 was on the ground floor in the fourth house on the left. When I had gone down a long dark passage, I came to a smell like washingday, though it was a Tuesday, and a pool of steaming water across the bricks. Then I knocked and out came a man about seven foot high and four foot wide, in a blue flannel shirt without a collar, red braces and cream corduroys. His bald head was as white as a peeled almond, but his face was the colour of prune juice; and he had a large waterfall moustache like a spray of nico-

tine mixture. His nose was like a pear with a dent across the small end as if someone had chopped it with a hatchet; and his eyes were as green as bottle-stoppers. He had a black leather strap about three inches wide on his right wrist. Genus, walrus Londonius; species, Longus Bottomus. A fine old bull from the Isle of Dogs.

'Ullo,' he barked at me. Then he thought a minute, opened his mouth and barked, a good deal louder, 'ULLO.'

I knew what he meant, and I was just going to explain that I hadn't come to murder Sara or steal the silver, when I saw, in the little triangle between the crook of his elbow and his shirt, Sara waving her head at me and making a face as if to say, 'Not a word.' So I answered, 'Excuse me, but is this 123?'

He thought a bit and answered in a bellow, 'NO.'

After another half minute's pondering he came to a further decision, and shouted, 'NO, IT AIN'T.'

'What a pity,' I said. 'Thank you very much,' and I went out again. But Mr Byles followed me to the top of the steps and when I reached the asphalt he spat on my head. But it may have been an accident due to bad aim. I don't want to think evil of a man like that.

When I got to the ground, I went round the corner into the next staircase, as if looking for somebody, and walked slowly up. You could see the railings out of the windows. I stopped at the top window for twenty minutes before some woman began to take an interest, and put her head out every few seconds to see that I wasn't stealing the bricks. So then I went down to the next window. And after about forty minutes, I saw Mr Byles come out of his door below with a spade and a fork on his shoulder, and make for the allotments. So I nipped down again and nipped into Sara's.

It was a long time before she opened to me, and then she was in her petticoat with a sack tied over it, and bare ankles. Hair all coming down in grey streaks, and face streaming. I thought her face had shut up a good deal since I'd seen her last, shorter in the chin and bigger in the nose. And when she turned round she had a regular charwoman's back, the high hump.

'Well, so there you are, Gulley,' she said. 'Fancy. You did give me a surprise. And I was just in a twitter lest you might say something to Byles. Not that he would mind you

203

coming in, except perhaps just when he was going out to his allotment. Well, I've often wondered what had happened to you.' So she fussed off into the kitchen, chirping away, but not in the old style or even the old voice. Never looking at me or talking to me, but sometimes at the wall and sometimes with her back turned, here, there and all round, as if it didn't matter very much what she said or whether I heard her or not. Hullo, I thought, this is new. Sara's really getting an old lady, running like a millstream late in winter, when there's no mill to turn.

'Oh dear,' she simmered, bobbing at the corners. 'What a mess—I was just having a turnout.'

And, in fact, the kitchen was all upsides. Chairs standing on the table, a pail in the middle of the floor, mops and brooms. Rows of beer bottles against the wall behind the door. Smashed chair propped up by the window. Two other chairs standing on the table and everything steaming wet.

'Yes, just when you're having a real turnout, somebody's sure to come,' said Sara in her old woman's way; a gay voice and a sad forehead; wrinkling up her eyebrows and champing her jaws. 'Not but what I'm real glad to see you, Gulley—well, of course,' giving me sometimes her back and sometimes her shoulder.

Yes, I thought. Sara's going away from this life, she's going from me, growing old. She's applied for the Chilledstern hundreds. She's climbing on the shelf.

I put my arm round her apron string. 'I hope you are glad to see me, Sall,' I said. 'And what sort of a mess? What's happened to you—what's happened to the life policy, I mean Fred?'

'Well,' said Sara, pulling down a chair and wiping the seat. 'It was the bills. They came out before I'd expected.'

'Bills always do—haven't you learnt that yet?—how much did you owe this time?'

'I don't know,' said Sara. 'It wasn't Fred, it was that sister, Doris—she got hold of him. Well, his weak side was always petty cash. No, I don't know how much it came to—but they took all my things—there's a dry chair for you. Wait, I'll put this mat on it. You don't want to get lumbago.'

'Took all your things, Sara?' for I was surprised. And I thought, So that's the end of the pictures if she had

204

'em. I might have expected that. You never know where it's coming from, but you always get it.

'All my things,' said Sara, 'two armchairs, two tables, the carpet that Monday gave me for my drawing-room, seven silver teaspoons and the tea caddy, four damask tablecloths and nine napkins, three silk cushions—'

'They can't do that, Sara. You must get a lawyer.'

'They said there wouldn't be enough to pay and I didn't want an argument. Well, that Doris said she'd go to the police, and I didn't want any more trouble. I suppose it was my own fault. You'll have some tea, Gulley? I wish I could give you something better, but there isn't anything in the house.'

And as she turned round to fill the kettle at the sink I saw that she had a black eye. A real damson. Blue with a bloom. And shut right up. A blinder. 'Hullo,' I said. 'What's wrong with your glim, Sall?'

'A wasp stung it. I haven't got any cake. But wouldn't you like a piece of bread and jam, or bread and bacon?'

'A wasp in April,' I said. 'More like a friend. What is Mr Byles like as a master—is he particular about drinking level?'

'Mr Byles has always stood by me,' said Sara, 'and he took me in at short notice when I'd nowhere to go and didn't know where to turn.'

'Why didn't you come to me, Sara?'

'What would you want with me when you hadn't enough to feed yourself much less a useless old woman that's only fit for a coffin? No, even when Mr. Byles was lodging with us he always stood up for me against that Doris, and he said that if ever I was in trouble I'd only got to come to him, and so I did, and he took me in. He may be a bit rough, but he's a Christian in his inside, Gulley, and I won't hear a word against him.'

The old lady was getting warmed up and forgetting the weight of her grey hairs. 'No, Gulley, I honour a man like Byles that stands by his word to a woman when he might fairly take it back, for the truth is that when he gave it to me, I still had a young bone or two in my flesh, but when I came round to his door and asked for a bed, I was a poor old castaway and a sight to boot, for I'd been crying my eyes away over poor little Dicky and my things and it all happening so sudden. Well, it makes me cold still to think what I must have looked like—I wasn't fit for the gypsies much less human company. And Mr Byles just threw open the door and said, "Mrs Monday, I said I'd make you welcome, and so you are, so come in and say no more about it. Least said," he said, "soonest mended." And here I've been ever since.'

'A man of few words, Mr Byles,' I said, 'his fist is quicker than his tongue. But I'd sooner he tried it on Fred than you. And I've half a mind to tell him so. I know you sometimes have a provoking way with you, one way or another, but I don't like to see you with that eye, Sara. Even if you aren't my property any longer I've got a kind of husband's feeling about your amenities.'

'I never said Mr Byles hit me in the eye, for I'm sure he never meant to, and even if he had I'm sure he had excuse with the amount of trouble they give in the department. The young ones putting all the heavy work on him just out of spite because he won't admit he's getting a bit stiff and short of breath. I shouldn't wonder if they didn't kill him one of these days, with his heart. He's often as blue as this apron after only climbing the steps, but it's no good telling him he ought to see a doctor. He can't bear doctors, and though I tell him doctors aren't hospitals, you can't expect him to change his ways at his time of life. I can only thank God he'll never make me go to hospital, and if my time is due it will come on me in my own home. I have to thank Byles for that, even if he does go and kill himself out of obstinacy.'

'Come on, Sall,' I said. 'We're not dead yet, unless we like to think so. And I daresay you had a few pounds put away in your box—they didn't get your box, I suppose.'

'They didn't leave me a shilling, Gulley. Even to bury me. Well, would you believe it, they came upon me in my bed, and that woman, God forgive her, she even went through my stays. Yes, she took seventeen golden sovereigns out of my stays, my funeral money that had been saving up for eleven years, ever since poor Rozzie died. Why, they even took up the floor, and they'd have broken in my box, but Fred thought it might be against the law. Not but what they didn't keep my box—yes, with all my things, even my mother's Bible. They kept the whole box, and if it hadn't been that Mr Byles went to fetch it for me and threatened to break the door in, and wring that Doris's neck—'

'So you got your box.'

'Byles brought it away, thank God, or I really don't know how I should have got over it. Well, Gulley, you may say it's a sign of being old, and perhaps it is, and I know I'm an old woman, but I don't think I could have borne it, to lose my box. Why, I got that box when I first went out to service in the year before the old Queen's jubilee and it's been with me ever since. In my grand days when indeed poor Monday wouldn't let it out of the attic for shame of its being such a poor servanty kind of thing, and in all my coming-down days since.'

'I seem to remember, Sara, that you used to keep some of my old drawings and sketches in your box—sketches of yourself—'

Sara began to shake her head, so I held up my hand and went on talking fast. I knew my Sara. Never to let her tell any lies until she understood the position. Because afterwards she might feel obliged to stick to them, even when she didn't want to. Sara was a woman all through. She had a sense of honour even in drink, and she was always particular not to change her mind or admit to a lie, on the same day. 'Wait a minute, Sara,' I said. 'There's money in this— Do you want to make twenty pounds?'

Sara's face changed and she turned her good eye on me with quite a sharp look. 'I should indeed,' she said, 'if I could do it honestly and without upsetting Byles. For 'tis the least I can do for him, not to put him out. But how can you get twenty pounds, Gulley? I'm sure you yourself could do with a new fit out from top to toe—'

'It's an offer, Sall. For one of those canvases which don't belong to you, anyhow. But Hickson seems to have said that you could keep my property, and you and I are old friends.'

'Canvases. What canvases?'

'The ones in your box.'

Sara looked me in the eyes. She was trying to make out if I knew anything, or was only guessing. But of course by the way she looked, I knew that she had something in her box. Sara was never a good deceiver because she never took enough trouble. She had the natural art; but she never improved on it. Relied too much on her charm and the inspiration of the moment.

'There's nothing in my box,' said Sara.

'No?' Hickson seemed to think there might be. And there certainly was when you first went off from me and took up with old Mr W. Drawings at least. You admitted it.

'Oh no, Gulley. I couldn't have. I never went off from you. It was you went off from me. And as for poor Mr Wilcher, I never thought but to be his housekeeper only. Oh dear. But there's the gas going down, and goodness knows if I've got a shilling.' And she went bobbing about again. She was in such a fluster what with the pictures and Byles in the background, and my talk of Mr W., that I could have laughed. She never could bear me to talk of Mr W., because she would always swear she had never been anything but a housekeeper to him. But she knew that I knew differently.

'It's funny you should forget about the drawings, Sara,' I said. 'Because it was the day I had that explanation with Mr W. about you.'

'Oh dear, oh dear, I'll never get done.' And she went clump, clump down the cellar steps with two brooms clattering on the walls and a pail creaking in her hand. Strategic retreat, with equipment intact.

But it was ten minutes to eleven and I knew she would be back to her tea. Not the devil himself could keep her from her morning tea.

28.

Wilcher was a rich lawyer, with a face like a bad orange. Yellow and blue. A little grasshopper of a man. Five feet of shiny broadcloth and three inches of collar. Always on the jump. Inside or out. In his fifties. The hopping fifties. And fierce as a mad mouse. Genus, Boorjwar; species, Blackcoatius Begoggledus Ferocissimouse. All eaten up with lawfulness and rage; ready to bite himself for being so respectable. He popped in one day when I'd called on Sara, and I thought he was going to run me through with his umbrella. His little hornet's eyes were shooting fiery murder. But I rushed up to him on the front door mat and seized him by the hand. 'How de do, sir? My name's Gulley Jimson. I hope you're quite well—quite.'

Sara had slipped away and he brought his umbrella to the order. Armistice. 'How do do, sir? I know your name. As an artist. I am honoured,' with a little clockwork bow, as if to say, 'You are ticked off.'

'Not at all,' I said. 'I called to see Mrs Jimson about some drawings.' This had a good effect. The little black devil put his umbrella in the stand and you could see that he was surveying his ground. Like a lawyer. His insect face became as blank as an insect's. Which meant that he was planning something—a lawyer's face always gives warning of an ambush. Like a blockhouse. Used to conceal the artillery.

'Mrs Jimson,' he said. 'Or Mrs Monday,' I said. 'I don't know what flag she's sailing under now.' 'She came to me as Mrs Jimson, but the registry office gave the name as Monday.' 'Both flags, in fact.' 'She was a widow, I believe.' 'Not mine, not yet.' 'Ahem. Then I understand that her name legally is Mrs Jimson.' 'No sir, legally, her name is Mrs Monday. Though, of course, she lived with me as Mrs Jimson.'

There was a short pause while this news filtered through the loopholes of the blockhouse to Mr W. within. Who then stood on one leg, put his finger in his ear and gave a loud halloo, followed by uproarious and uncontrollable laughter; that is to say, he wanted to do so; but being a respectable blackcoat, he could only place his hands together, press them so hard that they cracked, and remark, 'In-deed. Ahem. In-deed. As Mrs Jimson. Ahem. *As* Mrs Jimson.'

And I nearly burst out laughing in his face. It's easy to see, I thought, your kind. A housekeeper-keeper every inch. But I looked very grave and reserved, that is to say, demure, which was the proper move at this stage of the game, as played among the blackcoats. And Hot Nobless. '*As* Mrs Jimson,' I said.

'Not being, ahem, in point of fact, legally speaking, ahem—'

'I quite agree, Mr Wilcher.'

'And yet, I should have thought—I feel sure, a woman of principle.'

'Oh,' I said, 'very much so. The best. Sara was quite

ready to go to church. Always has been. The impediment
was on the other side of the family. If I may say so.'

At this Mr W. sprang clean through the ceiling, turned
several somersaults in mid air, sang a short psalm of
praise and thanksgiving out of the Song of Solomon, accompanied on the shawn, and returned through the letter-
box draped in celestial light. That is to say, he raised
his right toe slightly from the carpet, said 'indeed' in mi-fa,
and relaxed his ceremonial smile into an expression of
tolerance. 'Indeed,' he repeated, this time in mi-do, 'an
impediment.'

'I had the misfortune to be married before,' I said,
'several times, in fact.'

'So that Mrs Monday was in no way to blame.'

'Not for not being married. Certainly not. By no means,
never.'

'A truly religious woman,' said Mr W. using *vox humana*.

'Yes, you might say Sara had some religion, female religion.'

'I esteem Mrs Monday very highly,' he said then. He
was now preparing for the general assault. 'Very highly
indeed.' 'She always had a something,' I said, 'and so on.'
'A true woman, Mr Jimson.' 'You've only got to look at her.'
'The true old country stock.' 'Let us say breed.' 'Now, Mr
Jimson, I have a suggestion to make to you,' charging
down on me with all arms. Yes, a regular Boorjwarrior.
London is full of them. Infuriated blackcoats. Lying low
in some ambush with a dagger in one hand and a bomb
in the other. And the fires of death and hell burning under
their dickies. When you meet them, they're all clockwork
bows and hems and how-de-do's, until they've got you
where they want you, and then out come the claws, and
bang, they're at your throat like a Bengal tiger.

Mr W.'s proposition was that if I came near Sara again
or wrote to her for the money she owed me, he'd put me
in charge; but on the other hand, if I would undertake to
leave her unmolested, he was prepared to come to an arrangement.

'A financial one,' I said.

'Certainly.'

'You want to buy Sara—cash, I presume.'

'Nothing of the sort, sir.' And he burst into stars and
rockets. For of course I'd dropped my match right on the

spot where the gunpowder was kept. 'A most abominable suggestion. I have the deepest respect for Mrs Monday. My object, sir, is to protect her from a ruffian, sir, a blackguard. Which I intend to do, in any case, whether you accept my terms, or not.' And he folded his arms and stood on tiptoe and fairly crushed me with his glance. Or at least that was the intention.

'That's all right,' I said. 'So long as you don't expect me to protect you from Sara or versa vice. And the price is satisfactory.'

'A pound a week. And you will sign an undertaking not to write or communicate in any manner.'

'Thirty shillings for the whole property as a going concern.'

'I do not intend to bargain with a person of your sort. A pound is my highest offer. A pound or the police.'

And do what I would, I couldn't get him above twenty-two and six. But to tell the truth, men like Wilcher, the real old blackcoat breed, out of Hellfire by the Times, get on my nerves. They frighten me. They're not normal. You never know what they'll do next. They're always fit for rape and murder, and why not? Because they don't look upon you as human. You're a Lost Soul, or a Bad Husband, or a Modern Artist, or a Good Citizen, or a Suspicious Character, or an Income Tax Payer. They don't live in the world we know, composed of individual creatures, fields and moons and trees and stars and cats and flowers and women and saucepans and bicycles and men; they're phantoms, spectres. And they wander screaming and gnashing their teeth, that is, murmuring to themselves and uttering faint sighs, in a spectrous world of abstractions, gibbering and melting into each other like a lot of political systems and religious creeds.

> But all within is opened into the deeps of Entu-
> thon Benython,
> A dark and unknown night, indefinite, unmeas-
> urable, without end,
> Abstract philosophy warring in enmity against
> Imagination.

I was glad to get away from that little black scorpion. Ringed with hellfire. I feel my hair rise still all over, where it used to be, when I think of him. No wonder

211

they invented religion. Nothing but the heaviest dogma cast in the thickest metal can keep such demons, afreets and poltergeists bottled in their own juice, which is the only acid strong enough to disinfect their virtues.

29.

Sara was still knocking pails and brooms about in the cellar, and I saw that she was trying to drown the voice of conscience with household noises, a common trick among the ladies. But it gave me an idea. If she can't hear herself, perhaps she won't hear me. And I went out very quietly into the passage and tried the first door.

But a woman doesn't need to hear somebody prowling through her domains uninvited; she has a special organ, situated just under the diaphragm, which detects him five miles away even when disguised as a relation by marriage. I had barely half opened the door, before crash went the broom, bang went the pail, and Sara was coming up the steps like a gas explosion.

'I was just looking round,' I said. 'Nice place you have here.' In fact, it was a dusty bare little room with nothing in it except one cane armchair, a new wheelbarrow, some matting on the floor, and a lot of empty beer bottles. 'The parlour?'

'It could be,' said Sara, sighing and panting. 'If they'd only let me have a bit of carpet and a soft chair.'

'Nice photograph on the mantelpiece—nice girl. Where did it come from?'

'It's me—it was in my parlour at Fred's. It's always been in my parlour. I used to have one in a silver frame, but somebody took it.'

'That silver frame. The one you gave me for your photograph. Well, Sara, to tell the truth, I picked it up again. I needed a little cash, and I thought you wouldn't mind.'

Sara took it like an old lady. She only drew in her lips and wrinkled her forehead. 'A good thing I had another copy,' she said. 'That's me in my wedding frock—the one I had when I married you. I mustn't say married, I suppose. But that's what I meant, God knows.'

'Of course it's you,' I said, 'now I look again. It's sunk

in a bit, that's all. I couldn't forget that figure—a real figure. Ah, you were a woman, Sall, in the times when there were women who even looked like women. And I'll get that frame back for your picture.'

'Oh well,' said Sara, not believing me, 'I've got the photo, and it was a nice dress. I had a piece of the silk for a long time. I always had a feeling for it. But there, I was properly in love with you.'

'Or in love with getting married.'

And Sara didn't contradict me any more. She was too tired. 'Well,' she said, 'there was that too, I daresay. What woman doesn't? But not because of what you thought, Gulley. No, it wasn't the bedding part of it. It was being your wife.'

'Anybody's wife.'

'Well, a home needs a man I suppose, just like a cosy needs a teapot. And I always did like someone to do for. It's natural.'

'There's something boiling over,' for I'd had a good look round, and I knew the box wasn't in that room.

Sara listened and said, 'Bother it,' and hopped out quicker than you might expect. But she'd always had a dislike to things boiling over. And as she went into the kitchen, I skipped through the other door. Sure enough, the family bedroom. Italian brass bed with three knobs missing and most of the brass. Yellow cupboard with blisters. Little crooked table with a tin basin and a blue jug. Strip of worn-out carpet in front of the fireplace. Christmas supplements pinned on the walls. Cherry Ripe. Christmas Eve, with snow and postman and little girl. Raphael Madonna. Smell of matrimony. Two burst hatboxes on top of cupboard. Two boxes under bed. One solid wood bound with black iron strips. Old navigator's chest. Byles. One yellow tin, battered like crumpled glovepaper. Slavey's first trunk. Sara.

I knew that box. Sara had always kept her treasures in it. Old ribbons, old rags of velvet, old photographs, baby's first shoes, her mother's Bible, a broken fan, a pair of stays (what a waist I had at seventeen) and bundles of letters, hotel bills (honeymoon), dance programmes and bits of yellow linen. Her bridal nightgown at the bottom, to be buried in. The last nest of an old bird. It was locked, of course. Sara always had it locked. But the lock was a woman's lock; half off its hinge and full of rust; the tongue was ready to jump off the hasp, at a touch. I had brought a little box-opener with me, in case of having to open something, and I had the lid back in half a minute. A shawl on top. Then a pink silk dress, style of about 1900. And underneath that two great rolls of canvas, and a portfolio of drawings.

I spread out the canvases on the wall. The first was a sketch of Sara in a green dress, one of her old pre-war dresses with a full skirt. A knock in, nothing finished, except the hands and the bodice. But the other was a gem. The first study for the Bath. And in many ways better than the big one, fresher, more sensitive, more lively in the touch, and more character in the tones. More come and go. I was so pleased with it that I forgot all about Sara. Until she opened the door into my back, took one look at the open box and grabbed at the canvas. For a minute it was a pull devil, pull Gulley. But then Sara suddenly let go and the canvas fell down on the carpet. She said, 'Oh, Gulley, what's that?'

She'd seen the box-opener in my hand, and perhaps I'd waved it at her. But she was not so much frightened as shocked. She quite woke up all at once and forgot how old she was feeling.

'You weren't going to murder me?' she said. Then she put her hand to her side and leant against the bed-post. 'Oh dear,' she said, 'I'm too old. And then you looking like that. And looking in my box and taking my things.'

'They're not your things, Sara. They're mine, and I need them too—very badly.'

Sara gave a sigh so big, it was like a heartbreak. Except you knew that Sara's heart couldn't break. It was too soft. But she made the bedframe creak, or perhaps it was her stays. And then she said, 'You with a jemmy, Gulley.'

I saw that she was changing her feelings. Sara could always change her feelings very quickly. And I said, 'It's not a jemmy. It's a box-opener.'

'Oh dear, what's the difference?'

'It's a box-opener when an honest man uses it and a jemmy when a thief uses it.'

'How you can laugh and make jokes when you were just going to murder me?'

She screwed up her cheeks and one and a half tears rolled down her cheeks, the half one out of the shut eye. It surprised me. And I sat down on the bed and put my arm round her as far as it would go. 'Come, Sall, old girl. What's wrong? You know you hadn't any right to those pictures and both of us need the money.'

'Oh dear, it gave me such a shock when you looked at me like that. We're too old, Gulley. We oughtn't to go on like that at our age.'

'Well then, let's go off—there's twenty pounds for you and a bit for me too—enough for a week at Brighton.'

The old lady took another one-eyed squint at the canvas and gave another screw to her cheeks. I was afraid she was going to cry again. But instead she let out a kind of groan and said, 'Wouldn't the other one do, Gulley?'

'The one in a dress? No, Sara. That wouldn't get five pounds. No, you can keep that one.'

'Well, Gulley,' and she gave an old woman's sigh; a long quiet one. 'I suppose you have more right to it than I have; and we don't want to quarrel any more at our age.'

'We never really quarrelled, Sall, we only differed.'

'And I was a good model when you painted that—you thought a lot of me then.'

'Well, look at you.'

'Yes, perhaps we did quarrel—but it was nice to be young.'

'We're not so old now.'

Sara shook her head. 'If you knew how old I feel, Gulley. Grey in my very bones.'

'Cheer up, Sall.' What with the poor old girl's eye, and her griefs, and her good sense about the picture, I was touched. And I gave her a kiss. A bit sideways because our noses got in the way. I hadn't kissed anybody since Rozzie died, which was nearly ten years past, so I'd forgotten to allow for the natural obstacles. 'You were always my best girl, Sall,' I said, 'and my best model. An inspiration to the eye and everything else. Look at that pair.'

Sara smiled and the pink came into her cheeks, under the purple. She shook her head. 'Ah, Gulley, you could always get what you wanted. But my figure wasn't so terribly bad, was it?'

'And they're not so bad now, I daresay,' I said.

'Not so bad as you might think,' said Sara with such a look as made me burst out laughing. She still had youth in her old bones.

'The model wife.'

'And you never saw me as I was, Gulley. I'd had five children before you painted me like that. Why, look at my waist. It was a nineteen when I first went out to service.'

'Silly girl, spoiling your shapes.'

'Well, I do think you put a little bit on my hips, even then. I said so at the time, they're not my hips, Gulley. More like poor Rozzie's.' 'Of course they're your hips, Sall. Why, that's where you were strong. I wish all the world could have seen those hips.' 'They weren't bad for shape, but you made them a little heavy.' 'So they ought to be heavy. The hearth stone of the house. The Church's one foundation. The Creator of civilization. The Mediterranean basin. The Keel of the world.' 'The blue curtain is nice.' 'Meaning that it shows up a nice line along the horizon.' 'The horizon, Gulley. Oh, you mean—' 'The left cheek.' 'Oh, you are awful,' said Sara, getting quite lively. 'But the colour, I didn't think I was so pink as that, unless I'd been sitting on the pebbles.' 'Why, it's a lovely skin like a baby's.' 'Yes, it wasn't too bad then. When I went to have massage after my first, the nurse said she'd never seen such a skin. But you made my chin too long, Gulley. I know it's a bit thick, but gracious, you've made me look like the villain in *Maria Martin*.' 'I improved your nose though.' 'Funny that bit of white just there, how it brings it up,' said Sara, pointing with her toe at her breast. 'Yes,' I said, 'your left is your masterpiece.' 'Well, now you mention it, for a woman who'd nursed five and such suckers too, it's a wonder I didn't come out like an old purse.' 'I did that bit between the arm and the breast rather well, it's a lovely bit that, the foothills—' 'You'll admit they were wonderful firm, Gulley.' 'By God, firm as a Dutch cheese.' 'And wonderful white too.' 'As curdled cream.' 'Well, do you know, Gulley, the monthly nurse used to stare at them till I was quite shy, and then she would say she'd never seen such sweet lovely shapes. And of course she'd seen thousands and thousands. You might say they were as common as turnips to a dairy farmer.' 'Look at the vein there, just a drag of the brush across the grain. Yes, I could handle the paint then.'

'That's what Mr Hickson says—he says you had a wonderful gift, but you never used it properly but once, when you did me. And you never did anything better than the Bath.' 'Anything more slick, you mean.' 'If you never did anything else but those you did of me, you'd be famous in history, that's what Mr Hickson told me.' 'If I never did anything else, Sall, I'd shoot myself for a lipstick merchant.' 'I'll never forget how you used to tear the clothes off my back and I never knew whether it was to put me down or to make me sit. You were mad to paint me, weren't you, Gulley?'

And there she was, the old cyclops, making a glad eye at her own image. The tear marks still on her cheek.

'I suppose you have this canvas out every night, Sall. It looks a bit dog-eared.'

She shook her head. 'I'd forgotten about it.'

'Tell me another, Sall, and I won't believe that one either.'

'I used to take a peep now and then, just to remember our happy times. But not since I came here. I've been too low.'

'And now it's doing you good. Why not, it does me a lot of good.'

'You won't say I wasn't a sweet armful for you, Gulley.'

'So you were and God bless you, He gave you all a woman could want.'

'And glad I was for your sake.'

'And all the others.'

'No, Gulley. For I never rejoiced with any but you. No, I never gloried in myself but when we were together.'

The old lady was getting so warm I thought she might argue.

'Come, Sall, I must go. I've got an appointment with an agent at one o'clock. And shall I send you your twenty pounds in notes or a money order?' I stooped to pick up the canvas.

But Sara stooped down too and took hold of it on the other side.

'Now, Sall,' I said. 'You're not going back on your word?'

'Wouldn't the other one do?' said Sara.

'No, it would not. No dealer would look at it. Be sensible, Sall. What good is the thing to you hidden away in your box? You're not such an old stupid that you'd rather go looking at yourself as you were twenty years ago than have twenty Jimmy O'Goblins to play with.'

'Have you looked at the other one? It's very nice the way you've done the silk. It's really much nicer than this one.'

'Listen to the old trot. She wants to go on staring at herself still. She's still in love with herself.'

'Oh indeed, Gulley, it's not for pleasure. It makes me so sad I could cry.'

'Is there anything you care about in this world except yourself?' I said, for I was growing exasperated.

'Oh, Gulley, how can you ask? I was a true wife to you, and a true mother to your Tommy.' 'I was yourself, and so was Tommy. I was your best bed-warmer and Tommy was your heart cordial.' 'I nearly died when you left me.' 'Yes, as if you'd lost your left leg or your front teeth.' 'Well, you did what you liked with me. God knows. You broke my poor nose and I came back to you. And the times you pinched me and stuck pins in my poor behind, long ones, I wonder how I stood it. You were a cruel husband, Gulley.' 'You were a bad woman, Sall.' 'God knows I had my faults, but you shouldn't call me a bad woman, and even if you say I was bad, wasn't it all for your pleasure?' 'And you won't even give me back my own property—now when I need it.' 'Whatever you say, Gulley, I did make you happy, Gulley, often and often you said you were the happiest man in the world.' 'Come, Sall, wrap it up and let me get off.' 'Why, even the day you finished that, you were so mad after me—' I picked up the picture quickly and rolled it up under my arm. Sall gave a little cry, 'Oh, Gulley, you can't take it like that, all screwed up.' And I could see that she was nearly crying over her precious picture. I was sorry for her. This sketch, I thought, is the chief exhibit in the old museum. It's the treasure of the temple. She looks at it every day and says, 'What a girl I was, and what times I had. All the men after me. And no wonder. Look at my this and my that and my, etc.' Yes, it's a loss to the poor old dear. And so I gave her another squeeze or two. 'Oh, Gulley,' she said, 'you won't crack it, will you?' 'Crack it?' 'Crack the paint—let me do it up for you proper with a newspaper inside. As I used to. I wouldn't want your nice picture to get cracked.' 'My picture or your portrait?' I said. She made me laugh with her tricks. But I let her wrap the canvas in brown paper, which was just as well. For while she was tying it up in the bedroom, Byles came ramping in at the front door, and I was glad that he didn't catch us together.

As it was he just stood and looked at me. You could see the steam was turned on; and the wheels might move any minute. ' 'Ere,' he said at last, and lifted a fist like a coal scuttle.

'Good morning, Mr Byles,' I said. 'I was just calling on Mrs Monday, an old friend of the family.'

' 'Ere,' said Byles, and the wheels gave a jump. 'GET OUT.'

Sara slipped the parcel in my hand and I came away at once.

The Professor had actually been round that morning, while I was away, to ask for me. He was smelling out his fee. And I was just going off to Capel Mansions, to deliver the goods, when, by a piece of luck, I thought I would take another look at the canvas and see if it wouldn't be better on a stretcher. Amateurs like Beeder, and even dealers, often can't tell what a picture is worth, unless they see it on a stretcher.

So I unrolled my parcel. And there was nothing inside but four rolls of toilet paper done up in newspaper. I got such a surprise that I couldn't even swear.

Then, of course, I remembered that Sara had gone into the bedroom to look for string to tie up my parcel. And that she'd been some time about it. And I laughed. It was either that or wanting to cut the old woman's throat. And even to think of cutting Sara's throat always put me in a rage. Because, I suppose, I'd got her in my blood. I'd been fond of her. And it's very highly dangerous to murder any-one you've been fond of, even in imagination. Throws all the functions out of gear. Blocks up your brain. Might easily blow the lid off.

I took a little walk along Greenbank and snuffed up the breeze. And I admired the view of the spring trees on the towpath side, burning in the evening sun, like copper flames in a brass sky. Sun-dirty old brass. And the river like brandy.

30. The next afternoon found me at Chatfield Buildings again. With a bigger box-opener. I wasn't annoyed with Sara, but I wanted to come to an arrangement. But just when I was making a reconnaissance at the front door, I had a special providence in the shape of a small dog which bit me in the leg. I'm used to dog bites. Dogs always bite the ragged. But I've never liked them. And when I turned round to fend off the dog, there was Byles about two yards away coming for me with a garden fork. He chased me about half a mile round the buildings, and he might have caught me if he hadn't wasted so much breath on telling me what he was going to do to me. As it was, I managed to dodge into another staircase and I sat in a lavatory with the door bolted, for two hours, until it was dark enough to make my getaway. I wasn't going to take any risks with my new Fall. It would have been a crime.

It wouldn't have been wise to let the Professor know how Sara had diddled me. I wrote to tell him that the picture was at my agents, being stretched and cleaned, and I called the same evening to see Sir William and ask him to wait a few days for his masterpiece.

'Oh dear,' said the Professor when he met me in the hall. 'You're too late.'

'Too late?'

'They've gone to America, and they won't be back for three months.'

'Never mind,' I said, 'I'll use the time to find a frame. And I daresay Sir William wouldn't mind paying a hundred in advance.'

'I rather think,' said the Professor, 'Sir William will want to see the picture first.'

'In that case,' I said, 'I hold myself free to accept other offers. I believe Mr Hickson would make me a better offer.'

This worried the Professor a good deal, and he assured me that Sir William would certainly pay more than Hickson, if only I would wait.

The Professor was staying in the flat for the week-end.

He had nowhere else to go until Monday when he was visiting an old friend in Devonshire. And nothing much to eat. For the Beeders had locked everything up except a piece of cheese and half a loaf of stale bread.

He was put out when I suggested staying with him. But when he found that I was prepared to do the catering, he became more hospitable.

'You might have the sofa in the studio,' he said, 'I'm sleeping in the drawing-room.'

'What about Sir William's bed?'

'The bedclothes have been locked up.'

'Never mind,' I said, 'I can make allowances while Sir William is away.'

Then I showed the Professor how to pawn his winter overcoat and with the proceeds I bought beer and bacon enough for two. The plan was to take the overcoat out of pawn as soon as I had the picture. So we lived in the land of Beulah on bread and cheese and bacon, and bread and dripping and bacon, until the Monday. When his old friend called for him in a 40-50 Rolls to take him to Devonshire. The Professor's friends all seemed ready to give him every luxury when it suited their convenience, except clothes and money.

I was still in bed when the car came, and the Professor was worried. 'Excuse me, Mr Jimson,' he said, 'but I ought to lock up and take the key to the police.'

'Never mind,' I said. 'Give me the key and I'll attend to it. Don't keep your friends waiting.'

And, in fact, the friend was walking up and down in the studio, getting himself into a great state of impatience. Because his wife was waiting for him. The wife, I daresay, didn't like his friend the Professor very much; she was not prepared to wait very long for a gentleman with holes in his trousers.

'Come on, Alabaster,' he called, rushing out and in again. 'We've got a long way to go before lunch.'

'The Beeders are very particular,' said the Professor, quite pinched with agitation. 'They gave strict instructions. They naturally feel anxious about the safety of a unique collection like this.'

'They're quite right,' I said. 'Tell the porter to keep an eye on the door. Tell him that Mr Gulley Jimson will be responsible for handing over the key.'

The Professor was quite distracted. He was packing a cardboard box with the other socks, spare collar, notes on the Works of Gulley Jimson, toothbrush, etc. And every moment he ran to the door and said, 'Just coming, Sir Reginald,' and then he would run back to me. 'You'll be locking up this morning,' he said.

'Very likely,' I said. 'It depends on my poor stomach. But you can be sure I'll defend the place with my life. I look upon it as a sacred trust. And of course you must tell the porter that I'll give him the key.'

'Today,' said the Professor. And Sir Reginald was making noises like a horse that wants to win the Derby before the starting gate goes up.

The Professor kept on looking at me. But every time he looked I was looking at him. Straight in the eyes, sign of a clear conscience.

'Perhaps I'd better tell the police to call,' he said. 'You'd feel more comfortable, wouldn't you, Mr Jimson, if the police were in charge—less responsibility?'

'A good idea,' I said. 'Tell them that I'm in charge of the key, and will see to the locking up.'

'Are you coming, Alabaster?' cried Sir Reginald from outside. 'I can't stand your friend's pictures any longer—where did he get such trash?'

'Coming now,' said the Professor, quite horrified. 'Very well, Mr Jimson, I'll tell the porter, and the police, and you'll leave the key at the station. That will save you from all further anxiety.'

'Thank you,' I said. 'You're a good chap, Professor. For I do certainly feel a lot of responsibility. I like the Beeders and I appreciate their anxiety for all these fine things.'

'Yes,' said the Professor. 'Just coming, Sir Reginald. Here's the key then, Mr Jimson. And you'll be sure not to forget to close the windows and put on the burglar alarm, before you lock up.'

'Trust me,' I said. And Sir Reginald whisked him away, poor figment. So I took a late lunch on bread and cheese and smoked my pipe in the land of Beulah. And after I had opened the linen cupboard with a bit of stiff wire, I made up her ladyship's bed which seemed to be softer than Sir William's.

The porter and I had a little chat and a couple of gallons next morning at the Red Lion and he was so good as to call up the police for me, and to explain that I had been left in charge of the flat for the present, and took full responsibility for the property.

The porter had been very polite to me ever since he had discovered that I was a distinguished person. Now, when my boots flopped, he looked the other way; like a young lady when a baron shows a fly-button. He was most delicate in his feelings for the great. And beer. One of the old guard. A True Blue.

On the next morning after my bread and dripping on the mahogany, I took down the family portraits in the dining-room to see what the wall was like. For I hadn't forgotten my promise to Sir William of a mural above the sideboard. Tigers and orchids for a hundred guineas. The wall was not what I expected, and when I knocked in the tigers, lightly touched, with a piece of charcoal from her lady-ship's box, they wouldn't stay on the shape. It was too square, like a backyard. It asked for hens and daisies.

But afterwards, when I took down the water-colours in the studio to have a look at the other walls, I made a discovery. A good wall is often ruined by pictures, and I have found most excellent material in unexpected places, for instance behind a collection of old masters. And this was a gem. It was on the right side of the studio, near the entrance hall; framed between two doors and perfectly lighted by reflection from the ceiling. One of the sweetest walls I had ever seen. It made the remaining pictures look like fly-blows. I took them down and stacked them in the bathroom.

A good wall, as they say, will paint itself. And as I looked at this beautiful shape, I saw what it was for. A Raising of Lazarus.

I jumped up at once and sketched the idea with a few touches of a pencil, where it wouldn't show behind the pictures. This gave me a parallelogram on a slant from top left to bottom right, the grave. And I saw it in burnt sienna with a glass-green Lazarus up the middle stiff as an ice man; cactus and spike grass all round, laurel green; a lot of yellow ochre feet in the top corner and bald heads in the bottom triangle—one small boy looking at a red beetle on a blue-green leaf. But it was the feet that jumped at me. The finest feet I'd ever seen, about four times life-size. I only had to put a line round 'em. Then I got out her ladyship's nice little colour-box and rubbed on some body colour. It would all wash off. And I couldn't go wrong with those feet. They came up like music. Down on the left, in foreground, about a yard long and two feet high to the ankle bone—a yellow pair, long and stringy, with crooked nails; then a black pair, huge and strong with muscles like lianas; a child's pair, pink and round, with nails like polished coral; an odd pair, one thick and calloused, with knotty toes curled into the dust, one shrunk and twisted, its heel six inches from the ground, standing on its toes, a cripple's feet, full of resolution and pain; then a coffee-coloured pair with a bandage, an old woman's feet, flat, long, obstinate, hopeless, clinging to the ground with their bellies like a couple of discouraged reptiles, and gazing at the sky with blind broken nails; then a pair of Lord's feet, pink in gold sandals with trimmed nails and green veins, and one big toe raised impatiently.

When I fell down into a chair about tea-time and looked at those feet, a voice inside me said, They're good, good, good. Nobody has done better. The Works of Gulley Jimson. Jee-sus, Jimson, perhaps you are a genius. Perhaps the crickets are right.

And a masterpiece like that on the Beeders' wall. To be covered up by a lot of drawing-room pictures. The Hon. Mrs Teapot by Reynolds. Here's mud in your eye, your ladyship, and all down your left cheek. Lady Touch-me-not by Gainsborough, in one flitting, what soul in the eyes; the soul of a great baby. In milk and dill water. Poor sole, it's a flat life. One flatness on another. Flattery to flats.

But I'll get my feet on canvas I thought. And I went into the kitchen for the teapot and the bread and jam. Lady Beeder had left only the tin teapot out. But I'd found a nice piece of Sèvres in a glass case in the studio. Tea out of tin. Not in the land of Beulah. And the Sèvres made good tea, though a bit on the simpering side. But there were only two slices of bread left, and when I'd eaten them, I was still hungry. I tried a few cupboard locks with a bent sardine key and opened two of 'em, but nothing inside except the best dinner plates and a lot of odd silver.

Then all at once I had an idea. To sell Lazarus to Sir William instead of the tigers. It was a better bargain for him. He'd get a masterpiece worth thousands for a hundred guineas or, say, a hundred and fifty. And I could still make a copy on canvas.

And as for getting payment, I'd take an advance. In the only way open to me. Under the circumstances. Damme, I thought, looking at those feet, I'm giving him immortality. The glories he's tried to buy all his life. The Raising of Lazarus by Gulley Jimson, O.M., in the possession of Sir William Beeder. People will point at him in the street. One or two dealers, anyhow. Waiting for him to pop the hooks.

So off I went to the pop shop with the Sèvres teapot and a few apostle spoons. Two quid. And stood myself the best dinner I'd had in five years. No more scrimping and scramping, I said, for Gulley Jimson, O.M. His navel shall no longer shrink from the light. Not when he carries it in front of him like the headlights of an express train. Puff, puff. That's the secret. Meet the Professor. My publicity agent. And fetch another Aristotle, waiter. The philosopher is full of drink, as well as meat.

But I played fair by Sir William. Always treat a patron well so long as he keeps his bargain. And doesn't try to cheat you. By getting a masterpiece that's going to be worth ten thousand pounds for a couple of hundred dirty money and two of soft soap. I put the pawn tickets in an envelope and wrote my account on the outside. Raising of Lazarus by Gulley Jimson, £157 10s., advance £2.

Next day I went out and ordered what I wanted, paints, brushes, trestles, planks, canvas, and got down to making a real job of those feet. Of course, they didn't seem to be so easy when it came to the details. I had to run round for models. And the first negro I hired turned out all wrong, his feet were so damned impudent that I had to make a separate study of them. 'How did you get such feet?' I asked him when we were having a rest about dinner time. 'What kind of feet, sah?' For he was a sad and polite sort of chap, six foot high, three foot wide, and full of consumption. 'Cheeky feet.' 'I don't know, sah.' 'What do you do in life?' 'I been a steward, sah, on a ship, sah.' 'So that's where it came out?' 'I no know how you mean, sah.' 'It's got to come out somewhere when a chap waits on other chaps' feeding. It's my belief,' I said, 'that if you took all the waiters' boots off, their feet would make such rude remarks to the customers that nobody would be able to enjoy his dinner.' 'Just how you say, sah,' said the poor old

Joe, and he swallowed another half glass of champagne. It was only sec, but I hadn't time to get in some of the real stuff.

And when I got the feet I wanted, I couldn't get them to lie on the wall. Those toes stuck out like a row of fists. And then the females. I hunted three days for Sozie MacT., who used to have very good feet. But she'd got married and gone to the devil. Been wearing women's shoes for five years and more. Her Feet were like something in a doctor's museum. And when Bisson, a waster who calls himself a sculptor, lent me Carrie, the girl he calls his model, for an afternoon, he came with her and admired my Feet so much and talked so much about the Idea of the Resurrection, that he spoilt three days for me. I nearly scraped the whole thing off. On the third day I was ready to jump out of the window or cut my throat. And on the fourth Abel, who is a young friend of Bisson's, another sculptor, turned up and asked me if he could borrow one end of the studio for a job he had in hand; war memorial. A thin stooping young man, with a long crooked nose, and blue eyes, shoulder blades like wings, a backbone like a dying dog and enormous splay feet. His hands also were six sizes too big. He didn't talk much and all he said about Lazarus was, 'The left black foot has something.' I liked him. But I said I hadn't room for any bloody sculptors with their dust in the same room where I was painting. Then I went out to lunch and when I came back about six o'clock there were seven men with a crane swinging a four-ton block of Hopton stone through my studio windows. They'd taken out the bars and piled all the furniture and carpets and cushions at one end of the room.

Bisson, Abel and three more of their gang were directing the work, and when I told them to stop they didn't even hear me.

I ran into the middle of the floor and shouted, 'Hi, who lives here, you or me?'

'Lower away,' shouted Bisson, and the block began to come down on my head. Then Bisson, who is a big heavy man weighing seventeen stone, took me by the neck and the seat of my trousers and threw me on top of the furniture pile.

'Lower away, lower away,' he bawled. 'No, hold it.'

'Hold all,' Abel screamed, with his eyes coming out like

blue snails and his hair standing out like a bottle-brush. 'Hold it, you— Don't you see the block has three inches to drop. Do you want it to go through the floor and chip its edges. Here, you—get those rugs under. And the cushions.'

Down came the stone on top of all my precious rugs and fine cushions covered with priceless silk embroidery. And when I tried to grab off the last which was my favourite, Abel pushed me half across the room. But he hadn't even seen me. He was looking at the chains.

'Be careful of those chains, you— Don't let it swing. I've had stones ruined that way before by you—'

And nobody seemed to mind the way he cursed and swore. I suppose the workmen were used to sculptors. They knew that all real sculptors are insane; or they wouldn't have taken to sculpting.

'Damn it all, Bisson,' I said. 'Have you ever heard of the law? You can't come into an Englishman's house and treat it like this.'

'That's all right,' said Bisson. 'The porter won't know. He's round at the Red Lion with a friend of ours. And this is a commission. Abel's first real big chance. He's getting some real money for it, he'll make it all right about your pansy mats. That reminds me, if you want to get this stuff out of the way, I have the very man to store it for you.' He waved his hand at the pile of chairs and sofas. 'Keep it out of the dust. And you know what stone dust is.'

I always disliked Bisson. A big, cunning oaf. Born into money and tumbled young to the idea that the way to have a good time all his life and get away with murder was to be an artist. So he developed an artistic temperament at fifteen, stopped working, and came it over his people that he was a genius. At seventeen, he was playing at being an art student in Paris and keeping a couple of girls. At nineteen, he gave his first exhibition, imitations of Manet, etc. And at twenty-four, his second, imitations of the Cubists. Then he painted some walls in the style of Stanley Spencer, and did a little sculpture after Epstein and Henry Moore. But all with his left hand. Bisson never took any trouble about anything. He's never done a real job in his life. He doesn't mean to. He'd found out that it's more amusing to swindle, lie and swagger; to take advantage of his friends, and ruin the girls, who fall for his talk. They say he's driven three girls to suicide, and I believe he gets a kind of kick out of it. Makes him feel how impregnable he is. His very grin says, 'Nothing can touch me—I'm solid brass.'

But what is really annoying about Bisson is that he doesn't deceive himself. He knows he's a fraud. He knows he's getting away with it. And he enjoys the game. What I would wish Bisson, if I dared to hate him, is a complicated kidney disease, with chronic chordee. But I can't afford to hate him. He's too hateful. And I believe he knows that too, the bastard.

When Bisson calmly proposed to throw all Sir William's furniture out of the house, I said, 'Look here, Bisson. This furniture is in my charge. It belongs to Sir William Beeder, who's an honoured friend of mine. I honour him especially because he is a generous and devoted friend of art. There are too few millionaires nowadays who spend money and even time on the encouragement of art, especially young artists, and I'm not going to see him victimized by any dirty phony blackguard who takes advantage of the bloody imbecility and good-natured innocence of the public to pass himself off for a real artist, who is trying to do a real job. I like you a lot, Bisson,' I said, 'but if you try to come it over me, I'll cut your tripe out with a push-razor, and that wouldn't suit your book. Where would you be without your stomach? etc.'

'That's all right, my dear chap,' said Bisson, laughing and patting me on the shoulder. 'I know how you feel. I'd feel the same way myself. My idea was to avoid damage to the stuff. All this nice brocade won't be improved by Abel's mess.'

'That's true,' I said. 'But who is going to pay for storing it?'

'As for that,' said Bisson. 'You needn't pay. Do what I do when I want something well looked after for a few weeks. Pop it.'

'You can't pop sofas and chairs,' I said. 'I've tried. The only way to do business with stuffed furniture is to give a bill of sale and let the bailiffs find a market.'

'Nonsense,' said Bisson. 'You're out of touch. My friend is a real man of business—he'll do anything that's got money in it—but just as you like. Nice thing that of yours. Best thing you done,' nodding at the Feet.

'I don't like 'em much,' I said. 'They've gone sour on me.'

'Sir William is lucky if he gets it for anything under five hundred,' said Bisson, who believes in flattery. It costs him nothing. 'A masterpiece. But don't mind me, let him do you if you like. You can afford to give your stuff away —I can't.' And he went off.

Afterwards, of course, I saw that his plan for storing the furniture was a good one. Especially as I was rather short of ready cash at the time. So I telephoned to Bisson's friend, and he came that same afternoon and arranged to remove all the articles that might suffer by Abel's dust. He offered even to lend me a reliable man to take the porter to the Red Lion during the removal. But I preferred to do that myself. It was a task requiring a certain capacity.

And Bisson's friend not only brought a pantechnicon for the goods, but paid on the nail, in notes. No ledger entries to perplex accountants. His prices were rather low, but then I wanted only a temporary advance.

As for Abel, as soon as the stone was on the floor, and even before the workmen had got the chains off it, he was chipping away with his hammer. He was a modern sculptor. He didn't believe in drawings. Just went for the stone and made it fly. And while he was at work, you could have fired off guns in his ear, he wouldn't have heard you. I couldn't have got rid of him if I had wanted to.

So I hung up a lot of sheets and eiderdowns across the middle of the room and went on with Lazarus. We never spoke to each other all day. I could hear him singing and whistling when the work was going well, and swearing when he was in desperation. And once when I threw a china dog through the glass door because I couldn't see the baby's feet any more, he came in and shouted at me, 'What the hell. Can't you let me alone?'

'Get out,' I said to him. 'You humbugging rock-knacker. Who asked you to come in?'

Then he came up close to me, poking out his chin. His eyes were like bottle-stoppers. He had his hammer in his hand, and I thought he was going to brain me. So I snatched up my palette knife and aimed it at his breast. 'My God,' I said, 'I'll stick you through like a chicken, you miserable chop-and-chance-it.'

'What's wrong with you?' he said, stopping and taking in his chin, eyes, etc.

'Nothing, God blast your soul,' for seeing him drop the hammer I thought I'd come it over him. 'Well,' he said. 'You've been throwing things.'

'What's that to you? They aren't your things. You seem to forget you're a guest.'

Then he took a look at the Feet and said, 'You haven't done much this week.'

'Mind your own business.'

'But you've done more than I have.'

'What,' I said. 'Are you stuck?'

'My God,' he said, 'it's the damnedest awfullest job I've ever done. I've ruined the finest piece of stone I ever saw. It's a bloody crime. Come and look before I cut my bloody throat.'

31. Now the truth was I was so sick of those feet that I could have knocked my head on the walls. It wasn't that they were hopeless. They still had some sense in them. I could still feel that there was something there. Something real. But it kept on fleeing away from us.

So I was glad of any excuse to break off work and I went off with Abel.

There was the usual mess. Dust, chips, half a bottle of stout on her ladyship's Bechstein. The model's clothes hanging on the crystal wall-light and the model herself, a thick little blonde girl called Lolie, walking up and down and slapping herself with both hands to get back her circulation. Lolie has long hair and it was hanging down to her buttocks. Which was more than three-quarters of the woman, as she has the shortest legs in London.

'Isn't it good, Mr Jimson?' said Lolie. 'You tell him it's good.'

Abel paid no attention to her. He said to me, 'Look at that, Jimson. You see it was really a double block. A small one set into a big one at the corner. That was the character of the mass. Two levels on top—then the verticals of the small cube. Then the big block with the oblique left side—'

'Well,' I said. 'You've got that side all right.'

'I haven't touched that side,' he said, passing his hand over it as if stroking a horse. 'And I don't want to—it's a beauty. But come round here.'

He'd cut the little block into a woman's head and breasts and forearms. Forearms and breast on one horizontal plane. Head tilted sideways to get the cheek flat, and the hair flat down her back for the side of the stone. It was not bad for a young chap of thirty-four or so. 'That's not too bad,' I said. 'It's chunky.'

'Yes,' he said, 'but has it got the weight?' cupping his big hands like a pair of soup tureens. 'Can you feel her weight?'

'Heavier than the stone,' I said. 'Why, she looks about sixteen tons by herself—she's nearly as thick as Lolie.'

Lolie scratched herself with both hands at once, and said in a cross voice, 'It's coming on very nicely, and a nice subject too. Earth mourning for her sons. But he never will listen to anything I say.'

'It's a bloody subject, of course,' said Abel. 'But I haven't bothered with the name. It was the town council planted that on me. One of them was educated.'

'It's time for tea,' said Lolie.

'Just turn round a bit darling,' said Abel, 'yes, that's it.' And he turned her round by her shoulders. 'Look at that back. There's something there.' And he passed the back of his great knuckly hand down her spine. 'If you forget its meat.'

'Tell him he couldn't do it nicer, Mr Jimson,' said Lolie. 'He's only cross with it because he hasn't had his tea. That's what he wants. You tell him.'

'Look at what I've done with it—slop, just slop. Lost all the monumental. And that corner, oh my God—'

'Well,' I said, 'what did you mean—knocking that hole in the left side? What's it doing, that hole? What's it for?'

'Don't ask me,' he said, throwing his hammer on the floor and making a bit of the parquet jump right out of its socket. 'I thought I saw one of the dead there, sitting up with his head on his shoulder, I could feel him this morning, and this edge of the block is the line of his jaw and neck.'

'Well,' I said, 'I don't see why that shouldn't come out all right. You've got him square enough too. You could cut your fingers on his chin.'

'Yes, but what about the corner? I saw a lying figure at the bottom, with a flat back giving the side plane. Excuse me, darling.' He took Lolie by the shoulders, pushed her to her knees and pressed her head down on her shoulder.

'Oh dear,' said Lolie, 'he'll only spoil it. And it was so nice. Oh dear, if only he'd had his tea at the proper time. But what's the good of talking.'

'You see,' said Abel, combing down Lolie's hair with a chisel. 'If you forget the flesh, the planes come right out,' and he moved his great flat paddles in the air as if rubbing them on a surface. 'Solid as rocks. And so I cut into the block above it, cut out the whole corner. But it went soft. And it goes on getting softer. However sharp you make the edges. And now I can't even see the next vertical. Got to be a vertical there. That's the whole character of the block. Must have another cube. For the blockiness. But Christ, look at it now—it's gone soft—it's rotten. You could put your bloody fingers through it like bad butter.' And he gave the stone a prod as if he really expected his finger to go through it.

'What I keep on saying,' said Lolie, 'some ammunition boxes. It's on the battlefield, isn't it? Earth surrounded by her dead. And you can't get anything squarer than ammunition boxes. But you better tell him, Mr Jimson—he won't listen to me. Not since I married him.'

'Why, darling,' said Abel, 'I have the highest regard for your taste. Just bend over a little farther. That's it,' and he said to me, 'I thought I might do something with Lolie's head, by flattening it off a bit.'

'Oh dear,' said Lolie, 'why not a box? If you want a square edge. Oh dear, I wish you would have your tea.'

'My dear Lolie,' I said. 'You can't put a box of any kind in the middle of that group—any more than you could pin a bit of silk on a court portrait. It doesn't belong to the idea.'

'Not a real box,' said Lolie, shedding tears down towards her left ear. 'Oh dear, oh dear. He didn't have any lunch, not a real lunch. And now it's nearly six o'clock and no tea.'

'A box,' Abel said to me, 'has been suggested by that

ass Bisson. But I pointed out to him that you couldn't have a manufactured cube among natural chunks, it wouldn't look solid. It would look like an empty drainpipe in a forest, or one of those toyshop pieces where you have a lot of men and cannons mixed up.'

'He ought to stop now, or he'll spoil it. Tell him to have some consideration for himself,' said Lolie, who had been turning blue with the evening breeze.

'You're right,' I said, for it was an interesting point. 'It's got to be all meat or it would stop being stone, can't have a change of idea in the middle of the block, not from meat to plank.'

'Tell him to cheer up,' said Lolie. 'All he wants is a cup of tea, and he'll feel better at once.'

'Why not a dead horse?' I said, 'with the face flat up the front and the neck slewed round?'

'That is an idea,' said Abel.

'A box is much better,' said Lolie. 'It won't take so long. Make it an iron box if you don't like wood.'

Abel was bending down sideways and looking through his hands.

'He thought of a box himself yesterday,' said Lolie. 'But he had a proper lunch yesterday.'

'Yes, darling,' said Abel, and he lifted her up from the ground. But one leg had gone dead and she couldn't stand. 'Just hop over there dear, in the corner, and lie down on your side—yes, stretch out your legs and your arms, and twist up your neck. We want you to look like a dead horse.'

Lolie wiped her nose on her hand, which was all she had for the purpose, and lay down.

'I meant one that's been dead about a month,' I said. 'Not a bloated dead horse.'

'Just draw in your wind a bit, darling,' said Abel, pushing her stomach with the toe of his boot. 'We want to see your diaphragm.'

'Is that right?' said Lolie. 'Oh dear, he's so tired, Mr Jimson. He's just worn out—you can see he's ready to cry —he ought to be stopped, really he ought.'

'Not that way,' I said. 'Here, come next door and I'll cut it out in cheese.' So Abel came next door and I carved up a piece of cheese to show him my idea.

'It looks a bit made up,' he said. 'A bit as if you'd thought of it,' and we talked for a bit. Then we went out and had some beer at the Red Lion, and all at once I remembered Lolie.

'Lolie's changed a lot in the year,' I said. 'When I used to know her she looked like a pig, but now she looks like a dog-faced baboon.'

'Yes.' Abel agreed. 'She's changed—on the whole it's for the better. Her jaw's grown out more and her features have lost importance. The whole effect is flatter, more compact. It's a good face considering what most faces are—a mass of piffling detail.'

'Paint her white and cut off her ears and she'd do for a milestone.'

'Hardly, I'm afraid. But you couldn't expect it. Not with skulls as they are. A wretched job.'

'And you've really married her?'

'Yes, really,' he said. 'I mean we went to the registry. Of course my last wife may still be alive somewhere—I haven't had time to make inquiries. But Lolie has her lines, and I'm glad to get her.'

'Love at first sight.'

'That's it,' he said. 'As soon as I saw her I said, "You attract me a lot. Take off, will you?" So she stripped and—well, you've seen her. She's unique. "Look here, Lolie," I said, "you're practically made for me, but how much do you charge?" "Three bob an hour to a sculptor because of the dust," she said. "I can't afford to pay anything," I said, "but I'll marry you, and you can still sit in the mornings to anyone you like. I can carve all night." '

'And she accepted you.'

'Yes, she said she wanted to be settled. And she often makes four or five pounds in a good week. We do very well. It's been a great success. But as you see, we're both quiet people. Domesticated. We don't want to be rushing about amusing ourselves. Yes, there's nothing like marriage for an artist—if he can find the right woman of course.'

'I found her once,' I said. 'And what a woman, Rubens and cream.' And I began to talk about Sara. So we went on chatting about Sara and Lolie, and boasting of the virtues of our wives, as married men do, until closing time.

But then we went back to the studio, and while Abel was using one of his chisels on a cupboard in the dining-room that looked like a cellarette, I walked through and found Lolie in Abel's end of the studio holding her face on the floor. She was blue and purple with cold and as stiff as a corpse.

'Hullo,' I said. 'You look cold, Lolie.'

'I didn't like to move—not when he's got something in his eye. He might say I'd spoilt everything.'

'You wouldn't be any good to me, that colour,' I said. 'But I suppose a sculptor isn't particular.'

Then Abel came in and said, 'Hullo, Lolie, what, have you been waiting here all the time?'

'You didn't tell me to put on.'

'Didn't I? I'm awfully sorry. Why, aren't you hungry? Get up and have some tea. No, here. Just a minute, there's something in the sag of that left shoulder,' and he began to chip away. He was chipping away all night. I heard him singing and whistling to himself, and when I went in at breakfast time, I found him in the best of spirits. He was well away. Then we noticed that Lolie was crying, and when we asked her what was wrong, she said she was worried about Abel. He must be so tired, so we lifted her up and gave her a rub down with towels, and a cup of tea, and in ten minutes she was making breakfast for us.

'A girl in a thousand,' said Abel. 'She has the constitution of an elephant. She posed for me in the yard in December with three inches of snow on the ground. I didn't press her, but she insisted on it. And all she got was a chilblain on her nose which I never use, anyhow.'

And it was quite true that Lolie had a good constitution. Which is the chief thing in a wife. She posed for Abel all that day and most of the night. Until he couldn't hold a chisel or see out of his eyes.

Next day, of course, he struck another bad place; threw his hammer clean through Lady Beeder's long looking-glass; and disappeared. Lolie hunted him all over London. She used to come to me every night and say what a pity it was if he'd hanged himself again. 'But he's always so up and down. Oh dear, I do hate his downs. But there, everyone has his faults. And he's a good husband, I must say. Not like that Bisson, who knocks his girls about with an Indian club just for exercise.'

'I thought the carving was going rather well.'

'Did you?' said Lolie. 'I didn't. I think it's worse than the last. But all his stuff is rotten. Why, you wouldn't know me in any of them—I come out like a lot of bricks. But don't you tell him, whatever you do. He'll never learn, and it keeps him quiet. Poor old Abel,' she said sadly, 'I suppose he's about the rottenest sculptor that ever lived. But I think he's happy, don't you? I mean, as happy as a chap can be when he's got such bad health and never takes any regular meals.'

'I think he's happy,' I said. 'Now and then. But I don't suppose he knows it.'

'Oh, he likes sculpting,' said Lolie. 'Oh. I'm sure he does. He thinks a lot of me too, especially the back view. Oh, I'm sure he's happy.'

'As happy as a chap can be,' I said.

'I think so,' said Lolie doubtfully. 'Anyhow, in the ups. Oh, I know how to manage him when he has a new stone to hammer about and when he hasn't got his insomnia.'

'Did he hang himself before?'

'He started. But when his neck was beginning to stretch and just before he lost consciousness, he had an idea for a piece of modern gothic and knocked on the wall and the neighbours came in and cut him down.'

I didn't care for Lolie in her skin. She was a sculptor's shape, with no neck or waist and feet like ammunition boots. But I liked her dressed. Lolie's style is well known; bodices with buttons, long skirts, hats with feathers, in the old Phil May fashion. The fact is, as she told me, that as she had to have her hair long, and there was a lot of it, she put it up, and it didn't go with anything but a real hat. And as her legs were short and thick, she liked a long skirt. So she had taken to the style of 1890. And it suited her very well, with her pug face. Lolie dressed took me back to my youth when a woman was a female. Of course, she wasn't a real female, like Sara; she'd been brought up in the chromium-plate period and finished off with a synthetic spray. She didn't know sometimes whether she was a female or a dentist's chair. She used to say, 'Kids, not me, all that trouble for cannon fodder, not likely. Or just when you've worn yourself out on them they get saucy and tell you to lay off—it's time you were buried.'

To see her with a glass of beer down at the Eagle and her ostrich feathers shaking in the breeze of the gasworks made me feel like twenty again, in a curly bowler and chase-me trousers. But when I put my arm round Lolie, and squeezed her, she didn't giggle like a real old girl, or say, 'Do give over,' or throw her eye at me, as Rozzie used to do, as much as to say, 'Go further and fare better,' she only took a sip of beer and went on talking about Abel's nerves. She was out of touch with life, Lolie; I mean, female life. And she couldn't expect to know any other.

But I liked going about with that bodice and those feathers, and we hunted all the pubs in the likely spots —Chelsea, Hampstead and Hammersmith. We even tried Elsinore.

I thought old Plant might be able to help us, as he knew a lot of dosses and their regulars.

Plant and I were not so friendly as we had been because he didn't like my going to the Beeders', and he wouldn't come to see me there or even take a loan from me.

'I'm sorry, Mr Jimson,' he said, 'but I like to be independent. And I never cared to run into debt.'

'Yes, but how are you going to live?' I said. I'd found him in the kitchen at Elsinore with no money and nothing to eat.

'They give me a bed now for doing a bit of scrubbing.'

As I looked at the old man I thought he was about twenty years older. He seemed eighty. 'Look here, Mr Plant,' I said, 'Elsinore is killing you. You weren't born for a doss. You've got to fight your way in life, the lower the harder, and you've never learnt how. You're too much of a philosopher and you're too light.'

But old Plantie just kept on shaking his head. 'It means something, Mr Jimson,' he said. 'It means something or it wouldn't happen like this.'

'And what means dinner?' I said.

'Oh well,' he said, 'they're very wasteful here, you'd be surprised all the bits of bread and bacon that get into the bucket. And hardly any of them seem to know how to get all the meat off a herring or a kipper. I don't do badly.'

And he wouldn't take a farthing from me. 'No,' he said. 'Excuse me, Mr Jimson, but I never liked debt.'

'Trouble with you, Plantie,' I said, 'is that you're too proud. You'd rather feed out of a dustbin than own you're wrong.'

'Wrong about what, Mr Jimson?'

'About the meaning of the world. The world doesn't

mean anything to anybody except what the thrush said to the snail before she knocked it on the brick. GET ON OR GET OUT. LAZY BONES.'

But it was no good talking to Plantie. He was too far gone. And he couldn't even tell me if Abel had been that way, because he didn't seem to notice who came in or out. He sat in his corner all day, trying to find out what had happened to him, and why; until the boss came in and put a pail on his hook and a scrubbing-brush in his left hand; and then he went off to clean up the lavatories and the steps and the dustbins, just as if he were in a kind of dream.

But neither had anyone else seen Abel. Though he was easy to see with his eyes, his hair, his hands, his scarlet socks and green sandals. I began to think that he'd had an accident or even gone into the country.

But Lolie never lost hope. 'No,' she said, 'he wouldn't go into the country except just passing through on business, because he can't stand scenery. It reminds him of pictures. And I feel sure he hasn't drowned himself again. He left his tools behind.'

'Did he drown himself before?'

'Twice. First time he jumped off Westminster steps, but it turned out very well. Because the chap who fished him out had no lobes to his ears, and gave him an idea for an abstract bit of stuff he was doing, an urn or something; and the second time he put all his hammers in his pocket and jumped off Waterloo Bridge, but as soon as he hit the water, he got such a strong feeling of the horizontal that he shouted for the police. And he went straight home and did a thing called Plane Surface, which everybody thought was a joke. And between you and me, so it was. But it kept him happy for six weeks. And made a nice pastry board afterwards. Thank God he's chucked the abstract stuff,' said Lolie. 'He's still rotten, but he's not abstract any more.'

I was not surprised to hear that Lolie didn't admire the abstract; no more than if a coster's moke had told me it didn't take much interest in St Paul's dome.

'I suppose he doesn't need a model when he's doing the abstract?' I said.

'No, he only needs a woman. And the things it drives

him to. A little more of the abstract and we'd both have gone potty. What is there to bite on in the abstract? You might as well eat triangles and go to bed with a sewing machine.'

Lolie was right about Abel. He met us in the street one day on his way back to the flat. And he hadn't been in the country. He had spent the week in a drinking club down in Belgravia, drinking all night and sleeping it off all day. He hadn't had anything to eat but bread and cheese; his hair was full of flue off the floor and his beard was two inches long. His face was green, his eyes were crimson; and he had the shakes. But he was full of energy and enthusiasm. He had got a plastic notion. 'It's a feeling of declivity,' he said. 'I had just been sick,' he said, 'and I was looking at the bowl when it came to me. "That's what I've been feeling after—declivity." And I thought it was acclivity. You see, Jimson,' he said, waving his great hands as if he were wiping up a fishmonger's slab, 'I was trying to feel this thing upwards, against the grain, when all the time it was really downwards—like this. Here, Lolie, take off and I'll show him.'

And Lolie was so pleased to have her husband back that she began to take off in the street. I was glad to get her into the flat while she was still partly decent. And in two minutes Abel got Sir William's dining-table propped up on one edge against a pile of books, and Lolie hanging on the top edge by her arms and chin. 'I want the descending shapes,' he said, 'in a big way.'

He made such a noise, singing and swearing, for the next three days, that I couldn't think or feel. I thought I'd never be able to paint again. In fact, I was fairly driven out of the studio, and I would probably have given up the flat altogether if it hadn't been for young Barbon. I was coming out of the Red Lion one night, in a fog, when suddenly I saw a thin grey object in front of me, shaking in every inch. I thought it was the front of a cab-horse just about to fall off, when I heard Barbon's voice, 'Mr J-Jimson.'

'Why,' I said. 'It's you, Nosy. I thought you were a horse.'

'I've been waiting for you—I saw you through the window.'

'How are things? Are you working hard?'

'Very b-bad. I l-lost my s-scholarship, and I had to g-go for a clerk.'

'You go on for a clerk, Nosy. Steady pay and a dry life.'

'B-but I've g-got the s-s-sack.'

'What for?'

'I w-wasn't any g-good. I kept on being late.'

'Never you mind. You go for another clerk or office boy. Or kitchen man. You can always s-stay at home.'

'B-but, Mr J-Jimson, I c-can't go home any more. I c-can't tell my poor mother I g-got the s-sack.'

And in fact he had been going and coming home for a week pretending to be at the office. So I said, 'Look here, Nosy, I'm in funds just now. I've got a commission from Sir William Beeder for a wall decoration. Come along with me and I'll give you a job for a week or two till you get another clerkship. You can do secretarial work. Fetch my beer and answer the door. I'll give you a pound a week and your food. And you can go out for the beer.'

The poor boy couldn't thank me enough. And I put him into Sir William's bed the same night.

Of course, he thought the Feet were wonderful. He didn't know any better. But just by saying how wonderful they were, he got me criticizing them, and I thought I saw what was wrong. They were too low in tone. They wanted more jump. So I got started again. And forgot that Abel was in the same world, until he burst in upon me one afternoon with bloodshot eyes and his face and hair as white as a miller, and shouted, 'I've finished it, Gulley. It's done. For God's sake don't let me give it another touch. Come and take it away from me before I spoil it.'

'That's Lolie's job, isn't it? What's she for?'

'Lolie doesn't understand art,' said Abel. 'She was broken in with painters. Here, take my tools away while I telephone for the lorry.'

So I put his hammer and chisels into the fireplace while he telephoned for the lorry contractors and Bisson, and they swung out the group that afternoon through the same window, while Bisson and the porter tried a new pub farther off. Abel, of course, was going with the lorry, to watch over his precious Earth mother on the road, and see her safely delivered.

And as soon as the stone was in the air, he came in with his suitcase, threw his tools inside, on top of his smock, and made a run for the stairs.

'Good-bye,' I said, touching up the negro's toenails. But he didn't hear me.

And just then it struck me that I hadn't seen Lolie. 'Where's Lolie?' I called. 'Stop him,' I said to Nosy. 'Catch him,' and I shouted after him. 'What have you done with Lolie?'

'Lolie,' he said. 'Lolie,' as if he'd never heard of Lolie. 'Oh my God, is that rain?' And he tried to rush past me.

'Here,' I said, catching him. 'What have you done with that girl?' For though I liked Lolie, I didn't want her left on my hands. I couldn't use a girl all the time. I was much too busy.

'Let me go,' he screamed. 'Do you want it to catch cold?'

'What catch cold?'

'The stone,' he said, 'it's not even covered.' And he tore himself clear. However, when he'd got the stone on the cart, and covered it up with wadding and canvas, he came to himself and apologized. 'I have to be careful of that block. Of course, some Hopton stone will stand up to an east wind and take no harm. But this is a delicate piece. Beautiful grain, as you saw, but no real stamina. However, it's going into a good home. Municipal entrance hall. Central heating, and so on. So it can afford to be a bit soft.'

'And what about Lolie?' I said.

'Yes, of course. Where the devil is she? I shall want her along.'

'I'm glad you can find some use for her,' I said with irony. I've never liked the way sculptors treat women, who are, after all, an essential raw material.

'Use for her,' said Abel. 'Why, I *need* her. Don't you make any mistake. I know what Lolie's good for. I *value* Lolie, especially when there's a stone to be looked after. She once nursed a block of Portland for me, through ten degrees of frost, in the middle of Salisbury Plain, when a lorry broke down. Put her own clothes on it. Saved it. And caught a pretty severe chill too. Luckily only on the inside. Yes,' he said, as we climbed the stairs, 'you can't do without women when you're dealing with a job like that. They have a special instinct. Maternal. I've never been sorry, not really sorry, that I married Lolie.'

So we went to find Lolie, and there she was, hanging on the dining-table like a side of pork, cold as wet meat. Abel was enraged. 'Damn it all,' he said, 'I told her I was finished. I told her to get down and put on and have a cup of tea before we started. Now she'll want it on the way. Lolie,' he shouted, 'Lolie darling.' But she didn't move. She'd passed out. I thought she was dead, and it was just going to upset me when Abel saw my trouble and consoled me. 'Don't worry, old chap. She'll come round. And she'll be all right in two ticks. Lolie is good stock—Bethnal Green. I'll just ring up the hospital, and if you don't mind sticking her in the ambulance, I'll be grateful. Oh my God, what's that?'

And he rushed off in terror that some wall or thunderbolt had fallen on his masterpiece.

So I sent for the ambulance and Nosy and I put Lolie in an old mattress cover and carried her downstairs. Nosy was shocked. 'Is she all right?' he asked.

'Lolie's all right,' I said. 'She's attached for life. That's what she wants. To know where she is.' And we pushed her into the butcher's cart.

The diagnosis at the hospital was exposure, shock, displacement of the caudal vertebrae and malnutrition. I suppose the poor girl hadn't had a cup of tea for two or three days.

32. Abel's fussing about his lump of nonsense, and the trouble with Lolie, did not, as I had feared, put me off my work. In the next two days, I made a new thing of the Feet. Brought them up till they came right off the wall. And having got my key I decided to get on with the grave and Lazarus himself. That was a Sunday evening. I waited till eight o'clock that night, drawing. Then I was so tired I fell down. So I sent Nosy out to get two bottles of beer, a bottle of whisky, and a paper of fried fish and chips.

Nosy, as it happened, had to go some way off. Because we had run through our credit within the first half mile.

In fact, I had been right out of petty cash for the last fortnight. Luckily Nosy had brought his post office savings book with him, three pounds four shillings, and I had been able to take over the three pounds as an advance on his salary.

And as I knew that Nosy was a great man for a bargain, and might be an hour on his shopping, I went up to the gallery and lay down on the floor for a doze. It wasn't by choice that I had taken to the floor-sleeping again. We had had to part with the beds only to raise current expenses. For the prices we were getting for furniture from Bisson's friend were so bad that though we had nothing left to pop except the kitchen stove and a tin jordan, we were not up to my advance. In fact, allowing for expenses, and assessing the Feet only at two hundred guineas, Sir William still owed me fifteen or twenty pounds.

I had taken to sleeping in the gallery because Bisson's friend had removed all the window curtains. Bisson's friend had been a bit hard at a bargain, but he was certainly good at business. One had to respect a man who understood his public duty so well. He had taken even the bathroom taps, and the chain out of the W.C., at a shilling for the taps and twopence for the chain.

No one could overlook me in the gallery. And I gradually built up a comfortable corner for myself there, with a spring mattress of crushed dailies shoved into some old sacks and a dozen *News of the World*'s wrapped up tight and tied with string, for a pillow. A permanent pillow is the luxury of home. You can get it fitted to your ear. And I was having a sweet nap, the kind of nap which comes to a man who has had a good day's work and sees another in front of him, when the studio door down below the gallery opened and waked me up.

Being in good spirits over the Feet, I was just going to call out some nonsense to Nosy about a fete of celebration when I heard Lady Beeder's voice say in a queer tone, 'But I don't understand.' You'd have thought the woman was coming out of an anaesthetic. Then a stranger cracked off, 'My God, it's one of those new daylight robberies—they've taken everything.'

'I should so like something to sit on,' said Lady Beeder, still faint.

'There isn't anything,' said the stranger. And I heard him

running about. 'Yes, they've even taken up the linoleum.'
And in fact Bisson's friend had given us only four and sixpence for two almost new pieces of best quality linoleum
from the bathroom. The ticket was in the envelope.
'They've taken the lot, Flora—all your beautiful collection.
What a terrible thing. We must call the police at once.
Where's the phone?' And he rushed to the corner next the
door and began to ring up the house exchange and to
shout, 'Hullo—police. Yes, put me on to the police. It's
important—a big robbery.'

'But what is that on the wall?' Lady Beeder sighed. 'I
don't understand.'

'I think they're meant for feet,' said Sir William. I peeped
over the edge of the balustrade and there was Sir William
dusting the packing-case I used for a table and pulling it
forward for Lady Beeder to sit on. But she still kept gazing
round her and then looking at the Feet. For you understand that the grave and Lazarus and the bald heads, so
important to the composition, were only sketched in; so
that the feet appeared rather prominent. 'Feet,' said Lady
Beeder.

'Hullo, hullo. Yes, the police. My poor Flora. I can't say
how sorry I am. It's a dreadful misfortune. Irremediable,'
said the stranger, who was a little pink-nosed man with
pince-nez glasses and a pinch-waist overcoat. 'One of the
finest private collections in the country. So perfectly bal-
anced. Quite unique. Hullo.'

'Looks a bit queer, I'm afraid,' said Sir William, in a
reasonable voice. He was much more worried by Lady
Beeder's demand for a chair. Because obviously he wanted
to sit down himself. 'Do sit down, my dear. The box is
only slightly dusty.'

'But where are we going to sleep?' said Lady Beeder.
'Really, I do so wish we could have known about this
sooner.'

'It's come at an awkward time,' said Sir William, 'very
awkward. But I could ring up Aunt Lucy. She's always
delighted to have us.'

'A national calamity,' said Pinch-nose, who was fizzing
with indignation, like a soda-water bottle. Probably he was
a poor citizen, a Boorjay, perhaps even a writer of some
kind. He had none of the Beeders' repose in the face of
lost property. And again I said, 'God bless all Beeders.

244

God bless the millionaires, who can forgive everything unless it bothers them too much.'

'Oh no, Bill,' said Lady Beeder, 'I really couldn't face being entertained.'

'Shall I try the Savoy?' said Sir William, going towards the telephone.

'Aren't the Mortons there—they would be so terribly sorry for us.'

'Claridge's then—yes, excuse me, James.' And Sir William went to the phone.

'But the police—they're getting me the police,' said Pinch-nose. 'Every moment counts.'

'We really must have somewhere to sit, James,' said her ladyship, 'we can't live on packing-cases.'

And Sir William took the phone out of the little man's hand and said, 'Just a moment, James. Hullo, Claridge's, please. Never mind about the police just now. I want Claridge's. As soon as possible. It's rather urgent.'

And little Pinch-waist was in such a fury and a fluster that he shouted he would call up the police from the public phone. And shot out of the room in a passion.

Now Sir William and Lady Beeder were behaving so well that I had half a mind to call down to them and explain the situation. That all the pawn tickets were in the empty tomato tin on the top of the bathroom door, where the mice wouldn't get them. But the little man had given me a fright with his shouts for the police. A dangerous type, as I could see and hear. Probably a hanger-on. One of those rats who take advantage of good-natured gentlemen and ladies like the Beeders. Full of parasitic bitterness and bum-suck spite.

So I decided to explain myself from a distance. Luckily Claridge's had a room for the Beeders, and Sir William at once rang up a taxi, and while he was putting Lady Beeder into the taxi, I went quietly out by the studio door, grabbed my mackintosh and overcoat, passed down the back stairs and followed Nosy towards the fried fish shop.

I met him on the next corner and told him the necessary facts, that a quick move was essential. 'Preferably by country bus, from the central depot. No railway stations for me. They watch 'em in a case like this.'

'Whew—watch them?' said Nosy, who was greatly alarmed. He thought we were going to be arrested. 'It's all right,' I told him. 'We haven't got to be afraid of the police so much as the rain. I've got a bit of a cold in my head and a wet night in the rough might bring on my churchyard cough which is the worst of the five. How much money have you?'

'I have the f-fish and the chips, and the whew-whisky,' said Nosy, shivering with terror. 'And the change was ninepence and I've got a two-shilling bit.'

'And I have eightpence. We'll have to conserve our resources.' I held up my hand at the bus stop for a Victoria bus, and we went to the front seat on top. So that the conductor would take time to reach us. And I tried to put some heart into Nosy.

'It's not that we have done anything illegal,' I said, 'but there would have to be a legal investigation which would waste a lot of time. I'd be badgered to death by inquiries and solicitors when I ought to be at work. And then I might get irritated against the government. Which would be stupid. It's no good telling a government that an artist's time and peace of mind might be valuable to a nation, that is, of positive value, bringing in reputation and tourists and students and orders and friends and respect and allies and victories and security, and so on. It's no good telling it because it couldn't hear. It doesn't possess the necessary organ. It's no good running down the government,' I said, 'any more than swearing at a paralytic mule for having the habits appropriate to its condition.'

I admit that this language was injudicious; it's never wise to feel irritation against the lower animals, especially if they deserve it. But the truth was, that I was a trifle upset. For I kept on thinking, I'm getting on for seventy now, and I haven't the constitution I had at sixty. I'm in my prime as a painter, but how long will it last? Ten, fifteen years at the outside. Old Mike Angelo was at his best at eighty-five, but then he went and died. No, I can't afford to waste my time in jug, or hospital. The very idea made me angry.

'No,' I said, 'that's the very biggest mistake anyone can make, to get annoyed with government. Because it's so easy.'

Just then the conductor reached us and I held out two pennies and said, 'Hammersmith, two, please. Like my brother-in-law, Ranken—'

'Hammersmith?' said the conductor. 'Why, you're going the wrong way.'

Some of the passengers smiled, and I was greatly confused. 'But this is a No. 11,' I said, 'I saw it on the outside.'

'Yes, but it's going the other way. See? Sorry, sir. You'd better wait at the next stop—on the other side.'

'Oh dear, I must have read it backwards.'

And we got off. And took another Victoria bus. 'My brother-in-law, Ranken,' I said, as we made for the top front seats, 'was an inventor, God help him.

'And he couldn't get anyone to take up his patents. So he used to curse the government and say that it was a lot of Boorjuice Blimps starving the inventive genius of the nation. "All I want is a little progressive spirit—just a little—somewhere."

' "You can't get it," I said, "over the counter, not even in a special bottle. Progress isn't done by governments or spirits, but by chaps. A few rich chaps gambling on their fancy and a few young chaps backing them up in order to give papa and mama a shock. It's just the same in art," I said. "What keeps it moving is not a big public shoving its little foot forward, but a little mosquito biting a big public behind. If you left the world to itself," I said, "it would die of fatty degeneration in about six weeks. It would lie down in the nice rich mudbank where it finds itself and close its eyes and stuff its ears and let itself be fed to death down a pipe-line. But God, not intending to lose a valuable pedigree hog that way, has sent the mosquito to give it exercise, and fever and the fear of death." '

'Fares, please,' said the conductor. He was quite worried when he found we were on the wrong bus. A nice chap like so many bus conductors, especially London conductors. He got down to show us where to find the stopping-place and which side of the road to look for a Hammersmith bus. And we had to wait in a queue till he was out of sight. It was only polite. Then we crossed the street to the country-bus centre.

'B-but how are we going to p-pay for the tickets?' asked Nosy.

'That's the real difficulty,' I said, taking off my hat to wipe my anxious forehead. I was passing the queue at the time, as it happened, and several gentlemen put something into the hat. True, by a coincidence, I was simultaneously carrying a matchbox in my other hand.

And finding myself then at the top of the queue, which willingly made way for me, out of respect for my age or perhaps my appearance, distinguished by four days' beard and my habit of rolling my eyes and grinding my gums together, I took the opportunity of buying tickets for a considerable part of our way.

Providence had blessed us and we should have embarked at once, if Nosy at this moment, already slightly confused by the bustle of a great city, had not run into a policeman, and recoiled with such looks of horror and guilt, that the officer at once exclaimed, 'Here—what's this?'

But I quickly recognized the man. 'It's Tom Jones,' I said. 'How are you, officer?' 'Very well, thank you,' he said. 'But my name's not Jones.' 'No,' I said, 'but you gave me a shilling once for my kip when I was trying to sleep on a bench down by Millbank.' 'Did I?' he said, putting his hands together and grinding them a little. 'I thought I knew you. Well, how are things?' 'Not too good,' I said. 'Thank you all the same. But not too bad either. Me and my boy have got to get to Burlington tonight, and we've got a shilling towards our breakfast. But it isn't raining yet. We could sleep rough.'

'The Burlington bus,' said the officer. And he took us down to the bus. Then having seen us get on and made sure that I wasn't telling the tale, he took out a shilling and gave it to me, 'Here you are. This will give you a kip.'

Nosy was much excited. He turned red in patches, like a bad case of scarlet fever, as usual when he was moved in his best feelings, and tears came to his eyes. 'How awfully k-k-k—'

'Yes,' I said, 'I hadn't quite expected that myself. But after all, one oughtn't to be surprised. My experience is that the police are pretty reliable, especially if they've ever done you a good turn before, or think they have.' 'D-didn't he help you before?' 'I don't know. Probably not. They all look the same to me in uniform. No, I rather think the chap who gave me a bob before was a sergeant with a red moustache. But that doesn't matter. Most officers have given something to an old bum like me. And naturally they take an interest in you afterwards. It's natural. Well,' I said, 'I honour policemen—as a class, they're nice chaps and a good deal better than the government deserves, but I suppose nobody gets his deserts.'

For the bus was shaking up my bones, and my rheumatism was beginning to shoot, and I was wondering what would happen to my palettes and colours and drawings; all my gear left behind at the Beeders'. I'm too old, I thought, to be poor. And too hardworking to be deprived of my tools and my studio. It's an outrage. And I said to Nosy, 'To accuse government of being selfish, cruel, blind, deaf and dumb, is simply stupid; because what else can you expect? What is a government, Nosy? It's a committee of committees and a committee hasn't even got trousers. It's only got a typist, and she's thinking of her young man and next Saturday afternoon at the pictures. If you gave a government imagination, it wouldn't know where to put it. It would pass it on to the cat or leave it out for the charwoman to be taken away with the tea leaves. The only good government,' I said, 'is a bad one in the hell of a fright; yes, what you want to do with government is to put a bomb under it every ten minutes and blow its whiskers off—I mean its sub-committees. And it doesn't matter if a few of its legs and arms go too, and it gets blown out of the window. Not that I've personally got a bad opinion of governments, as governments. A government is a government, that's all. You don't expect it to have the virtues of a gorilla because it doesn't belong to the same class. It's not a higher anthropoid. It has too many legs and hands. But if you blow off some of the old limbs, well, imagine. There you have a piece of government lying in the middle of Whitehall, and it says to itself, "This is most unusual. I distinctly heard a bang. I must inquire at once—yes, immediately—I must appoint a commission." So then it opens its eyes and looks at the crowd and says, "My God, what has happened, what are these creatures?" And the people say, "We're the people, you're the government, hurry up and do something for us." And the government says, "I'll have a committee on it at once." And the people say, "You haven't got any committees—they're all dead—you're the government." And the government says, "Haven't I got a secretary?" And the people shout, "No, we've just chopped her up with a rusty axe." "Or an office boy?" "No, we've pushed him down a drain." ' "But I can't be a government all by myself." '

' "Yes you are, and you've got to do something."

' "But one man can't be a government, it isn't democratic."

' "Yes it is," the people say. "We've sent for another bomb. But you've got ten minutes still, so you'd better do something."

'So then the government looks round and thinks. It uses its imagination because it hasn't got any committee and because it hasn't got a secretary. It gets an idea all by itself, and it says, "Jimini Christie, look at all these people. Look at their trousers and their gamps. What squalor. It seems that they aren't in the government." And then it makes a law that everyone is to get a steel-stick umbrella and a trouser-press free. And all the old clubmen who used to be in government say, "It's impossible, it can't be done. The people won't stand it." But it is done, it is possible, and the people not only stand it, they ask for trousers as well, to put in the presses. And then the old clubmen themselves ask for new trousers and take it all as a matter of course. And then the bomb comes and the people blow that government into cottage pie and start again with committees. For the people is just as big a danger as the government. I mean, if you let it get on your mind. Because there's more of it. More and worse and bigger and emptier and stupider. One man is a living soul, but two men are an indiarubber milking machine for a beer engine, and three men are noises off and four men are an asylum for cretins and five men are a committee and twenty-five are a meeting, and after that you get to the mummy-house at the British Museum, and the Sovereign People and Common Humanity and the Average and the Public and the Majority and the Life Force and Statistics and the Economic Man brainless, eyeless, wicked spawn of the universal toad sitting in the black bloody ditch of eternal night and croaking for its mate which is the spectre of Hell.'

33. For we were waiting for another bus to take us anywhere, somewhere down in Sussex, and it was as dark as the inside of a

Cabinet Minister. 'Give me another drink,' I said to Nosy, 'I've got a chill on my bones.' And I took a little whisky out of the bottle. I hate whisky, it burns up the blood. But I didn't want to get irritated against the government, and especially the people. 'If I wasn't a reasonable man,' I said to Nosy, 'I should get annoyed with Governments and the People and the World, and so on. I should get into a state and wish that the dirty silly bitch had a nose so that I could kick it between the eyes. I should say that bugs have better manners and lice have more distinguished minds.' And then I began to say what I might have said about governments. And Nosy took me by the arm and steered me away from the lamp-post where the people were waiting. 'Someone might hear,' he said. 'Let them,' I said, and I was just going to tell them what I thought of the People, when I gave a stagger. Nosy caught hold of me. And I noticed my head was aching. And I thought, it's a stroke. So they've killed me after all—they've done worse than kill me. I daren't speak or move. In case I should find I was dumb or helpless. And I felt my indignation so hot and strong it was big enough to blow the stars out of their nail-holes.

But I saw the danger in time. And I said, 'Hold me up, Nosy, and keep cool. No malice intended. Revenge has a green face, he feeds on corpses. The king on his throne must never groan. One jump from death to life. Is my face all right?'

'What is it, sir?' said Nosy. 'What do you mean?' For the lad was frightened. 'Is my face crooked?' I said. 'Like usual?' 'Yes, just like usual,' said Nosy, peering at me in the light of the lamp. 'And am I touching your nose?' I said, putting out my finger at his nose. 'Yes, dats by dose,' said Nosy, sneezing. Then I knew I was all right. 'A narrow escape,' I said. 'The government nearly got me that time.' 'Where are they?' said Nosy, looking fiercely at a chap in a bowler. 'They nearly knocked me off my pins,' I said. 'Put me into a temper. But by God, I beat 'em. Yes, there's spunk in the old louse.'

'I suppose it's only their job,' said Nosy. 'I mean the police.'

'I forgive 'em, Nosy. And tomorrow I shall forget 'em. To forgive is wisdom, to forget is genius. And easier. Because it's true. It's a new world every heart beat. The sun rises seventy-five times a minute. After all, what is a people? It doesn't exist. Only individuals exist—lying low in their own rat-holes. As far apart as free drinks. Further because nothing can bring them into the same space. And what is a government individually, a hatful of prophets and murderers dreaming of bloody glories and trembling at the grin of the grave. I forgive it, the belly-ripping abortionist, the batter-brained, cak-handed, wall-eyed welsher, the club-foot trampler, the block-eared raper that would sell its sister for a cheer, the brick-faced hypocrite that would wipe art and artists off the face of the earth as it would skin an orange, and cut the balls off the genius of the Lord to make a tame gee-gee for the morning Park. I forgive it,' I said, as we got on to the bus. 'I forgive government, with all its works, because it can't rise out of its damnation, which is to be a figment.'

'That's rather strong,' said a gentleman in shammy-gloves, opposite.

'A figment,' I said. 'A spectre living among a spectrous world—a satan in a mill.'

They were all looking at me as if I were cracked or religious, and so I said to them, 'I also stood in Satan's bosom and beheld its desolations.'

> A ruined man, a ruined building of God, not made
>   with hands:
> Its plains of burning sand, its mountains of marble
>   terrible:
> Its pits and declivities flowing with molten ore and
>   fountains
> Of pitch and nitre: its ruined palaces and cities and
>   mighty works:
> Its furnaces of affliction, in which his angels and
>   emanations
> Labour with blackened visages among its stupendous
>   ruins.

'Excuse me,' said the gentleman, 'but I don't hold with attacking the government. Mr Chamberlain seems to me—'

'Who is Mr Chamberlain?' I said, for I knew I had heard the name. Yes. In connection with orchids.

They were all very surprised. But respectful. Thinking I must be cracked. 'He is the Prime Minister. The Head of the Government.'

'God help him,' I said. 'He had better be the head of a mop, pushed by a lot of dead wood behind and nothing in front but loose dirt and flat-faced paving stones.'

'Moreover,' said the gentleman, putting his shammy-gloves well forward on the top of his umbrella. And I could see what he was by birth and profession, a real old Boorjoe. Rusticus, Moreoverus. 'Moreover,' he said, 'it's my opinion that this is a good government—we need a strong government in these times. Strong for peace.' 'Hear, hear,' said a lady in pince-nez, sitting beside me with a man's portfolio. Lecturer. Boorjwas Pacificus Furiosouse. 'And not afraid to stand up to the warmongers in the army and navy and air force.' 'Men like this Air Minister,' said the Boorjoe, and his gloves were quite fiery with indignation. 'Just provoking Germany with their aeroplanes and battle-ships,' said the lady, amid enthusiastic cheers from a representative audience; that is, two grunts, and an approving sniff from a thin little woman opposite in goggles, with a little red nose and a basket of eggs on her knee; small farmer's wife.

'Thank God we *have* got a strong government,' said the lady, looking round to see if anyone dared to contradict her. 'Thank God you have,' I said. 'A government can't be too strong. I hope your government is a lot of devils. Or they won't have much chance against devils like you and me, ma'am. Look how we treat a government, worse than rats or bugs. The poor creature hasn't a real friend in the world. And the more it does for us, the worse we abuse it. Why, after a really long and glorious life, a government had better hang or shoot itself. And even the little boys in the street will spit on its coffin. There ought to be a branch of the Cruelty to Animals Society to protect governments, with special homes, of course, where the prevailing wind blows out to sea, and a lethal chamber. It's kinder to put them out of their misery before they retire. For of all the ungrateful spiteful cruel savages in the world, when it comes to dealing with governments, give me a Free and Sovereign People.'

'Speak for yourself,' said the egg woman.

'I can't speak for anyone else,' I said, 'I don't know the language.' And just then the bus stopped and the conductor told us our tickets wouldn't take us any farther. So we got out, and there we were on a road in the middle of a forest. Through the forest we could see the sea. And the bus went off like a comet, like the flaming world. We were alone, and Nosy said in an alarmed voice, 'Where are we, Mr Jimson?'

'There,' I said.

'But where shall we sleep?'

'Here,' I said.

'But it's raining, Mr Jimson.'

'Not where I am,' I said. 'I've got my mackintosh and overcoat. Or if they aren't mine, they're Sir William's, which are better.'

'But Mr Jimson, you know how you suffer in your chest.'

'You don't know how I suffered in London, neither did I,' I said. For the country was a bit of a surprise to me. It always is. And I hadn't seen a real wild tree for twelve years. I couldn't take my eyes off 'em, bulging out into the moon as solid as whales. By God, I thought, no one has seen a tree till this moment. And I believe I could paint it. And then again I felt that shape of the big fish and Churchill's hat. I felt an idea, a big one.

> *'Thou knowest,' I said, 'that the ancient trees seen by*
> *thine eyes have fruit,*
> *But knowest thou that trees and fruits flourish upon*
> *the earth*
> *To gratify senses unknown? trees, beasts and birds*
> *unknown;*
> *Unknown, not unperceived, spread in the infinite*
> *microscope,*
> *In places yet unvisited by the voyager?'*

That is, until the voyager arrives. With the eye of imagination. And sees the strange thing. And throws a loop of creation around it.

'What we want is a place between the roots where leaves have drifted,' I said. 'This will do. No, don't touch 'em, don't turn 'em over. They'll be wetter underneath.'

'But your chest, Mr Jimson,' said the boy, playing the nurse of genius.

'Give me that bottle and go back to your mammy,' I said.

I spread out Sir William's overcoat and curled it round us. And put the mac on top, and we slept like birds till the morning, one eye open, and knowing all the time which way the wind blew, and how the clouds sailed. And came so wide awake at sunrise it was like flying off into the dirty sky.

There was Nosy rolling his eyes at the forest which was only a dozen trees round a petrol pump; with a villa opposite, and a parade down below, with some bathing-boxes and the sea coming in as grey as solder.

'We've got to get away from here,' he said.

'No,' I said, 'It's a good place. I've got to earn our living.' The beech over our heads had boughs so long it made my shoulders ache.

'But you haven't any paints, Mr Jimson.'

'Painting isn't a livelihood,' I said. 'Not if you paint anything worth the trouble. Give me a lift—my legs won't bend.'

So he got me up, all of a piece, and I took out the newspapers.

'There's a policeman,' he said.

'Never mind the police,' I said, for I wasn't going to let the government interfere with my notions. 'Go home to your mammy.'

'You don't want me to do that, Mr Jimson.'

But I didn't answer him. The wind in the leaves was removing my landmarks. A big idea, I felt it grow. The whale of an idea.

'A nice mess you've made of your life,' I said, 'throwing away that scholarship.'

It was drizzling rain and Nosy stood on one foot like a young horse, with the drops sticking to his nose and his ears flopped, meditating.

'Come on,' I said, jingling Tom Jones's shilling against three sixpences, 'I'm hungry.'

'I don't think it's a mess,' he said. 'It's only starting.'

'Wait till they jug you,' I said. 'Five years. And come out creeping or cracked. How much money have you got left?'

Still meditating, he put his red knobby boy's hand into his pocket and took out a shilling, fourpence halfpenny in coppers, a front stud and a Napoleon ten cent.

'The French copper will go in the machine for a packet of chocolate. We'll call it one-and-six,' I said, 'and you can charge it to expenses.'

'Perhaps it would be good for me,' he said.

255

'What would?' I said. For the waves kept breaking into my stiffness.

'Prison,' said he.

'My God,' I said, smelling the coffee outside a chromium restaurant. 'You ought to be a bath bun sitting on the road and waiting for the steam roller to expand your soul. Come on.' For the chromium restaurant was full of snotty girls with permanent waves, Deadheads. And the sea was on the move, rattling my shells and making jewels of my pebbles. Knocking away my fences. Strokes of the prophet.

> *I stood in the streams*
> *Of Heavens bright beams,*
> *My eyes more and more*
> *Like a sea without shore*
> *Continue expanding.*
> *The Heavens commanding.*

'I beg your pardon, Mr Jimson,' said Nosy.

'This looks a good place,' I said. 'Flyblown all over the windowpanes and three night lorries at the door. Yes, two women that ought to be girls half dead with worry and work and grease and noise and desperation. That's the place. Back to the wall. Quality, quantity, or death. Spit on the floor and say your grace to the cabbage stumps.'

So we went in and ate a meal. And when Nosy had forked down two rashers as thick as a bank door, two old eggs as strong as floor polish, half a loaf of bread and a half pound of marg., he said to me cheerfully, 'It's all experience.'

'So is a brick to a dead cat,' I said. 'The question is, what and what for?'

For I had eaten so much my wits were like drums and gave off only echoes.

'Prison,' he said.

'Yes,' I said, 'but a hatchet would be better to let some daylight into your loaf,' and I was so angry I was nearly rude to the boy. But then I thought, Keep cool. He's young. He's earnest. He's empty. He's like a new sawmill with nothing to cut—all buzz and bust. Ready to fly off its own steel, so I said, 'Have you thought how we're going to eat?'

'Yes, Mr Jimson—I'm sure you oughtn't to sleep in ditches.'

This surprised me. But there's a lot of child in a boy, and children are always practical. 'And what are you going to do for money?'

'I thought I'd get a job.'

'What kind of job?' I said.

'A navvy,' he said, 'or something like that.'

'For the experience,' I said.

'I thought perhaps it's what I need. To touch the bottom.'

'Navvies are not at the bottom,' I said. 'Government is at the bottom. But they wouldn't have you. You can't get in on the ground floor without a scholarship.'

'Or an errand boy,' he said.

But I couldn't listen to him. The wind had come off my belly as sweet as an infant. The clouds had poured away. And as we went along the road the sky kept jingling my bells.

'This must be somewhere near Somewhere,' said Nosy, getting out of the way of a Rolls Royce full of butcher's meat in pin stripes. Looking for larks in lounges, at three pounds a day. 'By the downs,' said Nosy.

'A wonderful place for larks,' I said. For there were two of them taking their first rise out of a sleepy morning.

> He leads the choir of day, trill, trill, trill, trill,
> Mounting upon the wings of light into the great expanse,
> Reechoing against the lovely blue and shining heavenly shell,
> His little throat labours with inspiration; every feather
> On throat and breast and wings vibrates with the effluence divine.
> All nature listens silent to him, and the awful sun
> Stands still upon the mountain looking on this little bird
> With eyes of soft humility and wonder, love and awe.

I said, 'That's better even than bacon. Talk of nature. What is Nature to a man like old Billy Blake. To the imagination of genius. A door to glory.'

'There's a man following us,' said Nosy. 'He looks like a detective.'

'Very likely he is,' I said. 'Let him follow. Following is the government job. Ours is to lead the way. And you

257

ought to be selling insurance. Nice safe work—in five years you would have your own Rolls Royce.'

'I shouldn't want one.'

'Don't despise the good, the true and the beautiful.'

'I don't, but I want to be an artist.'

'Art is the biggest luxury of the lot,' I said, going into a post office. 'Like keeping alive. Which costs the earth.' I had one-and-fourpence over from the breakfast bill, and I bought a dozen postcards of the Burlington sights, the Promenade, the best churches, the piers. Good stuff. And six envelopes.

Nosy gazed at me with round eyes. But too polite to ask a question.

'Souvenirs,' I said. 'You wait at the corner here, and if you see a man with a blue face, ask him what's the time by his clock.' I put two cards in each envelope and stuck them up. A door to glory. The larks had stopped singing. Coming down, I supposed. A Memorable Fancy.

> How do you know but every bird that cuts the airy way,
> Is an immense world of delight, closed by your senses five?

Yes, I thought, fixing my eye on a superior pub. The angels must always be surprised when some man dives head-first into dirt, and then just by a twist of his imagination comes out again as clean as a comet with two wings bigger than the biggest in all heaven.

I had my eye on the saloon bar, and just then a young man came out.

Nice young man in a blue suit, with a dark blue hat, and new shoes. But green silk socks. So I drew up level with him and let my arm touch his and all at once I showed him an envelope and gave him the wink and said, 'Want any postcards, mister? Beauties of Brighton. Nice new views. For artists only. Plain envelope.'

'No,' he said. 'Go away. How much?'

'Five bob to you, sir. They're worth five pounds to a real artist. Art photos.'

'Half a crown,' he said.

I turned away, but he said quickly, 'All right, you old blackguard, hand over.'

He gave me two florins and plucked away the envelope.

258

It went into his pocket so quickly that it seemed to vanish in the air. The young man gave me a glance and said, 'You get off or I'll call a copper.'

I got off. I didn't trust that young man. But I was angry at the mean way he had swindled me. I hate the meanness of a man who throws away his self-respect for a bob. 'He thought I was a dirty old blackguard,' I told Nosy, 'and so he cheated me. There's a glimpse of human nature for you—a fellow that will make a shilling out of a dirty old blackguard.' And I was growing hot and furious when I saw how I was forgetting myself. 'I could kill that man,' I said, 'but why poison my wells with his nasty corpse?' So I went in and had a couple of pints and that man seen through the bottom of a pot seemed so small that I could dote upon him like any hair-leg of a flea. 'He was a fly-flat,' I said to Nosy. 'Poor little basket, he'll have but a hard life. Fly-flats fill all asylums and gaols and morgues and unions in the world. The flat is a flat, he keeps on the rails and carries only registered luggage. A fly man is a fly man, he spreads his wings and dives on his prey. But the fly-flat is a flat that thinks he's fly and even the worms bite him for the price of a workhouse coffin.'

Nosy kept on looking at me, and every time he looked he blushed.

'But the postcards were only twopence,' he said.

'So they were,' I said.

'Why did he give you four shillings for them?'

'Because I needed the money and you needed the money.'

'Was it charity?'

'No, it was commerce. Luxury trade. Due to the imagination. Ships, motors, wars, bankers, factories, swindles, taxes and ramps are all due to the imagination. For or against. A man who cuts a throat because of imagination is hanged by a judge who is appointed to keep imagination in order. If it wasn't for imagination,' I said, 'we shouldn't need any police or government. The world would be as nice and peaceful and uninteresting as a dead dog full of dead fleas. That's what I said to Ranken when he sold his patent regulator to a rich firm called Rackstraw, who were going to put it on the market. And then they found out that it wouldn't suit the market. "We're sorry, Mr Ranken," they said, "but your regulator is rather too sensitive—

there is no demand at present for anything so delicate. Our customers prefer something cheaper, even if it doesn't do the work so well." And when Ranken told them how to make his regulator cheaper, by making a lot at once, they shook their heads and said that there wouldn't be a demand. "Then make a demand," said Ranken. "Advertise." But they put him off and put off the regulator too. They couldn't be bothered. Why should they? Old rich firm. Chief in Parliament, eldest son in the Guards, another on the county council.

'Ranken had a fit, and when my sister got him round again, he wanted to shoot old Rackstraw, who'd probably never heard of him. "Keep cool, old chap," I said. "Look at the bright side. They didn't put you in quod or burn you alive. That's what happens to most pioneers. And serve 'em right for upsetting people and business and old-established markets, which means private and domestic family affairs. And you've still got your imagination. You can go on inventing things. You don't have to make out with parliament and pedigree bulls and social importance like those poor devils the Rackstraws." '

'But excuse me,' said Nosy, who like all good virtuous people, is a bit persistent. You might as well try to divert him as a colic. 'Those p-postcards.'

'Not at all,' I said. 'But I see what you mean. Now if you don't mind, will you go into that shop over there and ask them how much credit they'd allow you on a bottle of whisky for half a crown, taking due account of the Scotch rate of exchange.'

And I went out and sold another envelope to a serious-looking gentleman in a blue collar. But he had patent leather shoes with white insertions. He paid five bob without a word. And a fierce-looking woman in pince-nez gave me six. She was all in black, but the back of her neck was powdered and her umbrella had a monkey carved up the handle.

I had to buy some more cards. Before tea-time I was worth three pounds. But Nosy had got wise and he was upset.

'It's not fuffit for you, Mr Jimson,' he said. 'I'd rather do it myself.'

'You couldn't, Nosy,' I said. 'It needs an artist—it needs a lot of imagination. You weren't cut out for any of the arts and crafts. You were born for a government job, and since you missed that scholarship, your only hope is superior drapery. Service. To distribute frocks. The latest creations. The new world of female vision. The prophecies of Paquin and Molyneux against the golden calf—last year's short skirts. And the glory of the Lord, that is, the new long skirts, eternally regenerated in Sion.'

My eye fell upon a long-faced young gentleman in a blue London suit, hand-sewn, crinkled all round the edges; with handmade black shoes, black socks, an Eden hat. Very distinguished. Just coming out of a first-class hotel. You would have taken him for the highest aristocracy, big business, or Wimbledon tennis, if it hadn't been for his pink silk shirt, tie, and handkerchief to match, arranged in two points. I felt for my cards.

'Because the world of imagination,' I said to Nosy, 'is the world of eternity.' For, as Billy says, 'There exist in that eternal world the permanent realities of everything which we see reflected in this vegetable glass of Nature.' And, I thought, in the works of Gulley Jimson. Such as red Eves and green Adams, blue whales and spotted giraffes, twenty-three feet high. Lions, tigers, and all the dreams of prophets whose imagination sustains the creation, and recalls it from the grave of memory.

'Just get me an evening paper, Nosy,' I said. 'I want to see the Academy news, if any.' And as Nosy went into a paper shop, I said to the young duke, 'Excuse me sir, but are you interested in art? I have here, at a great reduction, some of the finest reproductions of the photographic science. In plain envelope. Studies for students. Passed by censor. Latest lighting effects. For adults only. Half a guinea.'

'That's all right, old man,' he said, 'I was looking for you. Just step in here.' And he took me by the arm and pushed me up an alley. 'Fact is,' he said, 'I've had a complaint.'

'Have you?' I said. 'Well, look here.' And I opened an envelope and showed him my cards. Two local churches and a sunset over the sea. 'What's wrong with that?'

'Just what they told me,' he said. 'Why,' he said, taking me by the neck and giving me a poke in the stomach with his knee that nearly broke me in two. 'You dirty old crook —you son of a louse. What do you mean coming here on

261

my pitch and swindling decent people with your filthy tricks. My God,' he said, giving me a kick on the kneecap that brought the tears of remorse to my eyes. 'You make me sick, you hound. Taking advantage of a lady that you aren't fit to speak to. I've a bloody good mind to set about you. If I wasn't afraid of dirtying my hands.' Then he kicked me up and kicked me down; kicked me in the guts and kicked me on the jaw; kicked me into the road and danced on me three or four times. His feet moved so fast one couldn't see them. At last Nosy came up, panting, and shouted for the police. The young gentleman then knocked Nosy down, kicked him five or six times a second for five seconds, and went away in a Daimler limousine, with a liveried chauffeur and a bunch of fresh flowers in the vase.

After that the police came and took me to hospital in an ambulance. And Nosy was waiting on the pavement when they carried me across. Purple with running behind and two black eyes where our honest friend had kicked him on the nose, but full of grief for the misfortunes of genius. The tears were creeping round the new nose, which was shaped like a loganberry. 'You go back to Mammy,' I said to him, 'and ask her to forgive me.'

But he only shook his head, with looks of horror and despair. A terrible experience for Nosy. You could see he was suffering terribly and enjoying every minute of it.

When they put me to bed they found I had a broken nose, a broken arm, a broken collar bone, four broken ribs, three broken fingers, three or four square yards of serious contusions and a double 'rupture. The Sister thought I ought to die, the house surgeon thought I was dying, and the nurse was sure I ought to be going off before tea-time, as she hadn't a relief. And I was so angry that I might have done myself a serious injury, if I hadn't said to myself, Hold on, Gulley. Don't lose your presence of imagination. Wash out that blackguard till you're well again and get a new pair of boots. With nails in them. Forgive and forget. Till you have him set. Remember that he had a certain amount of excuse for his actions. Give him his due, but not till you are ready with a crowbar. Don't get spiteful. Keep cool. It's the only way to handle a snake like that. Approach the matter in a judicious spirit, meet him with a friendly smile, and a couple of knuckledusters. Don't let him get on your nerves, that counts him one; but get on his face and push it through his backbone, that counts you one, two, three and an old age without regrets. Your only resort in a case like this is the Christian spirit. Because you haven't got anything else.

Then I began to feel better and when Nosy came to see me next afternoon, I made him buy me a penny notebook and a threepenny box of chalks. And my left hand began to draw things that surprised me. 'Yes,' I said, when I saw them, 'that's it.'

'What is it?' said Nosy, who happened to be looking over my shoulder.

'It,' I said. 'Yes, that is to say, a fact, a poke in the belly, well, it's got a feeling, hasn't it?—in fact, unless I'm much mistaken, it's something, almost itself by itself.'

34.   Of course, while I was in hospital, Nosy went down hill. First down; and then up again. He began to show his true bent, which was for commerce. First he got a job as a dishwasher in a teashop, then he sold newspapers; then he was an errand boy in a grocery. Now, if he had gone into the postcard business under some arrangement with the gentleman who owned the local pitch, he could have made money, and set us both up again. But as I always said, Nosy had no imagination. He was born to be an angel of grace.

And I was desperate for a few pounds, because I knew that I had the biggest idea of my life. It had begun from those trees on our first night in the country. Something bigger than the new Fall. A Creation. And I saw it about fifteen feet by twenty, the biggest thing I had ever seen. It would need a special studio, a special canvas, or wall; a full equipment of ladders, scaffolds, etc.; and buckets full of colour.

This thing grew on me all the time I was in hospital, till I dreamed blue whales, like gasometers; and red women growing out of the ground, with legs like Lolie's roots; and trees putting out their apples to the wind, like little breasts.

'We'll want about a thousand pounds, Nosy, to do the thing as it ought to be done,' I said. And Nosy, who was just as excited about the thing as I was, would say, 'We must s-save up.' He made me laugh.

'No,' I said, 'I'll write to Sir William.'

'W-what?' said Nosy, with his eyes popping.

'Why not,' I said. 'He's rich—he's a connoisseur—it's his job to support art. Yes, I'll ask him to finance us, a thousand down; and say another thousand on delivery.'

'But the p-police,' said Nosy. 'What about all his things?'

'You don't understand millionaires, Nosy,' I said. 'A millionaire is nearly always wise. He doesn't let anything upset him. I remember when old Hickson was robbed by a blackguard of a dealer who sold him a fake. He made inquiries and found that it was no good running the man into court, because he had no money to pay damages. So he asked him to dinner and gave him the hint that he knew what he'd done, and asked for a tip the next time the dealer saw a good thing going cheap. And Hickson got several good things through that dealer. Because he had the sense to cut his losses.

'CUT YOUR LOSSES, CULLY GREEN, and start fair on Monday. That's pure Christianity. And I bet you,' I said to Nosy, 'that Sir William will say to himself, there's no point in quarrelling with Jimson, even if he was a bit careless with my armchairs. I can't have the armchairs made new by being rude to him, but I might still get a good picture out of him, by being reasonable.' So I wrote:

Dear Sir William,

I was very sorry to be away when you returned home; and I should certainly have called long ago, if it had not been for ill health which has kept me in the nurse's hands for some weeks.

I daresay you noticed that I had carried out your kind and generous suggestion for a wall decoration. I believe the suggestion was for tigers in the dining-room. But as the wall there proved difficult, I designed a Lazarus for the Studio. I think you'll agree that the change has been advantageous to us both.

I should have liked to complete this work for you as soon as possible, subject to some friendly understanding about price, but I find myself unable to spare the time, as I am engaged on a work of major importance, to be called the Creation. It has been suggested that I should reserve this work for the State, and I have had very large private offers. But I am prepared to give you an option for a thousand guineas (1,050, 10, including stamp fee); the completed work to cost 5,000 guineas (5,259, 19, with special stretcher, etc.) for the next seven days.

Please address care of my secretary,

H. Leslie Barbon, Esq.,
14a, Dog Lane Mews,
Burlington-on-Sea.

Yours sincerely, my dear Sir William,
Gulley Jimson

You have noticed that I sent the greater part of your furniture to store, to avoid damage during the painting, etc. The tickets were collected for safety in the safe deposit box on the top of the bathroom door, where you will find them in order. I feel myself entirely responsible for any damage, and I should like to be debited with such sums in view of a final settlement.

To this letter I received about a month later the following answer:

Dear Mr Jimson,

Sir William and Lady Beeder are at present in Cannes on a very necessary holiday. I forwarded your letter to Sir William, who has asked me to say how much he has appreciated your kind offer, and your care for his furniture, etc. But he would still prefer an easel picture; if possible, a study of the nude, in that inimitable brilliance of your Sara Monday period, to a mural. He fully understands the greater importance of the work proposed, but feels it unsuited to the modesty of his collection and his accommodation. He would be most gratified by a call from you on his return from abroad, of which however the date is at present uncertain.

I am yours most sincerely and respectfully,
A. W. Alabaster

'There you are, Nosy,' I said. 'I told you Beeder was fit to be a millionaire—and likely to stay one too. If he uses the same Christian rule on the Stock Exchange as he does in art collecting.'

And as soon as I was out of the hospital, I made a dart

for Capel Mansions. No one at home. But I dropped my card, giving for my address:

ELSINORE HOUSE, ELLAM LANE, S.W.

It was raining bayonets and fish-hooks, and when I got to Elsinore about six, I was wet both down and up. And my winter cough, though more melodious than my dust cough or spring cough, is also more trouble. I hadn't really got the time for it. So I arrived in a bad mood, ripe for the devil. And the first devil I saw, who was a great bum with a face like a warthog, standing in the kitchen door, I said to him, 'Get out of my way, you son of something or something else.' And when he turned around to kill me, I let out a scream like an engine whistle. Bad for your throat, but it causes surprise and consternation among the savages. ''Ere,' he said, falling back two yards, 'I didn't touch ya.'

About sixteen other bums were crowding round and some of them had the idea of taking me up by the area and putting me in the dustbin. But others wanted to carry me up the stairs in order to throw me down the front steps. I voted with the dustbin party. But the stairs party won. Another victory for imaginative art. And they had just got me by the legs and arms face downwards, and were pushing the kitchen door open with my head, when suddenly I heard a voice I seemed to know saying, 'Here, stop that.' The bums protested that I was a union rat, and had no business in a place like Elsinore. But they stood me on my feet and there was a little old man in blue overalls with one hand and one hook. He had a pail in the hook and a brush in the hand. That's funny, I thought, Plantie had one hand and did out the lavatories. Then I saw it was Plantie, grown about forty years older; and Plantie saw that it was me.

'Mr Plant?' I said.

'Mr Jimson,' said Plantie, dropping the broom and giving me his left hand. 'Welcome, sir,' and he shook hands with me in a distinguished manner. 'This is a great pleasure—come in—come in.'

He towed me across the kitchen into the scullery and the bums got out of his way as if he had been royalty. Warthog actually carried his broom for him.

'Here you are,' said Plantie, pulling out a chair for me.

'And stay as long as you like.' To Warthog he did not condescend to speak. He merely pointed at a corner. Warthog, leaning very carefully the broom against the wall, said, 'Excuse me, Mr Plant, but if I could have the key.' Plantie didn't seem to hear. Warthog shuffled about a bit, and then tried again, 'Excuse me, Mr Plant—'

Plantie didn't even look at him. He waved his book, and Warthog went out practically on tiptoe and shut the door behind him as gently as any chicken thief in the middle of the night.

'And how are you, Mr Jimson?' said Plantie. 'Pull up to the fire.' For he had a little fire in the copper grate.

He was smiling so pleasantly that I thought, He may be a bit broken down, but he's happy at last.

'You look well, Mr Plant.'

'I'm pretty well, thank you, Mr Jimson.'

'Same job?'

'Same job.'

It was like an echo from the back of a church. And I thought that the old gentleman needed encouragement.

'And I can see who's king of the castle,' I said. 'By Gee and Jay, what a change. I congratulate you, Mr Plant. How did you do it?'

'Yes,' said Mr Plant, smiling at the fire. But he didn't seem much gratulated.

'You keep the key.'

Mr Plant bent his head sideways; an old man's nod. And went on smiling at the fire.

'And what happens if you don't think a chap is worthy of your lavatory?'

'He can always go to the public gents down High Street.'

'About three-quarters of a mile and pay his penny. So that's how you got your hook in 'em, you old rascal.' I burst out laughing and clapped Mr Plant on the back. But Plant didn't laugh. He just had the same smile which didn't seem to be paying much attention.

'What they wanted was a philosopher to look after them,' I said. 'Why, that Warthog was almost human. It's a triumph, Mr Plant.'

Plantie was smiling at the ceiling. But he didn't seem to be noticing it.

'And how are you feeling, Mr Plant?'

'Very well, Mr Jimson. A bit older, of course. And that reminds me, there's some letters for you.'

And he went to his cupboard and brought out a packet of letters.

'Ha, ha,' I said. 'My fan mail—something from the Professor.' But they were all bills or circulars except one from Coker.

> *The Boathouse,*
> *22 Greenbank.*
> *31/7/39*
>
> *I'd be obliged if you pay me what you owe which is five pounds thirteen and tenpence. If you can pay a pound a week to that nasty Leslie Barbon who's broken his mother's heart you can pay me.*
>
> *D. B. Coker*
>
> *I'm on the make from now on, and don't you forget it. This means that I want my money.*
>
> *To Mr. Gulley Jimson, Esq.,*
> *Common Lodging House,*
> *Ellam Lane.*

'A very nice mail,' I said. 'Tells you that you're not forgotten.'

'There's something else too,' said Plantie, recollecting himself in the middle of some private thought. He took another dive into the cupboard and hooked out something like a sack of potatoes. 'Left here by a lady in a Rolls.'

The sack had a note tied to the neck by one corner. And when I read it I jumped in my boots for joy. The address was Gulley Jimson, Esq., Elsinore House, Ellam Lane, and the note: 'Sir William Beeder has asked me to remit these articles for you, and trusts that they are all in order.—M. B. M.'

And inside the sack there was a colour box, two palettes, two tins of bully beef and a cardboard stay box marked, 'Brushes and colours,' and sealed with tape.

'Just like a millionaire,' I said. 'I wish there were more like Sir William, with a lot of chauffeurs, cooks, secretaries, and M.B.M.'s to look after them and carry out their kind Christian thoughts. God bless his millions.'

But when I opened the colour box, there was nothing in it, not even a palette knife; and when I opened the cardboard box, it contained two worn-out brushes, a lot of old squeezed-out, dried-up tubes, and three empty oil bottles. Somebody had got away with about twenty nearly new brushes, and three or four dozen new tubes of colours. 'Just like a millionaire,' I said. 'Surrounded by a lot of barefaced robbers. God bless him and to hell with M.B.M. Unless he or she only came in after someone else had had the pickings.'

'Dear me,' said Plantie, shaking his head. 'But there you are.'

He was still smiling and I was a bit annoyed, so I said, 'It all means something.'

'Well, well,' said Plantie, as if he hadn't heard. So I thought it might be Spinoza again, and I said, 'A nice object of contemplation for the old tallyscoop.'

'Who?' said Plantie, smiling in the air and blinking his eyes. 'Who was that?'

'The glassy gazer—the old Popeye.'

But Plantie didn't seem to notice. And I thought perhaps he'd got over all his philosophies. Grown out of them. He'd stopped looking for a rabbit-hole and was feeling what you might call the nature of things, at last. Like my sister Jenny when her husband Ranken got his last knock. They were both very happy just then; the first time they'd been happy in their married lives because a keen young firm called Brouts had taken up the Ranken regulator. They were going to make regulators on a big scale in a special building, and Ranken drew some real money as manager of the department. But the South African war broke out and Brouts went smash. They had a lot of contracts with mines. Besides, they had been taking chances, giving a lot of credit and spending capital on developing new patents. An enterprising firm. Asking for trouble. And their stock, contracts, patents, etc., were bought up by one of the old steady companies which put the Regulator on the shelf. They hadn't any use for a flibbertigibbet gadget which had ruined Brouts already. They were a good forty years behind the times, building tried and trusty stuff for sound customers like the Admiralty and War Office.

The Rankens went bust for the third or fourth time. They had to pawn their clothes for food. And when Jenny came to borrow a few bob from me and to tell me the story, she didn't exactly smile. But she didn't cry either, as she'd done before; and blame the government, or the manufacturers, or her husband's enemies. She sat on my knee with her head on my shoulders, a comic sight, for Jenny, at thirty-two, looked like a worn-out char, and I was fresh from a casual ward; and she gave only one or two sighs. The kind they call heartfelt. But they really feel more than having your guts removed by the roots. And I said, 'Cheer up, old girl. Luck will turn.' But she shook her head. 'Why won't it turn?' 'It isn't just luck.' 'What else?' 'I don't know—just things, I suppose.' So she'd got a dim idea at last. 'Well,' I said, 'to hell with things. Send them to the devil.' 'But Robert is so wretched —it's awful to see how he suffers. I didn't know anyone could suffer like that day and night—and not go mad. He'll kill himself—I know he will.' 'Never,' I said. 'Especially if he says so.' 'He's often threatened to do it, and he will.' 'The trouble with Robert is he won't face facts, things if you like. He wants them to come and lick his feet. But they can't—they can't lick. They can only fall about like a lot of loose rocks in a runaway train. Your Robert has got himself in a state, and now you're in a state.' 'How can I help it when he's so miserable?' And, of course, there wasn't any answer to that. Jenny was a good lover. She couldn't get out of loving Ranken just by wishing it. She could forgive things for knocking her about, but not for knocking Ranken about. You couldn't expect it. And so she went just as she had come. No one on earth could do anything for her. She was pushed right up against it, as they say.

It's the same with a lot of old people; even the ones that used to have a pass key to eternal joy. All at once you find that they are rather quiet and thoughtful. And a bit inattentive to glories and triumphs. Like Plantie in his present authority. I thought he didn't set much value on the courtly attentions of such as Warthog; and I thought even his smile didn't mean what it had meant before. Old men when they begin to hear the last trumpet, on the morning breeze, often have a kind of absent-minded smile; like people listening. And their smiles are just politeness. They probably don't know whether they're laughing or crying, and perhaps they don't care so long as they're doing something or other. And they don't trouble much about what they're saying either, so long as it fills in the gaps of the conversation and expresses their general satisfaction at not being dead yet. So I didn't ask Plantie whether he was laughing at me or himself or anything else. I just went on keeping my own boiler warm, with my own feelings.

In fact, in spite of a certain rudeness in my cough, due to general indignation with the weather, and some anxiety about finance, I passed a very happy and peaceful evening with Plantie, in front of the copper fire. And a good night on a bed of chairs. For though I could not sleep, I had a good view, as Plantie pointed out, of the sky, through the top of the window, and the sky was like a cinema film gone mad. Great whirling heads and arms and noses, naked legs and trousered bottoms, guns, swords and top hats, rushing past all night. Sometimes you saw a lovely lady in a pose plastique, but before you could wink she had swelled out like a balloon, lost her leg or her head, and turned into an ammunition wagon galloping over the corpses.

Plantie himself did not sleep either. Whenever I looked his way I could see his little eyes glinting as he stared at the ceiling. But what he was thinking of, I don't know. An old man's thoughts are an old man's secret, and no one else would even understand them. He only once spoke to me, when he heard the chairs creak and said, 'You all right, Mr Jimson?'

'I'm all right, Mr Plant. Why aren't you asleep?'

'I've had my sleep. I wondered how you were sleeping.'

'Like a top,' I said. For it saves a lot of trouble between friends to swear that life is good, brother. It leaves more time to live.

35.

I didn't like Cokey's letter. It seemed to me that Coker might be turning dangerous. So I went down to the boat-shed next evening when Mrs Coker might be expected to be out at the late Saturday market, getting meat bargains, and took a peep through a side window. Nothing to be seen. But there was a sound like somebody pounding meat and cursing.

Now, when I had listened at the boat-shed, I could generally hear Mrs Coker's voice, grousing. A noise like the winter wind moaning softly through a broken jew's harp. But this sounded more like a wagon-load of railway irons being dragged along Pickleherring Street. It was more like Cokey in one of her old tempers. So at last I ventured to tap on the window.

'HULLO,' Cokey bawled. 'GET OFF YOU! OR IT'LL BE THE WORSE. WHO IS IT?'

'Jimson.'

'That's a lie, anyhow,' said Cokey, and she pulled the curtain. 'Hullo, Mr Jimson,' she said, 'it's you, is it?'

'Where's your mother, Cokey?'

'Gone, thank God. But you can't come in here now, I'm too busy.'

I could see that Cokey was in her apron mood, full of temper.

'When can I come in, Cokey? I want to see you badly.'

'You can come in now if you'll keep your feet off the floor.'

So I went in, and there was Cokey with a cloth over her head, house cleaning. And a kid of about two months was sucking its big toe in a smart new cradle over by the bed.

'Hullo,' I said. 'All the family. And I must say you look well on it, Cokey. Quite a figure.'

But Cokey was swearing at the dirt, at the broom, and the floor cracks and the job. 'Who would be a woman?' she said, 'chivvying dirt from morning to night, and changing nappies from night till morning. Yes,' she said, when the kid put his toe into his eye instead of his mouth and gave a squeak. 'You little bastard, you're good enough now when it doesn't matter, but what about last night? I didn't get a wink.'

'Here,' I said. 'You oughtn't to throw it at her, Cokey. It's not her fault.'

'Her? Does it look like a girl? Use your lamps, Mr Jimson. A boy, you bet. It knew what was what. And as for throwing it at the kid, he doesn't know English yet. Not that he won't, all right. If I don't tell him, everyone else will, and good for him too. Take him down a peg. He can't learn too soon that he's got to muck in with the rest of 'em.'

'Why, Cokey,' I said, 'I thought you'd be fond of a kid.'

'Oh yez,' said Cokey, 'I was waiting for the mother stuff. All I can say is Nature has done enough dirt on a woman without that. And don't you try it either,' she said to the kid. 'Don't you come it over me, you basket, or I'll leave you on the Union doorstep, like the Ellam Street girls do with their nasty little errors, that they don't even know who was their father—'

'Does Willie recognize his family?' I said.

'Mind your own business,' said Cokey. 'Willie has enough trouble with that slab-sided pork sucking the life out of him. And give me that dustpan. I don't know why I don't put myself in the river, with all the dirt. You'd think this bloody shed was a vacuum cleaner the way it sucks it up.'

'And a nice kid too,' I said. 'Look at the crinkles on it, like new pork sausages.'

'Just like a man,' said Cokey. 'You didn't have to have it. And that old Plant telling me that God sent me a baby. I wish they'd send Plantie a baby. He didn't send me a husband, did he? It was Willie gave me a kid, and only because he didn't take enough trouble. Come up, you nuisance.' And she took the kid out of the cradle and pulled off its frock. To wash it. But I could see she made a good job of the washing. And the kid cooed away as if it was being tickled by the angels.

'A good kid,' I said.

'So it ought to be,' said Coker. 'It's enough trouble. The district nurse says this is the finest kid in six months and the best looked after—she wanted to put it in the Show. But I wasn't going to hear people say, "Look at the little bastard." '

'How could they tell?'

'Why, you've only got to look at him. Or at me when I'm round.'

'You ought to wear a ring. Why, all the girls down Ellam Street wear rings, whether they've got kids or whether they haven't.'

'Ellam Street girls can do what they like, the dirty bitches,' said Coker, giving the breast. 'I got my pride. Come up, Johnny, take a long pull at it. I haven't got any time to waste.'

'Don't put him in the Navy, that's all. It's an insult in the Navy.'

'Well, I don't blame 'em. I shouldn't like it myself. Go on, Johnny, bite it off. It's only your mother. That's it, stick in your nails, I'm only another bloody woman.'

'Open up a bit more, I want your chest,' I said, drawing away.

'Don't you draw me,' said Cokey. 'You've no right to see as much as you do. It's only because I'm too fed up to go in the scullery and you're just out of hospital. What you ought to do, Mr Jimson, if you had any sense, is stay here and let somebody see you got looked after properly, for once in a way. You look awful, strike me, you're enough to frighten a sexton. As for talk, let 'em talk. They've been talking about me for a year, that whore Coker and her bastard. Now they can add a lodger to that.'

'I should like that very much, Cokey. You're a nice girl, whatever anyone says. And I was needing a model.'

'A model. What do you take me for?'

'If I don't get a model and studio you won't get that money.'

'Don't you talk models to me or I'll answer back. But why can't you do your stuff here?'

'Too small, this is a big job. Biggest I ever did in my life.'

'There's an empty garage down Horsemonger Yard—they might let you use it for nothing.'

'I'll try it. I'm going to get a thousand for this picture, Cokey, and I'll give you fifty out of it. Guineas.'

'Never mind the guineas if you give me my five quid.'

'All right, Cokey. What about a pound a week, bed and board? Paid in advance. Put it in Johnny's savings bank.'

'I'll take that,' said Coker, 'I told you I was on the make. But when will you pay?'

'Next week. Or the week after.'

'A month in advance is enough,' said Coker, 'but I'd like to see it—don't you do me down, Mr Jimson, because I'm not taking sauce from anybody. I'm on the make from the first of April round to All Fools' Day. I've got to be, with this little handicap.'

And she went to get the supper. Grilled chops, mashed

potatoes, and porter, bread, butter and cheese. I couldn't have done better.

'Thank you, Coker,' I said.

'It's all in the bill,' said Coker. 'You treat me fair, and I'll treat you fair.'

'And if you did want a little bit on account,' I said. 'You've only got to make Mrs Monday hand over that picture. I've a firm offer.'

'Now, that's enough. Time you were in bed, I should think, without any more nonsense.'

'I thought you wanted your money.'

'I'll get my money, but I don't need to be mixed up with any funny business. My character won't stand it. I'm lucky to have a job without one.'

And, in fact, after a few hours of Cokey in her new shape, I wondered if I was going to be as comfortable as I had expected. Cokey was a good housekeeper, and what they call a good mother. She kept her kid clean and fed it like a prize for the show. In fact, she was mad about the kid. It's always that way with a bastard, either all one thing, or all the other. And I would not say that Cokey's temper was worse. She used to smile sometimes, when the kid brought his wind up or hit himself on the nose. But she wasn't happy because she was not that sort. A million a year and a husband out of the films wouldn't have made Cokey happy. She took life too seriously. She was one of the Marthas. She was the salt of the earth, as they say, and too much salt makes a man dry. She did me good, but too much good and not the good I wanted. She sent me to bed at nine o'clock and when I tried to object that I wasn't sleepy, she pushed me about. 'I've no patience with you, you old bone,' she said, taking my clothes off as if I'd been another baby. 'You're not fit to be up at all, with that cough, much less running about the town after all sorts. You'll go to bed and stay there.'

It was no good arguing with the girl, and I let her lay me out in one of her nightdresses. 'You go to sleep,' she said, 'or it'll be the worse for you. I don't want a funeral on my hands as well as that basket waking me up four times a night for his pint.'

Cokey had gone behind the armchair to get ready for bed. But her shadow was running up the walls, and I said, 'I've got to do you, Cokey. You're just the woman I want. You've got a figure now. You used to be like a boiler, Venus de Silo, but now you've got a front.'

But it was no good talking to Coker. She was like all young mothers. She never heard anything anyone said, not to understand it. Her head was full of kid and glory.

I was glad to find that Coker was back at the bar; in the Feathers half day for the evening rush. 'It's a respectable house, the Feathers,' she said. 'So long as you're a respectable shape, they don't ask for a ring. Which I wouldn't wear. And the pram goes nicely in the snug.'

She gave me orders to stay in bed and took away my trousers. But as soon as she was round the corner with the pram, I was out and about. I didn't need my trousers, with my long overcoat and a pair of long socks well pulled up, and though the people looked, I might have been a squire in plus fours, going round his estate.

And I had to be out in the air. Even one day in bed was putting a cramp on my ideas, tucking them up in a tight parcel. My imagination was working inwards instead of outwards; it was fitting things into a pattern, instead of letting them grow together. If I stayed in the boat-shed for a week under Cokey, I said, I could say good-bye to my Creation—it would turn into a little square picture with four corners and a middle. However big I made it on the wall, it would be a piece of art work. A put-up job. A jigsaw of the back room. Whereas a real picture is a flower, a geyser, a fountain, it hasn't got a pattern but a Form. It hasn't got corners and middle but an Essential Being. And this picture of mine, the Creation, had to be a creation. A large event. And no one can feel largely except in the open air.

Indeed, I was afraid that already, what with Plantie and Cokey, I might have got so compressed that I couldn't do anything but think about ideas and colours from the outside. And Cokey was still sitting in my brain, like a lump of lead ballast in a balloon basket, even as I turned down below the willows. But as luck would have it, the day was clear, with a sky as bright and grey as London water. And as soon as I stretched my legs Cokey began to stretch her shadow out of the basket; until she grew into the air ten foot high and the shape of life itself, living. That's what I want, I said, the woman-tree, with

something of Lolie about the roots. As round as a gasometer or Churchill's hat. Yes, Churchill's hat shall be a
blue whale. Suckling its calf. A whale with a woman's
face, floating in the green sea. And the black ring in the
middle shaped like a map of Australia shall just fit the old
'un who dreams it all for the first time. He shall be a
grey-bearded old man, just like the nursery pictures; like
something out of Blake but thicker, solider, and fitted
more closely. He must fit the shape like a nut in the
shell. But not too big. And the hollow rim of black, the
cave of the eternal rock, should have a broken edge on
which the she-whale rests while she nurses her calf. As
for the yellow uprights, they'd better be giraffes, a hundred feet high, browsing off the top of the moon which
should be covered with white flowers, the bigger the
better. Yes, a thing like this wants to be so big that people when they see it will put up their umbrellas to keep
the whale from falling on them. That whale wants to look
as big as the Tower of London, and the giraffes must be
bigger than life or they will look as small as photographs;
at least thirty foot high on the canvas.

I was walking up Horsemonger's Yard. I didn't believe
in Cokey's garage, but I had nothing else to believe in. And
when I found, to my surprise, that there was an empty
garage to let, I wasn't surprised to see that it was a dirty
old shed, about fifteen foot from floor to ridge with no
walls at all. The sides were tin.

But I noticed a lot of boards up. Desirable site. Property coming down; and off the Yard, a little back alley I'd
never seen before.

I always go up a back alley. May be a tree there or a
girl sweeping out a yard. Moving herself in a nice way.
It turned round sharp right. Six dustbins, a stable and
an old chapel, Gothic windows, and a little tin vestry
like a cupboard next the porch. Peeped in to have a look
at the roof timbering and found a bare floor. Nothing
inside but a few old tyres. Some rotten planks. A low
lame pulpit like a dock. But what knocked me down was
the east end *wall*. Twenty-five by forty. Windows bricked
up and all smooth plaster round. Sent from God. Only
wanted some plaster on the window bricks. Do it myself.
And I thought, no, it can't be. It's another joke. They're
having me on. I can hear them getting ready with the

big big laugh. My legs were trembling so much I had to sit down on the pulpit steps. I was all in a sweat. And I said to myself: No, Gulley, it's a have. It's a catch. It's the old devil again. Don't you depend on anything. You got to be calm. You got to be free. But my legs kept on trembling and my heart went on beating. Jesus Christ, I thought, suppose it was true. Suppose it's meant for me. Oh for a drink. Four fingers of blue ruin and a chaser of rum. To put some armour-plating on my guts. I was getting worse instead of better. So I went out and knocked on the first gate. Young chap with forget-me-not eyes and a magenta chin, put his banana out of the gate and said, 'Yerrs?' I said, 'That old ruin there, who owns it?' 'Dunno.' 'What is it, anyhow?' 'Nothing. Used to be a garage, but now it's nothing. Dangerous building.' 'I should think so—you can see it stagger when the cats cough. Who looks after the rubbish?' 'Next door but one.' Next door but one was a little old man with grey eyes and one bandy leg. Nose like a pepper-pot, all over freckles. Said, yes, he looked after the chapel. 'Condemned?' 'Why yes, but there's nothing wrong with it.' 'How much by the week on no notice either side.' 'Say a pound.' 'Say half a crown.' 'Couldn't do it under a pound.' 'For religious purposes.' 'What religion?' 'Low.' 'What sort?' 'Peculiar.' 'Ten shillings a week.' 'Three-and-six.' 'Split the difference.' 'Right oh, four-and-threepence. Here's a bob on account.' 'That's not the difference.' 'Ten shillings less three-and-six is six-and-six. Half of six-and-six is three-and-three, and I gave you a bob. That's four-and-three.' 'Here, wait a minute, Mister.' 'Name of Jimson, Gulley Jimson. That's a bargain. I'll go and get my traps.' 'But look here—'

I left him talking and made a dart for the boathouse. Coker had just come in with the pram and was abusing the kid. I snatched a chair in one hand and the frypan and my colour box in the other and flew. 'Hi,' said Coker. But I didn't stop. I was back in the chapel in five minutes. Put the chair in the middle of the floor, the colour box and the frypan in the pulpit. Old bandy leg put his pepper round the door. 'You can't come in—not at that money.' 'Yes, I can. I have. I've taken possession.' 'Out you go.' 'Too late, old boy. It's legal. Essential furniture. Cooking utensils and tools of trade. Look at 'em.

You can't touch 'em. Send for the bailiff if you like. He'll tell you.' 'You're a rascal.' 'That's slander. You'll hear from my lawyers tomorrow. It's big damages to call a man a rascal.' 'There aren't any witnesses.' 'Are you going to deny it, you rascal?' 'Rascal. What about this rent?' 'Four-and-threepence.' 'You know that's not right.' 'You took my earnest.' 'It's a bad un too. A French nickel.' 'My God, my lucky penny. Here, I want that back.' 'Why should I give it back?' 'Be a sport.' 'You be honest.' 'What did you think you wanted for the old dustbin?' 'Six shillings it came to.' 'I'll make it five for the sake of your great-grandchildren. But I warn you it's robbing God. You'll get no luck with it.' 'Make it five-and-sixpence, and I'll take my chance.' 'I see you're a Christian yourself.' 'Never mind what I am. What I want to see is your money.' 'You shall, old boy, but meanwhile I want time for meditation. I want to pray myself in.' 'I've half a mind to fetch a copper.' 'Is that what's wrong with you? What happened to the other half?' The old boy was cross and went out muttering like Ma Coker, but with a different neck action, more like a tortoise than a snake. I shut the door after him and pushed the bolt. Then measured up the floor. Twenty-five wide. And the timbering on the walls sound as Pharaoh's coffin. When I looked at the east wall, I saw my stuff on it. Finest job of my life. Twenty-five by forty. And I felt giddy. A bit too much for the old pipes. I sat down and laughed. And then I began to cry. Well, I said, you old ballacher, you've rolled into port at last. You've got your break. First the *idea* and then the *wall*. God has been good to you. That is to say, you've had a bit of luck. Two bits. And all the time, the forms were growing out of my egg—like cracker snakes. Coker and Sara and Lolie and Churchill's hat, white and red and blue, legs and arms and bottoms and a great black shape like a relief map of Iceland, with a white oval just by the north-east corner. God knows what it would have to stand for—He would give me the tip. But that black up against the reds made my angels sing. Oh Lord, I said, only let me fix that black shape and those fat reds before some damn fool talks to me about people or money or weather. And I had out my box and made a sketch on the side wall, four by three.

It's one thing to see or think you see a set of forms, and

another to put it down. But this set came up nearly complete. Not a gap anywhere. No filling required. And as far as I could tell in the sketch, the shapes would fill the surface. But that, as every mural painter knows, is not very far. For the line that is as lively as spring steel in the miniature, may go as dead as apron string on the wall. And what is a living whole on the back of an envelope can look as flat and tedious as a holiday poster, when you draw it out full-size.

36. All at once I found it was dark.

And I was so hungry I could have eaten the frypan and tickled my gums with the handle. I put my box back in the pulpit, left my big brush in a cup of water, and slipped out by the vestry, leaving the front door bolted. In case Peppernose might try to make mischief. I closed the window from the outside, and there you were.

An evening by Randipole Billy. Green lily sky, orange flames over the West. Long flat clouds like copper angels with brass hair floating on the curls of the fire. River mint green and blood orange. Old man lying along the water with a green beard, one arm under head, face twisted up—vision of Thames among the pot-houses. I could use that, I thought—that blunt round shape like a copper St Paul's with a squeeze in the middle—like a teat with a long end. A bit flattened sideways—sweet as a baby's breath. Yes, it will come in just by the rock—the old un's cave. Yes, yes, just what I wanted. But not a cloud. Don't want solid cloud. How then? A dead branch. A rhino's horn. A gorilla's finger. Stump of a leg. And while I was eating sausage and mash with Walter Ollier at the Kosy Kot, it shot right out of the canvas like a bronze cannon. Here, I said to myself, how am I going to get a cannon into the Creation? When all at once it turned inside out and winked at me like a railway tunnel right through the canvas. A mole, it came to me at once. A mole for a good black. You've got to have a good black, somewhere down in the right-hand corner, a mole with four hands—

blind—feeling its way under the ground—and a man's face.

'Have another cup of coffee,' said Walter, who was doing the host. 'Thank you, Walter,' I said. 'But I suppose you couldn't lend me a hundred pounds.' 'I'm afraid it doesn't run to it,' said Walter. 'Not a hundred. Five I could.' 'No,' I said. 'I've got a big job on hand—and I need some capital.' 'A picture?' 'Yes, a picture.' 'I don't know,' said Walter, 'but seeing the government has got your picture up, I should have thought they might give you something on account.' 'You can't expect it of 'em,' I said. 'What does a government know about pictures?' 'They were glad to get yours.' 'But that was an old picture and they didn't know about it till they were told by the papers.' 'Well,' said Walter, 'I don't know about pictures, but if the papers know, why don't they tell the government to go after your new pictures?' 'But the papers don't know it, Walter. They won't know for another twenty or thirty years. A picture isn't like an illustration in a magazine. You can't get to know it by looking at it. First, you've got to get used to it—that takes about five years. Then you've got to know it, that takes ten years, then you learn how to enjoy it and that takes you the rest of your life. Unless you find out after ten years that it's really no good and you've been wasting your time over it. No, Walter, I've got a better bet than the government—a millionaire.' 'Better to call than write.' 'Takes too long—I've only got to phone and he'll fork out.' Walter looked at me round his nose; Walter, though army, has a navy nose, with a high bridge. 'Telephone?' he said, meaning in his polite way to warn me. 'Yes, telephone,' I said, 'I'm going to explain the situation to him.' 'What is the situation?'

'There's two, mine and his. His situation is a bit ticklish,' I said. 'He might get his throat cut.' 'Have some more coffee, Mr Jimson, do,' said Walter, turning quite red. I'd never seen him so brick. He was trying to keep me interested until he could discover some way of diverting my murderous intentions. 'It's good here, don't you think? At least I've always found it not too bad.' 'Thank you, Walter,' I said. 'I think I will. Mr Hickson is probably in his bath now, and he mightn't answer me personally.' 'Do you think he'll know about new pictures, like you said?' said Walter, waving to the waitress. 'I should think it might be better to try the government.' 'No,' I said, 'Mr Hickson never knew anything about my pictures—but he's a millionaire, and so he knows how to invest his money, or he wouldn't be a millionaire.' 'I wonder is he still a millionaire,' said Walter. 'I know they're getting a bit scarce. There's such a lot of people got a down on 'em.' 'Scarce as polecats,' I said. 'I've heard they're going to be stopped,' said Walter, 'though it's probably just the papers.' 'It's quite likely they'll stop themselves,' I said, 'they're a tough lot owing to the survival of the fittest—but even tigers and polar bears get discouraged when nobody loves them.' 'And what will happen to artists if there's no millionaires? Will art stop?' 'Not art—you can't stop art. But you can stop original art.' 'What happens then?' 'The people go on with the old stuff, and folk art and so on, until they get sick.' 'Sick of art?' 'Sick of everything. Though they don't know it. It's a kind of foot-and-mouth disease. The mouth gets very foul and the feet turn sideways, so that the patient is always going round to the pub, the same pub, of course. I'm told by experts that there's a lot of it in country districts where you only have old masters to look at. Young chaps kind of waste away, and all at once they go and throw boiling water over a dog or cut a cow's tail off. In the end they get so full of spite and bile that they can't digest anything but whisky and politics, and finally they die in great misery.' 'So you're for the millionaires.' 'The more the better, Walter. In my view, everybody ought to be millionaires.' 'Money troubles are sometimes the worst kind,' said Walter. 'That's true,' I said. 'Look at me and look at Mr Hickson.' 'Has he a lot of trouble?' 'I've given him a lot to think about, and I'm going to give him more as soon as he's out of his bath.'

Walter gave a sort of jump and looked round as if for help. 'Have another go of sausage and mash, Mr Jimson?' 'No, thank you, Walter, it's about time for my call.' 'You're not going to call up Mr Hickson tonight, are you?' 'Certainly, Walter. The situation can't go on.' 'What is the situation really, Mr Jimson?'

'Well, Walter, I can tell you, because you're a friend; the situation is that I'm getting on in years and I shan't do much more painting. But I've still got my biggest work in me—a picture that will be famous for centuries. Yes, and it will give England something to be proud of too, and let her look the nations in the face. She'll be able to say I bred Shakespeare and Milton, and Billy Blake, and Shelley and Wordsworth and Constable and Turner and Gulley Jimson. Only the trouble is, Walter, that it will take about five hundred pounds to make this picture, and twenty years to get it established—I mean respected. Of course, I'll be dead before that—a long time before, I should say, and that will be all to the good, as far as this picture is concerned. It will establish my reputation. I shall become history, and history is respectable. Oxford and Cambridge study history. So you see, Walter, the job is to get this picture painted and keep it from being cut up or whitewashed over or just left out in the rain until I've been dead a few years.' 'You'll want an attendant to keep the kids from doing it a mischief.' 'Yes, what I need is money—five hundred a year. And I'm going to get the first five hundred this evening.' 'On the telephone?' 'Yes,' I said. 'I don't know,' said Walter, 'but I never liked the telephone myself. I like writing letters.' 'Give me the telephone,' I said. 'It's quicker, and you can say what you like.'

When we got outside, Walter excused himself quickly, and went off at four miles an hour. This was half a mile quicker than his usual rate which is postman's regulations, three and a half. So I knew he was going for assistance, Coker or Mr Plant. And I didn't waste time. I jumped into the next box and rang up Mr Hickson. A lady answered. 'Excuse me,' I said, 'I am speaking on behalf of the National Gallery, could I see Mr Hickson?' 'Hold the line, please.' And almost at once a man's voice said, 'Hullo, Mr Hickson here.' He was disguising his voice; but I paid no attention. 'Mr Hickson,' I said, 'I am speaking on behalf of the National Gallery to tell you that it has come to their ears, through official but absolutely trustworthy channels, that the late Mr Gulley Jimson left behind him an extremely important work which ought to be the property of the nation.' 'Excuse me,' said the man, 'but is Mr Jimson dead?' 'Last week,' I said. 'That is the official account, but his secretary, Mr Barbon, will collect any money due.' 'That's a pity,' said Mr Hickson, 'because we've been looking for him with a view to the publication of a Life, in fact, the illustrations are in hand.' 'I shall make further inquiries,' I said, 'in case Mr Jimson's death should be a rumour.' 'I wish you would. My late uncle, as you know, left three of his pictures to the nation.' 'What late uncle?' 'Mr George Hickson.' 'But that's my Mr Hickson,' I said. And I felt so queer that I nearly fell down in the box. 'You don't mean old Mr George Frederick Hickson is dead?' 'Three months ago.' 'I don't believe it,' I said. For I couldn't believe it. 'I shall want proof of that.' 'You can find it in *The Times* or apply at Somerset House. The will has been proved.' 'And who the devil are you?' 'Mr Philip Hickson, at your service.' 'Never heard of you,' I said. 'You may think it's funny to pull my leg, but you'd better be careful. Mr George Hickson was one of my oldest friends. I've known him for forty years and he was my earliest patron.' 'He's dead all right. The house is to be sold next week.' 'Why sold?' I said. 'It has the best room in London for showing pictures.' 'It's too big for any of us to keep up. The estate has been divided between seven of us, and the collections are to be sold. Except six pictures left to the nation.'

I thought a bit. I was so upset that my legs were shaking against my coat. Hickson gone. I couldn't believe it. It made me feel as lonely as a man who loses half his family in a shipwreck. 'I shall apply at Somerset House in due course,' I said at last, in a severe tone. 'And if it proves that this information about poor Mr Hickson is official, I shall have to look into things.' 'What things?' 'I suppose you know Mr Hickson owed Mr Jimson a considerable sum of money—nearly forty or fifty thousand pounds to be exact. A debt of honour, of course. So I daresay that a settlement could be arranged.' 'You're not Mr Jimson yourself, by any chance?' 'Certainly not, but I should feel bound to protect his memory against any hanky panky.' 'I'll inquire about the creditors, if you could hold the line.' But I did not hold the line. I wasn't to be caught a second time. I hit the receiver on the wall as hard as I could to give the rascal's drum a shock. And went out, leaving the door open.

But I didn't feel any better. I was so shaky in the legs that as soon as I was round the corner, I sat down on a step. 'I don't believe it,' I said. 'Hickson dead—why, he can't have been more than seventy. There's some dirty work at the bottom of this.' But I knew that Hickson was dead. I knew it just as a man knows when he's had his leg shot off, though he can still feel his corns. And it upset me. I felt as if the ground had given a yawn under my feet. I felt like that little dog in the story who ran out of Lombard Street to do his morning pee against the Bank of England and found it gone. Gone to nothing. Not even a hole in the ground. But nothing at all. Nothing even to bark at. What would be the good of a bark at nothing? Nothing. Because it would be nothing itself as soon as it went over the edge. I refuse to believe it, I said. But then I gave a great sigh and I found that I was crying. This cheered me up a little. Yes, real tears. I can't be so old, I said, if I can still cry. There's sap in the old trunk yet. And I got up and hobbled home.

When Cokey saw me, she was shocked. She threw me into bed, with abuse. 'Look at you, you old bother, you've caught another chill. Going out like that.' 'No, Cokey,' I said, 'I've had a blow. I've lost my oldest friend. And it's damn nearly broken my nerve. If you were a real woman I'd throw myself on your breast and cry like a baby. You don't believe it, but I could. I never needed a woman more; not a female but a woman.' 'I'll give you something to cry about if you go off like that again.' Cokey didn't believe I had any real friends except herself. She had a lot of womanliness in her nature though she didn't indulge it.

37.

Cokey did not let me out for three days. And by that time I couldn't even see my Wall. I might have been dead and coffined. But what could I do without money? I had no respect for myself so Cokey paid no attention to my appeals. Luckily the fourth day was the fourteenth of the month, Rozzie's anniversary, and when I told Cokey that I had a grave to visit, she gave me my clothes.

And when I went to the florist's, I told him that I wanted a better wreath than usual. 'Make it a two-guinea one,' I said. 'In flowers,' said the florist. 'Yes, two guineas in flowers and three in the bill.' The florist looked sad out of respect. He felt that my grief was sincere. 'Bill to Mr Thomas Jimson?' he said. 'Yes,' I said, 'c/o Cox's Bank.' For Tom always paid for the wreath, and, in fact, he usually sent me a card to remind me of the date. 'Expenses are a bit higher this year,' I said, 'owing to the weather.'

The florist was an old friend of mine. 'It was three pounds eight last year,' he said. 'And the wreath was only a guinea and a half.'

'Last year included hotel expenses,' I said, for I was always very particular that Tom got a fair deal. 'Last year I had two windows blown out at the place where I was stopping—came to nine-and-sixpence.'

'And did the hotel make you pay?'

'It wasn't exactly an hotel, it was my studio, but I was stopping there at the time of the anniversary, so it came under expenses. That's all fair, I think—'

'Oh yes, sir, quite fair.' And he gave me a guinea change. So I took a taxi to the cemetery. I knew Tom liked to do the thing properly.

And when I had admired the grave which always had some nice daisies, and read the inscription, I was thinking of Rozzie and what a queer girl she was, all brass on the outside, and all bread and butter pudding within, when I looked up, and there was old Sara waddling down the path in her fusty blacks with a hat full of purple and violets, and a bunch of Michaelmas daisies and marigolds in her hand.

She had seen me already, and she was obviously afraid to come up. She went from side to side and her feet flopped outways without making any progress. Once she began to turn away. But at last she took hold of herself and gave herself a shake and came on like the old guard.

'Why, Gulley,' she panted, 'I never expected to see you here.'

'Or you wouldn't have come, you old thief. What about my picture?'

'Well, Gulley, it was a shame, and I never meant to play you a trick like that. But something came over me, and you know how it is with an old woman. It seemed like losing the last bit of those good times.'

'Why shouldn't I send the police to take my own property?'

'Is it your property, or ought the creditors to have it? Or Mr Hickson? I don't know.'

'You'd rather give it to anybody but me.'

'Oh no, Gulley. That's not so, and you know it's not.' And Sara was quite excited. Her nose turned purple; a sign that she was speaking the truth for once. 'I'd rather you had it than anyone, and I'm sure you could have it now.'

At these words my heart jumped like a little ballet girl and the wreath jumped in my hand like a tambourine. 'What?' I said, 'you'll give it to me, the bath sketch?' And I saw three hundred sovereigns flash through the air like Phoebus horses followed by the Peculiar chapel, like a gypsy van.

'I would indeed, if I could,' said Sara. 'But Byles's got it now. Locked up in his chest. He's got all my things, even my mother's Bible. He says that it's valuable, and it will do to keep us when he retires from the council, and bury us.'

'What's valuable?'

'My mother's Bible. He says it's an old one and worth a hundred pounds—though I know my mother only paid twelve-and-six at the S.P.C.A. But Byles thinks that all Bibles are valuable.'

'And what about my picture, Sall?'

'He says it's worth five thousand pounds—only he doesn't like to sell it in case of the police. He says the police would be bound to think that we'd stolen it if we got all that money for it.'

I nearly dashed the wreath to the ground. I can stand a lot from Boorjays, God knows; but I could never bear the way they value pictures. Either they're worth nothing at all, or thousands. 'My God, Sara,' I said, 'five thousand for a sketch like that—I might get fifty for it, by special influence. No, if you want your burial money you'd better make Byles understand that I'm the only man who can pass off that daub as a masterpiece.'

'What is it really worth, Gulley?'

'I tell you, if I signed it and polished it up a bit, I might get fifty—fifty pounds that is—from a friend, more out of charity than business.'

'I thought it might be worth more than that now that I'm in the Tate.'

'You in the Tate—oh, you mean Hickie's bath picture.'

'They say that one is worth thirty thousand pounds.'

'It will be, it will be. In a hundred years. It may be worth two thousand now.'

'Byles measured it up with his eye and it's five by eight, and this one is three and a half by two, which is nearly a sixth, he says. But of course I knew it didn't go by size.'

'No, it doesn't go by size any more than women. The biggest are often the smallest.'

'Well, Gulley, I would have given it to you—I'd give it to you now if I could—only for what you said. Thirty guineas, and that's only to bury me. For that nasty Doris ripped up my stays—will you believe the meanness of a woman like that who'd send a piece of her own sex to a pauper funeral—shovelled into the ground like an old can —look at the way you're handling that beautiful wreath. I'm sure there won't be a bloom left on it.'

I picked up the wreath and took Sara's arm. 'Come on, old girl, we're forgetting ourselves, and Rozzie.'

'You make me quite ashamed with that wreath,' said Sara. 'It must have cost two pounds.'

'Not too much for Rozzie,' I said.

'Oh, Gulley, you liked Rozzie better than you liked me.'

'Not a bit of it, Sall. I'd give you a five-pound wreath any day, if I had the money, wild roses with the thorns on.'

'Oh, Gulley, there you go.'

'The sweetest roses have the sharpest thorns, Sall. What are you going to do with that bunch, you'll need a vase?'

'A vase, I never thought to bring a vase. Last time I came this way I brought a pot of daffodils. I never came before on the funeral day, Gulley. I should have, but I never did. Not since the funeral itself.'

'Where we had a pint together.'

'Yes, you were at the funeral too. But then, Rozzie was your real doting piece.'

I said nothing for fear of saying too much.

'Her legs were better,' said Sara with an old woman's cast in her eye, a back cast. 'If you like that kind of leg, like a custard glass; and her hair was lovely, for colour, that is—she never had too much of it.'

'The vases are over at the lodge, where the sexton lives.'

'Well, I suppose I'd better find some water for my daisies. Though they're nothing to your wreath. But Byles grew them on purpose.'

So we went along together to the lodge where the gardener kept some flowerpots and tin vases for visitors' flowers, and a stand-pipe. And while I picked out for Sara a vase without a hole in the bottom, she said, 'I'm glad you remembered Rozzie's day.'

'I haven't missed it once since the old girl died, except when prevented by circumstances.'

'You and Rozzie had a lot in common,' said Sara. 'Yes, you were closer to Rozzie than you were to me. The way you laughed together. But Rozzie had such wonderful spirits. Well, I always thought there was something in it. You always made so little of it.'

I put my face in a vase and lifted it up to the sky to see if there was a hole in the bottom and to hide any holes in my expression. Sara had a woman's eye for holes in the expression. She could see them when they weren't there; which comes to the same thing to a woman when she means to pin something on you.

'And all those wires from somebody called Robinson in Brighton with a box number,' said Sara.

'Here you are, my dear,' I said. 'The rustiest, but it seems to hold water. Come along, and I'll fill it for you.'

I didn't want to discuss Rozzie with Sara. For I knew she wouldn't be fair to Rozzie, and I was feeling tender-hearted about that ancient fireship.

38.

Rozzie was the only girl in the world for me except Sara. They nearly finished me between them. The seven years when I had those two women on my mind and body were as good as fourteen penal. For each of them was a harem and you never knew which spouse you had to deal with.

Of course, I always liked big women. I suppose I was meant to be a sculptor or architect. And what attracted me to Rozzie in the first place was her size. She was bigger even than Sara in those days. It took several minutes to walk round her. You studied her from different aspects, like a public building. Something between St Paul's and the Brighton Pavilion. But though I may have had some idea of getting away with Rozzie, I didn't reckon to fall in love with her.

They say, of course, any woman can catch any man if she takes him at the right moment, on the bounce, in the air; going up or coming down. But Rozzie didn't try to catch me. When Sara refused me the first time, and I was suffering from temporary sanity, I went to Rozzie just round the corner and took her by as much as I could get hold of with my two arms and my teeth, and said, 'Rozzie, you've got to marry me, or something like that, or I'll cut both our bloody throats.'

Rozzie brushed me off like an earwig and said, 'I'd smack your face if I wasn't afraid of catching whatever it is. I'm Sara's friend, and don't you forget it. Do that again and I'll tell her.' But she said it very nicely. Rozzie was a nice girl. She couldn't be rough if she tried, in spite of her big fists.

'If you're Sara's friend,' I said, 'you'll be nice to me, because I'm going to cut my throat and that will upset Sara considerably. She's fond of me, though she doesn't know it.'

'Go on and cut,' said Rozzie. 'Sara and I want a good laugh.' But by this time I was sitting on her knee and making myself accustomed. And Rozzie didn't brush me off. I expected that smack every minute, but it didn't come. And Rozzie was so fierce in her look and rough in her tongue, that it was only after she was dead and I had time to think about her and to see her in the all round, that I realized she was all bark and no bite. Take off her clothes and she was like a port-wine jelly rabbit shelled out of the tin, a pink trembler; massive and shapely in the forms, but inclined to spread at the edges; firm to the eye, but soft to the touch. Deep but transparent; something like a lion, but not much.

Why did I fall in love with Rozzie? Most men fall in love because they want to; that's why they can't be stopped. But I didn't want to fall in love with either Sara or Rozzie. I wanted to get on with my work. I was the victim of circumstances.

Every billet has its bullet, there's a fatal woman waiting

for every man. Luckily he doesn't often meet her. I was born six men and I had six fates, but thank God, I only met five of them. As a religious man, I fell for a Sunday school teacher, but I converted her to Christianity and she ran away with a primitive Communist. As a Briton I fell in love with Mrs Monday, the mother and the wife. I wanted to rest upon the domestic bosom. But she turned into a bride and wanted to rest on mine. As an artist, I fell in love with Sara, and her grand forms, but she was an artist herself, and she appreciated herself so much that she couldn't bear me to paint anyone or anything else.

But the man who fell in love with Rozzie was the poor little Peter Pan who wanted to creep back into his mother's womb and be safe and warm and comfortable for the rest of his life. Isolationist. With navel defence. Sure shield. And lo, Rozzie only wanted to creep into my stomach. She was the softie, the girl who never grew up, the rabbit that lived up a tree and sang to herself all day, the prayer: Oh God, don't let me know anything, or think anything or be anything. Because I know I never could. Don't let anything happen to me because I'm really much too young. Have pity on the silly little thing and don't ask her to make up her mind about anything, because she really couldn't. Just let her make jokes and drink and laugh—

Sara was a tyrant who tried to put me in a bottle and cork me up into a woman's cup of tea; and Rozzie was a slave who said, 'Beat me, eat me, but never, never ask me to make up my mind.'

Sara was an empress. It was a glory to have that woman, and to beat her. Alexander never felt bigger than me when I thumped that majestic meat upon the nose. Rozzie was a Leah, a concubine, a man tickler, the world's harem; she was the valley of peace and joy. She was a pillow for your head and a footstool for your rheumatism. But of course pillows and mattresses are not the sort of baggage a man wants to carry with him on a long journey. You could never get your own way with Sara. You might think so, but that was only her cunning. Life with Sara was all on the diplomatic scale, between the grand contracting parties. Sometimes we were noble allies and carried on the war together, sometimes we were enemies; but you were always yourself and Sara was always herself, and making love to Sara was a stormy joy, thunder and lightning. There was an exchange of powers, a flash and a bang; Jupiter and the cloud. You gave something and you took something.

But life with Rozzie was a doze beneath the palm trees; and loving her was like a shower of autumn leaves on a paddock. It left you bare.

Sara was a palace outside, but when you went in, you found yourself in a convalescent home. All clean and wholesome, h. and c., and indoor sanitation, regular meals by our resident dietician, nothing to do but keep your nose clean and put your bottom in the chair that was meant for it. You respected yourself at Sara's. But Rozzie, who looked like something between Knightsbridge Barracks and Holloway Gaol, when you had dared to push at the iron gate, which collapsed like brown paper, was a club for retired gentlemen. I mean, gentlemen that had given up the job and didn't want to mind their manners any more. You could spit in the fender anywhere round Rozzie from the attics to the lounge, and eat sausage and mash in the gilded hall.

Sara was the everlasting trumpets, a challenge to battle and death, Rozzie was a cradle song, accompanied on the ocarina.

It was a pleasure to take things from Sara, even if you had to steal them; a double pleasure, because Sara liked giving; it was a joy to give things to Rozzie, because Rozzie liked presents. They gave her self-confidence. They made her feel that she was worth something. Sara never needed anyone to tell her what she was worth, she knew her value so well that I don't suppose she even thought of it. She never had any pride; and Rozzie was so particular that if only a man stared at her in the street, she would glare and swear for an hour afterwards; and say the rude things she would do to him if she caught him without his bathing drawers.

I still remember Rozzie's indignation when I unbuttoned her bodice. 'Here, what do you think you're up to?'

'I'm going to marry you, Rozzie, or the next best thing.' Then Rozzie raised her great knuckled butcher's fist and I ducked for the swing. But it didn't come. 'What do you take me for?' cried Rozzie. 'A bloody tart?'

'No,' I said, undoing another button. 'You're the nicest woman I ever wanted to meet.'

'Leave off,' said Rozzie. 'Get off, you—'

'I should like to get off,' I said. 'With you, Rozzie dear.'
And Rozzie only said in a kind of perplexed tone, 'When
you've finished with my bodice.'

But I hadn't finished, and as I went further, trembling
all over and expecting to be knocked out of the window
any minute, but getting madder and madder all the time,
Rozzie's shouts changed into complaints, and at last into
appeals.

'No, Gulley, I never thought you would treat a girl like
this—it's not right. I'm a decent woman, whatever you
may think. I may have started behind the bar, but I
always kept myself respectable—'

And at the end of it she was almost crying, as near
crying as Rozzie could get. 'Oh, it's a shame, Gulley. I'm
surprised at you, you nasty little man. And what's going
to happen to me now? What will people think? Suppose
I have a baby. My character will be dirt. And how am I
going to meet Sara? My best oldest friend. I'd be
ashamed—'

Rozzie had a conscience; Sara had a purpose and an
object in life. Rozzie was a God-fearing heathen that
never went to church in case of what might happen to
her there; Sara was a God-using Christian that went to
church to please herself and pick up some useful ideas
about religion, hats and the local gossip.

Sara was a shot in the arm; she brought you alive one
way or another; the very idea of Sara could always make
me swear or jump or dance or sweat. Because of her
damned independence and hypocrisy. When you knew
Sara, you knew womankind, and no one who doesn't know
womankind knows anything about the nature of Nature.
But Rozzie was only a female and she never stirred up
anything but love and pity. Sara was a menace and a
tonic, my best enemy; Rozzie was a disease, my worst
friend. Sara made a man of me and damn nearly a murderer; Rozzie might have turned me into a lop-eared
crooner.

I remember the day I heard Rozzie was dying. I got a
wire from her landlady in Brighton; I was down in Devonshire busy at a big job. But I told some lie to Sara and
went right across England. Rozzie wasn't dying, but she
was nearly dead. She'd tried to give herself a miscarriage. I
found her as white as a wall, all fallen away and flat as a

cod on the slab. 'My God, Rozzie,' I said, 'what have you been doing?'

'I didn't want that kid,' said Rozzie, and she kept smiling all the time. 'Am I passing out?'

'No, but you nearly did, a nice mess that would have been.'

'Go on,' said Rozzie. 'A bit of all right for all concerned.'

'Don't talk like that, Rozzie. You know you don't mean it.'

'That's just what I do mean,' said Rozzie. 'Here, what am I good for? A bloody old burden—out of Barnums—or the back of a motor boat.'

'But Rozzie, what the hell? You aren't worrying about your character, are you? You aren't worrying about people looking at you? You've got a legal wedding ring, haven't you? You've got a right to a belly, you ought to be proud of yourself. Why, damn it all, it's a grand sight anyhow, a woman carrying.'

'Not this one,' said Rozzie. 'No, Gulley, I don't so much mind about the character—but what a fuss about nothing. And what's going to happen to the poor kid? It'll have a fine start with me for a mother. And you for a papa.'

'Damn it all, Rozzie, you'll be a splendid mother with your good nature, and as for me, I'm very fond of kids. And I shall be a better father than a lot of these boorjoes. I'm not going to hand over this kid to the schoolmasters and get rid of it under the pretence of education. No, I'm going to teach it myself. No reading and writing and arithmetic for my kid.' For I was really keen on education at that time. And I had the idea that if you could only prevent a kid learning to read, it couldn't pick up all the rubbish out of the newspapers and books, that spoils children's brains. My idea was to teach kids first of all to sing, since Nature starts 'em singing before they can talk; and then to draw; and then to swim and box; and then when they got a bit older and could do more brain work, to dance and make poetry in their heads. Also I was going to teach my kid to know all Blake's poetry and what it means and what is wrong with it, and then, if he was a boy, I should have gone on to Shakespeare and navigation, so that he could be a sailor and see some of the outside world, and keep away from culture and all the rest of it; or if a girl, Milton and cooking; so she might go into service and see some of the inside world.

But Rozzie was afraid of something. I don't know what. Responsibility or the judgment of Heaven. She felt that she had no right to a kid, or that the kid would be too much for her. 'You don't see me putting a kid to bed, and hearing its prayers.' 'Well, damn it all, don't hear its prayers. Just teach it to sing something. Little lamb, who made thee, or Tiger, Tiger.' 'Go on, Gulley, I'd have to laugh and the kid would see I was playing the fool—kids are too bloody sharp.' 'Why, you damned old bag, you'll be so fond of this kid, you'll thank God for it.' 'It won't thank God for me, I'll be tight half the time.' 'Blast you, you don't get tight now, you old pudding. Why should you get tight because you've got a kid?' 'You know what kids are.' 'But I tell you you'll love a kid. It's natural— and of all the great lumps of nature I ever knew, you're the lumpiest.' 'That's what I'm afraid of.' 'What, having a kid?' 'Well, you know what it is, with mamas that get fond of their kids and then their kids wake up one fine day and say: Why should I have to go round with this common nasty fiery-faced old bitch?—she'd ruin a Mary Pickford's chances.' 'Why, you old hurdy gurdy, why do you think it's going to be a girl?' 'A boy would be worse, he'd take to drink.'

It was a pleasure to get away from that great gutless Jill pudding, back to Sara, even though it was going back from peace and fun to the battlefield. Even though I could see all Rozzie's works going round like the wheels of a Greenwich clock and her face always told me the exact time; and Sara's face was only camouflage for the war factory. It was bracing to deal with a soldier again. You knew where you were, and you had some respect for yourself. And you could get on with your work.

But of course I never could put Rozzie off my mind any more than a nursing monkey can get its big baby off its back. I used to wake up in the night in a cold sweat and say, What's wrong? I wonder if Sara has poisoned me, and then all at once I would feel that Rozzie had cut her throat, or jumped off the new pier, and I had no peace until I had wired. How I used to curse that great soft oaf, though not to herself. You couldn't curse at Rozzie in case she took it badly and did herself an injury. You can't put a backbone into a blancmange; if you try, you only cut it up. And after the boy was born, she was more than ever afraid; afraid to nurse it, afraid to wash it, afraid to touch it. I had to wash it myself until we got a good nurse. I might have wasted my life on Rozzie and that kid if it hadn't been for Sara. For that was the time I was maddest on Sara. Painting her and fighting her. Yes, Sara saved me for Rozzie. But what a life, making up lies all the time to keep Sara quiet while I dashed off to Brighton to see how young Tom was taking his bottle, and then making up arguments to keep Rozzie's conscience quiet and to stop her from throwing herself on Sara's bosom and confessing all. Never tell me that women haven't got a conscience. It's their most ticklish point, except a dozen others. Then back again to Sara in the blue horrors in case Rozzie should have wired or some kind friend written and exposed the system; and lost me my Sara, just when I was getting to understand her articulation.

I was down to six stone when Sara deserted me, and God knows what would have happened to my remains if it hadn't been for a nice young thing called Margaret, or Mud; a lady by education and a gentleman by birth, who had got the idea, thank heaven, after being thrown out of the College of Music, the Slade and the School of Dramatic Art, that she was born to be the wife of genius.

Mud got after me, and I let her catch me. She had an income. She could afford to indulge a thirst for glory. And a good wife she was until the money ran out and Hickson stopped my allowance; and her family threatened to run me in for bigamy.

Mud even squared Rozzie by taking over the boy. And after that, whenever I had the Rozzie feeling, I could run down to Brighton and have a drink with the old saloon front, and a laugh, and let her talk flow over me for a day or two; fruity as distilled bar-snug, rich as xxx. For no one I ever knew had such a give-away as Rozzie, she opened all the doors and windows, and you could walk about inside as if you were at home. And what a home; the complete female widow's museum.

When Rozzie fell under that bus, I suffered a loss which surprised me. I cried. Well, there I was, with my palette and brushes in one hand and the telegram in the other, choking; and Mud saying to me in that drawl which women always have when they haven't got any moral delicacy, 'But darling, she's not da-id—it only says, seriously injured.'

'She'll die,' I said. 'Boo-hoo. I know she'll die. I had it coming to me. Things were going altogether too well. And Rozzie will never make a fight for it. The poor bitch was murdered young—by her spots.'

'Her spots?'

'Yes, her complexion. She had spots, poor child, and so she had to marry a middle-aged publican who did the dirt on her for fifteen years—all sorts of dirt. No,' I said, 'Rozzie never had any guts—and she'll die like an express train, without stopping at the stations.'

And of course I was right. Rozzie died laughing at herself, so she shouldn't cry. She stopped crying young because, with her complexion, she had to keep her powder dry.

39.

When I found the pump by the sexton's house, I gave Sara the vase and told her to hold on while I pumped. 'And look out for your feet,' I said. 'These churchyard pumps and standpipes are regular death traps. Too many mourners come here and get their feet wet, and then they are so overcome by grief they think it mean to change their stockings and the next thing is they're being measured for a wooden two-piece in polished elm, with silver-plated handles.'

'Poor Rozzie never had even elm—a pauper's coffin.'

'What did Rozzie care so long as it didn't let in the draught. She never could bear a draught. That was the barmaid all over.'

'You knew her better than me, though we were such old friends. You liked Rozzie better than you did me.'

'Don't you believe it, Sara, you were my right hand.'

'Well, they often said Rozzie was another limb to you, but I wouldn't believe it.'

'Rozzie was a respectable girl, and I often wonder she didn't marry again.'

'So do I,' said Sara, 'and perhaps she ought to have

been married again though goodness knows I have no right to talk.'

'So you think Rozzie had her affairs,' I said.

'They say she had a baby.'

'They'd say anything,' and I took Sara's arm, as we wobbled back to the grave. 'You and I, Sall, are too old to worry about what they say.'

'So we are,' said Sara. 'I suppose it wasn't your baby, Gulley?'

'Me, what baby?' I said. 'When did all this happen?' I said. But I used the wrong voice, for Sara stopped and looked at me. 'Well,' she said, 'I never could have believed it, so that's what the operation was, she went into hospital for—'

'You mustn't blame Rozzie,' I said. 'She was the victim of circumstances.'

'Well, I should have guessed,' said Sara, as we walked on again. 'And so it was Rozzie you used to go off to.'

'Rozzie gave me a home when you threw me over.'

I thought Sara would fire up at this. For she always maintained that I deserted her, because I left the house before she did. Though the truth was, she had abandoned me, in spirit, about a month before.

But Sara was growing old and you never knew quite what new old thing would come up to her mind. 'You always liked her better for a randyvoo.'

It took me by surprise, and I burst out, 'Now, what do you mean by that, Sara?' 'Well, for a holiday visit. She was so big and looked so fierce. You always liked to triumph over the sizeable ones, Gulley, being so little and light-bodied. Yes, I always thought you'd like to conquer over Rozzie, like a little bantam on a big midden.' 'Poor Rozzie, if you want to know, had no more spunk than a net of lard.' 'She was nervous of trains and dogs, certainly.' 'And everything else.' 'Not men, Gulley. She'd always known how to handle the men ever since she went into the Case is Altered at sixteen, a proper rough place, nothing but a beerhouse it was then.' 'Rozzie was meat for the first man that got hold of her.' But old Sara shook her head. 'She turned you round her finger, Gulley. But there, she always meant to get you away from me. And I hope you made her happy. I'm sure she deserved some happiness.'

'Dammit all, Sara,' I said, for I could not bear to see the old woman twisting everything about to suit herself. 'You don't believe that, and you know Rozzie was a loyal friend to you and to tell you the truth, she was very unhappy when the thing came about, she said she could never face you again.'

'I'm not blaming her,' said Sara, 'I'm sorry for her.'

'She was the honestest girl that ever knocked back a can,' I said, 'a true blue—it was the only good thing about her except perhaps her legs, and as for stealing me away from you, she had no idea of it. I did the stealing.'

We had reached the grave, and I read the inscription:

Rosina Balmforth, beloved wife of the late
William Oke Balmforth

Born April 2nd, 1881. Died June 14th, 1928

Blessed are the poor in spirit.

It brought up Rozzie in front of me, and by Jove my eyelids pricked. It was a high-shouldered stone, just like the poor old engine herself. I'd chosen it for Tom when he wanted to mark the grave. And I thought, Who will remember Rozzie when I go? Sara is immortal. She will live in the National Galleries of the world for ever, or at least for a few hundred years. But Rozzie is fading away already. I have to look twice before I can see those powdered cheeks, like overripe strawberries under a sprinkle of sugar; or hear that hoarse bookie's voice, full of good nature and resignation.

Yes, that was the attraction of the poor old barge; her despair. She seemed to say, I'm done for, but who cares? It's only another laugh on the house.

Rozzie was a desolation. You loved her like a ruin that has to be propped up and railed round to keep the dogs off. And she grew on you like the ivy and the drink, digging out your mortar with her great, knobby roots. Loving Rozzie was a special vice, like eating between meals.

'You don't tell me you had your own way with Rozzie,' said Sara. 'She could have eaten you at one bite, even without her front teeth. I mean her false ones. For you know her teeth were a weak point with poor Rozzie.'

'Why, Sara,' I said, 'if you will think badly of poor Rozzie, I can't help it. But I'm ashamed of you, standing here before her very grave—and I'm surprised at you because I didn't think you would be so mean.'

'I'm not thinking badly of Rozzie,' said Sara. 'Rozzie Balmforth was my best friend, and I'll never forget her good kind heart.'

'Tom stands all my expenses and he'd like you to have something, Sara, so what about a half one to drink his health?'

But Sara didn't seem to hear me. She was waddling along so slowly that I had to stop for her. And when an old woman gets so slow as that, it means she's thoughtful of her latter end.

All at once she looked at me, quite sadly, and said, 'I suppose you'll be buried here, by Rozzie. Well, she gave you a boy.'

'To tell the truth, Sall, I don't want to be buried anywhere.'

'If you go with Rozzie, Gulley, I'd understand it. Indeed I should, though there was a time I never dreamed you'd lie away from me.'

And I thought: Yes, poor old Sall, she's an old aged woman. She's fallen over the last step. Her mind is running on graves as only old women's minds do. Graves and buryings. Well, she always liked to make a home, and now it's the last home. Complete with husband.

'Come,' I said. 'You know there'll be room for you, Sall, wherever they earth me down.'

'I'd like that best,' said she, 'as God sees me. Well, isn't it natural? But, oh dear, I don't know if I can—'

'Ah, I forgot all the other claims, there's Monday and old Mr W. and Fred, as well as me. But why shouldn't we all come, Sara?'

'You may laugh, Gulley. But I wouldn't mind it. You can't have too many friends round you in that cold place.'

'Not laughing, Sall, I think it's a good idea.'

'But they all have their own places. And what I was thinking, Gulley, though it goes against my very soul, I oughtn't to lie with you now. I can't help it, but my duty is to poor Byles. He never had a house or a wife of his own these thirty years. And I promised him. That's what he said, "It will bury us both." '

She stopped again and I saw that this last quick turn was a tactical gambit of some kind. And she knew I knew.

So we walked on arm-in-arm, feeling very kindly to each other in a graveyard way, and feeling each other's nature too. For I said to myself: The old lady, full as she is of love, tears, regrets, grief and religion, is up to something; and I knew she was saying to herself, Dear Gulley, how awkward he is. It's as bad as catching eels to get him fixed to anything. And as usual Sara won the first round. I couldn't wait any longer, and I said, 'What will bury you both? I should have thought your family might be glad to do something.'

'Oh dear, my family—where is it? Phyllis indeed—but where is she?—she may be buried herself. And Nancy with all her own troubles. I shouldn't like to come upon Nancy. I've been trouble enough to the poor thing already. No, it wasn't the family Byles meant.' And we walked on. Till I got impatient again, and burst out, 'You mean the picture, do you?' And I kept on squeezing her arm, but I had to tell myself not to pinch it or stick pins in the old carcase. For it would shock the old lady, at her age.

'Come on, Sall,' I said. 'Byles said that the picture, my picture, would bury you? And where do we go from there?'

'Though indeed,' she said, making the usual Salleonic diversion on the left flank. 'I can't bear to think of that money lying wasted, just in a bit of canvas, and you getting no benefit.'

'Neither can I, Sall.'

'And you think I've kept it from you?'

'Come, Sall,' I said. For I saw the grand bombardment was about to begin. 'Come and have that drink and we'll work out what you're up to.'

'But the thing is, Byles is afraid to sell it in case there's questions asked. Why, that Doris might put Fred on to making a claim.'

'She might indeed, you're quite right, Sara. Selling pictures that don't belong to you is a tricky business. It needs an expert to do a job like that.'

'And you know, Gulley, if we could get the money between us, I'd only want enough for a real funeral, and a bought grave and a stone. Well, perhaps I shouldn't ask for that, and you may say it's only a vanity. But oh dear, I don't know how it is, I can't get that pauper funeral out of my blood. It turns my very heart. And then to lie alone, among strangers—for ever and ever. No, it's too cruel for my old flesh.'

'Sall,' I said, pressing her arm, and I was pleased as you may think, 'If you can get that picture out of Byles, you shall have the best funeral money can buy—four coaches and an oak coffin. Two best funerals. And a stone six foot high with eight lines of poetry. That's four more than Tom did for Rozzie.'

'Oh, Gulley, may God bless you. You may have your laughs—but you don't throw a woman's weakness in her face. For you know that God made us so, and so we are, and we can't help it.'

The old lady was so warm that I was surprised. And I said to myself for about the hundredth time: Say what you like, women are a sex by themselves, so to speak.

'I shouldn't call it weakness, Sall, far from it,' I said. 'And as for being a woman, didn't I like you so? When it comes to a wife, give me a woman any day. A woman born and bred.'

So we took three more steps, waiting for each other to make the next move.

'But who would sell it for us?' said Sara, as if that little problem had just occurred to her.

'I would, Sall. Proud and pleased.'

'Oh dear, I'm afraid Byles would never agree to that.'

'What's your scheme, Sall?' For I saw that she had one.

'Well, I thought, we could go together to one of the Bond Street shops and they could send us a man.'

But that, of course, was just what I didn't want. Dealers. Publicity. All sorts of complications.

'Come, Sara,' I said. 'We don't want any third parties in this business. Contracts and bills and legal stuff. We're all friends together.'

'Yes, but I can't see any other way.'

'Give me the picture and I'll sell it this very morning.'

'I couldn't even get it. It's locked up in Byles's chest.'

'You don't trust me, Sara. Not even now, not with my own picture.'

'Oh, Gull, you know I do. It's Byles who's so mistrustful.'

We'd come to the main gate. And right opposite there was the usual pub you always see at a cemetery gate, for the mourners, quiet-looking place with a door as discreet as a coffin lid, and all as clean as a mortuary slab.

So I said, 'What about that drink, Sall?'

'Well,' said Sara, 'I shouldn't mind. I haven't to be home so soon because Byles is away.' This made me jump in my skin. 'Mr Byles away,' I said. 'Yes, he's in hospital.' 'I thought he didn't like hospitals.' 'Neither he does, but he fell off a ladder and they picked him up unconscious. He didn't come round before he was in hospital.' 'I'm sorry about that, Sara, I hope he isn't badly hurt.' 'I hope not, and they say not, but you can't trust them, can you? You never know what they have in their minds.' 'Here we are, Sara—the Blue Posts.' And I went in and ordered a couple of pints, and sat Sara down to them in the bay window. 'Just a minute, Sall,' I said, 'while I see a man about a rose.' 'It's just inside the front door,' said Sara. 'Drink up,' I said. 'Don't wait for me, I take my time on a cold evening like this.' And I went out quickly and hopped on to a bus. For I thought: Now's my chance if ever I had one. Byles away and Sara drowning her grief.

I stopped only at the ironmonger's to get a box-opener. And I was in the flat quicker than I had expected. But just as I worked the crow into Byles's chest, Sara put her head round the door. She had followed me home. Just like Sara to suspect me. And before I could creep under the bed she saw me and rushed down the passage, screaming 'Police.'

I got a big fright. I didn't want the police. It might have meant five years. And five years would have finished me. I ran after Sara and grabbed her by the back of her skirt. But she still kept on screaming 'Police.' So I gave her a little tap on the bonnet with the Iron Duke, to restore her to her senses; and a little push away from the window. Whereupon she fell down the cellar stairs into some dark hole. I said, for I was a bit surprised, 'What did you do that for?'

And to my relief she answered, 'Oh, Gulley, I never thought you would murder me.'

'Why,' I said, 'what about you, calling out police like that? You know I'd get five years if I went in again. And that would finish me.'

'Oh dear, oh dear,' said Sara, 'I never thought you

would murder me. Oh dear, what a pity—what a waste.'

And I was just going down the steps to see if the old lady had broken something, when I heard a voice in the passage, by the front door, and saw a policeman coming in. I had a surprise. But by good luck he put his head into the parlour door, and before he got it back again, I nipped across into the kitchen, shut and bolted the door quietly behind me. Then I took a dive out of the window among the cabbage stalks and hopped over the back wall into a cottage garden at the other side. I never noticed my rheumatism.

The cottage was in a terrace. No way out. So I went in through a back kitchen and found a little girl washing up plates. I looked at her, and she looked at me. Her eyes were as big as teacups.

'Good evening, my dear,' I said. 'I came about the gas—it's in the meter, isn't it? Do you mind if I get my mate, he's on the street?' The little girl didn't say anything. She just kept looking and wiping a plate round and round. She must have wiped that plate nearly through. I said, 'Thank you, my dear—that will suit very well'; and I went down the passage and let myself out, and made a quick move for the main road, where I could see traffic. I was back at the boat-shed before Cokey came in from washing up the supper.

Nosy Barbon was waiting for me. He was in such a state of excitement that for a long time I couldn't get anything out of him but vibrations.

'Hold on, old chap,' I said. 'Take it easy.'

'B-beautiful,' he got out at last, 'm-marvellous.'

'What is?'

'The p-painting, your m-masterpiece, in the g-gallery. They've hung it in the m-m-middle, the B-bath, b-beautiful.'

He'd been at the Tate, looking at the Bath, and it had gone to his head, as it always did with weak heads at a first pull. Like champagne. Fizzy stuff.

'All right, old boy,' I said. 'Keep calm. Yes, it's not too bad. But beautiful is about the last word—'

'B-but there was a ch-chap c-copying it, but so b-badly, I thought I c-could do it b-better myself.'

'I daresay,' I said, and then I had an idea. 'My God, Nosy,' I said, 'our fortune's made.' I nearly cried. 'What's tomorrow? Don't say it's Sunday.' Thank God it wasn't Sunday. And before four o'clock the next afternoon I had the prettiest early Jimson you ever saw. Sketch for the Bath. Or rather, from the Bath, but bearing on its face all those indubitable marks which as the crickets say, testify to that early freshness of vision and *bravura* of execution which can never be imitated by a hand which in acquiring a mature decision of purpose, has lost, nevertheless, that *je ne sais quoi*, without which perhaps no work of art is entitled to the name of genius.

I dried it off too quick on Cokey's stove. Poor Sara had a blister on her behind when I took it round to Capel Mansions. But what did the Professor care? He wasn't buying a picture, but an early Jimson with an irrefutable pedigree.

When I asked him if he thought I had better take it to Bond Street, he nearly went down on his knees. He cabled to Sir William that very afternoon, and Sir William cabled back before dinner-time, fifty pounds, for a week's option. The rest to be paid on receipt of photographs, and a second report, from a cricket.

I made the option twenty-four hours; and Sir William, with true magnanimity, always ready to trust, when, on a large view, he had a good chance of a bargain, paid up at once.

40.

I was so busy by that time that I forgot to cash the order. And Sir William, fearing that he had lost his promotion, wired the Professor to call. But when he called, we were right back in Genesis, creating worlds, and we had no time to give to Prophets unborn.

We were giving it to the old chapel which needed all the temporal support we could find.

I had meant to paint direct on the wall. It was a wall twenty-five by forty; of common rough plaster, direct from the trowel; a sheer precipice of dirty grey, slightly varied by bird droppings and cobwebs at the top, and spit marks at the bottom, which made my fingers tingle for a No. 24 brush. I could have embraced that wall, less or more.

But Nosy objected so strongly that no one could have stood up to him without a complete suit of oilskins.

'But you can't paint direct on the wall,' he said. 'It's not g-good enough. You must p-paint on c-canvas or s-s-s-s—'

'Yes, but if I use ceiling-boards, I shall have to wait a fortnight to get them up.'

'B-but you *must* wait—till we've p-propped up the roof.'

'And what I think is that the damned old ruin will fall down by itself any day and then what will happen to your ceiling-boards? For me to paint a wall on any building,' I said, 'is as good as asking it to catch fire, or get struck by lightning, or fall down. And as this thing I'm doing is the biggest I've done yet, it will probably bring up an earthquake, or a European war and wreck half the town.'

But Nosy was horrified by such talk. His nose turned pink, it seemed to swell up with distress. This was due to the pressure of his feelings which were so strong that at first he couldn't get them out, and then they came all together like a dust shoot. 'B-but that's why you m-must wait. You m-mustn't take any risks, Mr J-Jimson, with a p-picture like this. You've no right to take such a risk.' 'No right, Nosy, damn it all, it's my own picture, isn't it?' 'Y-yes. N-no, I m-mean, it's a n-national picture, it's a w-world m-masterpiece. Y-yes, it belongs to the w-world, to p-posterity.' 'Pup-posterity will probably not give a damn for pictures except the movies.' 'N-no, p-please, Mr J-Jimson, this is a s-serious matter. You've no *right* to take the risk. Until the roof is p-propped.' 'Not on your life, Nosy, I'm starting now right away.' 'But the whole thing may fall down.' 'It will fall down.' 'And then all your w-work will be lost for ever.' 'That's it, Nosy, but there'll still be a lot of bloody fools painting pictures, even wall pictures. You can't stop art by dropping bricks on its head.' 'You know that no one is painting anything as good as yours, not g-great pictures.' 'How do you know they're great, Nosy?' 'Why,' said Nosy, quite shocked. 'Nobody can help knowing it. You've only got to see them.' 'You haven't seen this one yet.' 'This is the greatest of them all —you know it is.' 'You'll never be any bloody good as an artist, Nosy, you were born for the Church or big business. Faith rather than works. You ought to be a rising Ford or an early Christian. And to hell with the lions. You can't please everybody.'

But the truth was that I myself was a bit roused up by the Creation. I had it on my mind. I hadn't really had any proper sleep or meals for a week, since the first lovely money fell from Heaven, via Beeder, into my pocket. I used to wake up at night shivering all over and thinking the vampires were eating my toes; but it was only the Creation sticking its great beak into me. I used to laugh all at once and jump up in the street, several feet or inches into the air, so that the kids threw orange peel at me and the girls drew back their skirts and looked round for a policeman to remove the offensive rubbish; but it was only because I felt cold hands down my back, hands of Creation. In fact, I'm not surprised that, in those days Cokey thought I was slightly touched, and used to run after me with bottles of stout, woolly combinations and rubber water-bottles. For I slept on the job, like every good general, and according to Cokey, the chapel, being built only for hell-fire religion, had no damp-course.

'Look here, Nosy,' I said, 'there's something in what you s-say about the—'

'S-s-s—' said Nosy, who couldn't even wait for me to speak.

'And if you can get them up before tomorrow night, I'll spend the time on the cartoons.'

The reason why I couldn't wait, of course, was Sara. In case the police were after me. And another five years, even two years in chokey, would finish me off. So I was in a bit of a hurry to get my stuff on the wall. 'I'll give you twenty-four hours, Nosy,' I said, 'to put your ceiling-boards up—but I can't wait longer than that. It's more than my life is worth.'

'Can I pay overtime?' said Nosy, the lance-corporal of industry. 'It will save in the end.' 'Pay what you like. Money no object,' I said; and he went to use his influence. He used it so well that the ceiling-boards and three plasterers arrived that afternoon. Also a wagon-load of scaffold poles, ladders, cement, rope, buckets, trestles, and paint. A school friend of Nosy's called Jorks, who, like all schoolboys, understood electricity, went into the roof and joined some new wires on to the old chapel cable, so that we were able to hang down dozens of big lights, which made the whole place as bright as a restaurant. And two other boys from Ellam Street, called Muster and Toogood, who being real London boys, were interested in ships, ropes, knots and blocks, set up a rigging in the east end from which they swung a couple of painter's cradles. That is to say, boxes with one side knocked out, in which one could sit and paint.

In fact, the whole job would have been finished by next evening, except Nosy's props, if it had not been for the usual accidents. First, a gentleman came from some committee or council to say that the place wasn't safe and to give me notice. 'But we're making it safe,' I said. 'And it's my business premises. You can't turn a man out of his business premises. I've got a three-years lease.' 'That wouldn't be valid, I'm afraid, against the council's order,' said the gentleman, who had a blue knitted waistcoat and a red face with smile, gold spectacles, fat nose and expression; full of committee politeness.

'Why do you want me to go?' I said. 'Because the place isn't safe,' said the gentleman. 'I don't mind,' I said. 'But it might fall down and kill you,' he said. 'I appreciate your kind feelings,' I said. 'But I won't hold you responsible.' 'So you really intend to defy the council's orders?' he said. 'Oh no,' I said. 'I'm a law-abiding citizen. I'll stay quietly.' 'You understand,' he said, 'that the matter can't rest here.' 'You c-can't do that,' said Nosy, appearing suddenly in a state of considerable excitement. We both looked at him with surprise and disapproval. 'What?' said the gentleman. 'What can't we do?' I said. 'It's a s-scandal,' said Nosy. 'D-don't you understand that this Mr J-Jimson is Mr Gulley J-Jimson. *The* Mr J-Jimson.' 'Certainly,' said the gentleman. 'That's just what we do understand.'

'You hear him?' said Nosy to me, throwing off a heat-wave like a radiator. 'It's b-because you're Gulley Jimson.' 'That's all right, Nosy,' I said, patting his arm. 'Go home and sleep it off. No one's noticed anything yet.'

'We'll appeal to the nation,' Nosy shouted.

'Certainly,' said the nice gentleman, smiling gaily. 'That's often done. When we wanted to turn some old almshouses into a garage the year before last, there was a national appeal. They collected over a thousand pounds to buy us out. But it all blew over in a week. And you can see the pumps there now. A lovely station, brings us in about a thousand a year in reduction of rates.'

'You d-dare,' Nosy shouted, getting more and more furious. 'You d-dare. Don't you unders-stand it would be in history? P-people would c-curse you for thousands of years.' 'That's all right by the council,' said the councillor, charming and friendly. 'The council don't mind about history because it won't be there. But it will be here on the appointed date, to do its duty by the ratepayers. Good evening, Mr Jimson.' 'Good evening, Mr Councillor. My respects to the family.' And I was just in time to prevent Nosy from rushing at the gentleman and perhaps doing him a fatal injury. Fatal to the Creation.

'Are you mad, Nosy? His person is sacred. He is democracy in its best trousers.'

'B-boorjaw b-brute,' said Nosy, waving his arms. 'They want to stop the whole thing, b-because they don't like your s-stuff.'

'Don't be s-silly, Nosy,' I said. 'He was quite a nice chap, that chap. Doing his duty as England suspects.'

'But it's a pup-plot,' shouted Nosy. 'They're all talking about it. They d-don't want your p-picture here—near the s-school.'

'Don't you du-dare to talk to me about pup-plots,' I said, losing my temper, just like Nosy. For talk of plots against me or anyone else is what I can't bear. 'Don't you dare,' I said. 'It's the wickedest, dirtiest thing you could do— you might ruin me for life. Why, a chap I knew had a plot against him, he was a chap who sold matches and they wanted to get him off his pitch. And somebody told him about it and he started writing to the papers. And making speeches against the government, and then he knocked a policeman's helmet off. And now he's in an asylum. And what's more, he's not really enjoying life.'

'B-but—' said Nosy. I took him firmly by the arm and interrupted quickly. 'You ought to go and apologize to that poor councillor.' 'But he does want to stop you,' said Nosy, turning pickled-cabbage colour. 'And why not?' I said severely, 'if he doesn't like my painting. To paint a picture that a chap doesn't like—a great big picture like this that anyone might see, is very inconsiderate. It is really an insult. It's just as if I stood out here in the road and shouted that I didn't like his waistcoat; or his manners; that his nose was all wrong; or his face ridiculous. Anyone has a right to defend his own waistcoat. That's what freedom means. So go away, Nosy, and don't try to put these wild ideas in my head or by Gee and Jay, I won't let you paint.'

This settled Nosy. And I knew how to manage the council. When dealing with men like that you have to TRUST IN THE LORDS—for there's no one else. I sent a note to the Professor telling him that all my influence was necessary, and forgot the council. So that it did not really upset me at all. It did not stop the work. But the other hitch was serious. It could not be overlooked. We had labour trouble, and I couldn't blame it. When the carpenter began to nail up his battens, several bricks fell on his head, a large beam detached itself from the wall and hung in the air, tiles flew off the roof; and finally a two-inch crack appeared in the north side of the chapel.

The workmen then left the place and said they would not go back because it wasn't safe for them. And Nosy was inclined to the view that it was not safe for my picture, until his famous props arrived.

But in this crisis I remembered Nelson. I put a roll of paper to my nose, directed it at the crack, and said, 'I cannot see any crack. And as for being safe, is it likely that I should entrust my life-work to a building that is just going to fall down?'

And while the workmen were discussing this argument, I went to Jorks and said, 'They say this building is going to fall down and I rather think it may. So what? I vote to carry on.' 'So do I,' said Jorks, who was a red-faced boy with a big mouth and a short nose. 'I've got a plan for another dozen lights right down the middle. It will take some doing though.' 'So it will,' I said. 'It will probably break your neck.' 'Yes,' said Jorks, turning up his eyes towards the roof. 'Everything is absolutely rotten up there.' 'That's what I say,' I said. 'What's all this fuss about a brick or two when the roof is only supported by the dirt on the cobwebs?' 'Don't you worry. I can do it,' said Jorks. 'I've got it all planned out.' 'You go ahead,' I said, 'and don't let anyone interfere with you.' The end of it was that the workmen propped up the wall and carried on. 'We didn't ought to do it, mister,' they said. 'This place is a fair death trap, but seeing that it's in a good cause.' 'The cause of art,' I said. 'No, sir, but we hear you've had trouble with the council.' 'The council told me to get out.' 'Well, sir, we shouldn't like to let you down against the council.' And they worked all night. British to the core.

The boards were up by next morning, the cracks were filled with putty, and the roof was secured by several more electric wires. Of course, a certain amount of debris was still coming down, and Nosy was still disturbed in his mind.

'It will f-fall any m-minute,' he said, 'and then w-what about your picture?' 'Yes, I was going to speak about that, Nosy, we have to transfer about six hundred sketches and a couple of dozen cartoons on to the wall by Saturday.' 'S-s-s—' 'Yes, Saturday.' 'Why S-s-s—' 'Because we haven't got time to waste. Especially if this damn place is falling down, which seems not improbable as it has actually started to do so, and what I want is about a dozen first-class assistants. Girls from the Polytechnic art class would do.' 'But the place is d-dangerous,' said Nosy. 'They might all g-get killed.' 'That's one of the reasons why I think they'll enjoy the job,' I said. 'It's dangerous, and the other reasons are it's dirty and it's painty.' 'And it's art,' said Nosy. 'I shouldn't say anything about that,' I said, 'to an art class. Better stick to the danger, the dirt and the paint.' And, in fact, before tea-time that day we had offers from twenty-five girls and four boys, the whole class, from which I picked twelve of the middle faces. My rule is, middle faces for the best graft. Pretty ones may be more sensible, but they are always lazy; plain ones may be more earnest, but they are particular.

The result was that the Professor found us busy. The plasterers and carpenters were still working on the bottom boards, while Nosy and I, on a thirty-five-foot scaffold, were painting at the top. Jorks and Muster, with a six-foot straight-edge, a level, two art-school angles and a plumb line, were stuck on painter's ladders, fifteen feet below, ruling the plaster into foot squares. On which the ten girls and the two art-school boys were knocking in the first lines from the cartoons. Cokey, who had just arrived with the basket, the day's shopping, and six bottles of stout, in the perambulator, was sweeping. Cokey began every afternoon's work, first by cursing us all round for making such a dirt, and then by sweeping and dusting all the dust off the floor into the air again.

There was also a good deal of noise. Jorks was singing, Muster was whistling, the girls were talking, laughing, talking, coughing, giggling, talking and abusing the boys for dropping paint on their heads; the three plasterers and the carpenters were hammering, talking, whistling and singing; Nosy was sneezing and I was trying to make Cokey understand that all the dust she was raising would stick to my paint. That is to say, I was shouting as loud as I could. And I will admit that I wanted to shout for standing on the top of a scaffold in front of a good new wall always goes to my head. It is a sensation something between that of an angel let out of his cage into a new sky and a drunkard turned loose in a royal cellar.

And after all, what nobler elevation could you find in this world than the scaffold of a wall painter? No admiral on the bridge of a new battleship designed by the old navy, could feel more pleased with himself than Gulley, on two planks, forty feet above dirt level, with his palette table beside him, his brush in his hand, and the draught blowing up his trousers; cleared for action.

41. It was just
then that I saw, through the clouds of Cokey's dust and the plasterer's smoke, and the kettle's steam, the Professor picking his way among ropes and poles and beds and buckets, followed by Sir William Beeder and half a dozen other people in whom I could perceive, even from the roof, marks of the highest distinction. Such as clothes from Bond Street, and intelligent expressions from the best finishing schools.

In fact, as soon as I set eyes on them I knew who they must be. The Lords. My Influence. Which had been growing very fast since Hickson's death got my name in the papers. The Professor, in fact, had been writing to me or calling on me almost every day since the sale, to discover more early Jimsons, or to get details about my life. For the Life and Works of Gulley Jimson was on the way. A publisher had been found public spirited enough to immortalize my genius, on a guarantee of all expenses from Hickson's executors, who still had several Jimsons to dispose of; and from Sir William, who was, of course, a rising man among collectors, and really deserved to have his name handed up, or down, to posterity.

That deputation, in fact, so expensive and important, gave me such pleasure that I nearly fell off my legs. Yes, I thought, this is indeed a triumph—it reminds me of history, of old Punch's visits to the artist's studio. I might be dead already. Why haven't I a velvet jacket and a beard?

And I began to think better of myself. For my opinion of myself had been rising for the last week. This was due partly to regular meals, no doubt, and the best of everything, but also, I admit, to the Professor. It is very encouraging to be written up, even by a writer. And the Professor was in good form. He'd spent his fifty guineas rake-off on a complete new outfit down to socks, shirts and pyjamas. He was a new cricket and a cricket full of chirp. He sang to me so sweetly about myself that I began to soften towards my own pretensions.

So, seeing my dear Professor and the Lords come to the rescue, I was not so much surprised as delighted. A rapid glow, resembling a measles rash, broke out all over my body. And I said to myself: This is not only fame; it is self-satisfaction. I shall now be able to leave off my winter vest, at least for the summer.

'Who are they?' said Nosy, glaring down with doglike suspicion, in his nose. 'Fans,' I said carelessly. 'Never mind them. Attend to your job. And just look what you've been doing.'

For he had been painting the whale's nose in the wrong place. 'Look at what you're doing, Nosy. Look at the sketch, you great looby.' 'B-but a whale d-doesn't have a face on the b-back of its head.' 'Yes it does. My whale does. It must.' 'B-but I c-can't just s-stick it on.' 'Oh, my God, that's just what you've got to do. Stick it on like a mask on the side of a gasometer. If you don't, that whale will be a corpse, it won't have reality. It won't live, it will just be a bloody illustration out of a whale book.' [1]

Nosy was a bad apprentice, because he was in such a state of enthusiasm that he couldn't see straight or hold a brush steady. 'Come, Nosy,' I said. 'You've got to take a pull at yourself. Keep cool. You can't paint in a frenzy— you have to do some hard brainwork—you've got to concentrate in about fourteen places at once. You've got to think with your eyes, fingers, ears, nose, stomach, all available limbs, any brain that may have been left over from school, and the end of your tongue. Many good painters do their best work with their tongues. Oh my God, look at you!' for he was putting in a high light on the whale's nose. 'My God, do you want that great pecker to come right off the wall?'

'I c-can p-paint it out.'

'No, you can't pup-paint it out—not on a wall, or the paint will lose all its wall quality—and the oil will float instead of going in, and the whole damn thing will shine like poor old Sara's nose over a fish kettle. You'll have to bring the tone up to it—it's a good thing you didn't put it in lighter. My God, don't you see the effect of that great black jib up there?' For I may say this beak was giving me a sensation of considerable pleasure. It was my pride and joy.

And I forgot about the Jimson fans until I turned round, some time later, to spit, and there they were, right in the line of fire. Entangled, and now quite brought to amid the debris they raised their noses into the air with expressions so intelligent and smiles so full of delighted appreciation that anyone but Nosy could have seen that they didn't know quite what was happening or where they were. And all the boys and girls looked at them with contempt and disgust, because for the moment they were as good as artists. Even the plasterers, who are a domesticated and civilized race of men, looked at the visitors with con-

[1] A description of this composition will be found in the Appendix to the 'Life and Works of Gulley Jimson,' published in 1940, soon after Jimson's lamented death, with illustrations from the Hickson collection. But as Mr Alabaster points out in his scholarly introduction, it is on works in his earlier manner, such as the first Lady in her Bath, that this artist must depend for any permanent niche in the history of art.

tempt and disgust. Because the influence of a piece of wall art forty-five by twenty-five is stronger than X-rays. It has profound and often permanent effects upon the character up to a distance of twenty-five yards. One of my early walls, only twelve by fifteen, turned a fox-hunter into a etcher. Bang. Afterwards he cut his throat. He hadn't the constitution for etching. Too risky. Couldn't throw his heart over the bullfinches.

'Oh, my G-God,' said N-Nosy, 'look at the b-bloody p-people, just when we were g-getting s-s-s-s-tarted.'

'Chuck a pot of paint on 'em, Nosy,' and Jorky, just below, shouted out to Muster who was only ten feet away, 'Hi, look behind at what the dog's brought in.'

Muster, who is a bit of a prig, said, 'The Philistines be upon us, gentlemen.' And the girls all laughed so scornfully that icicles formed upon Cokey's tea-kettle.

Only Cokey, who was in her county suit, and, being a young mother, was impervious to all influences of any kind, behaved herself like a lady. She went up to the gang of dukes and asked them if they knew where they were going. 'This is a private studio,' she said. 'Who asked you to come barging in?'

Alabaster then presented himself, introduced the rest, and Cokey came along to the ladders and bawled up to me, 'Mister Jimson, come down and have your tea and talk to this lot. They say they're real people.'

'Tell 'em to wait, Cokey,' I said. For I was knocking in the old man's forehead, and it was going along very well, a shining pink dome against the brown cave of the rocks. The outside of the cave against the whale's back took up the pink, but in a jagged line which I had brought up against the sky; to cut the horizon. And I saw that the sky itself would have to be as smooth as cream. Not flat but deepening in tone very quickly towards the top edge. Like the sea in a bad Japanese print.

'Tell 'em to go away,' shouted Jorky, Muster and the girls, who were so covered with plaster and paint drippings, that they looked like little Easter cakes, sprinkled with hundreds and thousands. Happy as angels in the thought that it would take them a week to get the dirt out of their hair and their finger-nails; that they were suffering in the noble cause of wall painting. 'Tell them to go away,' they shrilled. 'Who are they, anyhow? Some

315

dirt off the streets.' But the party, being real ladies and gentlemen, looked still more delighted and intelligent. One very pretty lady in the front row even began to point out the beauties of the scene to her gentleman friend, or spouse, or duke, aiming her slender finger at the nearest carpenter's back and exclaiming in a voice of ecstasy, 'Don't you love that bit—how marvellous where it curves into the blue—what atmosphere.'

And I forgot them again. Until a few minutes later, there was a crisis among the girls. About the tenth that hour. Madgie, the mouse on the extreme left, began to cry out loudly, 'Oh, Mr Jimson, oh, sir, oh please, I can't bear it.'

Jorky, Muster and the other girls at once broke into cries of derision and wrath respectively. Girls are very savage against girls who fall down on a job. 'Hold on,' I shouted. 'Hold up, Madgie, don't do anything rash. Poppa's coming,' and I slid down the ladders at top speed. Just in time to prevent the young biped from bursting into tears. 'Oh, Mr Jimson, sir. I *can't* see how it goes. It's got all wrong, and it won't join up, and I'm sure somebody's made a terrible mistake.' 'Somebody's made a terrible mistake, have they? Well, my dear, that's not what nobody wouldn't expect. Let's have a look at your sketch. I see, square No. 6, portrait of a fish with feet; and where's No. 6 on the wall, I don't see No. 6; I see No. 9.'

'Oh, Mr Jimson, oh what an ass I am, I'd got it upside down.' And all the boys and girls burst into cries of rage and disgust. 'Go home, Madgie.'

'Take it away, Madgie, you mucker.'

'Why did she come, that girl?'

'Throw her out, the thing.'

But the girl herself did not mind in the least. Owing to the influence of the wall, she was invulnerable. Like a young mother, even like Cokey. She hummed to herself while she rubbed out her pencil lines and started again, right side up. 'Oh thank you, Mr Jimson.'

'Don't mention it, Madgie. It might happen to anybody almost—history relates that Michael Angelo often got his squares wrong—numbers were invented by Arabs who hate art,' and it was at this moment that the Professor touched my sleeve and hastily called my attention to the Princess, the Duke, etc. And they were so rich, so nice, and already so dusty that I could not be unkind to them. '*How* do you do?' I said. 'How *do* you do, Duke?' 'How do *you* do, Princess?' 'How do you *do*, Mr Smith?'

'Mr Alvin Smith, the multimillionaire,' the Professor murmured in my ear. And I shook hands again with Mr Smith, twice. And gave him the famous Gulley Jimson smile. A special unlimited edition.

'We have been admiring your marvellous picture,' said the Princess. 'It's quite the biggest I've ever seen.'

'Yes,' I said. 'Though some of it is bigger than others.'

'And what does it represent?' said the Duke. 'Though perhaps I shouldn't ask such a question.'

It was indeed the sort of question a fan should never ask. But fortunately for His Grace, I was in a condescending and gracious mood.

'Don't apologize,' I said, 'I don't usually expect to be asked questions like that, of course, but I don't mind telling you, as a friend, anything that might be satisfactory.'

'Then we should so much like to know what it means,' said the Duchess.

'It means, Duchess,' said I, with my best social manner, which I believe is not unworthy of a President of the Salon or the memory of Charles Peace in the dock, 'you will be sorry to hear, getting up at seven o'clock every morning. I have to use all the light available. But joking apart, a surface like that is something and it covers an area, for instance, of a thousand square feet, and will involve the use of sixteen gallons of paint, three dozen brushes, and over twenty pounds' worth of scaffolding, ladders; that means a lot of money.'

'We understood,' said the Professor, 'that the subject was to be the Creation.'

'Very likely,' I said. 'That is a good idea, or whatever you call it. Hi, Jorks'—for I saw that the boy was getting above himself. 'Don't drop that paint on the girls—accidents can't be helped, but that viridian is expensive, we can't afford to throw it about—'

'And what's the price,' said Mr Smith, 'in dollars? Finished, delivered and ready for erection.'

'I'm sorry to disappoint you, Mr Smith,' I said, in that kindly manner which is peculiarly the secret of the great. 'But I cannot accept your kind and generous offer. As a patriot yourself you will, I am sure, understand those feelings of patriotism which have forced me to decide that a British masterpiece, of this magnitude, ought not to leave the country. And I intend, in fact, to offer it to the nation. Of course, for a suitable price. But I don't anticipate any difficulty about that,' I said, smiling confidentially at the Princess, who cried, 'Dear Mr Jimson, I do so agree with you.'

'Of course, I must make some conditions,' I said. 'A work this size is not suitable to a public gallery. It really needs a cathedral. You will say, no doubt, that none of the existing cathedrals would be able to give the necessary lighting. And, in fact,' I said, removing, with an open-hearted gesture, several more inhibitions, including my electric chest protector, cricket-proof waistcoat, etc., 'my idea was really a special building somewhere near Trafalgar Square. I don't know what your own plans are,' I said, and the whole party murmured that noise which means according to circumstances, either homage to Art or how long it seems till dinner.

'I don't wish to seem to dictate,' I said, 'but such a building, thoroughly modern in style, would really be cheaper in the long run. Lighted by daylight bulbs. Open day and night. Preferably with attendants in the royal livery. I particularly want the red-coats to bring up the greens. Also, if I may intrude on what is, after all, your business, I suggest free drinks should be provided while the pubs are closed. Limited of course. Let us say, to a pint for each visitor.'

'Free drinks?' said Sir William. 'You mean at the national expense?' I was relieved to see that none of the party felt the least surprise at my suggestion. I warmed to them. They were undoubtedly, taken all round, the most cultivated, that is to say, the richest people I had ever met.

And abandoning not only my waistcoat but my plot-proof dicky and friend-defying shirt, I admitted candidly that my idea was to get people interested in the supreme works of the native genius. 'For,' I pointed out, 'you could not expect them to come, in large numbers, without some *quid pro quo*. And if they didn't come, my work would be wasted.'

'I think that is a very good idea,' said the Princess, who was a darling in first-class practice, 'a lovely idea, to educate the masses.'

That hadn't occurred to me,' I said, and I was now quite recklessly exposed. 'My intention was more to give brewery shares a fillip, for I've noticed that any rise in brewery shares means a great increase in art appreciation —and art patrons—buyers, in fact.'

Nosy had now come down the ladders and was moving about on the outskirts of the group. He had a suspicious look about the eyes and nose, and I knew he was still suffering from persecution mania. But I was not even annoyed. I smiled like Jove upon the ministering ganymedes, and said laughing, 'You mightn't see the connection at first sight, but there it is. A fact of experience. When shares go up pictures sell. There is a rush for spiritual nourishment. But why I want to see steady national support for the market is because it takes time to make a patron. The first generation of profiteers are often, to put it frankly, merely human, what in England we call plain men. That is to say, chaps of whom you can't say anything except that they are good for nothing else, but are very pleased with themselves on that account. It's only in the next generation that you get the real collectors— the men of intelligence, sincerity, industry, perseverence, guts and scholarship—men who are really educated, that is, who know that they don't know anything that matters about anything that matters, and have learned where to find the experts who do.' And, out of that innocent trustfulness so often observed among the truly great, throwing away the last of my garments (and thus perhaps revealing some minor details discreet historians would prefer hidden) I laughed again and said to the Duke, 'But that, of course, hah-ha, is a special art.'

'And what experts do you recommend?'

'Dealers,' I said. 'Most decidedly. If you want a good spec, ask the dealers. It stands to reason, if you want the best eggs, you don't ask advice from the hens. Hens are prejudiced. You go to a reputable shop. It's the same with pictures. But of course you must choose a living dealer. Some, unfortunately, are mortal. And it's not always easy to tell that they have passed over merely by their expressions. For really successful collecting you want, as the poets say, a nose.'

The Professor had withdrawn a little and was making a note of my conversation. A pleased smile cricketed across his lower features. What an art biogrubber loves is a subject that talks. Because then he can fill up the gaps between the reproductions and the dates; and sell the thing as a Work at a guinea, instead of a catalogue at sixpence. And if the filling is polite conversation, which is rude nonsense, so much the better, because the readers will feel that it's given them their money's worth, and they won't have to bother with the reproductions.

'That's why,' I said, 'art reached such a high state of cultivation among the ancient Hittites, and in modern New York, so I've heard, appreciation is growing so rapidly that—'

'Ha ha,' said the Duke, who had the nose of a true aristocrat, a Solomon; and then instantly, with the practical art of a courtier, or first-class head waiter, became grave. 'But excuse me, Mr Jimson, we came upon a mission.'

'Yes,' said the Professor, quickly putting up his diary between his heart and his pocket-book, and giving it a little pat of affection. 'These ladies and gentlemen are among your chief admirers, Mr Jimson—'

I saw that he was coming to business, and I hastened to give them a lead, before they committed themselves, unwittingly, to something I could not approve. 'There are really,' I said, 'only two alternatives, either to buy the council out, and perhaps one or two adjoining sites, so as to give this building a more worthy approach. Or to transport the east wall, as it stands, to some central position in the city, and place it in a new building. I daresay you would prefer the second,' I said, 'but I myself am quite indifferent. Trafalgar Square, Millbank, have their attractions, but provided that proper surroundings and attendance could be secured, I should be quite happy to see the picture stay here, at least for my life-time.'

Nosy was shaking his head at me, and now exclaimed, 'Bubbubbub—'

'That is fairly obvious,' I said, frowning to show him that I had control of the situation.

'I hope, indeed, that it will stay here for your life-time,' said the Duke. 'And meanwhile we have a request, which I hope will please you.'

'It must be a full length, Duke,' said the Princess.

'A full length, for three hundred guineas, or, if exhibited in the Royal Academy, four hundred guineas. But we do not insist on the Academy.'

'I think you will realize, Mr Jimson,' said the Professor, smiling his new beige smile, 'that this is a great compliment to your position in the art world. Of course, this deputation would be glad if you could see your way to send the portrait to the Academy, but they don't insist.'

'A portrait?' I said.

'Didn't you get my letter?' said the Professor.

'Very likely,' I said. 'I've had three or four in the last month.'

'These gentlemen and ladies,' said the Professor, 'who are members of the London Association of Loamshire Bumpkins (or something like that), are delegated to make a presentation to their founder, General Rollo Rumchin (or thereabouts) of his portrait, in oils. And when they approached me for advice—'

'It would be a great honour, Mr Jimson,' said the Duke, turning to me.

'I know you won't refuse me, as a Loamshire man yourself,' said the Princess, darling me.

'So kind,' said the Duchess, with an endearing smile.

And I simply didn't know what to say. The tears were standing to my eyes; either of gratitude or some other feeling. Probably I should have made them a little speech expressing my sense of obligation, and so on, if Cokey hadn't been discovered boiling over in the corner by the stove.

Cokey boils over all at once, like a porridge pot. It may be due to the straight sides. 'I don't know about you,' she sizzled, 'but I can't wait any longer—I've got to open in ten minutes—anyone who wants tea can make it fresh. This is poison.' And off she went.

Cokey's indignation caused a panic to the highest ladder. For Cokey, at the afternoon opening, was Queen of the Feathers, and it didn't matter how old you were if she didn't choose to serve. You were under age; and it was outside.

Muster, Toogood and the girls fell off the scaffold so quickly that I had to shout, 'All brushes for washing, all pots to be handed in—look sharp, Jorky, on the door.' And while I was getting control of the work, I didn't notice what happened to the deputation. I had a notion afterwards that I saw the Duke being swept into the vestry with several old brooms and a few odd lengths of rope, but if so, he is there still. His bones are whitening among the plaster buckets. Another victim of art. But the path to the National Gallery is paved with Academy Dukes.

42. By good luck, it was an interesting sunset. The sky was extremely hollow; as hollow as a hat. And nicely graded from a dirty gold, westwards, like well-fried bacon; through leek-green and bottle-green to a real Life Guard's blue, on the east. No clouds. And the air extremely clear. It was so clear that you couldn't have painted it, you could only stretch your mind in it. And this, of course, is a great pleasure, when one has been cramped by conversation and easy politeness. It was giving me the greatest benefit, and would certainly have removed any slight stiffness remaining after my recent accident, which would have seemed almost as comic as it was, if it had not been for Nosy, who rushed up to me in the street and told me that the deputation had been got at.

'What do you mean?' I said sadly. 'Got at. What a strange expression.'

'They were s-seen,' said Nosy, hissing in my ear like a snake, like the old serpent. 'Madgie saw them out of the window talking to the man in a blue waistcoat.'

'Asking their way,' I said. 'And I'm not surprised in this part of town.'

'But you wrote to Mr Alabaster asking him to do something about the council, and he never said anything.'

'He hadn't a chance to say anything,' I said. But, of course, Nosy's argument was a strong one.

'They've got at him,' said Nosy, 'behind your back.'

Now this was the very voice of the original serpent. It is only too easy to believe that something is going on behind one's back; because, of course, it always is. But I was too tired to murder Nosy on the spot. I said to him only in a mild voice, 'Well, Nosy, you know very well the Professor doesn't like the Creation. Nobody does. Nobody that is, who is over twenty-five and has any money. You can't expect them to like a picture like that. It's dangerous. It's an act of aggression. It's really equivalent to going into a man's garden and putting dynamite under his wife. Or trying to kidnap his children. Many a man has lost his children like that—on account of some picture which has carried them away. No,' I said, 'if there is a plot, it's a fair and reasonable plot. And I won't have you abusing my friends, Nosy, even if they are enemies. When you are as old as I am,' I said severely, 'you'll take my tip, "BE FRIENDS WITH YOUR FRIENDS." It may not be prudent, and it is often difficult. But it is better for the liver, lights, and kidneys. After all, friendship has one great advantage; if you don't like your friends, you can always avoid them, and they won't mind. Not if there is really good feeling on both sides.'

Just then we came to the Feathers, and seeing Alfred's old white cat coming out at the door, I caught her and carried her in. I wanted some kindness. And no one is more kind than a cat. Her own kind. But she jumped out of my arms on to Madgie's neck, and then before Madgie could even scream, melted into the convivial atmosphere, always very thick at the Feathers.

And I recalled myself to the duties of enjoyment. 'Now girls,' I said, 'remember the law. No one in here under eighteen. Don't forget you're eighteen.'

And they sang back like little canaries, 'You needn't tell us, Mr Jimson. We've been here before.' 'And no ports,' I said, 'I don't believe in ports for young girls. Beer was good enough for Queen Elizabeth, and it's good enough for little pieces that ought to be in bed with a feeding bottle.' 'Oh, Mr Jimson, you do go on so.' 'Sixteen half cans, Alfred, and minerals to choice. How goes it, Walter?' For there was Postie Ollier and all his crowd. 'Seventeen half cans, Alfred. Take it out of that,' and I gave him a pound. 'Had a winner, Mr Jimson?' 'That sort of thing, Alfred.' For I didn't want a lot of explanation. I wanted a rest.

The cat appeared on the counter. Came up from somewhere without a sound, like a demon on the magic lantern. And walked across. She didn't look anywhere but she never touched a puddle. Keeping herself to herself. Tiger, tiger, burning bright.

'Here's luck, Mr Jimson.' 'Mud in your eye, Bert. Cheeroh, Walter.'

I thought we were going to have a good evening. I wasn't sure, but I was feeling I hoped so. When all at once a little old man with a crooked leg and long red nose like a badly scraped carrot came up to me and began to shout and wave his fists. He had a friend with him, a fat short man in a black coat, with black hair over his eyes, and a moustache like a seal, who tried to push him away.

'How do you do?' I said. 'Pleased to meet you.' And I tried to shake hands with them both. 'Telling me all those lies,' bawled the old man. 'Which ones?' I said. 'About you were hiring my chapel for religious purposes.'

I looked again and I saw the old man was Pepper Pot, but his nose had changed colour in the electric light, like a Michaelmas daisy. And I felt depressed. I didn't want to be tactful any more. I wanted a rest. 'Yes,' I said, 'religion. Religious art.' 'What, that wicked muck? Religious?' 'I hope so. But of course I can't be sure.'

Bert was tickling the old cat under the ear. Sometimes she liked being tickled. But tonight, I was glad to see she paid no attention. She just went on moving through the forests of Bert, Ollier and me.

Pepper was making a speech, very loud. 'He can't be sure,' he said. 'Well, we can. We've got eyes. We *know* it's muck.'

'No,' I said, 'I can't really be sure. Not just now. I'm tired.'

'And let me tell you,' bawled Pepper, getting triumphant when he saw he was winning. 'I've put in an information against you, at the magistrates. For blasphemy and obskeenity. So you needn't waste any more paint on the dirty muck.'

'No, I needn't,' I said, sighing so deeply that I blew half my beer away with the froth. For I couldn't help feeling that plots were going on. And I didn't want to feel them just then. 'But I think I'll get it down all the same,' I said. 'Somehow I like to get it down—get it out of my system.' 'The police'll do that for you,' Pepper screamed, warming up a bit. 'And get you out too.'

At this Nosy rushed up to Pepper and tried to shout

something. But all that came out was 'S-s-s—' He changed the shape of his face and tried something else, like 'M-m-m—' Then he changed his face again, burst into tears, and hit Pepper on the pot.

'Outside,' said Cokey, and before anyone could wink an eye, she had taken Nosy by the collar and thrown him into the road. Then she went behind the counter again and said to me, 'And you be careful, you two, or you'll go the same way.'

And there was dead silence for about a minute. Tribute of respect to Cokey.

'Seems a pity, when you have a tenant, Mr Herne,' said Ollier. 'I don't care,' shouted Pepper Pot, 'I'm not a bum. I put religion before rent. I stop at godless wasters that call themselves artists.' 'Modern artists,' said the seal in a quiet voice, as if he were afraid to find himself so brave. 'Modern artists,' screamed Pepper Pot, foaming like a Bass, 'fakers that can't even draw right and twist up God's works so you wouldn't know them. Blasphemy. Spitting in the face of the Lord.' 'I see what you mean,' I said. 'Ya,' said Pepper Pot, turning puce all over and shaking his fist at me. He was getting hotter all the time with his own fire. 'Ya. You can talk. But you've done for yourself. They'll take your dirty picture away and burn it.'

Cokey came through the slab again and took him by the collar. 'Here, what have I done?' he shouted. 'I warned you,' said Cokey. 'I didn't hit anybody,' said Pepper Pot. 'You can't shout in this bar,' said Cokey, throwing him into the street. And then she went back again and said to me, 'But you be careful, Mr Jimson.' 'I'll be careful, miss.' For if Cokey had been Princess in the Eagle, she was Queen of the Feathers. Because of the basket. But one girl's error is another's glory. Depends where she wears it, I suppose.

'Mr Herne is a true Christian,' said the seal, looking round as if he would fight us all, if he had to. But he hoped that he wouldn't. 'That's it,' I said, 'a good chap, loyal to his principles.'

The old cat came back again and sat down by my can. I suppose she had remembered that I hadn't tried to interfere with her. But she didn't look at me. Stretched out one arm towards the whisky bottles, like a salute. And gave her wrist a lick. Cherishing herself. A cat is a nice idea. Classical. Big lines and good detail. And she knows it too. All over.

The seal was still telling the crowd how Mr Herne as a young Christian had broken the windows of the Education Officer. 'Yes,' I said, 'I honour such men. People with real principles. Ready to lay down their rent for their religion. Warriors of the old faith or even of the one before.'

'Warriors all right, all right,' said Bert. 'Too many about if you ask me.'

'Any news since last time?' said one of the boys. 'Not much,' said Alfred. 'Things don't look too good in Poland.' 'They didn't look too good last time.' 'You'll have something,' I said to the seal. He was a friend of Pepper Pot, and I felt a sort of kindness for Pepper Pot. Because of his nose and his bad leg and his bad temper and his age. He was probably older than I was, poor devil. 'Nineteen half cans, Alfred. Gents and ladies, give it a name. This is an anniversary with me.' 'Anniversary of what, Mr Jimson?' 'Same day last year.' 'You get a lot of anniversaries that way,' said Bert. 'It's practically all anniversaries at my age,' I said, and while Alfred and Coker were making the handles jump, I felt such a sigh come up that I thought I had had too much beer. But I remembered Pepper Pot in time and recognized it as grief for mortal things. Yes, I thought, I'll never finish that wall—I may just manage the whale. But no. Probably not. The roof will fall in and break my skull. Or probably not. It will be something I didn't expect. But it's certain about the whale.

For my experience is that life is full of big certainties and small surprises. You can usually tell that the knock is coming; but the details are unexpected. You get it on the right ear instead of the jaw. Look at the Rankens. Everyone knew they couldn't last much longer after the last disaster. And they were quite right. But when the crash came, it was quite clever. It wasn't Jenny that left Robert, but Robert that left Jenny. He went back to his wife who'd come into some money, just enough to make some more working models and take out some more patents. For a new and improved regulator. And it was Jenny, instead of Robert, who put her head in a gas oven. I suppose, after all, she hadn't his resources. He had his new governor to think about. He'd always had his governors and regulators to think about. But she'd only had Robert and when he went off, she had nothing and no idea of anything. We can't all be inventors. And a good thing too.

'To you, Mr Jimson.' 'To you, Bert, with flowers.'

'I don't like it,' said one of the boys. 'Looks to me as if Poland was having trouble.'

'Chap in my paper, he's an expert, says that war is full of surprises.' 'It is,' I said, 'and also peace.' 'This bloody war,' said Bert. 'Which one?' I said. 'Haven't you heard about the war, Mr Jimson?' said Muster politely. 'Yes, of course,' I said. 'But I thought it had stopped a little bit after the Peace Conference.' 'It stopped for a time,' said Bert, 'but now they've got it started again all right, all right, and it's going something beautiful.' 'Who's the enemy, Kaiser Bill?' 'No, Kaiser Adolph.' 'It's Germany again, is it?' 'What they call the Nazis, Mr Jimson.'

The old cat put up its nose to my can, and then quickly pulled it back and shook its whiskers. 'Look at her,' said Bert laughing. 'Particular, ain't she? Hi, puss. Have one on the house.' The cat turned its head away with a dignity you can't get in humans. They try too hard. And they're so sympathetic. They feel what other people are trying to do to them even when they aren't doing anything.

'Puss, Pussy,' said Bert. He dipped his finger in the beer and offered it to her. 'Pussy.' And he laughed because she was putting him down, before the crowd. Bert is sensitive about his public position. In publics. A regular bachelor.

'She can't hear you,' said Alfred. 'She has been stone deaf ever since she had the distemper.'

'It's the Nazis, is it?' I said. 'Yes, I know all about them. They're against modern art.' 'And lipstick,' said Madgie. 'And examinations,' said Muster. 'They don't believe in examinations.' 'Hear, hear,' said Jorky, 'I never could pass examinations myself.' 'What do they have instead?' asked a girl in spectacles, with some of my green paint on her nose. Right off the eternal sea. 'Character,' said Muster. 'What's character?' 'What the boss thinks of you,' said Bert. 'Hitler is a boss, and no mistake.' 'They say it's his blue eyes got the girls.' 'Go on,' said Bert. 'They didn't start the war because of Hitler's blue eyes.' 'Well, he's got something too—he gives 'em ideas.'

'Puss, puss,' said Bert, but the cat stretched itself and then jumped off the counter. Disappeared without a sound.

What a shoulder, what loins. What a movement. The flying tiger.

'That cat has a lot of character,' said Alfred.

'Yes, you can see it's her own,' I said. Bert gave Pussy up and knocked his can on the counter, standing no more nonsense. 'What I say is: why did they start it? They know they can't win. Not against the French army and our navy.'

'Because of modern art,' I said, 'Hitler never could put up with modern art. It's against his convictions. His game was water-colour in the old coloured water style. Topographical.' 'I believe you, old son,' said Bert, meaning that he didn't. 'All wars are due to modern art.' 'Well,' said Ollier, 'I have heard that the Nazis are against modern art. But I don't know about the Kaiser.' 'The Kaiser couldn't stand modern art.' 'Well then, Mr Jimson, what about Kruger?' 'Kruger was all against modern art. He stood by the Bible, which is the oldest kind of art. And what he'd been brought up to.' 'Well, what about the Spanish Armada?' 'The Armada was all against modern art and the new prayer book.' 'According to that,' said Bert, 'it's got a lot to answer for.' 'Of course it has,' I said, feeling as flat as the floor which was also worn into knobs and holes. 'That's the trouble. It's a disturbing influence. Every time a new lot of kids get born, they start some new art. Just to have something of their own. If it isn't a new dance band it's a new religion. And the old lot can't stand it. You couldn't expect it at their age. So they try to stop it, and then there's another bloody war.' 'What do you go in for it then for?' 'I can't help it, gentlemen, it's like the drink. I shouldn't have let it get hold of me. But I was born very young, and I grew up with little experience of the world. Yes, gentlemen, until I was twenty-five I didn't really know the dangers of my position, that is to say, I was practically on my own, you might say,' and I drank my beer out of an empty can. Right under Cokey's nose. To use a figure of speech. For since I had paid Cokey her money, she had had a sort of kindness for me, and sometimes gave me a pint on the house.

But she didn't even see that I was dry. She was scratching her left cheek with her left little finger-nail, the county one, and frowning at the air. Her mind was in the snug, trying to make sure the basket was still asleep; or examining his features to see if he was likely to be a Prime Minister. Works of imagination. Cokey had grown a bit absent-minded these days. She used to be worried to fiddle-strings because her face was out of drawing, and now she was worried to fiddlestrings in case the kid was taking after her. And I thought, she's got something to live for, Cokey, and it will kill her by the painful method specially patented for lucky mothers. She'll be a hag in five years, and she'll never die till she's dead. She's forgotten herself already, poor bitch, and what a load off her mind.

I lifted my can upside down and licked the edge. Cokey took it from me and filled it. But without looking. All in a dream. And every wrinkle in her forehead said, Oh, these men.

'Thank you, miss,' I said. 'Bless your heart, etc.'

'You be careful with your etcs.,' said Cokey. 'This is a respectable house.' But she didn't put any kick into it. She was listening towards the snug door. And there were at least two more listening wrinkles in her forehead, vertical ones. The ones that make you look old. But no good warning her. What would she care?

'The Lady Mayoress of somewhere says she wouldn't give a cup of tea to a wounded soldier,' said Bert.

'Why not?'

'She's against war.'

'I didn't make the war,' said a soldier, young chap. 'Blimey, you can have the war. And let me get back to my job.'

'What's your job, old man?' 'Never you mind,' said the soldier. 'Here, you want to know a lot, don't you? Perhaps you'd like to see my birthmark.' 'I was only asking.'

The soldier went out and tried to bang the door. But it was a swing door. You can't bang a pub door. The pubs know a lot, almost as much as the churches. They've got a tradition.

'That's young Simpson in our office,' said Walter. 'He's just married and feels a bit sore about the war coming on just now.'

'On purpose, you might say.'

'What's he so private about his job for?'

'I don't know. He's like that, Simpson.'

The cat mewed at the door. Then it suddenly appeared on the counter, winding its way among the pots like a white serpent. Three of the girls stroked it in turn, but it didn't even look. It's coming to me, I thought. And it stopped and looked at me. Made a point. With one paw in the air. Then it looked through me for about thirty seconds or half an hour. I looked at the cat and the cat looked through me. I wasn't even in the way.

'Puss, puss,' Bert said, tickling her suddenly. A surprise attack. She jumped on Alfred's shoulder, went down half his back and sailed away to the whisky shelf. The individual cat. The private beauty.

'Getting a bit restless at sunset,' Alfred said.

'Spring time,' said Bert.

'No use to Pussy,' said Alfred. 'He's an it. Just nature it must be. She likes being round in the dark.'

'It?' said Bert. 'If it's an It, what do you call it she for?'

'Well, I'm fond of poor old Snow.'

'She doesn't seem to think much of you, Alfred.'

'I can't say that she does. She's a character, I can tell you. You can't tell what's going on inside her.' 'Probably cat,' I said, 'or that's what I should think.'

The seal had been looking at me for a long time out of the sides of his eyes. Now he made a big effort as if he were going to jump through the ceiling, and said in a small voice, 'A lot of people think modern art is at the bottom of a lot of this trouble we're always having.' 'They're quite right,' I said. 'It is. Right at the bottom.'

And I was on the point of bursting into tears when Mr Moseley came in and knocked on the counter with a half-crown. His face was as red as red ink; and he had a complete new colour scheme, all in browns. Brown suit, the colour of old ale. Golden brown tie like lager. Brown boots shining like china beer handles. Guinness socks. And a new brown bowler, the colour of bitter beer, over his left eye.

It cheered me up. I like a man who takes all that trouble for the public good. 'Good evening, Mr Moseley,' I said. But he didn't see me or hear me, any more than the cat.

'Twenty half cans, Alfred, and a double whisky for Mr Moseley, Miss Coker, if you please.'

But I was feeling absent-minded. What is it? I thought. Moseley's boots or Pepper Pot? And all at once I saw Hitler's blue eyes fixed on me. So that's it, I thought. Yes, that's what the whale's wanted all the time. Pale sky-blue in slate, to pick up the sky. Pretty large, too. But what a lot of trouble.

'Here's looking to you, Mr Jimson.' 'Here's luck.' 'Here's mud.' 'Here's hoping.'

Shaped like tipcats, I thought. Wide open. But it will mean a lot of work. And if the roof is going to fall on my napper.

'Cheerio,' said Bert, 'chin chin.' 'Your very good health, sir.' 'Thank you gentlemen, and ladies.' 'But what I want to know is,' said Bert, 'what's the cause of wars, I mean the cause of all these wars?' 'Fighting,' said Mr Moseley. 'You've said it, Mr Moseley,' said Alfred. 'But what's the cause of fighting?' said Bert. 'Fighting,' said Mr Moseley. 'You've said it, Mr Moseley,' said Alfred.

'But what I want to know,' said the girl with eternity on her nose, 'how are we going to stop people fighting?' 'You fight 'em,' said Mr Moseley. 'You've said it, Mr Moseley,' said Alfred.

'Twenty-one half cans,' I said, 'and another double for Mr Moseley, miss.'

But the beer had no more taste than liquid. Those eyes wouldn't let me alone. Yes, I said, I can see you. Curves as sharp as blades. And the right eye extended a bit to the left, so that the point would come up very nearly to the right side of the whale's face, which is against the white cloud. Or through it, to break the line there. Gives you a kind of cut in the side of the hat. But no, a bit too clever. That whale has got to be sincere—it's got to be an honest young cow.

I felt something brush my trouser leg and then the cat was sitting right in front of me, like a landseer lion; but with one paw curled up. She half closed her eyes, and sat like marble. And I looked at her. Deaf, castrated cat. What did she care? She never knew what she was missing. The only individual cat in the world. Universal cat.

I knocked my can on the wood; respectfully.

'No, I won't serve you any more,' said Coker. 'You've had enough.' 'But this is my birthday.' 'Yesterday was your birthday too, and you had too much. Every day seems to be your birthday.' 'Yes, every day's my birthday. Often twice a day. Due to art.' 'Art has a lot to answer for, all right, all right,' said Bert. 'Yes, and it doesn't answer. It only keeps on.' 'Keeps on?' 'Keeps on what?' 'Keeping on.'

I drank up Green-nose's beer while she was wiping her spectacles. And sighed most of it back again. I was very low. That damned Creation was pestering me. To get those eyes, those marble mountains down. Before they were lost. But I wasn't a kid. I wasn't to be caught with a milky finger. I've had some. I knew what happened when you began changing things on the wall—a lot of nasty new problems, no end of worry and work.

Green-nose took up her own can and found it was empty. Then she put it down again, hollowed her back, and gave her hair a pat. You could see she was pleased. She didn't like beer, I suppose, any more than the girls who were taking minerals. But had more sense of duty. Ambition, learning to be an art teacher. Senior school. Elementary would take lemonade and teach wash-drawing. And she'll tell the little lads and lassies about when she worked with Gulley Jimson, and when they grow up, they'll all say, 'Oh yes, Gulley Jimson, he's one of the old gang. The pre-wars. Stale stuff. Dead as Julius Caesar.'

The news had started again. We were having it every hour. And Bert said, 'Another raid on Warsaw, poor old Warsaw.' 'They say it's a nice town,' said Madgie. 'Got a famous gallery,' said Muster, 'but I suppose that's gone up already.' 'Not the pictures,' said Bert, shocked. 'Why, they'd be old masters.' Bert is very conservative. 'They'd look after those.' 'Yes,' said the seal, 'they're valuable. They've got beauty. Done by real artists.' The seal spoke quite loud, and looked me in the face. And I saw he hated my guts. It gave me a shock. '*Real* artists,' he said. 'They're not by modern artists.' There was nothing to say to that, so I gave him a friendly nod. To wish him luck. The individual seal. In a world all made of seal. The heart of seal-dom.

> *What the hammer? what the chain?*
> *In what furnace was thy brain?*
> *What the anvil? What dread grasp*
> *Dare its deadly terrors clasp?*

Concentrated seal. Winding like a black tiger through its own forest, with teeth of china and gold.

> *When the stars threw down their spears,*
> *And watered heaven with their tears,*

Did he smile his work to see?
Did he who made the lamb make thee?

I drank Bert's beer while he was proving that the old masters in Warsaw couldn't have come to any harm. Because the Poles were lovers of art; and besides, the director of an art gallery would get it in the neck if he let old valuable masters be bombed.

That beard, I thought, the old man's beard will be a much more important shape if the values come up; the range of tones will be bigger. Yes, I'll have a lot to play with there—I'll make it the biggest beard in history—an eternal beard. And that green shine will pick up the greens of the sea, it will sing very nicely among the pink rocks. And I began to feel hot again. I'd certainly caught something.

The wireless had got on to the police notices, and all at once it read out, Mrs Monday, the victim of a murderous attack on the tenth of last month, died today. Before she died, she became conscious for a short time, and she was able to give the following description of her assailant.

Bert was getting so angry that nobody was attending to the wireless except Cokey, and I saw her looking at me. But I felt so queer, I couldn't pretend not to be.

And all at once Cokey turned off the wireless. I don't suppose she knew anything. It was just on suspicion, or something. Cokey, I thought, going quietly towards the door, is almost a woman. No one knows how she knows what she does know. But it's definitely horse meat.

As I slipped out, something like a fiery comet whizzed past my left ear and I saw old Snow land in the light in front of me; all four feet at once. And then with one spring, in every joyful lovely muscle, ascend into Heaven; or the garden wall.

43. Having retired unobtrusively from social prominence, I went home. That is to say, I climbed the ladders, right up to the light platform, switched on the top light, got out in the swing, and began to paint the whale's eyes. And every now and then

I gave Jorky's patent rope a pull and wheeled along a bit farther. Till I was swinging about in the air, thirty feet from the ground, like an angel.

And as soon as those eyes took shape and I put in the pupils, they got me. They were so something, I don't know what. There they were, gazing at me like all the grief and glory in the world, about a yard long and a foot high; and they brought the tears to my eyes. Boo-hoo, I cried, putting a little more cobalt on the shadow side; and I didn't know whether I was more upset about Sara or the whale. And the more those eyes took shape, the more I felt sure that I had got something good; straight from the stable. The cut in the outline was just what the mass wanted. Of course, a shape like the right eye, bang among the dark purple, jumped like the moon.

I'm raising up some nasty difficulties, I said, with a great sob, probably for Sara. But who cares? Boo-hoo. There's no doubt I'm damned upset about Sara, worse even than about poor old Hickie. It's quite surprising. I feel as if I'd lost my right leg or even my left leg, which is, on the whole, the best one. Of course, that's just what she always wanted me to feel, the old succubus. Getting after me with all her hooks. So I ought to tell her to go to the devil. And I sharpened up the whale's upper eyelid. But what's the good when I feel like this? Yes, she knew how to dig herself in. She knew how to get on a man's brain—stomach rather, or liver, or whatever this pain is. And stay there. Boo-hoo, there's a tear on my palette. Who would have thought I could cry a tear as big as a halfpenny? At sixty-eight, for a battered old helmet like Sara Monday. Who would have thought that at my age and experience she could take me by the throat like this, and choke me? Boo-hoo. The whale looked at me with such something or other that I couldn't contain myself. The tears ran down my nose, and I said, It's a masterpiece. Perhaps. And as for the old un's legs, I shall have to make them as solid as rock, solider—yes, I've got a lot of work to do in the next twenty-four hours.

And I painted like six students at once. But under certain difficulties. For Sara kept interfering with my inside and upsetting my respiration, and the cradle was playing tricks. I hadn't been able to find Jorky's stay ropes, and so the whole machine kept swinging about. Sometimes when I had mixed a colour and was going to put it on the wall, I found myself trying to paint the air. In fact, the cradle kept turning round and turning back again, and then it began to jump up and down. And once it swung slowly in a circle like the big wheel, until I was upside down. Here, I said, there's something wrong—this is against gravity—it's illegal—I must have got a touch of the old trouble: delayed beer, or perhaps Alfred put some alcohol in it.

But I felt my wrist and it was as hot as a breakfast kipper.

'Yes,' said Sara. 'It's a fever. Just like when I felt your pulse at Bournemouth on the first Saturday we were on our honeymoon. You ought to be in bed.' 'Hullo, Sara,' I said. 'What are you doing out there in the middle of nothing? Mind you don't fall off.' 'Don't worry about me,' said Sara, 'I know how to look after myself. It's you you've got to worry about. You're damned ill.' 'You're going downhill with that Byles, Sara. I never heard you swear before. It's not like you.' 'No,' said Sara. 'It's not. You put that in my mouth.' 'I beg your pardon, Sall,' I said, 'I forgot you were dead.' 'Yes, I'm dead, and that shows how ill you are. You've got a temperature, Gulley—you must be delirious to see me like this. Get down like a sensible man, do, and go to bed.' 'I haven't time, Sall. I've got a lot to do before tomorrow evening. Be a good girl and let me alone.' 'I should never forgive myself if I let you catch your death on that silly bit of wood.' 'Go along, Sall. Go back to your nice warm grave. I should have thought you'd be glad to be dead.' 'Oh, Gulley, how can you speak so? It was a cruel thing for you to push me down the stairs and break my back.' 'I didn't mean to murder you.' 'Come now, Gulley, you can't swear to that.' 'Well, I was a bit annoyed—with you calling police and trying to get me put away for the rest of my life. Worse than murder, that would have been.' 'I didn't mean for the police to come. I'm sure that policeman had no business round the flat.' 'Come, Sara, you won't swear you didn't want to get rid of me.' 'Oh dear,' said Sara. 'How do I know? I was so worried and torn in half. Goodness knows I wanted you to have your rightful share, Gulley. But I wanted to have my little bit of funeral money too, for Byles and me, just to bury us and keep us from a cold-hearted grave.' 'Come Sara, you know I'd always have buried you. And as for being dead, you're not missing much at your age. With no money and that brute knocking you about.' 'Don't you call him a brute, Gulley. I wish there were no worse than poor Byles. His temper may be a bit short, but he's been a true friend to me in my old age.' 'You were happy with your Byles. You could be happy with anyone, Sall, anyone in trousers.' 'Oh dear, what's happiness got to do with it? You are the only one I ever loved, Gulley.' 'Why was that? I've often wondered. Because you needed me more? I certainly kept you busy, didn't I, I was a full-time occupation.' 'Oh dear, the times I've laid awake wondering what to do with you—I couldn't even cry my heart was so sore. Yes, Gulley, you broke my heart as well as my poor nose and my poor back.' 'And yet you always say it was a good time.' 'A lovely time.' 'We weren't happy, but we were all alive.' 'Oh dear, Gulley, but why weren't we happy? You know we could have been. Well, weren't we suited to each other? Did you ever like any other woman half as much? Why, even to pester me, or think about me when I wasn't there.' 'That's right, Sara.' 'Oh you properly doted on me, Gulley, didn't you?' 'Sometimes, Sall.' 'And that's why you hit me on the nose, didn't you, Gulley? Because you didn't like me being on your mind. You didn't like not to be free, did you?' 'No, I wasn't a meal for any old wife. And I had work to do. Now, Sall, you go away. You get off. I've got a job on—the biggest job of my life. And I've got to finish it before they hang me.' 'You might as well talk to me as pretend you're doing any good with that brush. Why, half the times you don't know where you're putting the colours. And you can't tell blue from green either, in this light.' 'But I'm getting in the forms and the tones, and I've no time to waste. Just look at this wall—two years' work, and I'll be lucky if I get twenty-four hours for it.' 'Twenty-four hours. You won't get one at this rate. Why, you're killing yourself. You're as hot as a stove. You're trembling all over. You can't go on like this at sixty-eight. You'll be falling off the ropes in another minute—oh, you make me cry.' And she did actually begin to cry, big tears rolled down her cheeks, each with a full moon on the left side, coming through a Gothic window. Crying for me, or perhaps I was crying for myself.

'And what for, I'd like to know,' she said. 'What for did you spoil all our happiness with your worrying about your painting?—whether you ought to make this blue and that green? When we might have been so happy.' 'It was a nuisance, wasn't it?' I said, putting in a nice sharp edge on the rocks where they cut against the whale, light ochre on the blue purple. I had to sharpen this up because of the new eyes. 'A nuisance to you.' 'And yourself, Gulley. Well, I mustn't say it, but I used to say to myself, if it makes him so miserable, it seems a pity. And he with such a gift for enjoying himself.' 'You're quite right, Sara. Art has been my misfortune.' 'It'll be your death unless you come down off that swing.' 'I shouldn't be surprised.' 'Now then, Gulley dear, be sensible for once. Just let me put you to bed and call that nice girl to tuck you up and keep you warm.' 'I don't sleep with Cokey, Sall.' 'Better if you did, it would do you good only to have her there, like King Solomon in the Bible. And as for me, you needn't mind me, Gulley. I shouldn't be jealous. I used to be jealous of all your girls, I admit, and of poor old Rozzie. But if I could give you a nice girl just to keep your old bones warm, I'd do it this minute.' 'I believe you would, you old rascal. You never had any morals.' 'Indeed, Gulley, you know I was brought up strict. As my mother said, a girl can't have too many good principles when she's going into service, and goodness knows, when I was a young maid, I had plenty. But I don't know how it is, when you grow old, they get worn out of you, like lumps in a mayonnaise sauce. When you're old, you're all for smooth-ness.' 'All for making the best of what's left.' 'Come now, sweetheart, you'll be sensible, won't you? Get down and wrap yourself up.' 'Sall, my dear, I'd like to please you, but I'm busy. Remember what happened when you inter-fered with me before. Go and mother your Byles or your Fred or your Dicky. They'll make you happy.' 'Happy. You make me laugh, and you make me cry. Happy, well, how could a woman be happy getting her teeth knocked out? Oh dear, those teeth, they were the last of my vani-ties.' 'Why did you stay with him then, Sara?' 'Oh dear, whatever would that man have done without me? So down as he was, about getting old and losing his job. And couldn't sew a button on for himself with his hands so shaky.' 'Fred did without you.' 'And did you ever see him since I left? Quite fallen in. Oh, he's missed me, poor Fred. And that woman wouldn't do the right thing by him if she could—too spiteful in her nature. And little Dicky back in hospital for his chest. Oh dear these last months, I've lain awake night after night, for that poor little lamb. And now there's you.' 'I'm all right, Sall. You've only got to look at me, full of jump.' 'Oh dear, aren't I looking and grieving? Don't I know that you know that you're done for? Come, dearie, give it up. Listen to your Sara. Didn't I give you comfort and peace often and often when you were fit to be tied with worrying about your greens and your blues and the rest of your nonsense? Yes, even though you did hit me on the nose, weren't you glad to come into my arms after, yes, with the very blood on your pyjamas, and think you were back with your mother again?' 'There you go, Sall, you old bluemange, you've thrown away your stays at last and taken the whole world to your bosom.' 'Well, I go on asking myself, why can't people be happy, poor dears? Why do they have to go moiling and toiling and worrying each other? Life's too short.' 'Now, Sara, old girl, if you don't mind—' 'And you don't really want me?' 'Not just now, my dear.' 'And aren't you sorry I'm dead?' 'Well, look at me, my dear, boo-hoo, with the tears running down my nose, real tears. A genuine grief. Yes, I'm sorry you're dead, my dear, and that I'm done for. But after all, we mustn't get too upset, must we? It's the way things are.' 'Oh dear, oh dear, I ought to know what life is.' 'Yes,' I said, putting another touch on the old un's nose, to give it more elevation. 'Practically A MATTER OF LIFE AND DEATH, you might say, or thereabouts.'

44. Then I must have dozed a bit, for when I waked up, it was daylight, a wonderful top light which made that whale look at me as if I loved her. A world's sweetheart, I said. Love her for yourself and what does it matter what she does with the milkman?

'Good morning, sir,' said an archangel. But when I looked up I saw he was wearing a policeman's helmet and had Gabriel with him, in a green hat. They had opened a skylight and were standing outside on a cloud or a ladder.

'I suppose,' I said, 'you've come about Sara Monday.'

'Sara Monday?' said the policeman. 'What do you know about Sara Monday?'

'Nothing,' I said, 'I didn't do it.'

'Do what?' said the policeman.

I saw the trap and answered, 'What you think I did. Not if she told you herself. The description is all wrong.'

The policeman took out his notebook and said, 'If you mean Mrs Monday who died yesterday in hospital—'

'That's her,' I said. 'What about her?'

'The description she gave is—wait a minute.' And he turned over some papers and read out, 'A man of about six foot high, with red hair and moustache, dressed like a seaman. Spoke with a foreign accent. An anchor tattooed on his right hand. Large blue scar as if from gunpowder on left cheek.'

I began to laugh. I was surprised. But I thought, just like Sara. To diddle a man with her last breath.

The policeman kept looking at me. 'You say this description's wrong?' 'Yes,' I said, 'the bit about the six foot high.' 'How do you know?' 'How could an old woman tell— probably he was only about five foot ten.' 'Did you know Mrs Sara Monday?' 'More or less, we'd met—we knew each other sometimes—we were acquainted in a way—' And then I carelessly gave Jorky's rope a pull and glided away about fifteen feet so that I could get a general idea of the whole situation. It wasn't as bad as I had expected. But the old un's left leg was showing too much activity, and of course the whale had far too high a value. Yes, I said, I'll have to keep that girl in her place and the only way to do that is to make the place bigger than the girl— the sea will have to roar upon the shore a little darker and the giraffes must elevate their horns to more surprising brassiness in the upper register.

A lot of talk was going on down below. There was quite an orchestra. I distinguished Cokey, like a kettledrum, Nosy like a cracked oboe, Jorky like a viola, and four or five of the girls like a glockenspiel of tea cups.

Yes, I thought, chrome on the giraffes will sing very nicely with the whale's nose, and I called out to Nosy for a tube of chrome. And he ran up the ladder. But when

I stretched out my hand towards the platform, I heard a voice say, 'Mr Jimson?'

'No,' I said, 'I'm painting.' 'My name is Goodman,' he said; or perhaps it was Manley. 'I represent the Borough Council.' So I looked at him, and it was the angel in the green hat.

'Excuse me,' he said, 'I am the borough engineer, and my orders are to demolish this building as unsafe.' 'That is impossible,' I said, 'it's against my agreement.' 'What agreement?' 'I have the Council's undertaking not to demolish it till next month—that gives me three weeks.' Then I pulled at the rope and glided away ten feet, towards the whale's right eye. Yes, I thought, she's got something, and I've got something; and I began to work on the baby which was taking its milk at her right breast. I wasn't satisfied with the expression in its eye. A sucking baby has a round blank eye. The inward gazing eye of a mystic which contemplates eternal joy.

The light was getting better all the time. But there was a lot of dust. 'Not so much of it, Cokey,' I shouted. 'Cleanliness is next to Godliness, and just now we're on the real job.' But when I looked round I saw that the dust wasn't coming from Cokey but from a cascade of bricks which were falling off the back wall. A couple of young walruses were standing on the top of it with picks and knocking it down so fast that it seemed to be melting under their feet. 'Take care, you chaps,' I said, 'I wouldn't guarantee any of that brick wall—very impressionist stuff, much of it.' But they didn't even hear me. Enjoying themselves too much. A couple of walruses on duty in full uniform, with knee-straps and wrist-straps and belt-straps, don't like to be talked to by the common herd.

Most of the roof at that end had also disappeared. Which greatly improved the light. I got on to the old un, and seeing Nosy on the platform about five feet on my right I shouted to him for the crimson lake. Nosy was also shouting, for what with the bricks and tiles coming down and the men rumbling and the boys and girls underneath arguing with the councillors, the noise was getting noisy. 'No,' I said, 'I know what you think, that the old un is too much like Santa Claus on a cracker box. But that's what I want, Nosy. That's how I feel him. When you get to the bottom you're very near the top. Well, look at Renoir's children.

Next door to the Christmas supplements. But no tricks—
no cleverness—no an't I smart, an't I slick. That's what we
don't want. That's what we've got to dodge—that's the
jaws of death—and it champs up a couple of promising
young geniuses every two minutes.' 'Yes, my pet,' I said to
the whale, 'nobody can call you slick, you've got a figure
like a barrel of stout, and now I notice it, your right eye
is twice the size of your left eye. Why did I do that?'

A large red object came between me and the whale's left
breast, and when I looked I saw it was a fireman's ladder.
There was a fireman coming up, so I shook down a little
green paint from the eternal sea on him and he went back
again.

Nosy and Jorky on the platform were arguing with the
councillor, and I told them to stop. 'Don't get excited,' I
said, 'or you'll do something that he'll be glad of, like breaking his neck. It's no good getting irritated against the
bureaucracy,' I said. 'That's giving it best, and it doesn't
deserve it. Hit it on the conk—forget it for it knows not
what it does. No more than you do. You've got to take
people as you find yourself and give your best attention
to something else,' I told them, or perhaps I only thought
I told them, because I was thinking. What it wants in the
top left corner is a lively passage in a strong green. Say
a field of cabbage. Yes, curly kale. After all, curly kale,
as a work of the imagination, beats Shakespeare. The
green, the tender, the humorous imagination. When the
old un dreamt curly kale, he smiled in his beard.

Nosy and Jorky were fighting three councillors and two
policemen. And I remonstrated with them. 'Don't go on
like that, boys. You'll end by creating a disturbance in
your tempers, you'll spoil your appetites, which in children
takes the place of a rational power. Besides,' I said, but
speaking in a quiet voice, to save my breath, because nobody was listening to me, 'it's unnecessary to make all this
fuss. Remember that dukes and millionaires are among my
fans and that I've got four pictures in the national collections. In fact, I shall write to *The Times* myself as soon as
I've got a moment. Don't you worry about the Council.
They may take out a few bricks from the back wall, and
the tiles off the roof, but that's an old trick. It's often
done to remove bad tenants with too many children or
bugs or wall painters. Notice that they haven't touched

the beams or the side walls. Because they daren't. Essential structure. If they killed me, I could run them in for damages. I've had some before, and I've never paid any attention. It's what you call the pischological attack. Everybody goes in for pischology these days. It started in Genesis, and it reached the government about 1930. But when anyone gives you pischology, you can always give it 'em back. Pay no attention. Look at me, here I am, and here I sit.'

My platform began to waggle up and down and I nearly put a splash of chrome on the whale's eye. 'Hi,' I said, 'don't do that. It's not safe. A wall isn't a canvas. You can't scrape.'

And just then the whale smiled. Her eyes grew bigger and brighter and she bent slowly forward as if she wanted to kiss me. I had a shock. I was touched, of course, to see this affection in a favourite child, but I thought I must be dreaming again. 'My dear girl,' I said, 'my petsie—do be careful—remember your delicate constitution.'

And all at once the smile broke in half, the eyes crumpled, and the whole wall fell slowly away from my brush; there was a noise like a thousand sacks of coal falling down the Monument, and then nothing but dust; a regular fog of it. I couldn't believe it, and no doubt I was looking a little surprised with my brush in my hand, and my mouth open, because when the dust began to clear I saw through the cloud about ten thousand angels in caps, helmets, bowlers and even one top hat, sitting on walls, dustbins, gutters, roofs, window sills and other people's cabbages, laughing. That's funny, I thought, they've all seen the same joke. God bless them. It must be a work of eternity, a chestnut, a horse-laugh.

Then I perceived that they were laughing at me. And I should have got up and bowed if my swing had been steady enough. But it was waggling more than ever.

'Hi,' I said. 'Don't do that. I'll come quietly.' For I didn't want to cause any trouble. I wanted a new studio quickly. I wanted to get that whale straight down again before I lost the feeling of her.

But of course they couldn't hear me because of the amusement. And all at once the swing turned right over and I fell off into a blanket held by six art enthusiasts or friends of democracy.

Unluckily I cricked my back or neck or something, and I did not fully understand what was going forward until I found myself in a police ambulance with a peculiar sensation in my arms and legs and a slight headache. Nosy was there too, with his face so much out of shape that at first I took him for somebody else after a serious accident. There were also, sitting in a row on the opposite cot, Jorky, a nun and a policeman. Jorky had an eye closed and his mouth was under his ear. He was whistling so sideways that it seemed like cheek. And probably it was. The nun was holding my wrist and looking professional.

'Excuse me, officer,' I said, 'but this is illegal. You can't arrest a householder for doing art, not on his own premises.'

'Please don't talk,' said the nun. 'You are very ill.'

'Right,' I said. 'Not a word, mother.'

Nosy, who was now and then letting out a sob or perhaps a swear, grabbed my other hand. 'It's a c-crime,' he said.

'No,' I said. 'It was a resolute act of anti-aggression.'

'Pulled down all my lights,' said Jorky, 'without even asking.'

'But they'll pay for it,' said Nosy.

'No they won't,' I said. 'They'll get another good laugh and a considerable deal of self-satisfaction at the clever way they handled an awkward situation.'

'You must not excite yourself,' said the nun. 'It's very dangerous.'

'I haven't broken my neck, have I?' For I wanted to scratch myself, and I couldn't manage it.

'No, you have broken a blood vessel.'

'So that's it,' I said. 'The stroke at last. It only shows that you've got to be careful. Or that it doesn't make much difference, anyway.'

'Oh sir,' said Nosy, he had a tear-drop on the end of what had been his nose. 'I c-can't bear it.'

'Yes, you can,' I said. 'Take a deep breath, hold your thumbs, count up to fifty and USE LARGE MAPS.'

'It's not fair,' said Nosy. 'They're all against you.'

'There you go,' I said, 'getting up a grievance. Which is about the worst mistake anyone can make, especially if he has one. Get rid of that sense of justice, Nosy, or you'll feel sorry for yourself, and then you'll soon be dead—blind and deaf and rotten. Get a job, get that grocery, get a wife and some kids, and spit on that old dirty dog, the world. Why, I can tell you, as a friend, if it goes no further, that I once had a sense of justice myself, when I was very young. I resented seeing my mother scrub the floor while her worsers went to take the air in Heaven-sent bonnets and shining two-horse chariots that were a glory to the Lord. Works of passion and imagination. Even when I was a young man older than you, I didn't like being kicked up the gutter by cod-eyed money-changers warm from the banquets of reason, the wine of the masters, and the arms of beauty, that hoor of paradise. I was a bit inclined to think it a raw deal. Yes, even the celebrated Gulley Jimson, the darling of fortune, much caressed by all classes except the ones that never heard of him, might have turned a bit nasty and given the dirty dog best, if it hadn't been for his fairy godmother sending him a wall. Walls have been my salvation, Nosy, not forgetting the new types of plaster-board. Walls and losing my teeth young, which prevented me from biting bus conductors and other idealists. But especially walls. And above all that wall which is now no more. Yes, I have been privileged to know some of the noblest walls in England, but happy fortune reserved the best for my last—the last love of my old age. In form, in surface, in elasticity, in lighting, and in that indefinable something which is, as we all know, the final beauty of a wall, the very essence of its being, Pepper-nose's wall was the crowning joy of my life. I can never forget the way it took the brush. Yes, boys, I have to thank God for that wall. And all the other walls. They've been good to me. The angel, in fact, that presided at my birth—her name was old Mother Groper or something like that—village midwife. Worn out tart from the sailor's knocking shop. Said, little creature born of joy and mirth. Though I must admit that poor Papa was so distracted with debt and general misery that I daresay he didn't know what he was doing. And poor Mamma, yes, she was glad to give him what she could, if it didn't cost anything and didn't wear out the family clothes. And I daresay she was crying all the time for pity of the poor manny, and herself too. Go love without the help of anything on earth; and that's real horse meat. A man is more independent that way, when he doesn't expect anything for himself. And it's just possible he may avoid getting in a state.'

'Please don't talk,' said the nun. 'That's all right, mother,' I said, 'they can't hear me because of the noise of the traffic and because they aren't listening. And it wouldn't make any difference if they did. They're too young to learn, and if they weren't they wouldn't want to.' 'It's dangerous for you to talk, you're very seriously ill.' 'Not so seriously as you're well. How don't you enjoy life, mother. I should laugh all round my neck at this minute if my shirt wasn't a bit on the tight side.' 'It would be better for you to pray.' 'Same thing, mother.'

The Horse's Mouth is ostensibly a memoir, dictated to "my honorary secretary, who has got the afternoon off from the cheese counter". One motive for this undertaking is self-justification. Gulley Jimson's reminiscences are, and sometimes insistently, a rationale for the kind of life that he has led, even when he maintains that as a career art is too hazardous. Certainly all autobiography, even when, and sometimes especially when, it is self-regarding and self-assured, is an implicit plea for approval of the courses of action that it describes; and *The Horse's Mouth* is characteristic of its form in being an apology. But the book has another reason for being as well. The other motive, which unhappily plays little or no part in many other autobiographical narratives, is artistic. From the beginning of the book Gulley is paralyzed by the stroke that he describes in its closing pages, and he keeps on keeping on in the only way left open to him. He talks. *The Horse's Mouth* is contrived as a self-portrait by an ageing painter reduced at first to neglect and at last to words.

Ironically, Gulley's achievement as an artist has come to be recognized. One of his paintings hangs in the Tate Gallery, and another has been sold at Christie's. Opaque but kindly patrons have supported him. He is to be the subject of a biography, however deplorably conceived and written, by the critic A. W. Alabaster. Nonetheless, he is at the same time an outcast, a dirty old man no longer able to paint, even before his stroke, the kind of thing that finally brought him recognition, the kind of thing that he had stopped doing ten years before, because its style seemed to him no longer sufficiently telling. Although he is pleased when he examines *Sara in the Bath* at Mr. Hickson's house, he senses that he has moved beyond that phase in his artistic development. "Rather better than I had expected" he reflects as he gazes at it. "But nothing to my real pictures. No, I thought, it's a masterpiece in its own kind. But it's not the kind I like. It's the real stuff. But in a small way. Lyrical. Impressionist. And say what you like, the epic is bigger than the lyric." In painting *The Fall* and *The Creation*, Gulley has moved on to the epic mode, but whether his new style represents an advance, as he thinks, or a decline, as the critics think, cannot be decided with perfect confidence. Joyce Cary's silence on this point amounts to implicit criticism of success as the criterion of merit and reinforces Gulley's complaints against those who judge him, favorably or not. In any event, whatever the ultimate artistic importance of Gulley's paintings, they are substantial, even if often imperilled and sometimes destroyed. Gulley may or may not turn out to be "an immortal", but he is no amateur and no dilettante.

The setting of the book is London, which Gulley loves and hates and cannot live without. To him it is the ground, the focus and the emblem of a civilization that he has helped to make, but one that poses a constant threat to his own sovereignty of the self. The Thames he calls "the old serpent, symbol of nature and love", but he does not try to evade this potent force. England and its apotheosis, the great capital city with its river, are compellingly important. Cary's contemporary James Joyce in *A Portrait of the Artist as a Young Man* draws a hero who will turn his back upon home, fatherland and church, a hero who will fly by the nets of Ireland to a kind of personal and artistic fulfillment denied him in his native land. By contrast, Cary causes Gulley Jimson to depict himself as incapacitated. There is no question of flying by the nets of England. In fact, captivity is an important strand in the fabric of the novel, as it is in the work of James Joyce as well. The prison from which Gulley is released on the first page of the book is no more and no less incarcerating than the police ambulance in which he is hauled away to the hospital at the end. Gulley is both captive and free, for such, the book is at pains to show, is the human condition.

That London provides the circumstances in which freedom and captivity are equally possible is a paradox, but no more so than the return of Stephen Dedalus to Dublin, where he takes his part in James Joyce's most important novels, *Ulysses* and *Finnegans Wake*.

In Cary's work the resolution of the paradox can be seen in the role that Gulley imagines for himself, that of the lonely artist in combat with a society that simply by being organized constantly threatens him. "After all, what is a people?" Gulley asks Nosy Barbon rhetorically. "It doesn't exist. Only individuals exist—lying low in their own rat holes." Accordingly, Gulley has no sense of history and little respect for civilization. To him the past offers no lessons that ought to be attended to. It is dead as is his own lyric period. As for the present, what matters is not government or even civilization; these, in fact, are the enemy, because they would constrain, constrict, forbid, tame and trim. "The only good government" he says, "is a bad one in the hell of a fright". And words, which formulate, define and mediate, are especially to be abominated. Words are only about the reality that is painting itself. "Talk is not my line" he reflects after spending the night at Plantie's. "Talk is lies. The only satisfactory form of communication is a good picture. Neither true nor false. But created."

Such thinking is consonant with Gulley's romantic notion of his role as an artist, the notion contained in the proverbial significance of the phrase that is the title of the novel. Gulley refers to himself as "the old horse", that is, as having an especial kind of authority by virtue of his calling. When he gets his first letter of inquiry from A. W. Alabaster, he says to himself "Old horse, you are now famous". He refers to God by the same term. God, too, is the old horse; and in so far as Gulley is an artist, he is God. "I had got the feeling" he says, as he repaints Adam, "straight from the horse". The essence of painting may be communicable, but evidently not in words, which are abstract, lacking in particularity and therefore untrue. What comes from the horse's mouth cannot, in Gulley's view, be articulated except with brush and paint on canvas or wall.

When in exasperation he begins to obliterate the fish in his painting *The Fall*, Nosy Barbon objects. " 'But Mr J-Jimson, you're not going to take them all out?' 'All of 'em.' 'Why?' 'They're dead. They don't swim—they don't speak, they don't click, they don't work, they don't do anything at all.' 'But why don't they?' 'God knows. But he won't go into details. The truth is, THE OLD HORSE DOESN'T SPEAK ONLY HORSE. And I can't speak only Greenbank.' "

Despite his sense of separateness and despite his perpetual war with his London, his England and his people, Gulley has no "Crusoe" longings. He is sophisticated, urbane, dependent; and he thinks himself a seer and prophet. He comprehends the shape of human destiny as a series of cycles, of creation and recreation, in which the artist plays a seminal and lonely but not single role. As the maker of the revolutions that are both life-giving and life-destroying, the artist is at war with the conservative forces represented by the female impulse to domesticity and by the male sense of history; but force and counterforce— issue, nurture and preservation—are the ground of being.

As he often acknowledges, Gulley owes much to William Blake, whose poems he recalls throughout *The Horse's Mouth*. Blake's "The Mental Traveller", many lines of which Gulley recites in the twelfth chapter, is of especial importance in this novel. It describes an imaginary voyage, during which the traveller observes the working of destiny, the meeting of male and female, the encounter, contest and outcome of the meeting. Sexual and artistic terms coalesce. Thus, when Gulley walks along the Thames, he sees a plain youth and a plain girl, obviously in love. "Green in her eyes. Spinal curvature. No chin, mouth like a frog. Young man like a pug. Gazing down at his sweetie with the face of a saint reading the works of God." Gulley thinks of Blake's lines in terms that go beyond the sexual to the artistic:

> And if the Babe is born a Boy
> He's given to a Woman Old,
> Who nails him down upon a rock,
> Catches his shrieks in cups of gold.

Like Blake, Gulley regards the male principle as the active and imaginative, the female principle as the passive and regulatory. The cups of gold are the durable issue of a fleeting and doomed encounter. They are works of art, "the countless gold", as Blake says elsewhere in the same poem, "of the akeing heart". And Gulley remembers this line too in his walk along the riverbank.

The Horse's Mouth is a comic novel but Gulley is often near despair. The world, he thinks, has cast him out because he cannot accommodate himself to its demands. He knows better than to think that he can paint to order for the likes of the Beeders, because to do so would be to surrender himself to the comforts of mendacity. Civilization is the enemy of art, because it fixes while art creates. But it is the necessary enemy. Gulley's father was "an artist, a real artist", that is, he had paintings exhibited at the Royal Academy. But his style became unfashionable, and he was displaced by the pre-Raphaelites and died penniless. Thinking that he knows better than to resent the injustice of life as did his father or to pretend that it does not exist as does Plantie, the unlucky cobbler, Gulley nonetheless rages against the world. Rage drives him to utter menaces against Hickson, to insult the Beeders and to despise his own son, who went to Oxford and became a banker with hand-made shoes. But he does need the world and weeps with real sorrow when he learns of Hickson's death.

Because a book must be understood in its own terms, *The Horse's Mouth* must first of all be read as a self-portrait of its professed author. Joyce Cary's genius at what has been called impersonation makes the job of assessment less easy than it might be, had the differences between author and hero been repeatedly underscored. Gulley's ability to express himself, his practice in the arts of persuasion, his mastery in eliciting sympathy for the case that he makes so ably—these arts are, of course, really those of Gulley's creator, who conceals himself, though only to direct matters in such a way as to make them mean what he intends. To confuse Gulley with Joyce Cary is a tribute to the sense of reality with which the author of *The*

Horse's Mouth manages to invest his art, but it annihilates the distance that stands or ought to stand between the reader and the novel.

The Horse's Mouth belongs in a wider context. It is the third and climactic volume in a trilogy with two other equally demanding narrators. The first of these novels, *Herself Surprised*, is the self-exculpatory account by Sara Monday of her career as wife, housekeeper and mistress to a succession of men, including Gulley Jimson. The portrait that Sara draws of herself is not only more sympathetic than Gulley's sketch in *The Horse's Mouth* but is also different in several important particulars. Although in her book Sara can be seen to have deluded herself about certain of the episodes in her life, she does know her own role as nestmaker. And she has been generous enough to play it for such diverse men as Matthew Monday, the respectable middle-class husband whom she cherishes for a number of years, Thomas Wilcher, the deeply conservative lawyer to whom she becomes housekeeper and mistress, and Gulley Jimson, the artist to whom she is attached and to whom she is all that a wife should be, so much so that Gulley feels stifled by the relationship— "Stirring all that fire only to cook her own pot". Sara Monday writes *Herself Surprised* in prison, to which she has been sentenced for committing a series of thefts. Characteristically these are for domestic reasons, to feed Gulley and to pay his son's school fees. Imprisonment is as much a fact of her life as it is of Gulley Jimson's.

Equally captive is Thomas Wilcher, the narrator of the second novel, *To Be a Pilgrim*. He receives little mention in *The Horse's Mouth*, because he is entirely antipathetic to everything for which Gulley Jimson stands. Gulley refers to him contemptuously as "a rich lawyer, with a face like a bad orange. . . . Genus, Boorjwar; species, Blackcoatius Begoggledus Ferocissimouse. All eaten up with lawfulness and rage". But to himself Wilcher is a man who understands or who hopes to understand history, a man whose sense of tradition makes him build, or rather find, his own prison, the house that is the solace and the symbol of his life. Continuity and the past are what Wilcher evokes in the "journals", which are the fictional device employed by Cary in *To Be a Pilgrim*. The title of the novel, taken from John Bunyan's well known hymn, points to the sense in which Wilcher understands his role in life as the sometimes reluctant but always devout and ultimately blessed maker of a pilgrimage toward the Heavenly City. All in all, the three volumes of what Cary later came to call *First Trilogy* depict what appeared to their author to be "the whole landscape of existence".

But art is not the last word in *The Horse's Mouth*, not Gulley's last word, not God's either. The last word of God, of Gulley, of the book itself, is love. "Go love", Gulley's hero William Blake insists, "without the help of anything on earth". Such is the secret behind all the relationships in the novel. Nosy Barbon is maddening, but his devotion to Gulley transcends his incomprehension of the old man's art. The pathetic and fierce characters of Greenbank, Plantie, Ollier, Bert and above all Coker, touch the imagination and the heart by their unselfish, indeed selfless capacity for devotedness. The world is unjust, and evil confounds the imagination as it makes men miserable. The lamentable Professor Ponting espouses the Greenbank version of Spinoza as the celebrant of a view of the universe that denies evil and makes love triumph over all. Gulley Jimson knows better. He knows that to love without the help of anything on earth is not easy, and Joyce Cary shows that it is not possible alone.

Andrew Wright

*The University of California
   at San Diego*

ABOUT THE AUTHOR

Arthur Joyce Lunel Cary was born in Ireland in 1888 of Anglo-Irish parentage. His forebears had gone to Ireland at the beginning of the seventeenth century and were resident landlords there until the latter part of the nineteenth century, when the land acts drove the English settlers out. This biographical fact is important in delineating the sense of exile that was to influence Cary's thinking throughout his life. By the time that Cary was born, the very phrase "Anglo-Irish" was becoming an anachronism; and, in fact, Cary was born in Ireland only for sentimental reasons, for by 1888 his parents were living in London. His mother went over to Londonderry for the delivery of her child so that it could be known as Irish by birth.

Cary attended Clifton, an excellent public school in Bristol in the west of England, and afterwards, hoping to become a painter, he went to the art school of the University of Edinburgh. But his experience there and later in Paris, where he painted and lived the artist's life, persuaded him that he was not good enough to make a career of art. He then went to Trinity College in Oxford University, where he took an undistinguished degree in law, for the law did not interest him so much as did philosophy, and he was not examined in the latter subject. After leaving Oxford, he went out to the Balkan War of 1912-1913 to see what war was like and was arrested as a spy. Following a brief return to Ireland, he joined what was then called the Colonial Service and was posted to Nigeria, where he was "magistrate, road builder, a general Pooh Bah of state". In 1916 he married Gertrude Ogilvie. Four years later he was invalided out of the service, and he and his wife settled in Oxford, where they had four sons. There his long career of writing truly began, and there in 1957 he died.

Cary's novels may be classified as follows: the novels of Africa—*Aissa Saved* (1932), *An American Visitor* (1933), *The African Witch* (1936) and *Mister Johnson* (1939); the novels of childhood—*Charley is My Darling* (1940) and *A House of Children* (1941); the chronicles—*Castle Corner* (1938), *The Moonlight* (1946) and *A Fearful Joy* (1949); *First Trilogy*—*Herself Surprised* (1941), *To Be a Pilgrim* (1942) and *The Horse's Mouth* (1944); the political trilogy—*Prisoner of Grace* (1952), *Except the Lord* (1953) and *Not Honour More* (1955). A novel on a religious theme entitled *The Captive and the Free* was issued posthumously in 1959, and *Spring Song,* a collection of Cary's short stories, appeared the following year. An illuminating series of lectures published under the title *Art and Reality* was brought out in 1958.

The following books have been written about Cary and his work: Andrew Wright's *Joyce Cary: A Preface to His Novels* (New York, 1958); Robert Bloom's *The Indeterminate World* (Philadelphia, 1962); Charles G. Hoffmann's *Joyce Cary: The Comedy of Freedom* (Pittsburgh, 1964); Golden L. Larsen's *The Dark Descent* (London, 1965); and M. M. Mahood's *Joyce Cary's Africa* (Boston, 1965). All these studies contain bibliographies directing the reader to other works by and about Joyce Cary.

A. Wr.